# DAUGHTERS OF BRITAIN

## BY

## S.M. CARRIERE

Renaissance

Cover art and design by Caroline Fréchette. Interior design by Caroline Fréchette. Edited by Meaghan Côté, Myryam Ladouceur, and L.P. Vallee.

Legal deposit, Library and Archives Canada, June 2017.

Paperback ISBN: 978-1-987963-22-9
Ebook ISBN: 978-1-987963-23-6

**Renaissance Press**
http://renaissancebookpress.com
info@renaissancebookpress.com
Gatineau-Ottawa, Canada

For my Saturday morning shield sisters.
There is a warrior queen in each of you.

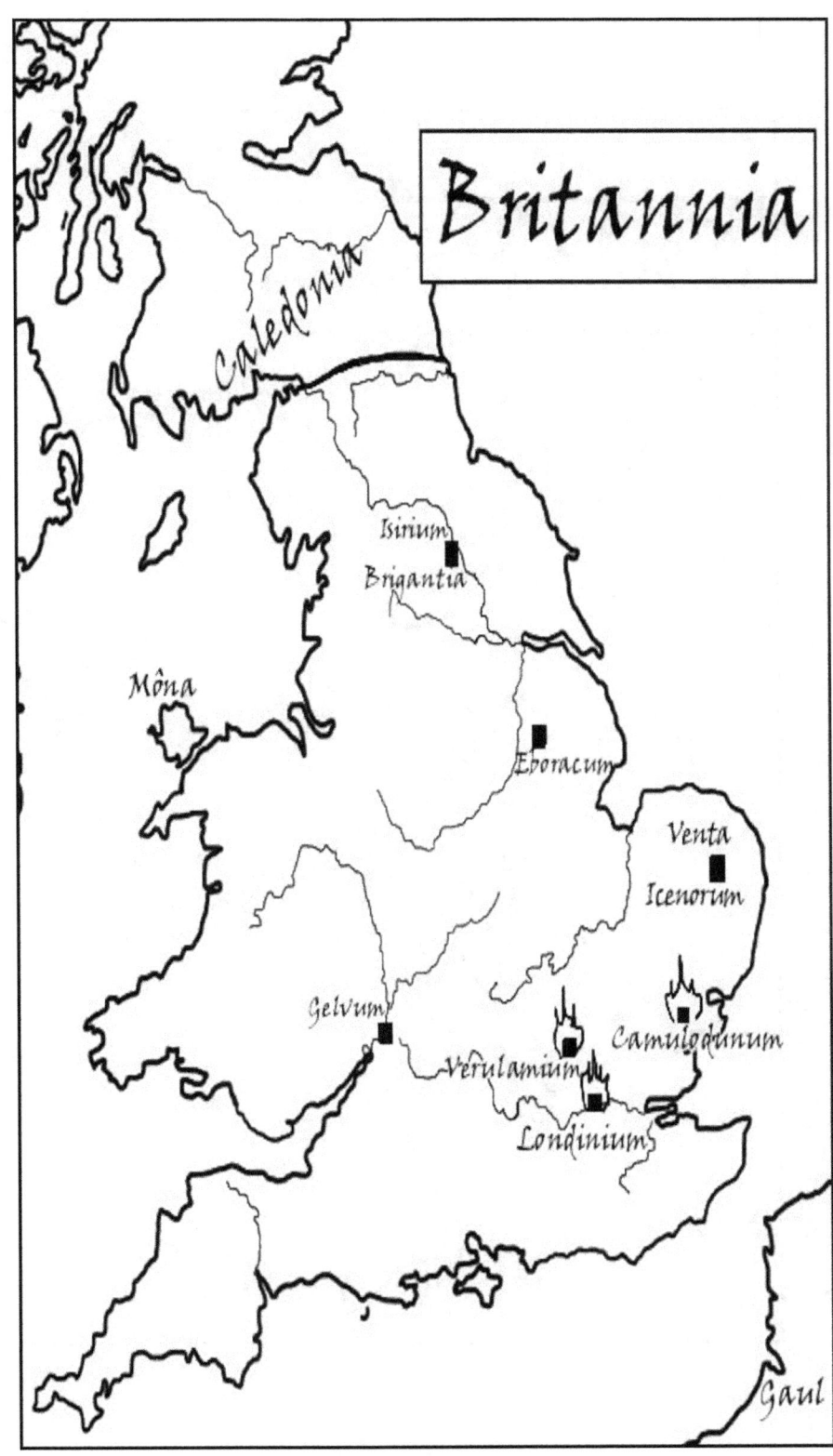

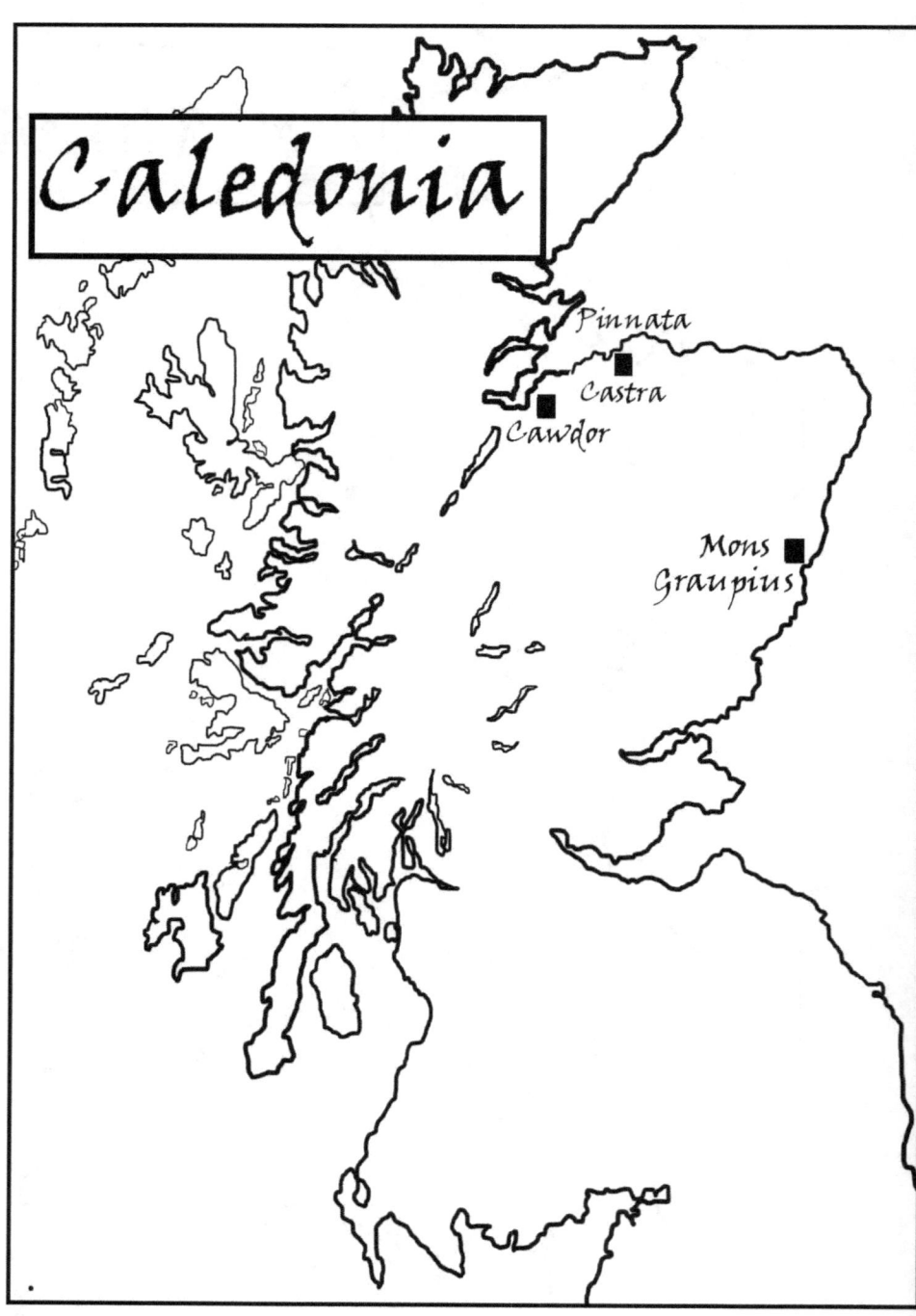

Caledonia

Pinnata
Castra
Cawdor

Mons
Graupius

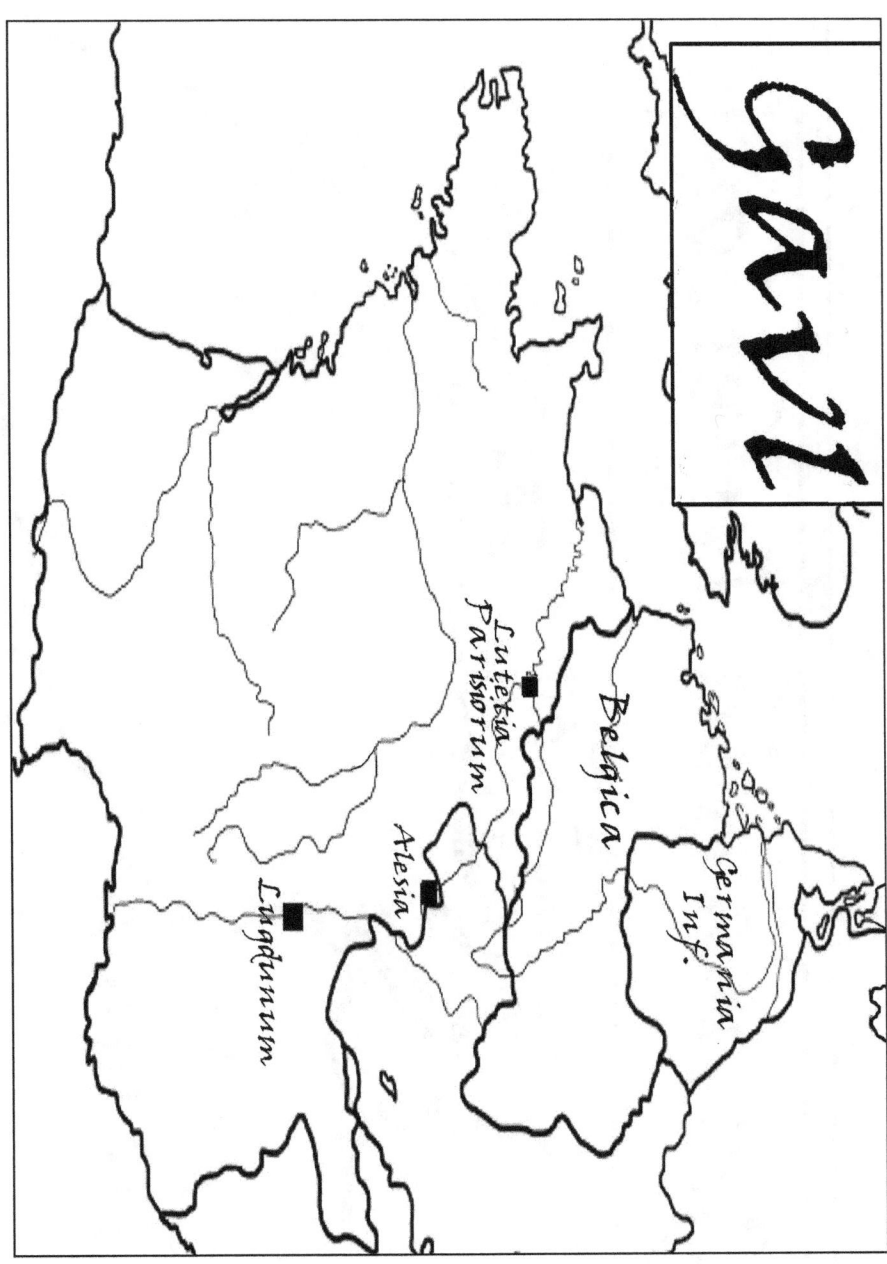

Germania Inferior

Lugdunum Batavorum
Noviomagus
Castra Vetera
Belgica

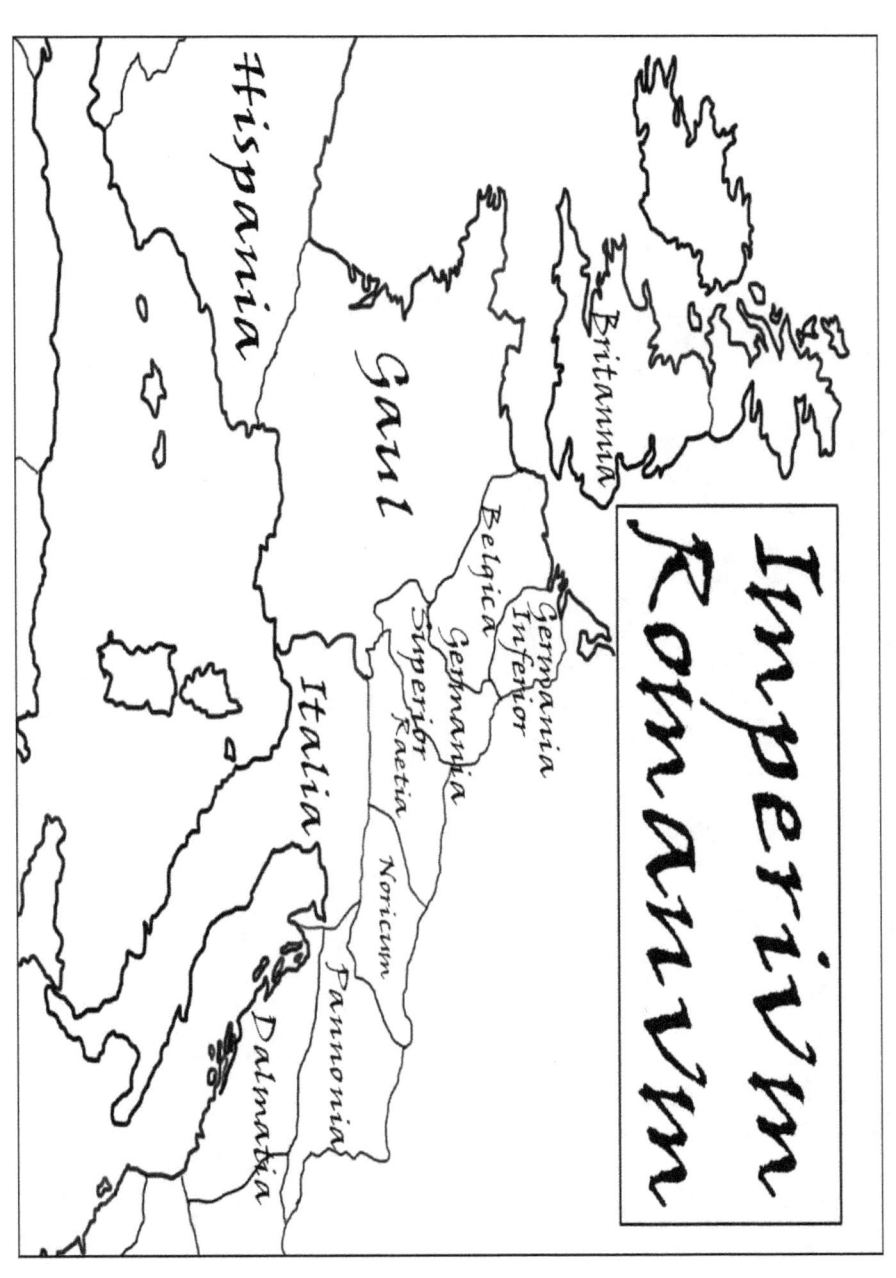

# DAUGHTERS
## OF
# BRITAIN

## Tri an llat Gughor Ynys Prydein.

rodi y ulkessar a g६yr ruuein ६e y karneu blaen y eu meirch ar y tir ym p६yth meinlas.

a r eil gadel hors a heyngyst a ronn६en y r ynys honn.

a r trydyd rannu o arthur y wyr deirg६eith a medra६t yg kamlan.

    — Trioedd Ynys Prydei, Llyfr Coch Hergest, c. 1382 AD.


## Three Unfortunate Counsels of the Island of Britain:

To give place for their horse's fore-feet on the land to the men of Rome, in requital for Meinlas;

and the second: to allow Horse and Hengist and Rhonwen into this Island;

and the third: the three-fold dividing by Arthur of his men with Medrawd at Camlann.

    — The Welsh Triads, Red Book of Hergest. c. 1382 AD.

# PROLOGUE

The people of Britain suffered beneath Roman oppression for over a hundred years. Small rebellions in Britain were crushed each in their turn, until a new hope for British freedom arose; the vengeful Queen Boudicca.

Born of a powerful druid, Boudicca had married the king of the Magni Ceni, a mighty tribe in the south east. Their seat was Venta Icenorum and had been for generations beyond count. For all their pride, however, young king Prasutagus had bent the knee to Emperor Claudius when Caratacus lost the battle at the River Tems and so the Magni Ceni languished beneath the oppression of Rome. Hatred for their subjugation simmered beneath the skin of every member of that proud tribe.

Sensing their malcontent, Rome's heavy hand grew yet heavier. Icenian men were forbidden to carry weapons, and more than once Rome marched on Venta Icenorum to steal cattle to feed their armies, and children to die for them.

In the year 60 AD, King Prasutagus died, leaving his kingdom to his two daughters by Boudicca. In a bid to soothe Roman greed, he named Emperor Nero as co-regent.

But it was not enough. Rome marched on Venta Icenorum and demanded that Boudicca relinquish the throne that rightly belonged to her daughters, claiming the kingdom was theirs. They claimed they did not recognize female rulers. Knowing them for liars—after all, they were keen supporters of Queen Cartimandua of the Brigantes—knowing what terror awaited her people should she leave them to absolute Roman rule, and knowing her daughters' rule to be sacrosanct, Boudicca refused.

There was great tragedy that day.

Boudicca was seized, her two daughters torn from her side. She was taken outside, stripped naked and flogged before all her people who loved her. Her two daughters were brutally raped and left barely conscious in the palace, which was then set ablaze. They were but girls of seven and ten.

The Romans laughed as they marched away from Venta Icenorum, taking with them all the wealth of cattle and burning the crop fields on their way. Only when Rome had turned their back did the people of the Magni Ceni dare move, swooping in to collect their queen, who had been beaten into unconsciousness, and rescuing their princesses from the burning building.

Shock at Rome's cruelty echoed across the south east. Tribesmen gathered in secret to ponder their fate should Rome choose to take their lands next, and hate like ice grew in the breast of every Briton.

The queen of the Magni Ceni survived her flogging, and her two daughters survived their rape. They stood tall, their pride unbroken before the greed of Rome. Boudicca's name was whispered in awe throughout the isle, until it grew into a rallying cry.

Brave Boudicca would not lie quietly down. She was not a meek Roman woman. She was a daughter of Britain, and she loved the island and its people with fierce gravity. Moved by her tragedy and the love she had for her daughters, the island and the British people, the Trinovantes, the Catuvellauni and the Coreltauvi joined her. Some one hundred thousand Britons took up arms against Roman oppression. In the sacking of Venta Icenorum, Rome had created its own greatest foe.

In the summer of 61 AD, they marched. The governor of the Province of Britannia, Gaius Suetonius Paulinus, had led his legions in a campaign to destroy the heart of the British people. They laid siege to the Isle of Môna, centre of druidic learning and a sanctuary to the British way of life. Their destruction of the druidic heart was totally and utterly complete. This act of violence against the British people brought yet more warriors to Boudicca's side. She, the mother of Britain, represented their brightest hope of driving out Rome.

She very nearly succeeded.

While Gaius Suetonius Paulinus was campaigning in the west, Boudicca and her angry hordes marched first upon Camulodunum, which had once belonged to the Trinovantes. That proud city had been turned into a *colonia*, an insult the Trinovantes could bear no longer. It was sacked and razed to the ground, the gutters running red with the blood of Roman soldiers and their traitor wives and mistresses. Quintus Petillius Cerialus led the Legion IV *Hispana* against Boudicca, but that legion was at last struck down outside the burning walls of that city, their past atrocities remembered upon their flesh by British blades.

No longer would the sons and daughters of the isle sit meekly aside as Rome ravished her. Boldly did Boudicca march on, sacking and razing Londinium and Verulamium both before the druid-killer Gaius Suetonius Paulinus met her upon the battlefield.

Disaster befell the British that day, and their angry army was defeated.

Boudicca rallied her troops, reminding them of her love for them, and of the hope of a future without Rome, a future where Britons would be ruled by Britons, in British fashion. She reminded them of all Rome had done to her and her children, and that she was the isle, and her daughters were the daughters of Britain.

For all her valiant speech, and for all the courage of her army, Rome's greed was more powerful still. The British broke and fled, hoping to survive long enough to regroup and battle once more.

Alas, Boudicca was struck in that battle as she desperately tried to shield her two daughters from harm. She fled with one of her commanders and her two daughters in a chariot, reaching the charred remains of her palace, where her people awaited news of victory.

Boudicca had no such news to give. She wept as she explained the loss to her people, pleading with them to remain proud, to remain brave, and to remain defiant. Rome would be broken. Britain would be free.

Gravely wounded and knowing Rome would chase her down, Boudicca arranged for her daughters to flee north and find refuge amongst the tribes there. They knew freedom and with Venutius, Cartimandua's ex-husband, they were fighting for it still. The girls fled in a chariot piloted by Boudicca's most trusted commander, disappearing from view a day before the Roman army descended.

As the Romans crested the hill outside the destroyed gates, Boudicca stood upon the steps of her ruined home in a ruined city, wearing a dress of white to signify her mourning, her red hair loose and blowing in the breeze. She smiled at Gaius Suetonius Paulinus and bid him welcome to the Britain that Rome had wrought; a hell of ash and death.

Standing with her were a select few warriors who refused to leave her side, such was their love for her. In that ruined city, many of the Britons remained, showing great courage in facing the wrath of Rome against their beloved queen.

When Gaius, governor of the Province of Britannia, dismounted to place the queen in shackles, she laughed at him and from her robes produced a phial of poison. "I am a daughter of this island," she declared, her eyes fierce. "Rome will never know the love she has for me, nor the love I have for her, and for this I pity you. And I curse you. Rome will never have this island. For as long as her sons and daughters stand with her against you, you will never claim her. Britain will be free. I am this island, Roman. You may beat me, but you shall never break me. But you, you shall be broken. With my life's blood do I see it so."

She drank down the phial and there, upon the steps of her ruined palace in her ruined city, did Boudicca rid herself of life.

Enraged by the insult, Gaius laid waste to what was left of Venta Icenorum. All those who had insisted on staying by their queen's side were slaughtered, down to the last infant. Any riches left were stolen away. Leaving Boudicca where she died, the Romans sacked the rest of the territory, leaving it desolate. When they left, their rage and greed sated, those who had hidden themselves went to Venta Icenorum to pay homage to their queen. Boudicca was buried in the sacred woods beyond the city, her body becoming one with the land she had so loved.

Across the strait in Gaul, farmers raised their heads to the sound of the keening cry of the Magni Ceni. Robbed of their lands, their children and their queen, the Magni Ceni were no more.

In the north, Boudicca's daughters lived on.

## 61 AD, AUTUMN, CALEDONII TERRITORY, FREE BRITAIN

Lord Rhys, the elder of the two heirs to the throne of the Caledonian Federation, raised his weary head. He had been at training all morning, and was exhausted. But the wind had whispered in his ear, urging him to look up.

There, on the crest of the hill, silhouetted against the setting sun, stood two young girls. They were thin and filthy, but the sun caught the sheen of golden torques around their necks, the glistening of golden rings in their hair.

Caught for a brief moment, the young Lord Rhys merely stared until one of the girls collapsed. With a shout, he rose to his feet and ran, fast as his long legs could carry him. His shout of surprise alerted the other men in the training fields, and they too began to run.

The first to crest the hill, Rhys stood before the girls, breathing hard. The girl on the ground, hair straight and the colour of flame, did not seem to realize he was there. The standing girl, however, did, and her pale dun eyes met his defiantly, as if demanding he kneel.

"What creatures have blown in, then?" Rhys's trainer, and father's shield-bearer, demanded. "Who are you, and what do you mean by so boldly entering lands that are not yours?"

The girl with the savage eyes turned to Geraint, and Rhys noted the broad man flinch back slightly.

"Sanctuary," the girl croaked through cracked lips. "I demand sanctuary."

"Oh, demand, is it?" Geraint snapped. "On what authority?"

The girl held out a clenched fist, and unfurled it, revealing a golden ring with a red stone. Carved in that stone, visible only because the sun now shone through it, was a hare.

"Andrasta's mark," one of the men breathed. "There's only one who would carry that mark."

"She's dead," Geraint said.

"I am Mederei," the girl declared, her voice gaining strength. "Daughter of Boudicca, Queen of the Magni Ceni. I demand sanctuary."

The short speech took all her strength, and she swayed. Rhys dove forward, catching her as she fell, starvation and exhaustion robbing her of consciousness.

Geraint turned to one of the men. "Fetch the druid, Alwyn. Cadeyrn, send word to Lord Brennus."

"What are we going to do?" Rhys asked, looking down at the gaunt girl in his arms.

"These are Boudicca's daughters, my Lord," Geraint murmured. "We will give them sanctuary."

## 62 ad, Spring, Fortified City of Lindon, Caledonian Territory

The argument was heated. Rhys felt sorry for the girls standing in the centre of the circle of shouting elders. The younger of the two, Modron, merely stared vaguely out past the circle of men, her head tilted as if the empty horizon held something particularly interesting and mildly amusing.

Mederei, however, kept her eyes up. She looked at each of the men in turn, according to who shouted the loudest. Her expression remained impassive, but her eyes flashed dangerously. There was fire in that girl, and Rhys found it all the more saddening. What manner of queen would this girl have made, if only Rome had not interfered? Surely the Magni Ceni might own the whole island. Better them than Rome.

Though the elders now fought as to what to do with the girls, there had been no argument as to their identity. Their story had proven true. The body of the charioteer, who had died of his wounds shortly after crossing the border into Caledonian territory, had been discovered, though the wolves had gone to work on him. Not far from that lay the chariot, overturned with the dead horse still attached to the pole. The faithful beast had run until it died, carrying the most precious thing the island had to safety.

At least, Rhys felt they were the most precious thing they had. Rome attacked the Magni Ceni because they feared that great tribe. They feared their beloved queen, and the power she could wield, and they feared, Rhys had no doubt, her beautiful daughters, who could have driven Rome from the island if given half a chance.

The arguing irritated Rhys. Some elders claimed that they had done their duty as prescribed in the law of the island. They had fed and clothed the girls, nursed them back to health. Now that they were healthy, some of the elders argued, their natural contract had ended, and the girls should be sent away, lest Rome come crashing on the federation with the full force of its might.

At last irritated beyond reason, Rhys stood. The sudden movement silenced the elders, and all eyes turned to him.

Ignoring them, Rhys turned to his father.

"We must give them a place amongst us, father," he said, bowing low.

"You were not asked to speak, Rhys," his father answered, his voice kind and his eyes sparkling. There was pride in that gaze, for a bold man would make a good king.

"I know, and forgive me, but I could not remain silent for fear of condoning cowardice."

"Cowardice, boy?" one of the elders demanded, incredulous.

"The Lord Rhys is speaking!" Geraint snapped, silencing the elder with a sharp voice and stern gaze.

"Yes, cowardice," Rhys answered. "For only cowards would turn away their countrymen for fear of Rome—Rome, who is not of our island. Are we to let these foreigners dictate our actions? How can we call ourselves men, if we are so unwilling to give aid to the children of our neighbours? And if you are too cowardly even now, remember that these are Boudicca's daughters. Have you no idea how they may lift the spirits of the people of this land? Can you not imagine the warriors we could call to our aid when they learn that their queen yet lives?"

Silence answered Rhys's declaration. He looked around, suddenly unsure.

"It is strange," a voice cracked with age said from beyond the circle of elders. The elders turned to find the druid leaning on his staff, grey eyes sparkling with life though age had folded his skin and bent his back. "That wisdom often comes not from men of might and experience, but from children. I have conferred with the spirits in this matter, Lords of the Federation. Do not send these girls away. There is much yet they can do for the island and her people."

"That settles it," Lord Brennus said, turning to address the elders. "They stay. Are there still any who dissent?"

No one spoke. Gainsaying a druid was not even for the foolhardy, and none wanted to lose face before the child Rhys, who would call them cowards.

"Good. Then this council is dismissed. Let each find their rest, and return here on the morrow for a feast. We have two new tribeswomen to celebrate."

# 68 AD, AUTUMN, BATAVIA, PROVINCE OF GERMANIA INFERIOR

The door to the mead hall slammed open, turning the heads of the gathered chieftains of the Province of Germania Inferior. Aullus Vitellius marched in, surrounded by a substantial force of Roman legionnaires as a bodyguard.

The chieftains of the Chatti Federation tensed.

"Gaius Julius Civilis," Vitellius said, sounding bored.

"Legate," the chieftain answered, standing slowly. The scale maille he habitually wore hissed like a pit of angry vipers as he moved.

"You are under arrest," Vitellius said.

The chieftains of the Chatti Federation exploded into angry shouting. Civillis himself remained silent, watching the new governor of his province with flinty brown eyes. At length, he held up a hand and the German chieftains fell silent.

"On what charge?" Civillis inquired mildly.

"Treason against Rome," Vitellius said.

Again the chieftains let fly, shouting at the governor in a loud cacophony of bass and baritone voices. Tall, broad, and powerfully muscled, the chieftains of the Chatti Federation would give even the most seasoned veteran of the Roman legions pause. Together, clad in their maille and furs and leathers, they appeared as a pack of angry bears, roaring together. It took Vitellius all of his considerable self-control not to reel back under their collective ire.

"Legate," Civillis answered, speaking to the governor as if speaking to a child. "We have danced this song before. Last year I was arrested on the same charge and brought before Rome. I was acquitted. Do you propose we do it all again?"

"What is this gathering if not to plot treason?" Vitellius demanded.

Civillis lifted his shaggy brows and looked around at the chieftains in his hall. "Do Roman men not have friends, Legate?"

"Do not play coy with me, savage! I am no fool."

"You are trying to arrest me for treason, Legate, a crime for which, as I've said, I have already been acquitted."

"You were never tried. Emperor Nero would have taken your head."

"Emperor Nero is dead," Civillis replied. "And Emperor Severus Galba has acquitted me of all charges."

"Is that so?"

"Yes," Civillis replied.

"Then tell me why Galba has disbanded the *Corpore Custodes*?"

This gave Civillis pause. "I beg your pardon?"

Vitellius produced a scroll from the belt he wore. With great pomp, he unrolled the scroll and began reading. "In accordance with the wishes of Severus Sulpicius Galba, the *Germani Corpore Custodes* are hereby disbanded, the members thereof permitted to travel home."

"We have served in the honour guard since the days of Julius Caesar!" Civillis said, unable to hide the surprise and hurt from his voice. Though tensions between the Chatti Federation and their attached Legion *XIV Gemina* had grown over the last few years resulting in some clashes between the two, the Batavi had always served with pride as the *Corpore Custodes*. They were men of honour, and they honoured the treaty that had been signed by their kings and by Rome when Julius Caesar began his march across Europe.

The current emperor had first professed love for all the Batavi had done on Rome's behalf when he acquitted Civillis last year. That he should now so disgrace Civillis's people by disbanding the positions of honour they held within the empire was a slap in the face to the Batavi.

"And you are no longer," Vitellius drawled. "What a shame. I am not certain that Galba would be terribly upset by your arrest. Nor will he be surprised, for it is suspicion that has made him send your warriors home. Now enough of this. Come with me, Civillis."

The announcement of the disbandment of the *Corpore Custodes* had silenced all the chieftains of the Chatti Federation. They stared at the legate, bristling in their silence.

"I will remind you," Civillis said quietly, "that I am a Roman citizen. I demand a trial."

Aullus Vitellius ground his teeth. The savage's arrogance had always grated on his nerves. He despised having to first consult with the chieftain on enacting laws in his own lands, but the Batavian people would not acquiesce unless the chieftain spoke the laws. He would not speak them if he disagreed with them. This arrest should put an end to that nonsense.

"Or have you so little regard for your own emperor that you would defy his laws?" Civillis asked this question in a low growl. A man could never be a bear, but Gaius Julius Civillis came very close in that moment.

"Not at all," Vitellius said. "A trial you shall have."

"Good. Because I would hate for word to get out to your emperor that you have overstepped your bounds."

Vitellius offered a tight smile. "I would not dream of it. Now, remove your weapons and come with me."

For a moment, Civillis did not move. He stood, surrounded by his peers, the temptation to unleash his battle prowess on the legate and his legions writ plain on his features. The guard surrounding Vitellius placed their hands around the hilts of their blades.

Deciding against starting a war at present, Civillis unhooked the large short-handed battle-axe he carried at his side.

"You know he means to kill you, do you not?" Brinno, chieftain of the Cananefates, said quietly to his friend in their native tongue.

Civillis nodded. "I do," he answered. "Brinno, it will fall to you if he tries anything."

Understanding Civillis's meaning, Brinno nodded. "I swear it."

"Good. Thank you."

The chieftains stood together, permitting Civillis to pass. As he did, he removed weapon after weapon from his person and handed them to each until all the chieftains of the Chatti Federation held one of his weapons. The symbolism was lost on the Romans, but the Germans understood. They would defend Civillis's people with those weapons should any evil befall him.

"This," Civillis said, hefting his war axe, "is for my son."

"I will bring it to him," a chieftain said.

"And my shield to my daughter."

"It will be done."

"Then it is good." Civillis walked forward to stand before the legate. Their differences might have been comical had they been friends. Civillis was, as all men of Germania Inferior, tall and powerful, made lean by the rigours of life as a Batavian man. Like most men of the region, he wore a well-groomed beard, grown long in preparation for the coming winter. His dark brown hair was pulled back in a single plait that ran down to the middle of his back.

Vitellius was, by contrast, short, plump, and bald, and his skin turned bright pink at the slightest exertion or northerly breeze. The chieftains had joked that Rome had sent an apple to govern them when Vitellius had come to Germania Inferior.

Now, however, the sight was anything but comical. Civillis stood head and shoulders above the legate, glowering down at him. The legate had to crane his neck to look the chieftain in the eye. Had he not his legions for a guard, Vitellius would have died for his insults. For now, however, Civillis permitted him to lead the way from his mead hall.

The sun shone brightly outside the hall, the summer not yet defeated. Members of the Legion *XIV Gemina* stood to attention as Vitellius marched outside. Beyond them, the people of the city of Batavorum stood in silence, grim faces watching as their chieftain was led from his mead hall. The Roman soldiers could not make out their intent as they stared impassively at the legion, and it made them uncomfortable. The uncertainty stretched to the Batavian chieftain, his features sombre, his brown eyes intelligent.

A man with light brown hair and dark brown eyes, tall and only just grown into his breadth moved forward, concern etching his features. The chieftain locked eyes with the man and shook his head, a movement barely perceptible. A young woman, blonde haired and blue eyed joined the man. Together, they stood and watched as the chieftain was led away.

"What is going on?" the woman murmured to the young man.

"They're arresting him," he answered.

"Again?"

The man scowled, but said nothing else as his father was led away.

# 69 AD, Spring, Brigantian Territory, Northern Britain

Mederei opened her eyes and smiled. Rhys lay beside her, his slow, regular breathing indicating he still slept. One strong, tattooed arm lay around her and she could feel his chest graze her back as he breathed.

The prince of the Caledonii had been a constant in her life since she fled north with her sister following the failure of the Icenian Federation's revolt against Rome. It was he who had argued so eloquently to permit Mederei and Modron a place amongst the Caledonii. At first, Rhys had tried to find a place for her with the women, but Mederei had proved too broken, too wild. She would fight her caretakers. The only way they found to calm her was to put a sword in her hand and to have her train with the men.

The men of the Caledonii had laughed at first. Mederei was but ten years old and thin from the starvation she endured in her flight north. But the rage of a wronged woman burnt deep in her breast, and those who did not come to respect Mederei soon learnt to fear her.

Only Rhys could calm her rages and she had blossomed some under his care, though Mederei's terrible temper still erupted unexpectedly. Even so,

Rhys's gentle voice and kind eyes had won her over, as did his promises of a free Britain.

To that end, Mederei joined the fight, standing as one of only four women in the ranks of the Caledonii. A warrior, just as her mother had been. Mederei sighed at the memory of her flame-haired mother.

Moving carefully to avoid waking her lover, she slipped from the bed and dressed in her under-armour. Looking back at Rhys briefly, she glided from the hide tent and stepped out into the cool air.

It was not yet first light in the highlands of the isle, though the first blush of iron grey had begun its slow advance on the horizon. The land was rugged, a scape of mountains and rocks, valleys covered in ancient forests and impossibly long lakes. It was not the landscape of her home, but it was still breathtakingly beautiful.

Mederei turned her gaze south, towards home. Or, at least, it used to be home. She remembered the splendour of her city, a beautiful oppidum with a grand palace worthy of the wealth of her tribe; the Magni Ceni, the people of high birth. They had once been the most powerful force in all of the south, perhaps all of the island.

Prasutagus had reigned as king, and he had done well for his people. They had become wealthy and strong under his rule. Rome had become jealous. They moved to rid the Magni Ceni of their power, emasculating the men by denying their right to keep their weapons about them, shunning the women, and laying such oppressions on the people as to smother them. What choice had they but to fight back?

When Rome marched on Venta Icenorum and demanded the throne, what people would not object? And when they did…

Mederei pulled her mind sharply back from that day, when the Romans dragged her mother outside by her fiery hair, and threw herself and her sister down on the floor. She could not bear to remember her sister screaming and thrashing as they were both raped, beaten, and raped again until they lay senseless on the ground. Mederei closed her mind to the memories of her mother's cries as she was flogged outside.

It was done. It would not do to relive it.

Modron approached, the sound of her light footfalls on the soft grass pulling Mederei from the horrors of her past. She turned to Modron and smiled.

Her sister smiled in return. In the folds of her skirts she had a pile of wildflowers. Large, vacant grey eyes, just like their father's but without the wit and sorrow, implored Mederei. Modron held up a small comb. Mederei sighed and smiled. She took the comb.

"Come on then," she said quietly, inviting her younger sister to sit on the ground before the cold fire pit.

Modron's smile widened and she emptied her pile of flowers beside the log seat before skipping around it to sit on the grass. Mederei sat on the log and began to comb through her sister's hair. Modron was blessed with the same fiery hair as her mother, a shining brilliant red. That was where their similarities ended.

When Rome snatched the throne away from her daughters, raping them, stripping away her clothes and flogging her before all her people, when Rome had burnt the crops, stole the cattle and sold her family into slavery, Mederei's mother had marched to war.

Modron lost her mind.

She had lain prone and unmoving after the rape, staring up into the rafters of the great hall even as the flames Rome had set inside the walls began to eat at the wood. It was Mederei who moved to act, struggling against the pain and the smoke to drag her sister's limp body from the burning building. That was when she had seen her mother, naked, her back stripped of flesh, lying unconscious at the foot of the steps.

Again, Mederei forced her mind away from that day, focusing once more on her sister's glorious hair. Sadness crept across her. Modron had not spoken a word since the rape. She had stared into nothingness, compelled neither to eat nor drink until Mederei was certain she would lose her sister.

It seemed Modron heard or saw nothing at all, not the cries of the Romans as they were slaughtered by the brave army of Britons who rose against them, not the flames of the three cities their mother razed to the ground, not the marching Roman legions, fresh from the slaughter of the druids, not their brave and beautiful mother's death.

Modron had remained silent and dreamy-eyed the entire time. She had stared up at nothing, smiling as their tearful mother hugged them one last time. She had not answered her mother's loving goodbye, the apology and the promise. She remained smiling as they were loaded onto a chariot and whisked away, fleeing north out of Rome's grasp as their mother faced the oppressor one last time.

Anger flashed through Mederei in a powerful wave. She paused in her combing, struggling to push the rage back. She was fighting a battle today. She must save her ire for it. When the wave passed, she returned to combing her sister's hair, plaiting it in the style of the women from northern Gaul.

In truth, Mederei was glad for Modron's insanity. It was better than the alternative. When memories came, she would scream; scream and cry and scratch at her own skin and make herself bleed. In those moments, only Mederei could be counted on to calm her. Such fits were increasingly rare as Modron slipped further and further from reality. In its place were the dreamy eyes and mild smiles of a girl who lived in a world free of Rome and Roman horror. Still, Mederei would not change places with her sister, however enticing the serenity of Modron's insanity seemed at times.

Mederei had promised her mother two things: that she would care for her sister, and that she would never yield to Rome. This oath was the reason she yet lived. It was the reason she refused women's work and took up arms. She would live and die by this oath, and it filled her with strength.

Modron had inherited their mother's hair, but it was Mederei who had her fire.

Movement at the edge of the camp caught Mederei's eye and she glanced briefly to find Venutius, exiled king of the Brigantes, exiting his tent, a young woman scurrying out behind him. Mederei's lips twisted into a smile as Venutius caught her watching. She returned her attention to her sister as the exiled Brigantian king approached.

"May I sit?" he asked.

"Of course, my Lord," Mederei answered, not looking up. She did not need to look up. She had seen his face a thousand times over. He was handsome, as all the men from the north seemed to be, with a mess of once dark brown hair and pale blue eyes that sparkled. Exile had turned much of his hair white, and his eyes sagged with the weight of his hope.

"And how fares the lovely Lady Modron this fine, gloomy morning?" Venutius asked the girl sitting at Mederei's feet. Modron turned her head and stared up at Venutius with wide grey eyes. She smiled at him, and said nothing, before facing around again and turning her attention back to nothingness.

Venutius smiled sadly. He rested his elbows on his knees and stared at the empty fire pit. "I can get this started for you. It's chilly here in the north."

"That is not necessary," Mederei answered, keeping her voice quiet to avoid waking Rhys. "I will do it as soon as I'm finished with her hair."

Venutius nodded. He observed Mederei a moment. "More and more you look like your mother," he said. "I almost forget you are not her sometimes. She was an incredible woman."

"Yes," Mederei whispered. "She was. But I find I look more like my father. I have his build, and his hair."

That much was true. Mederei's hair was brown, with only a little red in it. It was more rust than flame, and it fell in great thick waves rather than a silken sheet. And while Modron had grey eyes, closer to their mother's bright blue, Mederei's eyes were pale dun; not quite green, not quite brown.

"But you have your mother's face. Any who has seen your mother could not mistake it, and though your eyes are not blue, they have the same spark which enchanted so many."

"How oft and how long have you gazed upon my mother's face, Venutius?"

Smiling, Venutius answered, "Often and long when I was a lad and before I married Cartimandua." He spat the name of his ex-wife as if it burnt his tongue.

Mederei smiled slightly. "I'm sorry. I did not mean to cause you to mention her."

Venutius sighed. "The fault is not yours. It has been almost twenty years since she turned me aside for that fool Vellocatus. I should not be so bitter still."

Mederei picked up a wildflower from Modron's pile and considered it a moment. "Did you love her? Cartimandua, I mean."

Venutius stretched out his legs and looked towards the thin line of yellow that announced dawn. "I thought I did. And perhaps I still do, considering how fresh the hurt is. But I could not stand idly by and do nothing when Rome came to slake their greed. I invited Caratacus to find refuge amongst us, and Cartimandua betrayed him to Rome. She betrayed me. She betrayed our customs. And she betrayed our people. I cannot let that go unpunished."

"No," Mederei agreed. "You cannot. And you will not. You have the finest warriors in all of Britain on your side, Venutius. We will take back Isurium, and your people will be free from the rule of the traitor."

"It saddens my heart to hear the bitterness in your voice, Mederei," Venutius said, smiling gently. "And still it exults to hear it. I think Britain might yet be free so long as you are here to defend it."

"As I intend to do for always."

"Good. Britain needs women like you."

"Britain needs men like her, too," a voice said from behind them.

Mederei smiled at the sound of it. Rhys had awoken.

"Good morning, love," she greeted.

"Good morning, love," Rhys answered. He wrapped one arm around Mederei's shoulder and kissed her neck.

"Good morning, little Modron," he greeted.

Modron did not seem to hear. She tilted her head to peer at nothingness from another angle.

"What colour flowers would you like in your hair, love?" Mederei asked her sister, bringing the dreamy girl back from the brink of nothingness. Modron looked to the pile of flowers, running her delicate fingers lightly over them before closing upon a white wildflower and holding it up.

"No, Modron," Mederei said, sighing. "You cannot wear white flowers in your hair. White is the colour of death. Choose another."

Modron scowled and shook her head, raising the white flower again.

"Modron," Mederei said, more firmly this time.

"There can be no harm in it," Rhys said gently. "Does not the intent of the wearer matter as much as the colour?"

"No," Mederei snapped, but she relented, taking the flower from her sister and placing it firmly in the girl's plait. Modron picked another white flower from her pile and held it up. Mederei found a place in her sister's hair for the white flowers as Modron handed them to her until, apparently tired of being bedecked, Modron rose to her feet and wandered off back through the camp. She would wander around the camp until someone took pity on her and sat her inside a tent to eat something. Mederei watched her slow walk a moment before turning to help her lover with the fire.

"I have this," Rhys said. "Go put your armour on. We will march as soon as we have broken our fast."

Mederei nodded, leaving the fire to finish dressing. Rhys and Venutius watched her leave.

"She has come a long way," Venutius noted, rising to help Rhys build the fire.

Rhys nodded, not trusting himself to speak. His expression betrayed him all the same.

"You are worried for her." It was not a question.

"She is so filled with hatred," Rhys answered softly.

"She has good reason to hate; more than most of us, and we all hate Rome."

Rhys nodded, glancing briefly at the tent entrance, before fetching the fire bow.

"But," Venutius prompted.

"But this is her first battle as one of our warriors, Venutius."

"You are worried she will succumb to terror?"

"No," Rhys replied, smiling softly. "There are many words that can be used to describe Mederei. Coward is not one of them. No, it is her temper I fear. I am afraid it will carry her away. I am afraid she will do something rash. I fear that her own hatred will end her."

Venutius nodded. "Her end is inevitable. The same is true for every one of us. Even Rome will end in its time. If she does fall in battle, at least her end will be on her own terms. We can rejoice at that."

"And that I died free," Mederei said from the edge of the fire pit. "You should speak softer if you do not wish to be heard," she added when both men looked at her, startled.

"I am properly humbled," Venutius said. He smiled up at Mederei. She did not smile in return. Her face remained a mask of disinterest, but her pale hazel eyes burned. Sensing a taste of Mederei's temper, Venutius excused himself. "I should go prepare for battle. My Lord," he bowed to Rhys. "My Lady." Bowing to Mederei, Venutius made a hasty exit.

"You think I cannot handle myself?" Mederei asked her lover. Though her voice was soft, it contained an icy metallic quality that told Rhys she was bristling for a fight.

"Save your anger, my love," Rhys replied gently. "I am worried for you, that is all."

"I don't need your worry," Mederei snapped.

Rhys rose, the fire unstarted. "Please, let's not fight. We both may be struck down in today's battle."

"For my part, I hope it is you." Mederei spun on her heel and stalked away, heading towards the horses.

Rhys sighed and hung his head briefly. He knew better than to chase her down. She needed time alone. He would go to her later.

"She must be amazing beneath you," Geraint said as he wandered up to Rhys's fire pit. "Otherwise I don't know how you put up with that dragon."

"Shut your mouth, Geraint," Rhys said. He tossed his burly shield-bearer the fire bow. "And start the damned fire."

"Yes, my Lord," Geraint said, his full lips twisting in a smile.

"You're not funny," Rhys snapped as he stalked back to his tent.

"What's upset him?" Calgacus asked as he approached the fire pit.

"He and his dragon are fighting," Geraint replied.

"So? Aren't they always fighting?"

"No, little brother," Rhys said as he exited his tent, carrying his weapons. "We are not. Why aren't you in your armour? Go dress. Now."

"Armour restricts my stomach," Calgacus replied. "And I need room for breakfast."

"Calgacus," Rhys said in warning.

"You don't want me to tell mother you've deprived me of breakfast, do you?"

"I don't want to tell mother that you died of your wounds because you were too stupid to put your armour on. Now go. This minute, Calgacus."

"All right, all right," Calgacus said, raising his hands, palms out in a signal of submission. "I'll go. I'll just ride into battle starving and let you deal with mother's wrath."

Calgacus easily dodged the small stone his older brother lobbed at him and ran down to his tent, grinning like a fool.

"You shouldn't be so hard on him," Geraint said. "He's only trying to make you feel better."

"He is trying my patience," Rhys growled.

"You're starting to sound like Mederei," Geraint noted, before kneeling at the edge of the pit and blowing gently on the ember he had just placed in the kindling. His words gave Rhys pause, and the elder prince of the Caledonii sat heavily on the log by the fire.

"She has a good heart, Geraint," he said. "If you could only see how good she is."

"How can we?" Geraint said. He did not look at his lord, but stared at the growing flame, blowing gently until he felt satisfied it no longer needed his intervention. "All she shows us is anger and fire."

"What reason has she to show you anything but? None of you gave her welcome when she took up a blade, and you have all yet to do so now that she's proved herself with it."

"Aye, so her kindness is dependent on getting her way, is it? I've known a few women like that. Not worth the time of day."

Rhys bristled. He rose to his feet. "You will not speak against her in my presence, Geraint. Not ever. She has lived through horrors that would have broken you long ago."

Geraint shook his head. "Hand me your weapons and I shall strap them on. You always manage to do it wrong."

Remaining coldly silent, Rhys held out his sword belt and stood still while Geraint affixed it to him.

"No one is saying she isn't strong, my Lord," Geraint said. "There's not a man in this camp who does not admire her strength. But being strong and being respected are two different things. A good ruler must learn this. Mederei seems to think that being fearsome is the only quality she needs. If we achieve the impossible, if we manage to rid this island of Rome forever, and she is reinstated as Queen of the Magni Ceni, she must be capable of ruling justly. I fear that in her present state she is not."

"The Magni Ceni are a people no longer," Rhys replied, shaking his head. "They have been torn asunder by Rome's violent retribution. I fear there will not be a kingdom for her to rule should we win our island back from Rome. And she has promised to be my wife."

Geraint fumbled with the buckle he had been working on.

Rhys smiled slightly. "Her terms are impossible, of course. She has agreed to be my wife should we win the entire island back."

"That is impossible."

"And it's the only reason I stay in this fight some days. On the days I lose faith, I roll over to see her beside me, and the sight fills me with fire. You have much to be thankful for on her account, Geraint."

Geraint finished arming his lord and stepped back. He nodded to himself in satisfaction. "If it helps you, my Lord, we do not hate her."

"Who?" Calgacus demanded as he returned from dressing himself.

"No one," Rhys said.

"Mederei," Geraint said.

"Ah, yes. The divisive woman." Calgacus pulled a face. "She has pretty eyes." He shrugged. "When she is in a good mood. What's for breakfast?"

"Sit down," Rhys said, smiling. "I'll get you fed."

"Thanks, big brother. I knew you cared for me."

Rhys laughed and shook his head. He ruffled his brother's hair and took a seat beside him. Geraint set to task, heating up a pot of barley gruel and cutting the remnants of last night's dinner to mix in. It did not look appetizing, but every northerner knew it was hearty and warming and would last them the day. It was the best thing to eat on a morning before a battle. Before long, the three men were happily chewing on mushy barley, wild mushrooms, and overcooked meat.

"Save some," Rhys demanded of his brother as the young man took a third helping. "I will bring a bowl to Mederei."

Calgacus looked across the camp to the solitary figure of Mederei as she stood with her spotted horse, staring across the craggy landscape. Her horse stood patiently with her, grazing at the grass by her feet. The horse had been a gift. Mederei had been asked to choose a foal from amongst the births of the Caledonii's prized mares her first year in the north. Mederei had in turn consulted her vacant-eyed sister.

By some miracle, Modron had understood her sister and the situation enough to walk amongst the foals. They had no fear of her. By this did the Caledonii know that for all her insanity, Modron could be trusted. Horses knew evil. Modron was not it. The fire-haired girl emerged moments later leading a multi-coloured spotted foal, its concerned mother keeping pace.

"This one," Mederei had declared. The foal had walked boldly up to Mederei, seeking kindness. Mederei obliged. That day had been the first day she had smiled since arriving in the north.

Horse and rider became inseparable. Mederei took over all duties in caring for the foal, refusing to allow the stable hands to do so. Despite knowing that the Magni Ceni were famous horsemen, the depth of Mederei's knowledge of horses and the speed with which she bonded with hers had taken the men of Caledonia aback.

"Perhaps I should take it," Calgacus said. "She won't appreciate your presence if she's still angry with you. And I might be able to talk her down a bit before you approach."

"Now that is a good little brother," Geraint said. "Braving the dragon to spare you."

"Call her that once more, Geraint, I dare you," Rhys growled. He looked at his younger brother. Calgacus and Mederei were roughly the same age, and he worried that his brother might have designs on her.

"I'm not going to try and steal her, Rhys," Calgacus said, rolling his eyes. "I'm not as patient as you, and we'd fight more often." He stood and took up a fresh bowl of gruel to bring to Mederei. "Idiot," he added as he snatched up a spoon and marched away.

"Am I really that easy to read?" Rhys asked Geraint. Geraint merely grinned at his lord.

"Here," Calgacus said, sticking a bowl of steaming gruel under Mederei's nose.

"I'm not hungry," Mederei replied, still staring out at the green lands of the Brigantes.

"That's entirely beside the point. You will need it for the upcoming fight."

Mederei turned, her eyes hard as flint. Calgacus did not flinch from her, as so many others would have. He simply offered her a bright smile and waved the bowl beneath her nose.

Sighing, Mederei took the bowl. "Thank you."

Calgacus shrugged. "So, what did he do this time?" he asked.

Mederei smiled slightly, but did not answer. Instead she took a spoonful of the barley gruel and munched quietly.

"I mean, you don't have to tell me if you don't want to. I just want to make sure that I don't make the same mistake when I finally fall in love with a girl."

Mederei twitched.

"He does love you, you know."

Shaking her head, Mederei glanced at Rhys's younger brother. "You should not ask me. I am not like most women, Calgacus," she said quietly. "How can I be?"

"Oh, I don't know, you have all the right parts."

The spoonful of gruel Mederei had just placed in her mouth stuck in her throat as she laughed. Her laugh turned to violent coughing as her lungs tried to repel the gruel. Calgacus grinned at her as she struggled to get control of herself.

"Bastard," she snapped between coughs.

Calgacus laughed. "Not true!" he declared. "My parents are wedded!" He continued to grin, chuckling occasionally as Mederei coughed. His grin widened when her coughing at last slowed then ceased. She wiped the tears from her eyes.

"You are lucky your cheek is endearing," she said.

Calgacus laughed, the brightness of the sound echoing from the grey stones around the camp.

"Are you trying to kill my beloved?" Rhys asked from the edge of the horse enclosure.

"Damn," Calgacus said. "My plot has been discovered. I must flee!" And with that, Calgacus pranced away from Mederei, flouncing ridiculously.

Rhys sighed, trying hard not to laugh at his younger brother. "Ever the child," he muttered.

"It is a good thing," Mederei answered. "Too often childhoods are cut short in these times."

Rhys entered the enclosure. "I have come to beg for forgiveness."

Mederei looked down at her bowl and toyed with the gruel. "I am the one who should be begging for forgiveness," she said. "I should not have snapped at you as I did. I'm sorry. I don't know why I keep letting my anger loose at you."

Wrapping Mederei in a tight embrace, Rhys said, "You have a right to be angry. And I would bear all of your rage if it means I get to hold you at night."

"You are too good to me," Mederei whispered. She let herself lean against Rhys a moment. "And I am so harsh with you."

"You deserve goodness," Rhys answered.

"I don't," Mederei replied.

Rhys could hear tears in her voice, so he pulled her closer. "You do, and nothing you say or do shall ever convince me otherwise."

Mederei turned so that she could press her chest to his. They embraced for a long while, saying nothing. Mederei fought tears, and Rhys's silent strength was both a boon and a bane to her struggles.

"My Lord," Geraint said from the edge of the enclosure. "The men have finished eating. We're ready to ride out when you are."

Rhys nodded at his shield-bearer and sent him away. Mederei stood upright.

"Hurry up and eat," Rhys said. "I'll saddle Canu for you."

Mederei nodded. She ate as quickly as she could manage as Rhys saddled her noble spotted horse before moving on to his own strong mount.

"Come, Canu," Mederei said, holding out her hand. Understanding the gesture, Canu trotted over to Mederei's side, coming to a stop so that Mederei could mount without so much as taking a step.

"Your horse," Rhys said, tightening his horse's girdle, "is uncommonly thoughtful."

"She is a good mare," Mederei replied, patting Canu's neck appreciatively. "If a little bossy."

Rhys smiled and mounted. "Leave the dishes," he said, noting that Mederei still had her bowl and spoon. "The camp girls will clean them."

"And here I was thinking they served only to warm beds," Mederei replied.

"Are you a camp girl, then?" Rhys asked. "For you warm my bed."

"I am your camp girl," Mederei answered, making her lover smile. He said nothing as he kicked his horse into an easy trot. Mederei followed suit.

The warriors of the Caledonii and allied tribes gathered behind a hill. Beyond that hill, across the plain stood Isurium, the capital city of the Brigantes. There sat Queen Cartimandua, universally reviled by her own people. Indeed, Cartimandua was so hated, that the Caledonian army was able to hide by virtue of the pretend ignorance of the rest of the kingdom. Farmers, huntsmen, and milkmaids had been by often to ensure that the army was well fed and healthy prior to battle. The majority of the army were made up of Brigantian warriors, with a large contingent within the walls of Isurium, ready to turn upon their queen and open the gates of the city to Venutius, their exiled king.

"The plan remains unchanged," Rhys began to say as his officers gathered close. His speech was interrupted by the running approach of a huntsman.

"My Lords," the huntsman said, huffing and puffing. "I come now from the city. Cartimandua knows of your imminent attack. She had sent for aid from Rome."

"We expected as much," Venutius growled. "The woman could not command her way through a flock of chickens. What legion has come?"

"No legion, Your Majesty," the huntsman said. "But auxiliaries. Light cavalry, mostly. They are attempting to extract Cartimandua. Fighting within the city walls has already begun."

"Change of plans," Rhys said sharply. "Calgacus, Mederei, take the Caledonian riders south to the road. See if you cannot ambush Cartimandua's escort should they evade us. Calgacus, the command is yours."

Calgacus's face lit up, a smile hovering around his lips and his posture improving. He turned his horse and began the ride south.

"Take care, my love," Rhys said as Mederei prepared to follow. "Come back to me."

Mederei nodded. She offered her lover a small smile. She turned and joined the rest of the Caledonian cavalry as they thundered through the woods to the southern road.

"The rest of us will take the city. No doubt Rome's lackeys will fight to keep it. Let's give our friend his kingdom back."

Geraint raised a horn to his lips and blew a musical call. The army moved forward at a trot.

"This is as good a place as any," Calgacus noted, peering over the rocky outcrop onto the road. "We can have the archers on higher ground here, and the cavalry has space to hide. We should—" His schemes were cut short by a cry of alarm.

"Ambush!" Mederei shouted, scrambling down from beside Calgacus and running to the aid of her countrymen.

"Bastards," Calgacus spat. He slid back down the rock and drew his weapons as the Romans flooded the space he had made for his warriors. The horses screamed shrilly, bucking several of their riders off. Canu, however, saw her rider running for her. She turned in her flight to meet Mederei.

"On your horses," Mederei barked as she mounted. "On your horses!"

The startled Caledonians responded, seeking their mounts and drawing their weapons. Mederei led the counterstrike, cutting a wedge through the attacking Romans before the Romans closed ranks and pushed back. A piercing scream caught Mederei's attention and she saw on her left Calgacus's horse buckle, a thick Roman lance piercing its noble chest.

"Calgacus!" Mederei screamed as the young warrior disappeared from view.

"My Lady!" another rider shouted. "We are routed! We must fall back!"

Mederei looked about her and saw that it was true. She nodded, but the sound of clashing weapons turned her head. Calgacus was on his feet, fighting hard. Mederei's heart soared and she said, "Not without the prince! Take the right flank and push north. Let me get Calgacus on a horse, and we can fall back."

The cavalryman nodded. "Taexali!" he barked. "With me!" To Mederei he said, "Get him out quickly. We are sore pressed."

The Britons moved swiftly, swinging around the ambushing Romans and drawing them off so that Mederei might be able to fight her way through to Calgacus. She rode forward, cutting through the Romans with practiced efficiency. Her first battle and neither the sight of blood nor the screams of the men she maimed and killed troubled her in the least. This fight was for Britain, every Roman slain was penance for the crimes of their empire against her people, punishment for her rape and the death of her mother. All of Rome would have to crumble into ash at her feet before retribution would be hers; and she intended to see it done.

She reached Calgacus, though not as quickly as she had hoped. He was gravely wounded and half-blinded by the blood that poured from his head into his eyes.

"Calgacus!" she barked. The prince turned in time to see the knife of a Roman soldier strike down on her thigh. Mederei screamed as she was dragged off her horse.

"Gods damn everything," Calgacus spat. His sword strokes flashed with renewed vigour, hoping to reach his brother's beloved before she was killed.

He found her, on her feet and fighting savagely.

"Canu!" Mederei called, when she turned to find Calgacus at her side. "My Lord," she said to him as Canu came to her side. "Get on."

"What? No! You get on."

"Calgacus, I am struck," she said.

It was then that the young prince noticed that Mederei had one hand pressed to her side, blood streaming through her fingers all the same. He looked up at her in alarm and saw that her face was pale and twisted with pain.

"You must ride north to your brother, return with reinforcements if you can. I will not survive that ride. Besides, the Caledonii need their princes more than they need me."

Calgacus swallowed past a lump in his throat. "I can't just leave you here," he said.

"You must. If you are swift enough, I may yet be saved. I will try and hold the Romans for as long as I can, but you must ride. Ride now!"

Knowing her words for truth, Calgacus mounted.

"Bear him well, Canu," Mederei said. She turned and re-entered the fray, sparing not a glance for Calgacus. Swearing, Calgacus turned Canu's nose and kicked her rump. The spotted mare bolted forward in a desperate flight to reach Rhys in time to save Mederei.

The fighting was bitter, and Mederei had long ago begun to feel the effects of the loss of blood caused by her wound. Still she pushed on, her and what was left of the warriors formed a solid barrier so that Calgacus could get away safely. Her vision narrowed and so it took her some time after her last kill to realize that the fighting had stopped. She blinked and looked around. Naught but five of the warriors who had departed to ambush Cartimandua still stood, and all of them were bloodied.

The Roman ambush had been defeated, but there were too few of them now to have any hope of capturing the traitor should she slip past Venutius and Rhys. One of the warriors nodded approvingly at Mederei. It was the last thing she saw before blood loss and exhaustion claimed her.

"Miserable ingrates!" Cartimandua fumed as she slowed her horse to a trot once it breeched the forest line. With the aid of the Roman auxiliary, she had managed to escape the city and had galloped south at great speed. She now rode amongst the Roman troops, safe on the south road, shrouded by thick forest. "My peace with Rome was the only thing keeping them from slaughter! And now I have lost my home and my birth-right, not to mention my husband! May Rome rain justice upon them!"

"No doubt they will," a tired commander answered. He did not look Roman, having the ruddy complexion of a northerner. From his accent, he was likely from somewhere in the Province of Germania. As was Roman policy, the auxiliaries were not Roman citizens, but taken from those kingdoms that had submitted to Rome's might.

"And what does Rome send to me to reward my loyalty? An auxiliary! There are no legions to spare, they claim! Damn them! I have defended them to my own people, and when I need them, where are they?"

"Look, Lady," the commander snapped. "You are lucky to have left that city with your head still on your shoulders. Rome is at war on four fronts, and there is no stability at her heart either. You are lucky Rome spared us at all."

Cartimandua clamped her mouth shut and sighed. "My apologies, good commander," she said. "I am understandably upset. I had thought that my people understood the value of Rome's favour. I had greatly overestimated them, I am afraid, and now find myself without a home and without a husband."

"Space has been made available to you in Rome," the commander answered, not losing the edge in his voice. "You will live the rest of your years in wealth and honour."

Another soldier, also German, from what Cartimandua could tell, muttered something in his native tongue, prompting snickers from the men nearby. Their commander barked something at them in their native tongue and discipline was restored.

They had not travelled through the woods long before they came across a scene of much bloodshed. The commander halted his troops and dismounted to survey the mess.

"Britons," one of his men said, turning over a corpse with his foot.

"Yes," the commander replied. He sighed. "They attempted to send an ambush, as we suspected they might." He shook his head. "Search for survivors."

It took almost an hour for the Britons and Romans to be separated. All the Romans the commander had left behind in the case of an ambush were accounted for. The Britons had slaughtered them to the last man. Of the Britons, only one had been found alive, a female champion. Some of the British force must have survived, for the woman was found hidden behind a large rock, her wounds treated.

"Put her in the wagon," the commander said. "And tend to those wounds properly. We might earn enough from her sale to make this venture worth the trouble. Hurry up, I want to be at camp before sundown."

Calgacus fought against nausea and unconsciousness as they flowed over him in waves. His wounds were more grievous than he realized when he let Mederei convince him she would not survive this ride. She may well have been telling the truth, for Calgacus was struggling himself, and her wounds had been greater still.

The gates to Isurium were thrown wide open, and there was much clamour in the streets. A celebration, Calgacus realized as he approached. Venutius and Rhys had retaken the city, and the anti-Roman majority were thrilled.

"Make way," he croaked. He had meant to bellow the order, but his voice had refused the work his mind had allotted it. "Gods," he whispered, keeling over in his saddle. The world spun as he began to slide off the horse.

"Whoa there," a friendly baker said, pausing in his dancing long enough to ensure Calgacus did not crack his head on the paved road. The man pushed Calgacus back into the saddle.

"Rhys. I need to talk to Rhys. Quickly," Calgacus managed to tell the man.

"Aye," the baker agreed. He turned to the crowd. "Make way!" he bellowed.

Finally, the revellers took note of the bloodied prince on horseback and the crowd immediately parted. Calgacus kicked Canu's flanks and the horse bolted forward once more.

"Rhys!" Calgacus screamed. "Rhys!"

"Calgacus!" Rhys said, running from the steps of the palace as he spied his bloodied brother on Mederei's horse.

"Rhys! Mederei…. We were ambushed," Calgacus started to explain. He fainted. Sliding once more from the saddle. Rhys hauled his brother off the horse.

"Healer!" he screamed. "I need a healer!"

The celebrating crowds had fallen silent, their eyes on the two princes of the Caledonii.

"Rhys," Calgacus whispered, having briefly regained consciousness. "She could not ride. They need aid." He fainted again.

The healer arrived, a young, hollow-eyed man who had trained at the druidic sanctuary on the Isle of Môna. He had only just departed to spend his allotted time amongst the people as his training dictated when Rome attacked the sanctuary. He had lost all his friends and family in that cowardly attack. The loss plagued him still.

"Go," the healer said softly to Rhys. "I will care for him. Our people need your aid."

Rhys nodded and stood. "Caledonii!" he bellowed, running to his horse.

His loyal men left their places amongst the revellers and returned to their horses, mounting quickly.

"Our friends need aid," Venutius said. He began to descend the palace steps. He paused.

"Go," a Brigantian guard said to him. "I will start the clearing of the streets."

"Thank you," Venutius said, running forward. "And someone care for that horse!" he ordered as he ran. Before long, the healer and his aides had lifted Calgacus onto a stretcher and carried him inside the palace for treatment. The royal stable hands had collected Canu, whose sweaty flanks were flecked with blood and foam, and led her away for care. The riders of the Caledonii along with Venutius, his new shield-bearer and a few of the Brigantian warriors, galloped south.

They rode hard until they came to the place of slaughter. Rhys pulled his horse up short, dismounting before the beast had time to properly stop. His gaze swept the carnage.

"Mederei," he whispered, seeking her form amongst the dead.

"My Lord," Geraint said, pointing north. There, moving through the trees, the remaining warriors of the northern federation stumbled towards them. They were all heavily wounded.

"My Lord," a Taexali horseman said, bowing before Rhys. There were tears in his eyes as he stood. "We were ambushed."

"Mederei?" Rhys demanded. He cared for nothing else.

"Rome has her," the horseman replied, his voice cracking. "They came in great number after the ambush, the traitor queen with them. We tried to hide Mederei, but they discovered her and took her away."

"And you just let them?"

"My Lord, we are but five and heavily wounded, and they were a hundred strong. There was nothing we could do."

"And you just let them?" Rhys demanded again, his voice growing louder.

Geraint dismounted and immediately went to Rhys, placing a comforting hand on his lord's shoulder. Rhys twisted away from Geraint and walked away, trembling with rage.

"You did what was right," Venutius told the horseman gently. "It would not do to throw your lives away in a fight you could not win."

Muttering darkly under his breath, Rhys spun around and marched to his horse. He mounted, pushing the beast forward. Geraint grabbed the reins and pulled back. The horse stopped moving, issuing an irritated snort at the interruption.

"What are you doing?" Rhys demanded of his shield-bearer.

"I ask the same of you," Geraint replied.

"I am going to get Mederei back."

"Don't be foolish," Venutius said. "You would not stand a chance against one hundred auxiliaries."

"I'll be damned if I do not try," Rhys snapped. "I will not leave her to Rome!"

"I will go," Geraint said, interrupting Venutius before the king could formulate a reply. "I will try and find a way to help her escape the Romans. My Lord," he said to Rhys, "you are the heart of this fight for our people. They cannot do without you."

"Mederei is the heart of me," Rhys answered, his face twisted with anger and grief.

"I know," Geraint said gently. "I know. I will do all I can, I swear. But you must remain with your people. They need you."

"It is good," Venutius said to Rhys. "Geraint will not be goaded into foolishness as a lover's heart would. He will be better for retrieving Mederei than you, who might be called to rash action for love of her."

Rhys knew this was true. He looked between Geraint and Venutius before swallowing past the lump that had formed in his throat and nodded. "That is true," he whispered. "I would not be prudent. Geraint, you must go in my stead. Bring my beloved back to me."

"Tomorrow," Venutius said. "You all need tending now that the fighting is done, and I will not see you out of Brigantian lands without having cared for you to the best of my abilities. Geraint, you must be at full strength for this undertaking."

Geraint and Venutius both looked to Rhys, who nodded. "Tomorrow," he whispered.

Seeing his lord so close to tears hurt Geraint's heart. He had known Rhys since the prince was a babe. He had trained him and served as a mentor and guide until the prince was old enough to take control himself. Of all of Geraint's many accomplishments, the young prince Rhys was his grandest. Tears struck Geraint's own eyes as he gazed upon Rhys's miserable features. He offered his lord a small, sympathetic smile before releasing his lord's reins and mounting his own horse. The party turned north, riding slowly back to Isurium. Rhys said not a word the entire journey.

The morning dawned brightly as if in mockery of Rhys's grief. The prince of the Caledonii sat at the table in the main hall of the palace, staring down at his untouched food. No one knew how to breech his wall of misery, and so they feasted, ignoring him as much as possible.

All except Geraint.

The shield-bearer sat beside his lord, eating slowly and ignoring the joviality of the feasters around him. He did not speak to his lord, for he had no words of comfort that might soothe the prince's broken heart. There were no words that could ease the worry that had kept the prince awake all night. Nothing could be done to calm the fears of what might happen to Mederei, who had already suffered so much at the hands of Rome.

The wounds of most of the warriors had been well tended. Geraint's wounds were slight, and would heal well even if disrupted by travel. He would hold by the promise he made to his lord. He would do all in his power to restore his lord's love to him.

He said as much after breakfast as he prepared to leave.

"Please," Rhys answered. "But Geraint, it would ruin me as much if you were killed. Be careful."

"It does my heart glad to know that my Lord loves me," Geraint replied. He offered a smile to Rhys, and it was returned, though Rhys had tears in his eyes. Unable to bear seeing his prince so miserable, Geraint wrapped the young man in a strong embrace.

"You must be strong now," he told his lord. "Your people will look to you to keep them safe from Rome's wrath. You must concern yourself with more than the fate of one woman."

Rhys nodded. "For your sake, Geraint, I will try."

"That's a good lad," Geraint said. He released Rhys from his bear-like hug and patted him on his shoulder. "I do not think Mederei would want you to crumble, so if all else fails, try for her sake."

This brought a smile to Rhys's face. "I can imagine what words she would fling at me should I yield to my grief."

"Aye," said Geraint. "They would not be kind."

"No," Rhys replied. "No, they would not."

Geraint mounted. "I will send word when I can. Try and be patient with me, my Lord. This will take some planning and a good deal of luck if I am to steal her back from under Rome's oversized nose."

Rhys nodded and grinned. "Good luck. And thank you."

"Thank me when I return with her. A title would show your gratitude, I think."

Laughing Rhys stepped back. "Geraint, if you return her to me, you can have mine."

"Oh, aye? Me? A prince? Hah!" With that, Geraint spurred his horse on, leaving Isurium at a gallop.

## 69 AD, SPRING, BATAVI TERRITORY, PROVENCE OF GERMANIA INFERIOR

"What?" Vitellius demanded, his eyes bulging in his head as the news was relayed to him.

"Emperor Severus Galba is dead," the messenger replied. "Emperor Otha wishes you to turn away from your quest for Rome and to offer your allegiance."

Vitellius narrowed his eyes at the messenger.

"Legate," said the commander of the Legion *XXI Rapax*, leaning against the table where Vitellius was currently seated. "My sources have told me that Otha had Galba killed in a bid for the throne. This treason must be punished."

"Is that so commander?"

"It is. You will have no better opportunity, unless you feel Otha shall make a better emperor? Or perhaps it is that you endorse this treason against yourself?"

Vitellius sighed and rested one plump elbow upon the table. He stared at the messenger, who looked between the legate and the commanders of the two legions Vitellius commanded.

"It is the treason that bothers me most," the commander of Legion *V Alaudae* said. "There are many things a man might do to win a throne. Treason is the most foul."

"And here I was thinking that Gauls did not care for the Roman throne."

"We don't," the commander said, "but for all we owe Julius Caesar. We made a vow, and we are men of honour. Besides, treason even amongst foes is to be condemned."

"Bravely put," Vitellius noted, smiling at the commander. "In the presence of a Roman."

The commander smiled. "Has Rome ever had any reason to doubt our legion?"

"No," Vitellius admitted with a sigh. With Galba dead, Vitellius saw a chance for his own advancement. He looked to the messenger. "Run back to Otha, and tell him that the true emperor is on his way to Rome. He will answer for his crimes."

"Otha is the emperor," the messenger replied stubbornly.

"I am the emperor," Vitellius answered with a sneer. "And it is fear of my legitimacy that guided Otha to kill Galba I have no doubt, so frightened was he that he might lose his position of privilege. Well, I will not back down from what is rightfully mine. Otha will kneel, or he will die. Now run along, before I lose my patience with you and send you back without your head."

The messenger quailed, turning a peculiar shade of white, before bowing and fleeing the encampment.

"Tell me," Vitellius said to the commander of the Legion *XXI Rapax*. "What do your sources say of Otha's forces?"

"He has the loyalty of the Praetorian Guard, who did his killing for him, the coward. Legions *I Adiutrix* and *XIV Gemina* are with him as well. There are rumours that he has promised freedom to every gladiator who fights for him."

"Indeed? *XIV Gemina* is with Otha?"

"Yes, Legate."

"If I may suggest, Legate," the commander of Legion *V Alaudae* interjected. "The Batavians know Legion *XIV Gemina*. They were the auxiliaries for them since the days of Julius Caesar. They would know best how to fight them."

"Do not even suggest it!"

"Legate, call the Batavians to arms. Have them fight for you."

"They will not," Vitellius said, bitterness making him spit the words. "Or you forget I arrested their beloved chieftain."

"Then release him in exchange for this fight. Civillis will honour the agreement."

"Just whose side are you on, Gaul?"

"Your side," the commander replied. "Only the Batavians will know how best to deal with *XIV Gemina*. And thanks to the bitterness between the auxiliaries and that legion, the fighting will be hard."

Vitellius scowled as he pondered the words of the commander of the Gaulish Legion *V Alaudae*. "I am not over fond of the idea," he admitted.

"I imagine not. Call for him all the same. Civillis will aid you if it promises his freedom."

"Very well," Vitellius agreed. "Send for Civillis."

It took only a matter of minutes before the burly chieftain of the Batavi stood before Vitellius. He glowered at the legate, his dark brown eyes flat and untrusting. His standing as a Roman citizen had afforded Civillis luxuries other prisoners were denied. Still, his silent regard emanated a deep threat.

"Gaius Julius Civillis, you are looking as robust as always," Vitellius said with a small smile.

"What do you want, Vitellius?" Civillis demanded, his voice harsh from disuse.

"Well, many things, but for now I want to set you free."

Civillis's brows knitted together as he scowled down at the plump legate. "In exchange for something, I assume."

"Nothing gets past your sharp mind, does it?"

"Save the flattery for the mindless fools upon which it works. Do not insult my intelligence."

"Very well," Vitellius replied. All veneer of false nicety vanished from his features. "Otha has killed Galba, who so graciously acquitted you of treason. He claims the throne for himself."

"And you want it, is that it?" Civillis smirked at the surprised expression Vitellius momentarily let slip. "Aye. I thought as much. A grasping worm as you ever were, Legate."

"Legion *XIV Gemina* fights for Otha."

This captured Civillis's attention. The great bear of a man straightened.

"I understand you fought beside them in the Province of Britannia during the red witch's rebellion."

"I did."

"It was there you earned your distinction, and was awarded with Roman citizenship was it not?"

"It was before then, when we forded the river and slew the charioteers of Caratacus."

"Oh yes. You were instrumental in forming the battle plan, as I recall. Not bad. It was your first year in the army. In any case, I understand that you do not much like that legion."

"I do not."

"Good. Then you will not be sad to fight against them."

"Them? No. But there are Batavian auxiliaries amongst them. I will not raise my weapon against my own."

"Not even for the price of your freedom?"

"So, if I have this correct, you want me to lead the veteran Batavian auxiliaries as part of your bid to defeat Otha and claim the imperial throne."

"And I'll be out of your hair and your province forever."

Civillis grinned. It was a smile devoid of humour, a flashing of teeth that served as a warning. "I will have your word on that, Legate."

"Whatever do you mean?"

"My freedom assured, forever. And never will you bother the Batavi again."

"I swear," Vitellius replied. "You shall be free to live your days in peace, and all previous treaties between the Batavi and Rome shall be honoured."

"I will have that in writing, Legate," Civillis growled.

Sighing, Vitellius waved imperiously at a serving boy, who ran to fetch parchment and ink. He returned momentarily, setting the pieces hurriedly on the table, as if frightened that moving any slower would earn him the brutal lick of the lash.

Making a show of it, Vitellius rolled up his sleeve and took up the stylus.

"A warning, Vitellius," Civillis said quietly. "I can read."

Vitellius smiled tightly at Civillis before returning to his work. He wrote carefully, to avoid any errors. He blew on the ink once he was done, willing it to dry faster, before turning the parchment for Civillis to inspect.

"Your seal?" Civillis demanded.

"Of course," Vitellius said. "How remiss of me." Taking off the ring he wore on his little finger, Vitellius took a small round of coloured clay from his box of writing tools. He affixed it to the bottom of the paper and pressed the face of his ring upon it.

"There," he said, turning the paper once more to face Civillis. "Are you satisfied now?"

Taking his time, for indeed Civillis's skills in reading were not profound, the chieftain looked over the parchment.

"It seems in order."

"Then you will fight for me?"

"I will fight for my freedom," Civillis growled. "You be damned."

"Lovely," Vitellius said, clapping his hands together in delight. "We march tomorrow. Someone unlock those shackles and see our brave Batavian freedom fighter back to his family."

Civillis held his hands out as another serving boy ran forward with the keys to release the shackles that bound his wrists. The thick iron cuffs dropped to the rug with a heavy thud. Civillis rubbed his brutalized wrists, trying to bring feeling back to the flesh there. Those shackles were not made for thick northern bones. They had stopped much of the flow of blood to his hands.

"You have a day to muster your warriors," Vitellius said.

"I need a fortnight," Civillis said.

Vitellius raised his brows at him.

"My men are all veterans, their time in the auxiliaries served. They have returned to their homes, not to some barracks to await further instruction. Have you any idea how long it takes to cover the length and breadth of our land?"

"We are supposed to be marching tomorrow."

"That is not my problem."

"I cannot spare two weeks. Otha will be marching on us even as we speak."

"Then you will meet him in Gaul instead of Rome," Civillis said. "And that suits my men just fine. It's terrain we know."

Vitellius scowled.

"There is no way I can have an army ready to march come the morrow," Civillis said. "Even if magic were real and I was in possession of it, it could not be done."

"Fine. You have a fortnight."

"Thank you, Legate."

"You are dismissed," Vitellius said.

Civillis nodded and turned.

"And Civillis," Vitellius added, "I am the emperor. You will show the proper deference."

"You are not the emperor," Civillis said. "Not yet. Good day, Legate." With that, Civillis turned and strode from Vitellius's halls, free at last.

"I genuinely hate that man," Vitellius said.

"Father!" Gyða said, dropping her basket of dried fish as she spied the enormous man lumbering through the streets. It took her brother a moment to understand that he, too, saw his grim-faced father. He smiled, moving swiftly on his sister's heels as she ran for the man.

"Gyða!" Civillis said, opening his arms wide, permitting his daughter to fly into them. He laughed brightly as he hugged the woman close. "How fares the fairest?"

"Oh papa!" Gyða said, almost weeping. "I am so happy to see you!"

"Father," Adalbern greeted.

"My boy," Civillis said, drawing him in to share the glad embrace with his sister.

"How are you free?" Adalbern demanded. "Who did you have to threaten?"

"We have the pretender Otha to thank for that," Civillis said, pulling away. "Vitellius has traded my freedom in exchange for aid in putting him down. We have a fortnight to gather our forces."

Adalbern shook his head. "You have served your time in the auxiliaries."

"Many of us have, but I will fight again, if it keeps Vitellius away from Batavia and puts my arse back in my own hall."

"Those were the terms?"

"Those were the terms."

"The treaties with Rome remain, then?"

"Yes. Rome has been good to us in the past. Perhaps they will be again."

Adalbern smirked. "Let's hope. Come, Mother will be pleased to see you."

The family moved towards the large hall which served as the seat of the chieftain of the Batavi, talking of pleasant things. Once inside, Gaius Julius Civillis was greeted by his devoted wife and his grandson, a bold lad of eight.

"Mamma!" the lad squealed when he spied Gyða enter the hall.

"Hello, handsome!" Gyða answered, kneeling and spreading her arms wide to welcome her son into her embrace. "Look who has come home!"

The boy's blue eyes grew wide as Civillis stepped through the door. "Opa!" he squealed. He leapt from his mother's arms into his grandfather's, who greeted the boy with his booming laugh.

"Have you not stopped growing?" he demanded of the boy. "Look how big you've gotten!"

"Adalhard!" Brygda said, calling him by his birth name. She gathered her skirts and ran down the stairs to meet her husband. "How come by you your freedom?"

"My beautiful wife," Civillis said, pulling the woman close to him. "I have missed you so."

"Adalhard," Brygda said again, tears spilling down her cheeks. "I thought he was going to kill you."

"He certainly tried," Civillis said. "But I have Roman laws to thank."

"Roman laws did not save your brother," Brygda reminded her husband, withdrawing.

Civillis winced. "No," he said. "They did not."

"So, you old goat. How are you here?"

Civillis looked at his wife and sighed. "My love, we must go to war for Vitellius."

"What?" Brygda demanded. "No!"

"That was the bargain," Civillis said.

"You have served your time with the Roman army! Vitellius is entitled to you no more. You are mine now!"

"If I wish to remain free," Civillis explained, "and if we are to be free of him as legate, we must fight for him."

"How can you bargain to bleed for that hateful man?" Brygda demanded, her voice made breathless by grief and worry.

"Do not fret, wife," Civillis replied, brushing a silver strand of hair from her face. "If we succeed, Vitellius will go to Rome, and life will return to normal."

"And you will conscript our son, who has only just returned home from his tour, I suppose."

"He is a fine warrior, Brygda. And still in his youth. More or less. I pity the man who faces him on the field."

"He has not yet found a wife!" Brygda snapped. "Would you deprive me of more grandchildren?"

"I have every intention of returning from battle, Mother," Adalbern said, smiling.

"Intentions are one thing, eventualities another entirely."

"There is nothing for it now," Civillis said. "I have given my word. Now I want some drink, a hot meal and a night of love, in that order."

Brygda sighed, but turned to ensure her husband's wishes were fulfilled. Provisions would be made tomorrow. Tonight, Civillis intended to enjoy time with his family.

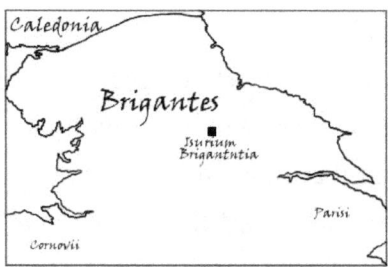

## 69 AD, SPRING, ISURIUM, BRIGANTIA

It was a week after the liberation of Isurium, the Brigantian Capital, before Calgacus opened his eyes. He breathed deep, his aching body moving to stretch before realizing the extent of his wounds. He grimaced.

"Hello, little brother," Rhys said from his place in a chair beside Calgacus' bed. "You slept long."

Calgacus smiled up at his brother, then frowned. "Mederei?" he asked. He regretted asking immediately.

Rhys's eyes welled with tears, and he could not bring himself to look his younger brother in the eye when he said, "Rome has her."

Though Rhys's eyes had welled, it was Calgacus who wept. "Forgive me," he said through the sudden tears. "I should not have left her side. Perhaps Rome would have claimed me instead."

"There is a choice that would kill me to make," Rhys whispered. "My brother or my betrothed, both of whom I love so well." Tears slid down the prince's cheeks. "No, you did what was right. And Geraint, who is good to me, has gone south in search of her."

"It is my fault," Calgacus whispered. "Forgive me."

"There is nothing to forgive, little brother."

But Calgacus would not believe him. "I will be your shield-bearer," he said. "And serve you as penance for my error until brave Geraint returns with your wife."

"She is not my wife," Rhys said. "Not yet. You need not lower yourself, Calgacus. You bear no blame."

"It was my command. I did not so much as even check for a possible ambush, and ambushed we were. Now you have lost both your lover and your shield-bearer. It is right that I do what I can to ease the losses and since I cannot, and will not, be your lover," he said, trying to find some humour, "I will be your shield-bearer."

Rhys wrinkled his nose. "That is a disturbing thought," he muttered. "Very well, since I am deprived of a shield-bearer, and you seemed determined to pay for crimes that were not yours, you may serve me until Geraint returns."

This seemed to settle Calgacus's grief some. He let his body relax back onto his bed. "I am so sorry, Rhys," he whispered. "I am so very sorry."

"Peace, little brother," Rhys replied. "We both must save our grief. Rome will not let Isurium be lost forever. They will try to claim the north as soon as they can. We must be strong for our people, and ensure that there will be a free north for Mederei and Geraint to return to."

Calgacus nodded. "Rome would be wise to stay away," he said, his anger made comical by the sleep that had taken hold of him once more. "They will..." It was all Calgacus managed to utter before sleep took him under and he began to snore.

## 69 AD, EARLY SUMMER, PENINUS PASS, CISALPINE GAUL

Vitellius's army marched through the Alps with great resolve. The Legions *V Alaudae* and *XXI Rapax* moved in silence. The Batavian auxiliaries had no such compulsion. They sang ancient songs in their mother tongue in their deep voices as they rode and walked. The sound bounced from the rocks of the mountains, adding some thousand voices in echo to the music. The Gauls of Legion *V Alaudae* smiled at the sound. They had such songs they sang also, though rarely in the company of true-blooded Romans. Rome, for all its arrogance, was still uncertain about the peoples they had entreated or conquered, and to sing in Gaulish would be to arouse suspicion the legion could ill afford.

Word had arrived that forces loyal to Vitellius awaited them at Cremona, and so they made their way at a good pace. They arrived to find their expected allies had gone to Locus Castorum and there clashed with legions lead by Gaius Suetonius Paulinus. Civillis bristled when he heard the name of the commander, Suetonius.

"Did you not serve with him?" his son asked when he heard. He, his father, and the chieftains of the Chatti Federation had sat down to dinner. "During the revolt of the red witch in Britain?"

"Her name was Boudicca," Civillis said, rolling his shoulders. His voice was soft when he spoke her name. It hardened when next he spoke. "Suetonius was our commander."

"I take it you do not like him."

"He is a brilliant tactician," Civillis said. "And I am alive because of his schemes."

"But?"

"But he is everything wrong with Rome today." Shaking his head, Civillis looked beyond the flames of the fire pit through the dark night towards the west. "He is proud, not a thing to decry for all men must have some pride. But in him it is wedded to hatred and cruelty. The entire war could have been avoided had he not sought to throw down that woman and her daughters. Such bloody slaughter and loss of life could have been spared."

Adalbern placed aside his bowl and applied more wood to the fire. "The contract ended with Prasutagus's death," he said softly.

"It did," Civillis agreed. "But a new treaty could have been struck. Rome recognized the queen Cartimandua, they could have recognized Boudicca. Suetonius would have none of it. He should have known that the women of Britain do not fear a warrior's death. And we all paid for it; Roman, Briton, German." Civillis shook his head. "And then, at the end, with the queen dead at his feet, he needlessly laid waste to an entire people, down to the last child. There remains nothing of them."

"They defied Rome," another chieftain said.

"Yes," Civillis agreed. "And yet I think on my own family. Boudicca's daughters were just children. What would I risk had Rome raped my daughter, flogged my wife? I cannot judge her harshly for what she did. I would not have acted differently."

"Was she beautiful?" Adalbern asked suddenly.

"Rome talks of a screeching harpy, with over large limbs and a fierce countenance," Brinno noted.

"Yes," Civillis said in answer to his son. "She was beautiful. Her daughters too, were beautiful children. They would have grown into lovely women."

"What happened to them?"

Civillis shrugged. "No doubt Suetonius had them slaughtered with the rest of the children of that kingdom."

Adalbern turned his eyes from his father's unhappy face to the fire. He knew that story well enough, though his father would rarely speak of it. The Batavian auxiliary had performed honourably, but Civillis had no pride in the victories they helped ensure. The ill will between Legion *XIV Gemina* had begun during the revolt by the British queen. The Batavians had looted the ruins of Boudicca's city with its parent legion, but had refused to draw their weapons against those who lived there still. There was not a warrior amongst them. Legion *XIV Gemina* had no such scruples. They slaughtered infants in their cots, cutting through their desperate mothers or, sometimes, forcing those hapless women to watch as they slaughtered the babes. The Batavian auxiliaries had withdrawn from the city when the murders started.

Memory of the screams plagued Civillis now. Adalbern placed his hand over his father's to stop their tremble, offering the greying man a smile.

Adalbern himself had served in Britain, but he had arrived after the revolt had been quelled. He had seen none of the fighting, only its aftermath. He had worked alongside his father for the first two years. When Civillis's tour ended, he returned home and left his son, then a lad of eighteen, to the command of the new governor of Britain, a man who did not hate the Britons and sought to use reason instead of slaughter to control the island's inhabitants. He was, for the most part, successful in this regard, and the auxiliaries moved north to defend Roman lands from the ad hoc attacks by the free men of that region.

Five years Adalbern had fought in Britain, moving to Gaul with the auxiliaries when the legion was withdrawn from the island. A further five years was spent with the Batavians in Gaul. After ten years of service, Adalbern returned home, electing to find a wife and father children before serving the rest of his time, a further five years, with the Batavian auxiliaries.

It was not uncommon for the Batavian men to work their time in this manner. Civilis himself had done it. Rome permitted it mostly because the terms of the contract were fulfilled—fifteen years' service in the auxiliaries— and it ensured that the Batavian people would keep birthing strong warriors to supply the Batavian cohorts. That he had yet to find a wife or found a family plagued him a little. He did not want to return to the ranks without having done either.

It was another week of marching before they arrived at Cremona. It was not a happy sight. The leader of the army there had already fought and lost one engagement with the Othanian forces. Upon seeing the famous grim-faced Germans, however, the despondent mood cleared.

Two days later, the armies clashed. Otha's forces, led not by Otha but by his brother Titianus, marched in from their camp in Bedriacum to Cremona. Weary from the journey, they fell to Vitellius's army, fleeing before the onslaught back to their camp.

Otha took the news hard, killing himself before Vitellius could march on his location at Brixellum.

The Batavian veterans performed well, eager to return home to their wives and their more peaceful lives away from the Roman legions. They had clashed against Legion *I Adiutrix* and the Legion had no choice but to give way, such was the fierceness of the Germans against which they fought.

Civilis led the auxiliaries well. Knowing Roman tactics better than most, he outwitted the foe, sparing most of his warriors serious harm. His command did not go unnoticed by Vitellius.

When the Roman Senate sent word to Vitellius that they were prepared to welcome him into the city and crown him emperor, the former legate of Germania Inferior summoned Civilis to his command tent.

"You called?" Civilis asked, his deep voice soft yet still somehow threatening.

"I did. I wanted to congratulate you on your command in the battle. Surely now I recognize why you were extended the honour of Roman citizenship."

Civillis lifted his shaggy eyebrows and said nothing.

"In any case, the Senate has informed me that I am to be crowned emperor upon my arrival in Rome."

"Congratulations," Civillis replied. A short, uncomfortable silence followed.

"Of course," Vitellius said with a tight smile. "I will honour my word. You and your veterans may return to Germania Inferior. I will march on to Rome."

Civillis shrugged. "As you like." When Vitellius scowled at him, he added, "Your Grace."

"Good. I will march on the morrow. You may leave whenever you wish."

Civillis nodded, a curt single bob of his head. "Thank you." He paused, if only to irritate Vitellius, before once again adding, "Your Grace."

"Dismissed, Civillis," Vitellius said acidly.

Civillis offered a short bow and left the command tent.

"We leave," he said in the typical blunt fashion of the German people.

Smiling, the Germans immediately began to walk from the camp. They had packed up their camps, their armour, and their weapons the moment Civillis was summoned to Vitellius's tent.

"You know he doesn't want you in the triumph because he knows that all of Rome will know that his victory was in fact yours," Brinno said as he rode beside Civillis. The pair led the enormous column of German auxiliaries away from Cremona, eager to return home to their wives and their fields.

Civillis shrugged. "What do I care? I want only for my own bed and the warmth of my woman. Let the apple have his parade."

Brinno grunted, a grin parting his thick red beard.

"I genuinely hate that man," Vitellius said sourly as he and his generals watched the German Auxiliaries march away from the camp at Cremona.

## 69 AD, Late Summer, Londinium, Province of Britannia

Mederei stood, watching the crowds as they gathered in the market. Not all were here to bid, she knew. Many came just for the spectacle. This day, British slaves were for sale, brought low in their own land, and traded like little more than livestock.

The city was still rebuilding, Mederei noticed. There were still piles of blackened debris where once stood proud buildings of Londinium. The scent of ash lingered in the air, even now. It brought a mirthless smile to Mederei's lips. Her mother's army had razed this city. It was an act she was certain the world would never forget.

That thought fortified her and she straightened, squaring her shoulders despite the tug of the chains on her shackles. She closed her eyes and recalled the victory over Londinium. She had witnessed it from her mother's chariot. In that moment, she had felt power run through her, throbbing along her veins, reminding her of her proud heritage.

Mederei felt it again, and that sense, that feeling of righteous belonging stayed with her, even as she was dragged up and onto the auction block.

She stood, her back straight and her expression proud, and the citizens of Londinium would long remember the queen they saw sold into slavery.

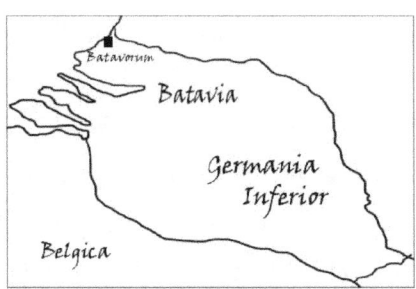

## 69 AD, EARLY AUTUMN, BATAVIA, PROVINCE OF GERMANIA INFERIOR

Adalbern and his father walked quietly together, their shirts removed and slung over one shoulder as they returned from the river fresh from the day's swim. The still hot sun beat upon their bare backs, browning their skin. Being of a ruddy complexion, they were far more fortunate than either Adalbern's mother or his sister, whose skin turned red and painful beneath even the winter sun.

Civillis carried a large pole with the day's catch, a mix of large pike and trout. It had been a good day for father and son, and the silence they shared on their journey home was comfortable and contented.

Until they reached the city.

Mayhem had erupted in the streets, Batavian men and women brandished weapons and were fighting. The chieftain and his son were ignored. Shock kept Civillis inactive for only a moment. The chieftain peered through the chaos to find Roman centurions battling back an angry mob of Batavians.

Civillis marched forward, Adalbern close behind. "Stop what you are doing!" he bellowed. "All of you!"

"Make them give us our boys back!" someone in the crowd shouted.

"And cut off their cocks for what they have done!" someone else demanded.

Adalbern scanned the crowd to find those who had spoken, but was met with stone-faced Batavians, each bristling for battle. He turned to the centurions.

"Would you mind explaining what they meant?" he asked mildly.

One centurion straightened. "By order of the emperor," he declared loudly, "we are here to raise an army to fight the pretender from the east."

"Vespasian," Civillis said. "The general in Persia. I've heard of him. Marching on Vitellius is he?"

"Yes," the centurion said.

"Well, his Grace has Batavian auxiliaries already at his command and attempting to recruit now will exceed the maximum number of warriors we are to contribute according to the treaties we have with Rome; a treaty, you will remind his Grace, he swore to uphold when we won him the throne."

"You haven't the authority to deny Rome!" the centurion barked. "Now stand aside and let us to our work."

Civillis raised one shaggy eyebrow. "I will not," he said softly, his deep voice becoming a growl. "You will stand down, you will release the boys I see you have rounded up—boys I will note who are well underage according to our treaty—and you will tell me why my countrymen want to cut off your cocks."

The centurion drew his gladius, pointing it at the unarmed chieftain. "You will stand aside," he commanded. "Now."

Civillis looked at the blade and smirked. "Don't be stupid, Centurion," he said. "Or you will start something you will deeply, deeply regret."

"By order of the emperor," the centurion said again.

A scream from the great hall turned everyone's attention and three centurions burst from the door, stumbling down the steps, carrying Civillis' struggling grandson between them. Two more centurions followed holding Gyða between them. The princess spat curses in between demands to release her son.

Civillis breathed deep in an effort to control his temper. He turned back to the centurion. "Stop this madness," he growled. "That boy is half the age required by Rome."

"No one is above service to Rome," the centurion snarled. "Not even a German princeling."

Gyða planted her feet. She was a least as tall as the centurions against whom she struggled, and just as strong. She also had the advantage of being a woman, a gender which the Romans constantly underestimated, and Batavian women had the Celtic woman's love of martial training—a result of their blended heritage. They were a force to be reckoned with in their own right. She twisted free of one centurion, knocking him back with a powerful kick and, in a single fluid motion, threw the other, fully armed and armoured as he was, over her back and hard onto the ground. Now free, she ran for the three centurions who held her son.

The boy was unceremoniously dropped to the earth, landing with a hard thud. Reacting instinctively, Civillis lifted one long leg and kicked the centurion who had drawn his blade against him full in the chest. The man flew backwards, dropping his weapon and sliding in the dirt some distance.

The Batavians leapt into action, surging forward with a roar.

The fighting was hard. Civillis and Adalbern both struggled to reach Gyða, who fought well against the centurions. Father and son broke free of the crowd, but too late.

The centurion smirked at Civillis as he pulled his gladius free from Gyða's back. Civillis's heart stopped for several beats as he watched his blue-eyed daughter fall lifeless to the ground. His grandson's scream blended with the cry of his wife as the woman charged forward, her husband's battle-axe held high. The centurion stood not a chance against the woman, aged though she was. She had seen her daughter murdered, and there was no salvation from a woman's rage and grief.

Moved to action, Civillis leapt forward with a roar, Adalbern at his side. More centurions arrived to aid their fellow recruiters but, against the anger of the residents of Batavorum, found themselves quickly overcome. It was a short battle, and at the end of it, there remained not one centurion alive.

The young men the centurions had taken captive were freed. Fathers and mothers hugged their rescued sons close, and the Batavian people cheered.

In the centre of the celebration, immune to the cheers of the crowd, Civillis, chieftain of the Batavi, and Adalbern, his heir, knelt in silence beside the body of the fair-haired Gyða, Batavian princess and Civillis's joy. Her son, a boy of eight, lay across his mother, weeping uncontrollably, his tears mingling with her blood as it ran in a rivulet down the front stairs of the great hall.

Brygda stood, her husband's battle-axe in hand, and stared down at her daughter. Blood dripped from the edge of the fearsome weapon, a proxy for the tears Brygda could not shed. The circle of grief made itself felt, and the celebrations slowly died down as one by one, the Batavians noticed their chieftain kneeling on the ground beside their beloved princess.

Afore long, the whole city fell silent. The only human sounds in the city belonged to the eight-year-old Diethelm, who had witnessed his mother's death.

"Adalbern," Civillis said softly, rousing his son from his grief. "Take the boy, please."

"No!" Diethelm screamed as Adalbern placed his hands around his waist. "No! Mamma!"

"Come, Diethelm," Adalbern said gently. "Come."

Diethelm lifted himself from his mother and threw himself at his uncle, uncaring for the spectacle of his grief. Adalbern pulled the boy close holding him a moment before rising to his feet with the boy in his arms. He walked slowly into the great hall.

Civillis lifted his daughter's body, blood running freely now the wound was free of the ground. Ignoring the gathered crowd, he turned and followed his son.

"Come, my love," he murmured to his wife, pausing at her side.

She looked up at him with grey eyes. They filled with tears at the grief she found in her husband's gaze. Her own misery at last found expression. Weeping, she walked by her husband's side, still carrying his battle-axe. They disappeared into the great hall, leaving their people to grieve for their princess.

Civillis sat in silence upon his seat in the great hall. His wife sat by his side, her presence a silent comfort. The chieftain did not hear the sounds of the funerary feast held in his daughter's honour. He touched not a morsel of food. He did not touch his drink. He simply sat and stared, brown eyes boring into the floor as if he might set the timbers alight with his gaze.

Brinno, chieftain of the Cananefates and a long-time friend of Civillis, sat next to him. For all the years that the two had known each other, Brinno could find no way to comfort his friend and ease his grief.

Adalbern sat next to his mother, also brooding. They were much alike in temperament, father and son, but the grief was harder for the father. Civillis had loved Rome. He knew the Batavi would have no home were it not for the generosity and respect of the first Roman emperor, Julius Caesar. For that reason, all chieftains had, since Rome had aided their relocation, taken on the name Julius. It was their way of honouring the man who had honoured them. For generations, the Batavians had proudly served Rome, sending their sons to die for the empire that was once their friend. Civillis himself had been specially honoured. It had been a proud day when Rome granted him citizenship, and Civillis had set aside his Batavian name of Adalhard and took up his Roman mantle, Gaius Julius Civillis.

Rome had betrayed him. Rome had assaulted Batavian children. Rome had murdered his daughter.

The love he had for Rome had been shattered, and in its place grew hate like ice, savage and cutting.

Adalbern had no such delusions about Rome. He had not been blinded by honours and accolades. He saw Rome as it was, not as it once had been. The growing hatred between the Batavian auxiliaries and their parent legion, Legion *XIV Gemina* had flowered during Adalbern's tour. He had fought his own legion alongside his countrymen. No, Adalbern had no love for Rome.

"Uncle," Diethelm asked quietly, drawing Adalbern from his thoughts. The blue eyes that stared up at him were red and puffy, the result of a long evening of mourning as Gyða's body was interred. "May I sit with you?"

Offering a small smile, Adalbern nodded and opened his arms to the boy, who climbed into his lap. He ignored his food and drink as he held his nephew, singing softly to him until the exhaustion so obvious in the boy's countenance won over and Diethelm slept. Adalbern pulled the boy closer, kissing the crown of his head.

"You will make a fine father one day, my son," Brygda murmured to him, stroking his arm. She tried to smile at him, but could not.

Taking pity on his mother, Adalbern opened one arm and pulled her close. Three generations of royalty held one another, closing out the world for a moment. That moment was broken when the Great Hall's doors swung open with a bang, rousing even Civillis from the depths of his thoughts. The swinging door briefly revealed a rainy evening. Even the Batavian sky mourned the loss of Gyða. A lone rider strode into the hall, his oiled cloak dripping with water. The man was not Batavian, but Frisian, a tribe friendly with the Cananefates.

"My Lord," the man said, bowing low before Civillis. "Lord Ellert of Frisia sends his condolences. We heard of your daughter's fate. We are very sorry."

"And what does Frisia care for the troubles of Batavia?" Civillis demanded.

The messenger shook his head. "Frisia has long been victims of the cruelty of Rome. We know all too well the heartbreak you are currently suffering."

Civillis opened his mouth to speak, his scowl already saying much, but it was Brygda who saved the messenger from her husband's injured temper.

"We thank you and your lord, Frisian. It is a kind gesture to send someone so far."

"Not very far, my Lady," the Frisian replied. "I was on my way home with news for my Lord when I heard of the terrible events here."

"What news for your lord?" Civillis demanded.

"Food and drink first," Brygda said. "Come, Frisian. Take off your cloak and warm yourself by our fire. Partake in our hospitality. Though we are grieving, we have not forgotten our traditions."

Civillis growled, but beckoned a servant to do as his wife suggested.

The messenger bowed low. "You are gracious, my Lady," he said. "Indeed, Rome knows not the same courtesy."

The Frisian removed his cloak, letting one of the servants take it to hang by the fire and dry before gratefully accepting a seat between Adalbern and Brygda.

"Now," Civillis said once the messenger had sated his appetite and thirst, "tell me, what news for your lord?"

"It is news of Britain, Lord Civillis. The men of the north of that island have long struggled against Rome, fighting even their own queen whom they feel has betrayed them. This spring past, they struck a major blow to Rome's hold on that island, taking the city of Isurium Brigantum and banishing the queen Cartimandua. She has fled south with the aid of auxiliaries and is rumoured to be making her way to Rome."

Civillis's eyes brightened briefly.

"Rome can be defeated after all," the Frisian said. "And I am headed to give my Lord word of this; that it might rekindle the hope the cruelty of Rome has beaten from our people."

"In what manner were the Romans defeated?" Civillis asked, leaning forward in his chair.

"The Brigantes revolted against their queen, using the recent struggles for the imperial throne to their advantage. Rome had no legions to spare, and could only offer the queen escape. The Britons were clever and brave, and the queen so reviled that even most of her own army refused to fight for her. Would that all the north of all the empire were so united against Rome. We might also have a chance against it. To live free from the heavy hand of Rome... Would that not be something? Still, my Lord Ellert may find some pleasure in the news of Rome's defeat somewhere."

"We all find pleasure in that," Civillis mused. "Thank you, Frisian. Though I am much aggrieved, this is still glad news."

Brinno looked at his friend. "Rome is defeated," he said. "They have fled south. I would hear those words again, but this time let them be said of a free Batavia."

"My Lord," Chlodulf, Civillis's cousin, said leaning forward, one hand resting on the top of his long leg. He looked his chieftain in the eyes and said, "Now is the time. We can free Batavia and all of Germania, perhaps even Gaul if they will stand with us. We can send Rome away and no longer will they fiddle with our sons or murder our daughters."

"Civillis," Brinno said. Before he could say another word, the chieftain of the Batavi spoke.

"Adalhard," he said softly. "My name is Adalhard." He looked across at his son, who grimly nodded in approval; one single bob of his head that told the chieftain his son would stand by his side. "To hell with Rome."

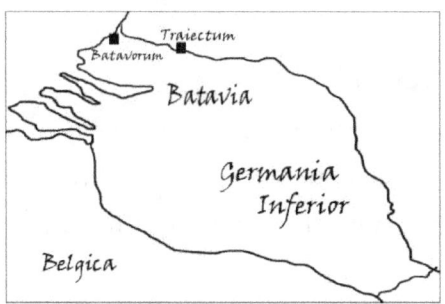

## 69 AD, AUTUMN, NEAR TRAIECTUM, GERMANIA INFERIOR

Adalhard looked over the battlefield, grim-faced and quiet. Yet for all of his impassive expression, his men knew he was pleased. The ruse could not have gone better. Brinno had returned to the land of the Cananefates after the burial of Gyða and had, taking the enemy by surprise, attacked several Roman forts. Each attack had been successful. The legate of Germania Superior, Flaccus, had sent auxiliaries to deal with what he thought was a small Cananefates revolt. Adalhard could not have hoped for a more arrogant and uninspired response. He led his army of battle-hardened Germans against the auxiliaries and devastated them. Now he sat on his horse and surveyed the slaughter.

Adalbern strode up the hill to his father. "Twenty dead," he reported. "Major injuries are near the hundreds, though."

"Send them home," Adalhard said. "They have earned their rest. They can rejoin us when they are well again."

Adalbern nodded and bowed, returning down the hill to relay his father's orders.

"Your son is just like you," Chlodulf said with a grunt. "Entirely too serious."

"My son loved his sister," Adalhard replied. "And considers this a sacred undertaking."

"Like I said, just like you."

Adalhard smirked. "Come, we can rest for a day or two, then we prepare to meet Brinno. Rome will not leave this unanswered."

"Good," Chlodulf said. "I would like more Roman heads for my collection."

"You are more Gaul than German."

Chlodulf grinned. "I am, and I am proud of it. Gauls are good people. Our grandmother was one, you know."

Work that evening was hard and varied. Adalbern spent his time with the soldiers, burying the dead, tending to the wounded, and organizing their return to Batavia. He joined his father and the other commanders at dinner to watch them strategize. His father proved a brilliant tactician, able to callously weigh the cost in lives for every plan considered against the potential of victory. Adalbern, though one of the most competent warriors in the Batavian freedom army, did not feel certain enough of his tactical abilities to contribute. He listened and watched, trying to absorb some of his father's brilliance.

"It is hard on your son," Chlodulf noted after dinner when Adalbern had withdrawn to aid the warriors once more. "To walk in your great shadow."

"What shadow? My son is an excellent warrior."

"Oh he is, but you were so excellent as to win Roman citizenship. He has not done the same, you'll note."

"Rome is incapable of acknowledging excellence that is not Roman anymore. They have fallen too far into their own worship. Julius Caesar would die of shame if he were alive now and saw what his empire had become."

"It's a good thing he's dead, then," Chlodulf replied.

"I would have liked to have met him," Adalhard mused. "If only to prove to myself that I was not a fool for loving Rome."

"Rome had done the Batavi much honour in the past," Chlodulf answered his cousin kindly. "You were not a fool for loving them for it."

"And yet I was blinded by it."

"Well, your son can take heart knowing that even you, beloved chieftain of our people, are not entirely infallible."

"Go to bed, Chlodulf. You're talking nonsense."

## 69 AD, LATE AUTUMN, CASTRA VETERA, BORDER OF GERMANIA MAGNA AND GERMANIA INFERIOR

"We march!" Prefect Gaius bellowed. He had received word from Flaccus of a growing uprising in Germania Inferior, led by Gaius Julius Civillis, chieftain of the Batavi. Together with the tribes of that province, along with the Chatti in Germania Magna, they had cleared northern Germania Inferior of Roman occupation, the carefully built forts now in German hands. Worse news arrived that morning, with the most northerly of the Gaulish tribes of Belgica joining in the Batavian revolt.

It could not come at a worse time. The pretender Vespasian was still marching on Rome from the east. Two legions had to be moved away from that front to fight the uprising in the north. Legions *V Alaudae* and *XV Primigenia* had been ordered by Legate Flaccus to deal with the revolt. North they would go.

They had one thing on their side—a Batavian auxiliary of their own, commanded by none other than Lebeo, a Batavian who was well known for clashing with the new traitor Civillis. The two were old enemies. Lebeo would know best how to deal with the Batavians in battle.

Prefect Gaius sat upon his horse, watching the army march north. They would clash within the week.

Whispers of a Batavian uprising had made their way through the ranks of the auxiliaries marching with *V Alaudae* and *XV Primigenia* weeks before the order to march was given. It surprised Lebeo to no end that Civillis was leading the uprising. The man's love of Rome was well known, and the reason they had clashed so often.

"Commander," a warrior said as he entered Lebeo's tent. "Forgive the intrusion, but there is a messenger here from Batavorum."

"Cut off his head," Lebeo growled. "Civillis can say nothing that I want to hear."

"Forgive me, Commander, but the messenger is looking for Gerlach, son of Godafrid, who was Gyða's husband. He was told the man was a warrior with your auxiliaries."

Lebeo raised his brows. "Bring the messenger in, and fetch the man he was looking for. If Civillis is looking to make my warriors sympathetic to his cause, it will be done in front of me."

The warrior nodded and left the tent to do as he was bid. Moments later, a tired-looking youth walked into the tent. "Commander Lebeo," he said curtly, bowing shortly.

"What is your name lad?" Lebeo asked.

"Forgive me, Commander, but I was told I may speak only with Gerlach, son of Godafrid, who was Gyða's husband."

"That extends even to your name, does it boy?"

The youth merely shrugged.

"Fine," Lebeo grumbled. "What do I care if even the great Civillis's messengers do not deign speak with me?"

Gerlach arrived after a long silence between the messenger and Lebeo where the two merely observed one another.

"Commander," Gerlach said, bowing. "You summoned me?"

"I did," Lebeo answered. "Your father-in-law has some words for you, and I demand they be said before me."

"It is a family matter, Commander," the youth said.

"In this army, we are all family," Lebeo answered. "Now whatever you have to say to my warriors, you have to say to me."

Again the youth shrugged, his nonchalance irritating the commander of the Batavian auxiliary. The messenger turned to Gerlach.

"My Lord," he said formally. "Adalhard, father of Gyða sends his love, and his deepest woe."

Gerlach stared at the youth, his heart threatening to revolt. "His woe?" he asked slowly.

The messenger nodded. "Forgive me, that I am the one to bear the worst news for a husband to receive. Gyða, your wife and Adalhard's beloved daughter, was murdered defending her son during a struggle in the city of Batavorum this fortnight past."

Gerlach's knees felt weak. He stared mute at the youth.

"Forgive me for bringing such terrible news to you at this hour and in this time," the youth said, his eyes filling with tears as he looked into the shocked blue eyes of the man before him. "It was evilly done, and your father-in-law strives now for retribution for the murder."

Gerlach shook his head. "I do not believe it," he whispered.

"It is true. I was there. I saw it happen." The youth reached into his satchel and withdrew something small wrapped in finely embroidered linen. "She fought bravely," he said as he handed the parcel to Gerlach.

The warrior took it, his movements made slow by the numbness that struck before grief. Before his commander, he removed the linen from the item. It was a ring, a finely wrought band of worked Gaulish red gold. It had been his gift to his wife the night of their union. Gerlach stared down at the ring, recognizing it immediately. His breath left him, accompanied by the almost audible crushing of his heart. The big, blond man sank slowly to his knees, tears now streaming freely down his cheeks, his eyes fixed upon the ring.

"Tell me how it happened," Lebeo asked of the youth, his voice now devoid of all hostility.

"Roman centurions, Commander," the messenger said, spitting the words out as if they burnt his tongue.

Lebeo stared at the youth, disbelieving.

"They had come to Batavorum seeking to recruit more than the number stipulated by the treaty Rome had made with Batavia, breaking not only the treaty but the emperor's word that the Batavi would be troubled by him no longer. It was then we learnt of the terrible deeds done to our boys by the Romans; that they had so abused them. When the centurions tried to take the young Lord Diethelm away, Gyða fought. Alas it was five against one, and though she fought bravely, she was struck in the back by a Roman blade. The coward! Neither Lords Adalhard nor Adalbern could reach her in time. The people of Batavorum took up arms. All the centurions were killed. The kidnapped boys were rescued, and Lord Diethelm remains safe in the city. But for his mother, our beloved princess..." the youth trailed off, his voice cracking with grief.

"You call him Adalhard," Lebeo said.

"Our chieftain has renounced Rome," the youth said. "The evil of the Romans has broken even his love of them. Had Rome behaved honourably, perhaps, he would love them still. But they murdered his daughter, and he intends to see that Rome murders no more Batavians, and keeps their filthy hands off our boys."

Lebeo turned away from the messenger and knelt on the floor where Gerlach had sunk to his knees. Through Lebeo's exchange with Adalhard's messenger, Gerlach had knelt, tears streaming down his cheeks as he took in the story of his brave wife's murder. The commander placed a firm hand on the man's shoulder. Gerlach looked up, his blue eyes hard and full of hate.

"Get some rest," Lebeo said gently. "We have a long march ahead of us."

"I will not fight for the men who murdered my wife," Gerlach growled.

"No," Lebeo agreed. "And I do not intend to force you. But if you try to leave the army now, you will be chased and killed for a deserter. Let us get you closer to home."

Gerlach frowned slightly and, realizing his commander was right, nodded. With Lebeo's help, he rose to his feet and walked slowly from the tent, his spirit defeated.

"That is cruel news," Lebeo murmured.

The messenger nodded.

"Did the Romans see you get into camp?" Lebeo asked the boy.

"I did not care to hide it. I imagine that to Rome one German looks a lot like another."

"That may well be true. Then you must march with us also, or Rome will have you and I both killed. We will say you are my shield-bearer should anyone ask."

"That is gracious of you, Commander," the youth said.

"Did Civil… Adalhard have nothing to say to me?"

The youth smiled slightly. "He did say that should you ask, I was to tell you that he still has Julius in his name to honour a good Roman, as does his son, and you should get used to that."

Lebeo's mouth twitched with the effort of containing a smile. Some thirty years past their warring youth, a daughter dead by Roman hands, and Adalhard still would not admit Lebeo was right.

"I have no bed for you. You can use my saddle blanket to keep the damp of the ground at bay, but you will have to sleep on the floor."

"I have slept in worse places than a floor, Commander. Again, I thank you for your hospitality."

"I might be marching with the Roman legions," Lebeo said. "But I am Batavian."

The messenger smiled as Lebeo left his side and searched the floor of the tent for a relatively dry place to sleep.

## 69 AD, LATE AUTUMN, LONDINIUM, PROVINCE OF BRITANNIA

Mederei's face twisted in a small smile. Her back ached from the lashing she had received. It was a pain she relished, for it reminded her that a man had tried to dominate her, and failed. In her mind's eye, she replayed breaking his jaw over and over, letting the satisfaction of that memory carry her, once again, to the auction block.

## 69 AD, LATE AUTUMN, NEAR NOVIOMAGUS, GERMANIA INFERIOR

Adalhard sat astride his great black horse, a gift from Lord Ellert of Frisia, and watched, his brown eyes hard as flint, as the Roman army approached. He recognized the crests of Batavian cavalry in the columns and grimaced. He did not cherish the thought of spilling Batavian blood, but his resolve to see his people free from the evil Rome had become proved stronger than any other consideration. They were not far from Castra Vetera, to which Adalhard had intended to lay siege. He still intended it. He would just have to fight a battle to get there. He had made provisions for such an event.

Adalhard was joined by his son, Adalbern, his cousin, Chlodulf, and his long-time friend, chieftain of the Cananefates, Brinno.

"They are already defeated," Chlodulf murmured. "Look at them. They do not want this fight."

"The Gauls do not want this fight," Adalhard replied. "But they will still fight. As for the rest, they think they can win. Look at that prefect. His arrogance could not be more obvious if it was made of smoke and flame."

"I feel sorry for the Gauls, then," Chlodulf said. "They look dispirited."

Adalhard shrugged. "Good. It will make our fight easier."

"The Batavian cavalry are not singing," Adalbern said. "Have you noticed?"

Adalhard straightened. It was true. Batavians always sang on their march to battle. Their deep voices could be heard for miles, a warning to all that Rome's elite were on their way. It did much lift the spirits of the Batavian warriors as they marched, and caused fear in the enemies who heard the powerful war tunes.

This engagement was different. Batavians would be fighting Batavians, brothers and fathers pitched against one another in brutal conflict.

"There is nothing to sing about," Adalhard said. "No matter the victor this day, the loss to Batavia will be great."

"Unless Lebeo has come around," Brinno replied.

Adalhard snorted. "Do not count on it," he growled. "The man is too stupid and too stubborn."

"Oh yes," Chlodulf said. "And you're not stubborn in the least."

Adalhard glared at his cousin before movement in the enemy's ranks caught his eye.

"Come," he said to his commanders as the prefect's dainty Arabic horse picked its way towards the middle of what was to become the battlefield. "Let us treat with these bastards."

Prefect Gaius looked over the enemy army with pursed lips, as if the tall, broad men standing in their scale maille and furs were an affront to his delicate sense of smell. They stood in rows, glaring at Rome's army with bestial hatred. Prefect Gaius spat.

"Savages," he muttered.

Sitting behind the Prefect on a thick-limbed spotted horse, Lebeo glanced only briefly at the man. To his left sat Adalhard's messenger. On his right, his shoulders slumped and his eyes red with grief, sat Gerlach. The man had not slept a night through since receiving the news of his wife's death. Around his neck on a thick leather thong hung his wife's ring. Even under the overcast sky, the ring was bright as if some small spark of the Gyða's love remained there still, wedded to the ring.

The prefect snorted, shook his head and said, "Let's get this over with, shall we?" He pushed his horse forward, riding at a trot to meet his foe in the typical pre-battle parlance that these northern savages were so fond of.

Adalhard drew his horse up short a few feet from the prefect who led the two legions on the field. He silently noted his messenger riding at Lebeo's side, and his son-in-law, who looked so broken it pained Adalhard's heart.

"Civillis," Prefect Gaius greeted. "What do you want?"

Adalhard said nothing for a time, his brown eyes masking the rage he felt at the prefect's tone. When he felt he had made the prefect sufficiently anxious, he spoke. "I want Rome gone from Batavian lands. I want our warriors returned home to their families. I want a guarantee that Rome will never again step foot in the north. The friendship between our peoples is over. Turn around and go home, Prefect. There is no need to shed blood here today."

Prefect Gaius smirked. "Batavia belongs to Rome."

"Batavia was allied to Rome," Adalhard snapped. "There is a difference. That alliance is over. Turn around. Go home, or I will send you to Rome in pieces."

"Come now, Civillis," Gaius chided gently. "You know you cannot win a war against Rome. Whatever your grievance, there are better ways to seek restitution."

"Restitution, is it?" Adalhard said, his brows raised. He growled his next words. "Restore the daughter Rome murdered to me, Prefect, and I will turn my army around and go home."

Prefect Gaius clenched his jaw and said nothing.

"I thought as much," Adalhard said. "It is not restitution I seek, Roman. It is retribution, and all of Rome would have to lay in rubble at my feet before that is done. I am letting the empire go lightly. You have your terms, now get out of my sight."

"You know I cannot accede to these demands, Civillis."

"Then die today. This parlance is done." Adalhard turned his horse and rode back to his army at a canter, followed by his entourage.

"Adalhard was never the most reasonable of men, Prefect," Lebeo noted nonchalantly. "Worse when his temper is roused."

"Shame," Gaius said. "Such a colossal loss of life could have been avoided if he was more reasonable." He turned his horse and rode back to the legions.

"Grief knows no reason," Lebeo said quietly. He caught Adalhard's eye as the chieftain wheeled around to face Rome's army, nodding once; a quiet mark of respect he would never have offered before now.

Adalhard scowled as Lebeo rode away, following the prefect back to the Roman army.

"Why does Gerlach go with him?" Adalbern asked as he watched his brother-in-law return to the Batavian cavalry.

"He means to defect," Adalhard said.

"Lebeo?"

Adalhard nodded.

"How do you know?"

"Judocus is with him still."

"Do you think the messenger had much talking to do to convince him to come to your side?" Chlodulf mused.

"Nothing could convince him of that," Adalhard answered. "But it would take next to nothing to convince him to fight for a free Batavia."

Adalbern allowed himself a small smile. He watched as Gerlach straightened, his grief giving way to determination, his broken spirit finding strength in purpose. Keeping his eyes on his brother-in-law, Adalbern began to sing. It was an ancient tune, a song celebrating the brave deeds of the warriors of the Batavi, deeds performed for love of their home, their sisters, and their wives.

"We are the Batavi!" Chlodulf bellowed raising his weapon high.

"Batavi!" the army bellowed in answer.

"For Gyða!" Adalbern yelled.

"For Gyða!" the rebel army answered. In the name of their murdered princess, the army surged forward, fighting to claim their home back from the overreaching grasp of Rome.

"Infantry!" Gaius yelled. He turned to Lebeo.

"Just as discussed, Commander," he said before retreating with his personal guard to a nearby hill to oversee the battle.

Lebeo's lips twisted in a cruel grin.

"Just as discussed, Prefect," he answered.

He lifted high his javelin and kicked his horse's flanks, charging forward. The Batavian cavalry followed, their silence speaking volumes over the tumult of their countrymen.

The Roman auxiliary split in the centre, a common tactical ruse designed to trick a charging army into becoming encircled in armoured horseflesh. The cavalry would typically pass the army, wheeling around and charging at it from behind.

Adalhard let the cavalry pass without heed. A full third of his own cavalry were waiting patiently in the woods that bordered the field upon which they now fought in case his guess at Lebeo's intentions proved ill-founded.

When the enemy cavalry had passed the army and charged at the rebels from behind, Adalhard bellowed his command.

"Horseman's channel!"

His army split in half, dividing to create a wide channel that could easily accommodate four horsemen abreast. Adalhard himself stopped charging and pulled aside.

With a great roar, Lebeo's cavalry surged forward, their javelins raised high. They rode the channel, sparing not a blow for the army they rode through. As each horseman reached the front of Adalhard's army, they launched their javelins, striking into the legions they had marched with moments before.

Adalhard's split his lips in a vicious grin as Prefect Gaius's expression changed from smug, to confused, to shocked and, finally, terrified.

"Now!" Adalhard bellowed, summoning his cavalry from the woods. They ploughed through the left flank of the Roman legions, who had been lost to confusion and terror long before.

The battle lasted just moments before Prefect Gaius turned his horse, and with his guard, bolted from the field. The Roman army broke, fleeing before the rage of the men of Batavia as ships flee an ocean storm.

"Let them go!" Adalhard bellowed when some of his men gave chase. "We have time to spare. See to the wounded."

The wounded were few and far in between, most of them belonging to the Roman legions. On Adalhard's orders, the Gauls were spared, their wounds treated when possible. Batavian wounded were given priority. Romans were slaughtered indiscriminately. It was Rome Adalhard wanted to frighten.

The victory was celebrated well that night, with the Batavian men singing and dancing around their fires. Raucous laughter followed many a retelling of the facial expressions of Prefect Gaius. The mood was more sombre in the chieftain's tent.

"It pains me that we reunite under such circumstances," Adalhard said to Gerlach, rising to meet the cavalryman as the latter entered the tent.

Gerlach nodded, accepting the crushing embrace of his father-in-law. He said nothing as he fought back tears.

"Come in," Adalhard said, releasing him. "Eat, drink, and rest. We can find comfort in each other's remembrances of Batavia's beloved princess."

"She was beloved," Gerlach said, smiling through his tears, "wasn't she?"

"How could she not be?" Adalhard replied. "With a heart as big as hers. The people show their love with grave gifts even to this day, I am told."

"How fares my son?" Gerlach asked, accepting the cup of drink Adalhard offered him and finding a place to sit.

"Grieving," Adalhard answered. "As well he might. He wanted to accompany us in this fight, of course."

Gerlach smiled. "He has his mother's courage."

"It is your courage he has," Adalhard replied. "And his mother's heart. A remarkable boy. You have good cause to be proud of him."

With a grunt, Gerlach downed his drink. "I wish I could have been there to see him grow. I returned to service before he could walk. I doubt he even knows me now."

"Gyða told him stories of you every night," Adalbern said quietly. "He knows you very well, Gerlach."

Gerlach nodded. "Can you imagine?" he mused. "How different it might be for fathers if we need not abandon our sons to fight another's battles?"

"I can imagine," Adalbern answered, though Gerlach had not asked the question of anyone in particular. "Perhaps I am too soft for a warrior's life, but nothing would please me more than to watch my children grow, that I might be there for their first laugh, their first words, their first steps. That I might be the one to teach them to swim and fish, instead of their mother."

"That does not make you soft," Adalhard said to his son. "For I regret that I was not there to see these firsts for you and your sister. The gods blessed me with twins, and a wife strong enough to bear them and live. And I was not there to enjoy those blessings. I have cut many lives short fighting for Rome, but none of them weigh so heavily upon me as this."

Adalbern looked up at his father in surprise. He had never heard his father speak thusly, and for the first time understood the great toll Adalhard's loyalty to Rome had on the chieftain's heart; the same toll he himself feared.

"A better father could not be found in all of Batavia," Adalbern answered.

Adalhard scoffed. "Hah!" he said, downing his drink. "Kind words for an aging man. And still, I shall take them." He looked up to find Lebeo standing at the entrance of the tent. He rose.

"Come in," Adalhard said. "Come. There is food and drink to share, and share it we will, for we have much to thank you for."

Lebeo stepped into the tent, his grey eyes scanning the space and noting the bunched shoulders of the men in the room. The rivalry between Adalhard and Lebeo was legendary, and they were thought to hate one another.

"Thank you for your food and drink," Lebeo answered, accepting the proffered cup.

Gerlach rose to his feet. "Commander," he greeted. His acceptance of Lebeo eased the tension slightly.

"Well, Adalhard. Who could guess that between us, you would be the one to start a revolt against Rome?"

"To be fair, it was Brinno who started the revolt."

Brinno waved from his seat and Lebeo smiled.

"Under your command, no doubt."

"Details," Adalhard said. "Sit, please. For the sake of our country, let us put aside our differences and stand together against Rome. When our freedom is assured, you may return to hating me."

"You would have to prove disagreeable indeed if you give me cause to hate you after freeing our country," Lebeo answered.

Adalhard laughed brightly. "If anyone can manage such a mighty feat, it would be me."

Lebeo grinned. "How did you know I would not fight you today?"

"In truth, I did not. I trusted your love of Batavia more than I trusted your hatred of me. I have known you were not evil and that you opposed me for love of our country."

"Yes," Lebeo said. "For love of our country, and hatred of Rome, but also hatred of you. Your German blood supplanted my Gaulish blood, and I had always seen you as the enemy."

"Batavian and Gaulish blood had long ago mixed," Adalhard said. "Indeed, our people benefit from both. There is a reason we were considered the elite of the Roman army."

Lebeo shrugged. "Enough of past hurts. You are marching to Castra Vetera?"

"That is our goal, yes. I intend to take all the forts in Batavian territory."

"I was stationed there, Adalhard. Taking that fortress will not be an easy thing."

"Then it is well we have you, for you have the best information about that fortress. It will help our cause greatly."

Grinning, Lebeo sat, accepting a plate of freshly roasted boar. "Then let me tell you all I know."

# 69 AD, LATE AUTUMN, CASTRA VETERA, GERMANIA INFERIOR

"My Lord," Judocus said, bowing slightly.

Adalhard looked up to find his messenger with a Roman standing behind him. Through the haze of cooking fires, the Roman fortress of Castra Vetera loomed like a great grey vulture.

"What does the Roman want?" Adalhard asked, taking his weight off the table that sat before his pavilion. Lebeo and Adalbern continued to look over the maps and plans of the fortress. A prolonged assault proved too difficult, despite Lebeo's knowledge of the fort. The cold did not help. Adalhard had since decided to draw back and starve the legions into surrender. He made sure to have his men fan the smoke from the cooking food towards the castle as they awaited their meals.

Autumn had made her stately march across the land, her cool touch turning the vestment of the trees brilliant shades of yellow, orange, red, and black. Only the noble oak had yet to succumb to the seductions of the season.

"I have a message from Emperor Vespasian," the Roman said.

"I did not speak to you, Roman," Adalhard snapped.

Properly chastised, the messenger clamped his mouth shut. Judocus cleared his throat. "My Lord," he said. "We have word from Vespasian."

"And what does he want?" This time Adalhard looked at the Roman messenger full in the face. In truth, he was little more than a boy, still awkward from the first blooms of manhood, and evidently anxious in Adalhard's imposing presence.

"Emperor Vespasian greets the most illustrious king of the Batavi," the messenger bowed stiffly, his words sounding painfully rehearsed.

Adalhard allowed himself a small smile. "King, is it?" he asked. "That is yet to be decided."

The Roman messenger blinked. "But do you not lead these men?"

"I do. That makes me a general, not a king."

"But… are you not born to the family who has always ruled?"

"Define always, boy," Adalhard replied. "Lebeo's family ruled these lands before the Batavi came to settle here and the lines mixed. Perhaps he has more right to kingship."

The Roman glanced over at Lebeo, who looked up. "If it was to be a popularity contest," he assured the messenger, "then Adalhard is definitely king."

Adalhard sighed.

"Um…" Having lost his place in his rehearsed speech, the messenger took a moment to try and remember the words he had been instructed to utter. He flushed red when he could not find his place, feeling afraid and foolish standing before the enormous bear of a man that was Adalhard.

"You needn't remember the words exactly, my boy," Adalhard said gently. "Just the gist. Speak that clearly and with authority, and no one will know that your speeches were not carefully crafted." He offered the messenger a smile.

The boy smiled slightly in return. "The emperor salutes you for keeping the villain Vitellius's forces away from the main fight. Loyalty to the true emperor does not go unrewarded. The Batavi are welcomed by the emperor as friends and allies."

"The emperor can kiss my Gaulish arse," Lebeo muttered, making Adalhard grin.

"We were once," he told the messenger. "Once the Batavi were honoured by Rome, and we proudly protected the emperors, we stood in their armies, humbly defending our friends. So deep was the bond between Rome and the Batavi that all men in our ruling class took on the name Julius in honour of Rome's first and mightiest emperor. But Rome broke her word, turned aside our friendship and now my daughter is dead. You can tell this Vespasian that the Batavi are a free people, and now wiser when choosing our friends."

The messenger clearly did not have a script for this. It had not occurred to Vespasian when the emperor was composing his message to the Batavi that the Germanic tribes once so friendly with the empire would turn him aside.

Adalhard sighed at the boy's dejected expression. "Come lad, it is not your fault we now think so ill of Rome. How could it be? You are but a boy and not responsible for her policies. You must have ridden hard to get here. Come, have some food and drink and a good night's sleep in a warm tent before you return to your emperor. The nights are getting cold as Old Father Winter prepares his sleigh and his frost deer breathe their frozen breath in anticipation of the chase."

"Who is he chasing?" the messenger asked. "This 'Old Father Winter' of yours?"

"The light, boy," Adalhard said. "He is chasing the light. Now come, let's get you something warm. Your lips are turning blue."

"Vespasian won," Adalbern said to his father, his breath frosting. The crystals of his frozen words sparkled prettily in the dying light. "We've had word from Gaul. Vitellius was beheaded by Vespasian's army in Rome. Flaccus sends an army to lift our siege."

"What now?" Chlodulf asked his cousin.

Adalhard scowled. He looked across at Lebeo. "I want Rome gone from our lands."

"Yes," Lebeo answered. "Give me the cavalry, Adalhard. I will take Flaccus at the border of Belgica. He will not lift this siege."

Adalhard took a moment to think. At length he nodded, making his once-foe's grin yet broader. "Be careful, Lebeo. Flaccus may be a Roman, but his inaction has been a result of caution, not foolishness or cowardice. Be on your guard."

"You worry too much, Adalhard. We will bring that man's head to you on a spike."

"Keep it. I am not in the habit of collecting heads."

"Rome has civilized you some. A shame."

"Go on with you."

# 70 AD, SPRING, GELDUBA, TERRITORY OF THE TUNGRI, GERMANIA INFERIOR

Lebeo spat blood, riding hard behind all that remained of his eight cavalry units. They had vastly underestimated the courage and size of Flaccus' army and now most of the Batavi cavalry was lost. Sparing a glance behind, Lebeo allowed himself a grim smile.

Defeated though they were, victory had cost Flaccus far too much. Either way, that army would not be able to lift the siege on Castra Vetera. In this, at least, Lebeo had been successful.

He would not be ashamed to face Adalhard in this defeat.

## 70 AD, WINTER, NEAR CASTRA VETERA, GERMANIA INFERIOR

The ruse of attacking Mogunticum had worked. Adalhard grimaced as he lay flat on the rock and watched the Roman army march past his hidden warriors on their way to relieve the stronghold they believed would soon be under attack.

Lebeo's loss had hit him hard. The eight best cavalry regiments of the Batavi had been all but obliterated, with only some forty riders returning, all of them bloodied. Lebeo had escaped that battle, though barely. Even now, he could do little without getting hideously dizzy.

It was then that the two men put aside all their differences and became friends in earnest. Adalhard had spent much time with Lebeo, ensuring he was well cared for and kept informed of the war for freedom. It was not going well.

Adalhard intended to expel Rome from all of Germania Inferior so that not only the Batavi may benefit from this fight. Some Gaulish tribes, and many of the northern Belgic tribes, had joined the fight for freedom. He intended to free them as well. For now, however, they needed to regroup and think of how they might best benefit from the various problems Rome had created for herself.

Sighing, Adalhard gave the signal, and he and his scouts returned to their camp.

"Father," Adalbern greeted, washing blood from his hands.

"What happened to you?" Adalhard demanded of his son.

Adalbern laughed. "A successful hunt, Father. Or would you have preferred to skin the beast yourself?"

Relaxing, Adalhard permitted himself a chuckle. "Ah, no. Next time. What did you get?"

"A doe," Adalbern answered, smiling. "Alas there's little meat on her this time of year, but she'll still feed a fair few."

"Good. I'm starving."

Life for the Batavian army proved quiet in the weeks that followed. They easily inhabited the camp, immune to the cold they had borne all their lives. Adalbern continued to move amongst the men, ministering to their various ailments. He had learnt the skill of healing from his mother, just as his sister had. Since he had returned from service in Rome's auxiliaries, he had joined his sister as she made the rounds in Batavorum, helping her tend to the ill or keeping the children company if she did not need any aid.

Memories of those happy days at home amongst the people he loved best ached in his heart as he walked. He loved his country; the smell of it, the fresh taste of the woodland air, the many rivers, streams, and even marshes where he had learnt to swim and fish as a boy. He loved the changing seasons, the bright green of spring, the deeper, more sombre greens of summer, the fiery autumn, and even the long night of winter. This was home, and he loved it all.

"You think a great deal," Chlodulf said, coming to stand beside Adalbern on the small hill at the edge of the camp. "It cannot be good for you." He followed Adalbern's gaze across the white scape that was Germania Inferior in the winter.

"It is beautiful, isn't it?" Adalbern asked.

"It's cold."

"And that, too, is beautiful."

Chlodulf snorted a laugh. "You are just like your mother. She never liked summer near as much as she loved winter."

"Winter is peaceful," Adalbern answered.

"That's what she told me. Me, I miss the sun, and the swimming, watching the women bathe when they think no one is watching them. Do you know how beautiful they look, river water glistening on their skin?"

"They know you're watching," Adalbern said with a smile.

Chlodulf grinned. "Then I thank the gods that they are not as frightened of a man's gaze as southern women. Have you finished your rounds?"

"I have. Only minor cuts and burns. We all remain in good health."

"Well and good. When you're finished admiring the scenery, your father would like you present for dinner."

Dinner had started by the time Adalbern returned to the tent he shared with his father. "There you are!" Adalhard said. "How fare the men?"

"Well," Adalbern answered. "Very well."

"They speak highly of you, you know."

"They appreciate that I know women's work," Adalbern said with a smirk.

"Actually, I was talking about how you've led them. Your regiment is very fond of you."

Adalbern scowled.

"Most people smile when flattered," Lebeo noted, smirking.

"I do not feel as if I am deserving of that flattery."

Adalhard and Chlodulf exchanged a meaningful look.

"How could you not?" Adalhard demanded. "Look how well they have come through every battle thus far!"

Adalbern shrugged. He sat heavily, accepting a plate filled with sizzling meat. No sooner had he started eating than Adalhard's messenger Judocus flew into the tent.

"My Lord!" he said breathlessly. "Flaccus is dead, murdered by his own legions! His second-in-command has fled the army."

The smile Adalhard gave would not have been misplaced on a wolf. "Eat well tonight," he growled. "Tomorrow we besiege Castra Vetera."

## 70 AD, SPRING, COLONIA AGRIPPINA, UBII TERRITORY, PROVINCE OF GERMANIA INFERIOR

Adalhard had smiled as he received word from Julius Sabinus, Emperor of Gaul. The man now had the loyalty of two legions, the Legion *I Germanica* and the Legion *XVI Gallica*, and had offered his aid in a mutual alliance against Rome. For his troubles, Sabinus demanded that Adalhard march no further than the border of Germania Inferior and Gaul, and take no Gaulish land for himself. It was a good treaty. Adalhard had no intention of ruling over Gaul. Nor did he much care for ruling over the other tribes in Germania Inferior, however much the chieftains of the Ubii, Tungri, and Cananefates swore fealty to him. His concern had always been with the Batavi.

That his army had secured the destruction of both legions formerly stationed at Castra Vetera, a fortress now in Batavian hands, had done much to bring other chieftains to his side. Now, encamped at Colonia Agrippina, Adalhard strove to bring the tribes of Gaul, Belgica, and Germania together in a unified fight against Rome. Rome could be beaten, if the tribes would but stand together.

It could only help that Rome was embroiled in a terrible war in the east.

The news he received the following morning caught him by surprise. Emperor Vespasian had elected Quintas Petillius Cerialis as general over an enormous army, composed of Legions *VIII Augusta, XI Claudia, XIII Gemina, XXI Rapax* along with newly formed Legion *II Adiutrix* and their attached auxiliaries. Further, Legions *I Adiutrix* and *VI Victrix* were on their way from their stations in Hispania, and Legion *XIV Gemina* had been summoned from Britannia. The force that Rome had sent against the rebellion was staggering.

Upon receiving the news, Sabinus lost his two legions, who made a poor showing of their first engagement and soon threw down their weapons. Another Gaulish ally, Tutor, surrendered upon seeing the enormous army. In a blink of an eye, Adalhard had lost his hard-won friends.

"We take to the water," he answered, when Chlodulf asked the chieftain what they were to do. "No one knows the rivers and coasts of this land like we do. We can still take Rome."

For some months, that is what Adalhard did. Keeping to the water and sending guerrilla raids against Rome from both land and sea, Adalhard and the Batavians successfully frustrated the enormous Roman force that had come looking to subdue the Germans. Legion *XIV Gemina* tried to take the province from the coast, but the Cananefates, long-time friends of the Batavi, destroyed that fleet handily.

The Batavi managed to capture the Roman flagship.

Rome refused to let go of their northern holds. They built a new fleet and, under the command of Quintas Petillius Cerialis, they landed on the shores of the island upon which stood Batavorum.

## 70 AD, EARLY AUTUMN, BATAVORUM, BATAVI TERRITORY, GERMANIA INFERIOR

Adalbern watched his father closely as a storm of emotions crossed the man's face.

"Are we lost?" Lebeo asked quietly.

Adalhard hung his head briefly. "Rome will come full force now. We might have held against Quintas Petillius Cerialis, but with Vespasian now victorious in the east and free to march, he will bring all of Rome's might to bear upon us."

"Can we sue for peace, still?" Chlodulf asked.

Adalhard sank onto his chair in the great hall that had been his home. "You understand what terms Rome will demand, don't you?" he asked his cousin. "You know the cost of peace?"

Chlodulf stared mutely at his cousin.

Adalhard looked around the room. "Rome will permit peace," he said. "I will entreat them."

"Wait," Chlodulf said. "What is the cost?"

"My head," Adalhard said quietly.

The hall fell silent. Adalbern spoke before he had time to think. "No," he said sharply. "We cannot permit that."

Closing his eyes, Adalhard remained silent and still. The only sign of life could be found in the steady rise and fall of his great chest as he breathed, his mind working to find another solution.

"There is no other way," he said, eyes opening. "Either I die, or all of Batavia is enslaved. It is one life weighed against many. Even the life of a king is not worth those of all his people. I will not leave the Batavi or her allies to suffer because I was afraid to face death."

"Father…" Adalbern said, but his father held up a meaty hand and stopped his words.

"This was always the cost should we fail. I knew it and I fought all the same," Adalhard whispered. "I do not fear to meet my fathers now, for I strove bravely against oppression, and for righteous reasons. I will be welcomed amongst them with strong drink, good food. and boisterous song."

No one in the hall could argue with the chieftain. They all sat in mute silence, staring at the man.

"I will stand with you," Adalbern said. "When they march you to the headman's block. I will stand with you."

"No, Adalbern," Adalhard said, smiling softly. "You are young yet, and have not taken a wife or fathered children. I will not walk to my fathers with you at my side. I need you to work still, wait and find the right time, then do what you can to free our people. You will be chieftain when I am gone. I need you to lead our people to freedom. This is your sacred undertaking. You must promise me you will do this."

Adalbern shook his head, his heart refusing to work beneath the weight of his grief. "I will not leave you to die alone."

"He will not die alone," Lebeo said, standing. "I turned upon my own legion in a bid for freedom. I will stand beside you, my king."

"I am equally responsible," Brinno said, rising to join Lebeo. "I was the first to rise against Rome. I will stand with you, my king."

"The pair of you sit down," Adalhard grated. "I am submitting to Rome in order to save lives. I will not have my friends throw theirs away needlessly!"

"Nothing I did in my life was needless," Brinno said. "And neither shall be my death."

"I'm not letting you get all the glory," Lebeo added.

Adalhard blinked at them both. "No. If it can at all be helped, you will not join me in death. Adalbern," the chieftain of the Batavi said, bringing his warm brown eyes full to bear upon his son. "Promise me you will do what you can to resist Rome. Give our people the hope of freedom; either by your hand or that of your sons."

Adalbern stared mutely up at his father, unable to speak.

"Promise me, my son. You are my last child. I cannot die in peace knowing you will join me with so much of my task left unfinished. Promise."

Slowly, though his heart ached enough to take away his breath, Adalbern nodded.

Smiling, Adalhard nodded in return. "That's my boy." He straightened. "Judocus!"

The messenger boy appeared, biting his lower lip. "My Lord," he said.

"Raise the flag. Tell this Roman general I wish to speak with him."

Adalhard watched the Roman general Quintas Petillius Cerialis approach with a heavy heart. He stood before the gates of his city, out of range of the

Batavi bowmen, beneath a canopy to shade from the surprisingly strong autumnal sun. Before him, as was Batavian tradition, stood a table laden with fruits, bread, and mead.

"General," he greeted solemnly when Quintas arrived.

"Civillis," the general said, nodding. "You were wise to sue for peace."

"I'm not sure that is true," Adalhard replied. "Please, sit. Let us break bread together and talk."

Quintas stared at the table, his suspicion writ plain across his features. Adalhard smiled slightly.

"It is all sound food," he said. "It is Batavian tradition that visitors to our lands are given food and drink, and shelter should they wish it, before anything is asked of them."

"The Gauls and Britons have the same, though it is rarely extended to Romans," Quintas noted.

"Perhaps it is from the Gauls we acquired this tradition," Adalhard said, seating himself. "Please," he said again. "Sit."

Sighing, Quintas removed his helmet, placing it on the table. He lowered himself down onto the cushioned chair and observed Adalhard a moment.

"You have made Rome very sore," he said, smiling.

Adalhard nodded. "The intent was to make Batavia very free."

Quintas shook his head. "Your people have benefitted much from Rome's favour, Civillis. It was ungrateful to turn against us so."

"Rome arrested me and murdered my brother, and I did not revolt. Rome arrested me again, and still I kept my peace and even fought for her, honouring the treaty struck between our peoples. Then Rome broke faith with us," Adalhard said. "Rome abused our boys, and took them too young, in numbers far too great. Rome tried to take my grandson, only eight-years-old, and you murdered my daughter."

"That was Vitellius, not Vespasian."

"It was Rome. Julius Caesar would weep for what his empire has become."

Quintas sighed. He watched as Adalhard tore a chunk of the dark loaf, offering it to the general. Still suspicious, Quintas took the piece, but did not eat until Adalhard had torn a chunk for himself and bit a piece off.

"I am sorry about your daughter," Quintas said at length.

"I had loved Rome," Adalhard replied. "Did you know that? I fought so hard for her because I believed Rome honest and true; a vision of goodness and honour in a landscape of pettiness and brutality. The honours Rome bestowed upon me were precious to me. Now they are as ash in my mouth. And still, I sit across from you and I cannot see evil in you. You fight bravely, and are clever. Your men clearly love you, and you stand loyal to your fellows. In another life, perhaps we might have been good friends."

Quintas found he could not swallow the bread in his mouth. It had gone dry. He knew Civillis. He had worked beside him, if only briefly, when in Britain. He had also seen the brutality of Suetonius in that region, just as Civillis had. He had seen the Batavi grow uneasy under the increasing cruelty of their parent legion.

"Civillis," he said. "I know why you fought, and I understand it. My heart grieves for how wronged you and your people were. Emperor Vespasian has granted me the power to negotiate a peace with you. Will you hear my terms?"

"Speak them gently, General. My heart is aggrieved enough."

Quintas nodded. "You must submit yourself to arrest and, as is the rule of law, a trial. Rome cannot offer the same courtesy to your co-conspirators, you understand."

"There were no co-conspirators," Adalhard replied. "I revolted."

"You had help."

"They aided me under duress."

Quintas glanced at the men who stood behind Adalhard as the two negotiated the peace. He saw Civillis's son Adalbern, broader and stronger than the last time he saw him in Britain. A larger man wearing furs, whom Quintas did not recognize, stood beside the youth, his head held high. Brinno, Chieftain of the Cananefates, whom Quintas had met only once and very briefly, stood near Lebeo, their severe faces failing to hide the love they had for their chieftain.

"You and I both know that is not true," Quintas said sadly.

Adalhard's eyes flashed. "There were no co-conspirators," he repeated.

Quintas put down his bread. "These talks will go nowhere if we cannot agree on this point, Civillis."

Behind Adalhard, Brinno and Lebeo exchanged a glance.

"Then let us speak of other things for a time."

Quintas shook his head, but pressed on. "Batavorum is to be deconstructed. The city is to be moved downstream to the camp of Noviomagus, and Legion *XIV Gemina* will be stationed there to keep the peace."

Adalhard twitched. He looked sharply at Quintas. "You know that legion has clashed with us before. Their cruelty is unsurpassed. You are asking my people to submit to abuse."

"*Gemina* will not harm your people, Civillis. I swear it."

"I will need to think on this. What else does Rome demand?"

"Rome's former treaty with the Batavi is to be reinstated and upheld."

Frowning, Adalhard waited for more. When Quintas said nothing, he spoke. "That is all you ask, that the treaty once held between our two peoples is reinstated, no alterations, adjustments or further tribute demanded?"

"Not entirely. These are the terms: You and your co-conspirators submit to arrest. You further submit to trial as per Roman law. Your people will dismantle Batavorum and move the city and themselves to Noviomagus. The treaty that once stood between Rome and the Batavi is to be reinstated. And last, your heirs are to submit as hostages of good faith. Your son is to go to a family in Gaul, your grandson will be taken to Rome to be educated as a Roman. Do we have an agreement?"

Mention of his heirs leaving Batavia bunched Adalhard's shoulders. "You cannot take my son from here. He is the last of my children. My wife—"

"Rome cannot risk your family leading another rebellion, Civillis. It is this or war."

"Will you let me speak with my council?" Adalhard asked.

"Of course, Civillis." He rose.

"No," Adalhard said. "You are my guest. Stay, avail yourself of my hospitality. I will speak with my council and return ere the sun begins to set."

Quintas nodded. He sat slowly down and watched as Adalhard and his men retreated into the city. He looked up at his entourage, down at the enormous spread on the table before him, and back at his men again.

"Mead?" he offered.

"No."

The council of men had barely entered the great hall before Adalbern rounded on his father and spoke.

"No," he said again.

Adalhard moved silently past his son and sat slowly down on his chair at the end of the hall, looking down at his lap a moment. His shoulders bowed with the weight of Rome's demands and the threat of the empire on his people.

"No what?" Brygda asked from her place in the door leading to the private chambers. She stepped into the light.

"Rome's terms," Chlodulf answered her wearily when Adalhard could not.

"What are they?"

Chlodulf answered. Tears struck Brygda's eyes when the demand for the hostages was announced.

"And what is the alternative?" she asked in a whisper.

"War," Adalhard replied. "And all of Rome shall crash against us. Against the army at our door now we might have stood a chance, but not all of Rome, not all of the empire. We will be obliterated."

Brygda walked to her husband's side and snaked one arm around her husband's shoulders. He shifted his weight and rested his head against her. For a moment they said nothing.

"And they cannot help but find you guilty in this trial," Brygda said to her husband.

Adalhard nodded.

"And they will kill you."

Again, the chieftain nodded.

"And so I am to lose my family to save our people."

"I am sorry, my love," Adalhard whispered. "I had thought myself equal to the task, but I was not. I am so sorry."

"Damn Rome," Brygda whispered, allowing tears to stream freely down her face. She knelt and took her husband's face between her hands and said, "You are not to blame, my love. You did what you could, what you should. It is Rome that bears the blame for our fates." She kissed her husband, briny tears on her lips before standing and facing her son.

"Adalbern, come," she said, extending her hand. Gladly, Adalbern took her hand and walked into her strong embrace. "My son, I am so proud of you. You have grown so strong."

"I do not want to leave here, leave you."

"There is little choice," Brygda replied. "If you disobey Rome now, it will spell disaster for our people."

Adalbern nodded. He knew. He also knew his protests were worthless. He would do this, not from a desire to please Rome, but to save his people. They had been strong and loyal. They deserved this sacrifice.

"I will stand as a co-conspirator," Brinno said quietly. "Rome will easily see I was, and if I give myself up as one, perhaps we can spare an investigation and thus save those Rome cannot easily connect with the revolt."

"What is true of Brinno is true of me," Lebeo said.

"Are you two determined to die?" Adalhard snapped.

"It will spare your cousin," Lebeo argued, "who is unknown to Rome. He will be able to help your widow help your people."

Adalhard opened his mouth to argue, but could find nothing to argue against. "For once, Lebeo," Adalhard said. "You are right."

"I've always been right, old man," Lebeo answered. He offered a sad smile.

"Then we tell Rome we accept these terms?" Chlodulf asked. "We should fight!"

"We would lose," Adalhard said. "And what would become of our people then? At least this way they will not be rounded up and sold as slaves. This way, at least, they can live their own lives in their own country. War is a game played by the aristocracy, but it is the common people who suffer most. I cannot gamble their lives away so easily."

"Gods," Chlodulf whispered. He shook his head and turned away so that his cousin would not see his tears. "We were so close, Adalhard," he said thickly. "So close."

He felt a hand on his shoulder and turned to find his cousin standing at his back, smiling sadly at him. "I know," Adalhard said.

The two men embraced roughly. After a while, Adalhard pulled away. "Come," he said. "Let us inform Quintas of our decision."

The arrival of the Batavians to the shelter did not put a smile on Quintas's face. The men were sombre, their faces grim and eyes hard. They walked with purpose, but their steps faltered beneath the weight of their decision. He watched, his heart heavy for them. The Batavians had been good to Rome, their warriors securing most of the victories in barbarous Europe, and they had been wronged.

Adalhard looked the general in the eyes when he spoke, proud even in defeat. "We accept Rome's terms."

Quintas swallowed. "I almost wish you chose to fight," he admitted. "It is hard seeing you grieve, Civillis. You were good to Rome."

"It is a shame I cannot say the same of Rome," Adalhard answered. "I submit to arrest. Brinno and Lebeo also. My heirs will go to the empire as hostages and our people will relocate as asked. The treaty between our peoples is renewed. We will have warriors ready to go within the week." The words were spoken hollowly, without emotion.

Quintas nodded. "It is easier this way," he said. "You may return to your home, Civillis. You are under house arrest pending the trial. Your friends are to go with you. They may receive no missive, nor send one unless I read it first. Your heirs are permitted to stay with you until the trial's conclusion. Deconstruction of Batavorum will begin shortly thereafter. You will now permit my army into the city."

Adalhard nodded. "As representative of the empire, General Quintas, I offer you the hospitality of my hall."

Quintas raised his eyebrows in surprise. He shook his head. "Thank you, Civillis, but—"

"It is considered rude to refuse an offer of hospitality," Adalhard interjected. "If Rome is to reclaim any of our love for her, she should learn our manners."

There was no argument to this that Quintas could make, so he simply nodded. "Thank you, Civillis. I would be honoured."

Saying nothing, Adalhard nodded. He noted that the Roman army, encamped beyond the river, was already ready to move. They had rightly guessed Adalhard's decision. He turned and led Quintas up to the keep, his entourage following. They walked in silence, their backs stiff against their grief.

Silence greeted Quintas upon entering the city. Batavian citizenry stopped in their work to stare at Quintas and his Roman entourage. They wore stony expressions, unreadable in their stoic facades. It became an eerie parade.

Quintas knew there could be no other outcome from Civillis's trial but a guilty verdict, and he knew well the punishment under Roman law. The Batavians knew also. Their eyes followed their chieftain, a dead man walking.

The trial did not last long. There was no investigation worth doing. Two men had come forward as co-conspirators; Brinno, Chieftain of the Cananefates who had struck out first, and Claudius Lebeo, who once commanded a fearsome Batavian cavalry and had helped Rome gain many victories before he turned on his commander mid-battle and fought for Civillis. These men were not Roman citizens as Civillis was. They would not be afforded a trial.

The chieftain of the Frisii had been arrested, his horses having been given to the Batavi to aid the revolt. But he was released when Civillis confessed to stealing the horses from the hapless old fool. Quintas suspected that the horses had been a gift and Civillis was only trying to spare the Frisian's family the grief of losing their patriarch. Yet Quintas could find no evidence that events were any different from Civillis's confession and so the Frisii were permitted to keep their aged chieftain.

Civillis himself pleaded guilty to all the charges laid against him, resigning himself to execution long before the trial had begun. It made Quintas uncomfortable to hand down the sentence in the man's own hall, looking down at the chieftain from his own seat. The words were spoken before the Batavi nobility, such that it was. They made not a move, their grim faces unchanged. They had known the outcome of the trial also.

So too did the people of Batavorum. The verdict was read aloud from the top of the stairs leading up to the great hall to the waiting crowd and was answered with silence. Unreadable faces stared up at Quintas. There was no wail of grief, no sobs or gasps, no angry murmurs. Not a sound answered the pronouncement save the cold autumnal wind.

The execution was set for the same day.

When Quintas returned to the hall, no one save the chieftain's cousin, a massive man by the name of Chlodulf, could be found.

"Our chieftain has retired to be with his family in his last moments," Chlodulf informed the Roman general.

Quintas nodded. "The executioners will be ready in a few hours."

"We know."

"I'm sorry," Quintas said. "I truly am. You must understand that Rome cannot be lenient when—"

"Save your excuses, Roman. Our chieftain speaks highly of you, but I would rather listen to ice rot than hear your miserable voice."

Quintas nodded. "Understandable," he said with a weak smile. He pondered briefly how ice could rot and what it might sound like.

Chlodulf turned away from Quintas and found a seat upon the stairs of the hall. He reclined, keeping one eye on Quintas. For two hours, each man sat in silence in the great hall, each keeping their peace until a Roman soldier entered, announcing that the preparations were complete.

Quintas stood.

"Stay where you are, Roman," Chlodulf said, rising to his feet. "I will fetch them."

Quintas nodded. Still standing, he waited patiently for the three condemned men to appear. He did not wait long.

Adalhard, Brinno, and Lebeo arrived together, dressed in fine clothing befitting honoured aristocracy. They had all bathed and, Quintas noted, been anointed with sweet-smelling oils. Each man wore a thick golden torque around their necks, an acknowledgement of their Celtic heritage, along with a strange axe-like pendant on a leather thong, acknowledging their Germanic heritage.

Finding he could not look the men in the eye, Quintas simply turned and marched from the hall.

He blinked in surprise to find the people of Batavorum standing before the great hall, surrounding the platform that had been built at the base of the stairs for the execution. The platform itself had been wildly altered.

The three chopping blocks had been draped with fine white linen, white, late-blooming flowers strewn all over them and the platform in so great a number they formed a perfumed carpet. Four flaming torches had been erected around the platform to guard against the fading light.

The Batavians themselves were all dressed entirely in white—the colour of mourning for most of barbarous Europe. They each held a white candle, unlit as yet.

All eyes fell to the three doomed men. They walked tall and proud, now at peace.

Adalbern, holding his nephew in his arms, stood with his mother at the base of the stairs. They, too, were dressed in white.

"Sorry, General," a Roman soldier said gruffly. "We tried to stop them but…"

"It's all right," Quintas murmured back, the soldier's words drawing him back from the grip of astonishment. "Civillis is a great man. Let his people honour him how they wish."

Quintas led Adalhard and his friends down the stairs. He stopped to permit the chieftain one last goodbye to his family.

Adalhard embraced his son first.

"You are strong, my son," he whispered. "And I am so proud of you."

"I love you," Adalbern answered in return.

Adalhard released his son and stroked his grandson's cheek. "And you Diethelm. You are strong and have made me so proud. When you go to Rome, promise me you will not forget that you are Batavi. Remember that for me, little one."

"I promise," Diethelm whispered, struggling against the tears that spilled down his cheeks nonetheless.

Adalhard turned last to his wife. He caressed her face with the back of his fingers. "You are so lovely. You took my breath away when I was but a boy, and all these long years I have never caught it again."

"Oh, my love!" Brygda said. She wrapped her arms around Adalhard's neck and pulled him in close.

"I will wait for you," Adalhard whispered. "But don't come too quickly. Our people will look to you now."

"I will come when I see fit," Brygda answered tartly. She pulled away from the embrace and kissed her husband fiercely. "And you better not have some young thing in your lap when I do."

Despite the grief that pressed in from every direction, Adalhard chuckled. "No sprite of the Otherworld could compare," he assured her.

Brygda smiled at her husband. He returned the smile, taking one last long look at his wife's face before moving off to climb the platform. The three men took their places behind the blocks, Adalhard in the middle. They straightened, facing the crowd in white.

"Where is Gerlach?" Adalhard whispered to himself, scanning the crowd. "Where is my son-in-law?"

Of the many faces in the crowd, Gerlach's was not amongst them.

"State your names and the nature of your crimes," Quintas said, no longer able to bear the eerie silence. "Then kneel."

Lebeo spoke first. "I am Claudius Lebeo, Commander of the Batavian cavalry. I have committed no crime, but that of loving my people and wishing them free." He knelt, bending over to rest his neck on the block.

"I am Brinno, Chieftain of the Cananefates. I began the revolt against Rome. It was right that I did." He knelt in the same fashion as Lebeo.

Adalhard lifted his gaze. Even from the base of the steps he could see the surrounding valley; her rivers sparkling like jewels in the waning light, the thick forests with their changing leaves, the snow-capped mountains, and broad, lush grasslands. Other than his wife's face, he would know no sight more beautiful than the land he loved.

"I am Adalhard," he said loudly, pride at his German name radiating from him. "I am father to a murdered daughter, chieftain of a wronged people, and my offence was my failure to prevail against those who committed these crimes. Forgive me. I tried."

Adalhard's plea was answered with silence, and he knelt down and rested his neck on the chopping block.

"That's not what they were supposed to say," Quintas's second-in-command growled.

"Leave it, Camillus," Quintas murmured.

The three headsmen stepped forward and raised their large axes.

"Wait," Quintas barked. "Wait until they're done." He nodded towards the crowd, each member of which were now lighting their candles. The pin pricks of light spread through the crowd, reflecting off the white robes of the Batavi until it seemed like they glowed.

As the candles were lit, Adalbern stepped forward, his candle flickering. With tears in his eyes he began to sing, an ancient Batavi hymn, a dirge sung by their people since long before they came to the Rhine Delta. Adalbern sung in a deep voice of heroes and gods, light and dark striving against one another, and three new names were added to the long list of Batavian heroes. The ancestors of the Batavi would welcome these men to their hall with open arms and glad hearts.

One by one, the Batavi began to sing until all of them lifted their voices.

They sang on, even after all the candles were lit. Quintas nodded at the executioners. The men raised their axes high.

"I never thought I would die beside you," Lebeo said to Adalhard, "as your friend."

"I am glad of it," Adalhard answered. He smiled. "We will meet again."

Quintas flinched as the axes came down. The Batavi did not. They continued to sing until the song had run its course. Their own voices rang back at them, returned from the surrounding valley, and the world fell silent again. The sun slipped behind the horizon. No one moved.

Quintas looked at Adalbern, who had served under him in Britain. The man's face was wet with tears, but he did not sob. Drawing his gaze back, Quintas noted that all the Batavi wept, but their tears were silent. They stood, weeping, their candles flickering in the cold night breeze.

"Come," Quintas said heavily to his soldiers. "Our work here is done. Leave them to theirs."

Quintas turned and walked up the stairs to the great hall. At the top step, he turned. None of the Batavi had moved. They stood, shrouded in white and glowing like ancestral spirits around the three corpses of once great men.

When Quintas woke the following morning, moments after the sun had fully risen, he stared up at the ceiling of the room, not wishing to move. Facing the grim expressions of the mourning Batavi would require more strength than he thought he had at present. He sighed when a polite knock at the door forced him from his bed. He rose and answered.

"Breakfast is ready," a solemn-faced youth said. "Queen Brygda sends her apologies, but her duties in preparing her husband's body for burial will keep her company from you this morning."

Quintas nodded. He forced back the apology that sprang so naturally to his lips and simply said, "Thank you."

The youth nodded. If he hated Quintas, he gave no sign. The youth turned and walked away, leaving Quintas to his thoughts.

Breakfast was grand. Quintas ate with his officers. The high-ranking Batavian warriors who would have normally been their company elected to break their fast elsewhere.

"We will start the deconstruction today," Camillus said, attempting to draw his commander back from the man's thoughts. "The sooner we do it the better. Winter comes fast in this part of the world."

"No," Quintas replied. "The Batavi have a funeral to attend to today, and it is their tradition that they celebrate the lives of the deceased for three days after. We will begin deconstruction on the fourth day."

"General, they are savages. Why care for their brutish traditions?"

Quintas put down his food and looked across at his second-in-command. "Not caring for our friends is what led to this whole mess in the first place," he said. "We will let the Batavi grieve. Rome has done enough harm to these people."

"My husband was right to speak well of you," Brygda said from the threshold separating the private quarters in the great hall from the main room. She wore robes of white, tied at the waist with an embroidered red cloth. White flowers adorned her braided hair.

Quintas rose to his feet. "Your husband did me great honour," he murmured. He tried to hold Brygda's gaze, but her large blue eyes were so filled with grief that he had to cast his down.

"I have come to invite you to the funeral for my husband and Claudius Lebeo. Chieftain Brinno's body has been prepared and is now making its way to his homeland for his family to bury. The funeral procession will begin soon."

"Thank you," Quintas said. He tried to swallow only to find his mouth had once again run dry. "I fear it will be wrong of me to attend."

"You should attend," Brygda answered, her direct gaze making Quintas tense. "Adalhard asked me to ask you to attend."

The Roman general shook his head. "I cannot imagine why."

"No one may know a man's motives but himself," Brygda answered. "He wanted you there."

"Then I will attend."

Brygda nodded, the impassive mask she had made of her face never once lifting. "That is good. I will have Judocus bring you to the site." With nothing else to say, Brygda turned and walked away.

Having lost all appetite, Quintas sank into his chair and stared down at his plate, brooding. It was not long before the youth that had beckoned him to breakfast stood before him.

"General Quintas," he said. "Queen Brygda has sent me to collect you. Come, I will take you to the site."

The boy turned and walked away, not bothering to check if Quintas followed. After a brief hesitation, the Roman general jogged to catch up with the boy. He tried to broach conversation with the youth, but found that he had nothing useful to say, so he elected to remain quiet. As he walked from the great hall, he noticed the Batavian citizenry gather along the barely visible path of packed earth that served as a road. They still wore their white robes and their unreadable expressions as they lined up, leaving the road clear. Down through the city Quintas followed, then out. The buildings fell behind as the pair walked quickly to the burial site. People lined the road, though the city was far behind. That was when Quintas saw the royal family, such that it was, standing atop a hillock beside a large hole. At the base of the small hill, a second hole had been dug. Quintas noted the young woman with two sons standing at the hole. Lebeo's family.

An old man stood apart from both families, wearing a hooded white robe. He, however, used a blue embroidered sash to tie his robes instead of a red one.

A semi-circular copse of oaks grew behind the hill, and Quintas immediately recognized the site as sacred. They were not burying any Batavi. They were burying heroes.

Quintas felt cowed by the towering oaks, and not a little conspicuous in his Roman military uniform; a brown and red sore marring the white parade.

He walked to where Judocus indicated, at the top of the hillock but apart from Civillis's family and turned. He swallowed. All of the people of Batavorum had arrived, from the warriors and workmen, shepherds and healers, they all stood in rows, each indistinguishable from the other in robes of white. Some of the Roman legion had decided to attend also. Civillis' story was well known now, and the soldiers wished to pay their respects. He may have become an enemy of Rome, but he had been a good and brave man and a worthy foe. The soldiers recognized this.

The general snuck a glance at Civillis's family. Brygda stood with her arms around her grandson, her grey hair tied back. The boy, Diethelm, stared numbly out, one small hand resting on one of Brygda's forearms. Adalbern stood at his mother's side, his expression, like the rest of the Batavi, unreadable. Each one stared back towards the city, down the road where, Quintas noted, two sets of beautiful horses pulled carts towards the burial ground. He watched as the carts drew near, and were pulled around the site three times to mark the turning of the sun.

The old man with the blue sash walked forward, first to the body of the chieftain, then to Lebeo's corpse. He anointed them both with some sort of strange-smelling liquid, muttering as he did.

Eight men walked forward, four to a body, and they hefted them from the wagons. Those at the base of the hillock waited patiently for those carrying the chieftain's corpse to the hill. As the old man lifted his arms to the sky and began to beseech the gods, they lowered the corpses into the earth.

Quintas did not know the language of the Batavi well, though he knew it well enough to understand and be understood. It did not sound all that far from Gaulish, of which he knew some, but of what was uttered here during the ceremony he could understand nothing. He recognized the name Wotan, whom he knew to be the Batavi equivalent of Jupiter—more or less. He heard the name Hel, and knew her to be a deity of the dead, though her exact form and function was unknown to him. Everything else, however, escaped him.

The priest held up a sword. Quintas recognized the weapon as belonging to the chieftain. The old man intoned something. He raised his knee and placed the sword across it.

"No," Adalbern barked suddenly. "Let his weapon be true. My father's draugr would only rise in defence of these lands. Let him defend it well."

The old man considered a moment. He nodded. "It shall be."

He laid the weapon in the ground, unbent, stepped aside and bowed his head. Brygda walked forward, picking up a goblet from the ground that Quintas had not noticed. She took a sip from the goblet, raising it first to the heavens before placing it on her lips. She passed the goblet to her son, who made the same skyward motion and drank. He passed it to his nephew. The boy took it as if in a dream, made the same motion, and sipped from the goblet. Brygda and Adalbern knelt at the boy's side, each taking a hold of the goblet. Together, they poured what remained of the drink over the body.

The old man stepped forward again and gave another short service. Two young girls walked forward bearing torches. Strapping young men, soon old enough to enter service in the Roman army, began the work of covering the body with oak planks. Quintas noticed that the body had been laid on planks of wood and woven mats of dried grass and weeds.

He watched as the young men stepped aside and the two girls laid their torches on the wood. They caught immediately, making Quintas suspect that they had been soaked in some kind of oil. The fire flared hot and bright.

Another flare turned Quintas's head and he realized that Lebeo's service had been conducted in perfect unison with Civillis's. This spoke volumes of the esteem the Batavi had for both men.

The mourners turned and began a slow procession back to their homes. Quintas moved but Judocus's hand on his arm stopped him. "Honoured guests and family are expected to stay until the fires burn themselves out."

"How long is that?" Quintas asked.

"If the priests have calculated correctly, sundown."

Quintas wanted to groan. The sun indicated that it was only mid-morning.

"You may sit, if you like," Judocus said.

Quintas looked over at Civillis's family and saw them settle on the grass. They watched the flames, holding one another, Adalbern, now the head of the family, wrapping strong arms protectively around his mother and his nephew.

Time dragged. The flames burned hot for a long time before the bulk of their hunger seemed sated and they cooled some. Diethelm had fallen asleep on the grass, his head resting on Brygda's lap. Brygda and her son remained awake, though they had said not a word to one another. They shared a mutual comfort in silence. That same silence bored through Quintas as if threatening to eat his soul. He needed conversation, if only to fill the horrible void left by the silence and the sucking flames.

"What is a draugr?" he asked Judocus, who had taken to examining the clouds in the sky.

"It is the spirit half of a person."

"The spirit half?"

"Yes, a person is made of two parts—the body and the spirit. A body without a spirit is nothing, just a mass of flesh and bone. It is the spirit that gives life to the body. A draugr is a spirit that has not gone on to the hall of our ancestors. Something keeps it trapped here."

"What would keep a spirit from eternal food and drink?" Quintas asked.

"Unfinished business perhaps, or perhaps someone has cast a spell and pulled the spirit from the hall. No one really knows, but if the draugr is angered, it may rise from the grave. That is why we normally bend the weapons before burying them."

"Adalbern did not want that to happen."

"No. His father loved this land and loved his people in life. His draugr will also. If the spirit rises from the grave, it will be righteous. Those it slays will deserve to die."

Quintas nodded, though he did not fully understand. "Are you not afraid that this spirit will slay you?"

Judocus's mouth twisted. "No," he said. "We are being moved, Roman. The draugr will have to walk many miles in order to lay a sword across my throat."

Quintas snapped his mouth shut. He turned his gaze to the flames still eating greedily in the pit. Adalhard's form had vanished entirely, replaced by glowing embers and white ash. There was no distinguishing between bone and wood now. He stared deep into the flames, perhaps hoping to catch sight of this draugr before it departed to the Batavi land of the dead.

"Do not stare too deep into the flames," Judocus whispered to him. "Or they may draw you with the dead to the Otherworld."

Quintas snapped his eyes away from the fire in alarm. He noted a shepherd approach the hill. The man stopped and waited for Adalbern to notice him. When the latter acknowledged the shepherd with a small frown, the shepherd bowed and approached. They exchanged words in low voices. Quintas watched as Adalbern's eyes closed briefly, his face twisted in pain, before the Batavian prince nodded to the shepherd and spoke, presumably to give instruction. The shepherd nodded. He reached out a strong hand and clasped Adalbern's shoulder briefly before turning away.

Judocus hung his head and Quintas turned to him. "Do you know what that was about?"

"They have found Gerlach," Judocus said, nodding his head towards the river, easily seen from the hillock. "Rome claims another victim."

Quintas's heart dropped when he spied four men carrying a body between them approach the city.

"He hanged himself," Adalbern said to Quintas. He spoke quietly so as not to disturb Diethelm's sleep.

"I'm sorry," the Roman replied automatically.

Adalbern shrugged. "It may yet prove to be better and wiser."

Quintas waited for Adalbern to finish the thought. The Batavian remained silent. "Than what?" Quintas asked him.

"Than life beneath the oppression of Rome," Adalbern answered, looking Quintas full in the face. His brown eyes were hard.

Quintas could offer neither rebuttal nor comfort, so he merely watched the men take Gerlach's body into the city.

"He will not be buried amongst the heroes of our nation and his weapon will be bent," Judocus said. "For a man to hang himself, there must have been great torment of the soul. He will be bound to that torment and unable to move on. His draugr will certainly linger, and it shall be a vengeful spirit. A shame. Gerlach was a brave and honourable man in life."

Adalbern stood with his mother, dressed in his furs and segmented armour, wearing the pale blue undergarment that had come to signify a Batavian warrior. He looked as if he might be preparing for his next tour within the Roman ranks, but for the single thick white band tied around his upper arm; a silent signal to other Batavi that he was still in mourning.

Indeed, all the Batavi had resorted to their normal dress, and all wore this white band around their upper left arm. Brygda had refused to wear anything but white, her silver hair tied back in the fashion of married women, though she was married no longer. She looked exhausted. Three days spent weeping and serving each in turn as her people mourned their fate had taken their toll. It had been Brygda who hosted the feasts all three days of the mourning period. Now it was over, her people had turned to her for direction. She had received no peace and no rest since the revolt ended.

The two Batavi were joined by Diethelm, the solemn-faced boy dressed in riding clothes and sporting a large knife. It had been his father's, Quintas was informed. The ring he wore around his neck on a leather thong had belonged to his mother. Quintas knew that both items were likely to be taken away from the boy once he arrived in Rome. Vespasian wanted the boy to forget his heritage and love only the empire. It was unlikely, Quintas mused. The Batavi had been friends of Rome, but they loved their lands and their fellows more than anything. They were proud and stubborn. This revolt had proven that much.

Still, Diethelm was young enough that any re-education may prove effective. Adalbern was a lost cause.

"We're ready to move out," Camillus said, keeping a careful eye on the Batavians as they dismantled their houses to take to the new location. The commander of Legion *XIV Gemina* would ensure the Batavians made it to their destination and everything was rebuilt according to the peace treaty Civillis struck with Rome.

Quintas was to escort Adalbern to Lugdunum in Gaul and then onto Rome to deliver the youngest Batavian to Vespasian. He nodded at his second-in-command and approached the family standing at the top of the stairs to the great hall, Camillus at his heels.

"We are ready to go," he said to Adalbern. The man nodded at him. He turned to his mother.

"My wonderful son," the silver-haired woman said. "It breaks my heart to see you torn from me so."

Adalbern had no words, so instead he wrapped his arms around his mother and pulled her close. "I love you," he whispered.

"I love you, too. Remember," Brygda said. "Remember whose son you are, and that you are Batavian. Never forget this, and I shall be content."

"I swear I will remember." Adalbern released his mother and stepped back, his eyes wet, though he did not shed any tears.

"And you, little man," Brygda said, kneeling down to face her grandson. "Remember your old grandmother. Rome will try and make you theirs, but as long as you remember us, and remember that you are a man of the Batavi, they will never be able to claim you."

"I don't want to go," Diethelm whispered, shaking his head as tears began to stream down his cheeks. "I don't want to leave you. I don't want to go to Rome."

"I know, little man," Brygda said. "I wish you could stay forever in the land you were born to. But you cannot."

Diethelm burst into tears and Brygda pulled him close. "Be brave," she said, tears of her own striking her eyes. "You must be brave."

Diethelm cried harder, clinging to his grandmother as if a breeze might carry him away.

Scoffing, Camillus stepped forward to take Diethelm away from his grandmother. Adalbern silently stepped in front of him, blocking the way. He said nothing, but his eyes bore into Camillus's, his impassive expression somehow threatening. Camillus had to crane his neck to look Adalbern in the eye. Not only was the man typically Batavian in height and breadth, but also on a step higher than Camillus.

"Step back, Camillus," Quintas said before Camillus could open his mouth and make demands of Adalbern.

Camillus snorted. "It's a pathetic man indeed who relies so much on the affection of his mother."

Adalbern drew himself up further yet and his already hard eyes turned icy. His glare could whither an oak.

"No one who has fought beside our men would ever describe them as pathetic," Brygda said acidly, rising to her feet. She fixed her blue eyes on Camillus, her bearing proud and powerful. "Perhaps Rome's men would be twice as brave and half as cruel had their mothers loved them half as much."

Adalbern's mouth quirked slightly, threatening a smile.

"But then," Brygda continued, "who could love such men as they? Our men, at least, are worthy of the love we give them."

This time Adalbern did smile. It was a vicious, mirthless sort of smile that reminded Quintas much of Civillis. Turning to his nephew, Adalbern opened his arms and knelt down. "Come," he said. "Rome is in need of a real man in their midst."

Diethelm went to his uncle, allowing himself to be picked up and hugged close. With one last look at his mother, Adalbern walked down the steps to where the horses waited. He ignored Camillus's glare as he walked.

"You have no one to blame but yourself," Quintas said to his second-in-command, turning from Brygda and following Adalbern down the steps. Camillus said nothing and followed his commander. As he mounted his horse, he heard Diethelm's unsteady voice ask his uncle, "Can I ride with you?"

Adalbern immediately and wordlessly placed Diethelm at the fore of his saddle before mounting. Surrounded by armed Roman cavalry, Adalbern walked his horse from Batavorum one final time.

"My son!" Brygda called from her place at the top of the stairs to the great hall. She raised one fist into the air and in Batavian said, "Sons of Batavia, stand proud!"

Adalbern turned in his saddle. He raised his fist in a salute back at his mother. "Proud I stand," he called back.

The Batavians ceased their work dismantling their homes and one by one raised their fists into the air.

"Proud we stand!" someone bellowed.

"Proud we stand!" the crowd answered.

Again and again they chanted the words, bidding the last of Civillis's blood farewell on their journey. The deep voices of the Batavi followed the departing Roman army like a ghost, dogging their march home.

## 70 AD, AUTUMN, LUGDUNUM, PROVINCE OF GAUL

Adalbern watched the Gauls as they went about their tasks in the city. They moved through the streets, barely smiling, on their errands. Adalbern's heart lurched when he saw a family of three blonde-haired sisters, younger than Diethelm, begging for scraps, their faces smeared with muck. The Gauls had forgotten their proud heritage.

Adalbern wanted to turn his horse and share the last of his travelling rations with the children. He needed them no longer. But his guard of Roman cavalrymen prevented him from walking his horse any direction but forward.

"It's not Rome," Camillus said with a smile. "But I am glad to be back in civilization."

"Civilization is letting children starve on the street, while others have more food than an army could eat in a month, is it?" Adalbern demanded of the second-in-command.

"They could find work," Camillus said, waving dismissively.

Adalbern took a deep breath in, but refrained from speaking his mind further. He looked down at his nephew, who stared around him at the city.

"He is to go to the emperor," Quintas said, drawing Adalbern from his thoughts. "He will never go hungry."

Adalbern's eyes flashed dangerously, but he remained silent. He knew he would not be able to make the Roman understand. How could he? Romans believed cruelty a default state for men.

The party rode up to the guard house of a large estate and they dismounted. Adalbern followed suit, helping his nephew from the saddle.

"Quintas!" a portly Roman said, walking from the compound with a big smile. "How lovely to see you again. And ahead of schedule!"

"We had little trouble on the ride in," Quintas said, smiling at the rotund man. The man's eyes shifted to Adalbern and down to Diethelm.

"This is the boy, is it?" the man asked.

Adalbern pulled Diethelm closer, mistrusting the greedy expression of the man observing his nephew.

"It is," Quintas said. "Diethelm, this is Governor Lilius. He will be accompanying us to Rome with his guard."

Diethelm scowled at the man.

"It is considered a great honour to be so escorted, young man," Lilius said.

"No prison is honourable," Diethelm replied.

Quintas sighed. Adalbern smiled.

Lilius turned to Quintas with raised brows. "Well," he said. "I can see that there is a great deal of work to be done to scrub this boy of his barbarism."

Diethelm opened his mouth to speak again. Fearing the governor having a brutal temper, Adalbern placed his hand on the boy's shoulder and, understanding, Diethelm clamped his mouth shut.

"At least your uncle has some sense," Lilius told the boy. Diethelm narrowed his eyes at him, glaring hatefully.

"You," Lilius said, "must be Civillis's son." He extended his hand.

Adalbern declined to take it.

Lilius let his hand drop and he sniffed derisively. "It's already too late for you," he said. "I cannot understand why Aetius decided to take you in. Still, he gains much favour from Vespasian for it. The emperor is rather enamoured of your father, I hear. I cannot understand why the emperor would so admire a traitor."

Adalbern could not contain himself. "It was Rome who betrayed us," he growled. So threatening was his demeanour that several of Governor Lilius's personal guard grasped their hilts.

Lilius mopped his brow. "I find the humidity of this place intolerable," he muttered. Adalbern smirked. He knew well the difference between the sweat produced from heat and that produced in response to fear. Lilius' was the latter.

"Well, as much as I hate to house barbarians, the emperor has entrusted me with your care for the evening. The servants are preparing food as we speak. Come in, rest in the courtyard. I can offer you some drink while we wait for the food. My boys will see to your horses."

"Thank you, Governor," Quintas said, smiling.

Lilius's boys, Adalbern learnt, were all young, well-groomed slaves. Their eyes were flat and lifeless, and they did not look up at Adalbern as they grasped his horse's reins and led the tired beast away.

"Why are they broken, uncle?" Diethelm asked him.

Adalbern shook his head. "I don't know, Diethelm," he answered softly. He did know, he just did not want to think about it.

The courtyard of Lilius's property was a pleasant space with perfectly trimmed trees, kept deliberately stunted for aesthetic reasons. Adalbern found it a miserable sight. Trees were made to stretch their branches. They were designed to reach the sky. But, in typical Roman fashion, these ones had been deprived of their liberty. It spoke much of the Roman mind and Adalbern found he sympathized with the trees. They were like the peoples Rome absorbed into their cancerous empire; aching to stretch to freedom, forever beaten back, forcibly confined and made to conform with the image that pleased Rome most. It did not please Adalbern. He found wild woods more beautiful by far than this carefully tended garden.

Quintas, Camillus, and Lilius walked to a paved area with stone seats, finding a place for themselves and sitting down. Adalbern instead went to the green, seating himself beneath a tree, near enough that he might be included in the conversation if they wished. It was barely large enough to fit him seated beneath it. Diethelm sat beside his uncle and immediately began playing with the grass before him.

Quintas watched the boy a moment. Diethelm wore a scowl that vanished any time he looked at his uncle. He took all his cues from the tall Batavian man, appearing relaxed only when Adalbern was, and alert when Adalbern was. This was how the Batavi instructed their children. No words or formal lessons were necessary. Men learnt to be men by watching men. Charged with the sacred task of remembering to be Batavian in the heart of Rome, Diethelm was learning all he could as quickly as he could.

"Well," Lilius said, smiling. "I'm very glad the whole mess is over. First the civil war, then the revolts, on three fronts, mind. The east is subdued, the north is subdued, and now we turn our strength to Britain. Those northern rebels will not last that long. The island will be ours."

"How could they?" Camillus asked with a scoff. "From what I hear, they are little more than a rabble of grubby mountain dwellers."

"It would be dangerous to underestimate them," Quintas said quietly. "They took back Brigantia, did they not? They might be few in number, but they are fierce and proud, and have already proved to be much trouble. No, derision is the wrong attitude to take when it comes to any of the peoples of the north, Britain or otherwise."

Adalbern smiled slightly. He listened but added nothing to the conversation. Northern Britain had a distinct advantage when it came to fighting Rome. The shores were rocky, the seas tumultuous. Crossing the straight was rarely an easy affair. The landscape was rocky and mountainous, with deep lakes that hindered travel in the valleys. It was perfect for tactics that Rome did not know how to counter—guerrilla warfare. Such tactics had the potential to destroy a legion with as little as a hundred men, some well-aimed projectiles, and clever traps.

Adalbern pulled his mind back from fantasizing about destroying Rome in northern Britain. It was not the discussion at hand, and he needed to concentrate if he was to find a weakness he could exploit to renew Batavian emancipation.

They had not been seated long when serving girls, Celts by what Adalbern could tell, entered the courtyard bearing cups and pitchers of wine. Adalbern refused the wine offered.

"I would prefer mead if you have it," he said. "Otherwise I will drink water."

"Mead," Lilius said with a scoff. Nevertheless, he waved one girl away to fetch Adalbern what he asked for. "And milk for the boy," he called after the girl, who scurried away at great speed.

Before long, Adalbern was sipping at the cup of Gaulish mead; not quite the flavour he liked but it was better than Roman wine. Diethelm took the milk, but stared down at it distrustfully.

"Drink it, boy," Lilius said. "Before it spoils."

Diethelm looked to his uncle for direction. Adalbern nodded down at him and Diethelm drank.

"You will have to learn to decide for yourself," Adalbern told his nephew in Batavian. "Soon they will take you away, and I will not be there to help you."

Staring down to hide his tears, Diethelm nodded. "I don't think I will be able to."

"You will," Adalbern said. "Being Batavi is in your blood. Trust your instincts and you will not be led ill."

"Speak in a language we can all understand," Lilius said.

"Why?" Adalbern asked. "Those words were not meant for you."

"So that I know you are not plotting some new treason and you get to keep your head."

It did not escape Adalbern's notice that Quintas turned away from Lilius in an effort to not appear sympathetic to the Batavians. Adalbern looked the governor in the eye. "Take my head," he said quietly. "Break the Roman treaty again, and watch Batavia rise. Again."

The contest of wills was broken when a serving boy, painfully young and well-groomed, entered the courtyard and whispered something in Lilius's ear.

"Aetius is here," he said, turning and stalking away, following the serving boy.

"A word of advice, Adalbern," Quintas said. "Don't antagonize your hosts. Rome is on her way to stability once more. There will be no sparing your people if this situation goes ill."

Adalbern looked away from Quintas, staring at the elegant pillars that surrounded the courtyard. His silence was acknowledgement that Quintas was correct, and it was good enough for Quintas.

Lilius returned with another man, much leaner and fitter at his side. Behind him walked a slender boy of perhaps sixteen, sullen and silent. They were all Roman, judging by their dress and features.

"Quintas," Lilius said brightly as the commander stood. "This is Aetius, the merchant who owns half the marketplace."

"I have heard much about you," Quintas said with a smile, offering his hand to Aetius. "This is my second-in-command, Camillus."

Adalbern sighed and rose to his feet.

"This is your hostage," Lilius said, indicating the Batavian. "Adalbern. Barbaric name. See if you can't fix that."

Aetius did not offer his hand to Adalbern, which proved a relief. Adalbern would not have taken it. Instead the Roman merchant looked him over appraisingly.

"You'll do," he said.

Adalbern raised his brows.

"Perhaps you'll be able to teach my good-for-nothing son how to be a man."

The boy standing behind his father folded his arms across his chest and rolled his eyes. Adalbern did well to hide a smile.

"That is your son?" he asked, indicating the sullen youth.

"Yes," Aetius said. "Ambrosius, this is Adal... what was it?"

"Adalbern, son of Adalhard, War-Chief of the Batavi," Adalbern supplied.

"I thought you were Civillis's son."

"I am," Adalbern said. "Adalhard was the name his mother gave him, and it was the name he was buried with."

"Ah. In any case, the emperor has given me directions to treat you as if you were family, and so you are welcome to my home and to my table. Alas, you are not to leave my property without an escort."

"Do you normally put members of your family under house arrest?" Adalbern asked mildly.

"Yes," Ambrosius muttered before his father could give answer. This time Adalbern did smile, though it was nothing more than a brief flash across his face. Ambrosius returned the smile, equally as briefly.

"Come," Lilius said, interjecting before the tension reached breaking point. "I am told lunch is served. Come and eat." He led the way into the house, into a room with a large round table laden with foods of all kinds. He took a seat, waving his hand vaguely in what was evidently an invitation to do the same, for the others also sat. Adalbern was the last to sit, with Diethelm safely at his side.

Diethelm and Adalbern remained silent as Quintas, Lilius, Camillus, and Aetius talked. In listening, Adalbern learnt that Aetius was a powerful man, well respected by the merchant class and well feared by the lower classes. Governors oft came to him for counsel, and few were ever put into office without Aetius' support. He was wealthy and he was hard, sparing little pity for those who struggled in the current climate. He was born and raised in Rome, and only headed into Gaul for the business opportunities it presented. He found the Gauls and other "barbarians" as distasteful as Lilius did. He was particularly disgusted by Gaulish women.

"Entirely too heavily set," Aetius said with a shudder. "They can hardly be described as women at all. They're more like oxen, and who wants to fuck an ox?"

The men laughed uproariously, except, Adalbern noted, Ambrosius.

"Strong women breed strong sons," Adalbern said, cutting through the mirth as effectively as a sharp sword cuts fine silk. Ambrosius did smile at this. There was a touch of amazement at Adalbern's boldness in his expression.

Quintas turned the conversation before Aetius could respond. "And how is business these days in Lugdunum?"

Aetius turned from glaring at Adalbern to answer Quintas's question.

"Is it true?" Ambrosius whispered to Adalbern. "Do you truly believe that sons are made strong because their mothers are?"

"How could it not be true?"

"Father believes that women merely carry the seed. The women contribute nothing."

Adalbern snorted. "Unless something goes wrong, I assume," he said. "And then it's all the woman's fault."

Ambrosius blinked. "You're not wrong," he said after pausing a moment to ponder. "Father blames mother for the way I turned out...." Ambrosius trailed off. He leant back in his chair and stared down at the olives on his plate.

"My sister looked exactly like my mother," Adalbern said, drawing the boy back again. "Everywhere I look, I see children who look like their mothers. The Batavi believe that men are no different to any other animal. In order to breed a strong horse, you need a strong stallion and a strong mare, or there is a risk that the offspring will not be able to perform to standard. Romans breed animals, do they not?"

Ambrosius nodded.

"I am puzzled how they can believe otherwise, then."

Ambrosius offered a sad smile. "I've never thought about it much, but it explains a lot I suppose. Is your mother strong?"

"Very," Adalbern said. "She bore twins and survived, and I saw her heft my father's battle-axe in combat. None of the men she fought stood a chance."

Ambrosius's eyes shone brightly. "I should have liked to have seen that!" he breathed.

Adalbern smiled at him. "In truth? It was a little terrifying."

Ambrosius grinned. "I think I like you, Batavian."

His words made Adalbern chuckle.

Romans, Adalbern discovered, preferred long, leisurely meals. The men lounged and talked for a few hours. Adalbern could tell Diethelm was bored, though the boy tried hard not to fidget. Confinement was difficult. Ordinarily, Diethelm would have excused himself and, with friends and a few of their older siblings, cousins or parents, would head to the river to swim and play until exhaustion drove them home again. There was a decided dearth of young men Diethelm could play with, save the young serving boys of the house, and there was no way to escape the city to run in the open air or swim in the river. Adalbern scratched his chin with the back of his thumb as he regarded the boy.

"Bored?" he asked him.

Diethelm nodded at his uncle. Adalbern nodded back. He turned to ask permission for his nephew to be excused. Before he could speak, Lilius rose. "Well," the man said. "I had told the emperor that I would leave for Rome today. We must be away before the sun sets."

Adalbern's heart skipped. He had not expected to be parted from his nephew yet.

"So soon?" Diethelm asked in a small voice.

"We cannot keep the emperor waiting," Lilius said, smiling at him.

Adalbern felt his shoulders tighten in response to the man's smile. Though his expression appeared benign, there was something in Lilius's countenance that sat ill with the enormous Batavian.

"Come on, then," Lilius said. "The servants have finished packing the carriage by now. We must be away."

"But—" Diethelm protested.

The smile worn by the governor slipped slightly. His voice took on an edge when next he spoke. "We must not keep the emperor waiting."

Adalbern stood slowly. "Come, Diethelm," he said gently. "We must honour the treaty struck between the Batavi and Rome. Let us show Rome how to keep trust."

Diethelm swallowed and slid off his chair. He took the hand Adalbern offered him and together they followed Governor Lilius out to the front of the building. A carriage indeed awaited them, pulled by fine white Iberian horses. There was room enough for two men to lay down inside, or six to sit upright. Servants waited patiently at the open door of the carriage, their eyes downcast.

Lilius moved forward, stopped at the open door of the carriage and turned. He stared at Diethelm, who still clasped his uncle's hand at the entrance to the house, with eyebrows raised in an expression of impatient expectance.

Two of the city guard, apologetic-looking Gauls, marched to Diethelm and, after nodding at Adalbern, took the boy and led him to Lilius. Diethelm paused at the entrance.

"Wait!" Adalbern said, walking forward. "Wait."

The two Gaulish guards stepped in between him and his nephew. "Let me say goodbye," he said to the men. They turned back to Lilius, seeking permission.

"Go on then," Lilius muttered waving his hand dismissively. The guards stepped aside and Adalbern walked forward. He knelt on the ground so that he might look his nephew in the eye. Diethelm fought tears as he stared at his uncle.

"Be brave," Adalbern said to him. "And remember what your grandmother told you. Trust yourself, and trust your Batavi blood. You will not be led astray."

Diethelm nodded.

"I love you, Uncle" Diethelm whispered.

Adalbern pulled the boy into a close embrace. "I love you too," he replied softly. "If you remember nothing else, remember that." He pulled away and kissed Diethelm's forehead. He rose to his feet and watched, his heart paining, as his nephew took a deep breath and climbed into the carriage. Lilius turned to follow, smirking. Adalbern caught his elbow and pulled him back.

"If any harm comes to that boy," he growled, "all the armies of the empire will not save you from me."

Ashen faced, Lilius managed a placating smile. "Harm the property of the emperor? I would not dream of it."

Fighting the urge to tear the man's throat out, Adalbern released him. He stood, helpless and heartbroken, as the serving boys shut the carriage door. He did not move as the driver lashed the horses, sending them from the compound at a trot. He watched until the carriage could no longer be seen through the dust and tumult of the city.

Quintas clapped Adalbern on the shoulder, yanking him from his grief. He turned to face the general.

"We must also depart. I'm to head north again, apparently, and oversee the building at Noviomagus. Then who knows?"

Adalbern did not respond, turning once more to the city beyond the compound.

"Will you accept my advice?"

Adalbern nodded absently, barely listening.

"Remain Batavian," Quintas said.

Adalbern turned to him in surprise.

"But don't let your pride lead you to stupidity. Pick your battles wisely." Quintas offered the Batavian a small smile.

"I will try," Adalbern said.

"Good." Quintas offered him his hand. Adalbern took it. "I have a great deal of respect for you and your people. I hope to visit with you whenever I am in the city."

Offering the barest of smiles, Adalbern stepped back and Quintas turned to mount his horse. "Treat him well, Aetius," he said. "The last thing we need is a second Batavian revolt. Rome may not be so fortunate the next time."

Aetius scowled, but nodded. He and his son waited for Quintas and his men to leave the compound before approaching Adalbern.

"Come on then, Batavian," Aetius said. "It is time I got you home. If you don't mind, I would like to stop by the market. There is soon to be an auction; freshly acquired goods from Britain."

"I am at your disposal, Aetius," Adalbern said.

Unable to tell from the impassive expression on the Batavian's face or from the dead tone of voice if Adalbern was being sarcastic, Aetius shrugged and walked forward, leaving the compound. Ambrosius and Adalbern followed.

The streets of Lugdunum were dusty and they stank, a product of the gathered poor and the number of animals that ran amok. The three men walked in silence, Adalbern towering over his hosts, though many Gauls almost matched his height, if not his breadth. Ambrosius walked beside the Batavian, lost in thought, his mood easily matching that of his companion.

"May I ask you a question?" he said at last. Adalbern nodded.

"Why was your mother brandishing your father's axe in battle? Is it common for women to join battle?"

"No," Adalbern said. "While it is not unheard of, it is not common. My mother took up arms because she had witnessed her daughter murdered at the hands of Roman centurions."

Ambrosius clamped his mouth shut. "I'm sorry," he said after a long silence.

Adalbern shrugged. "It is done and cannot be changed."

Sinking once more into melancholy, Ambrosius said no more. They walked a while before they arrived at the market. A crowd had already gathered, awaiting the commencement of the auction. Aetius made his way to the centre back, ascending the stairs designed to permit a clear view of the auction and waited.

Mederei walked silently from the dock, her feet still aching from the cane cuts she had received a week ago, punishment for escaping the compound that housed all of the master's slaves. The Roman bastard had tried to rape her and she had used the opportunity to crack his jaw and flee. She had almost made it to the forest and would have been free, but for the damned Roman guard that came after her on horseback.

That Roman had been the fifth owner in the months she had been captured by the German auxiliary and sold into servitude. All the trappings of her nobility had been taken and sold; her armour, her golden hair bands, her torque, all of it gone, sold off to fill the auxiliary's purse.

The pain in her feet numbed as she walked, a defence her body had miraculously acquired. She thanked the gods for it.

Her hands were bound before her in iron shackles, connected with thick chains to the slaves before and behind her. Her ankles were similarly bound. They shuffled along, a chain of aching misery and lost pride. Some slaves wept. Others trembled, muttering curses or prayers. Mederei remained silent and straight-backed, her dun eyes hard and unflinching even as faces leered at the chain of slaves making their way to market. Mederei cared not for them, for those leering faces were Roman and they filled her with hateful resolve. The looks from the Gauls proved harder to ignore; pitying looks of a people who understood the pain of slavery though they wore no chains. Mederei wanted to hate them too, but she could not. She had seen and experienced first-hand what Rome did to people in order to break their spirits.

She would have the last laugh, however. There was no spirit left in her to break, only a cold, endless pit of hate. It did not matter what Rome did to her, she would never submit. Not ever.

The market buzzed with life, Roman and other foreign merchants chatted to each other as they awaited the auction to begin. Mederei stood patiently in the pen as the slavers replaced her shackles on her wrists to be independent of the others. They removed the ones at her ankles entirely so that she would be able to take the steps to stand on display for the waiting crowd. While unlocking her ankle shackles, the slaver grabbed her leg so that she could not step away and dragged his tongue up her shin.

This had long ago lost its horror for Mederei. She had been raped by Romans when she was but ten years old, and they had tried repeatedly since her capture.

The man was smirking as he stood. Mederei returned his self-congratulatory expression by looking him over, twisting her brows to look as unimpressed as possible, and scoffing. She knew well there was nothing a Roman hated more than having their tenuous masculinity mocked.

The change in the slaver's expression was almost comical and extremely satisfactory. He slapped her hard across the cheek, cutting the skin.

"I'll teach you to mock me!" he snarled grabbing her roughly by her shoulders.

"How?" she replied. "Dogs are more man than you, Roman."

"Ho, there friend," another slaver said, pulling the angered man away from Mederei. He examined her briefly.

"Fantastic," he said sarcastically. "Now we'll have to reduce the price."

"She deserved it," the first slaver spat.

"And I deserve my gold. Get out of here. Go on. Find someplace to cool off, you idiot."

Spluttering curses, the slaver stalked away. Mederei's eyes followed him, a mirthless smile that looked like the snarl of a she-wolf showing her teeth.

"You'll end up dead if you keep that up," the second slaver told her.

Mederei turned her baleful gaze upon him. "Good," she said.

Shaking his head, the slaver moved on.

When her number was announced, Mederei walked to the display platform, her shoulders straight and her head held high. This was not her first auction, and unless she died soon, it would not be her last.

Adalbern straightened slightly as the hazel eyes of the woman on the auction block met his briefly. The fourth slave to be called forward, she proved a refreshing change from the broken women and men that had been dragged up to be sold off thus far. Her bearing was proud, her features strong and noble, good breeding showing through despite the obvious lack of food and the swelling on her left cheek. Adalbern's eyes fell to the tattoo of a hare on her shoulder. Deep blue and highly stylised, the design was instantly recognizable. The woman was from northern Britain, then. It did much to explain her countenance. She looked over the crowd, her expression of disdain silencing them a moment.

"Now here is a feisty find!" the auctioneer said. "From a wealthy family in northern Britain, she has been through five masters. Are there any of you who are man enough to achieve what the others could not?"

Evidently understanding Latin, the woman on the block scoffed. The anger in the crowd grew, becoming palpable. No one bid. Adalbern smiled to himself.

"Come now," the auctioneer said. "Have none of you the necessary parts to show this young Briton why Rome rules their island?"

No one missed the flash of pure hate that crossed the woman's face like a shadow of lightning.

"And you can have that privilege for only three aurei. Three aurei, a bargain at triple the price. Look at her! She is beautiful! She is proud! Three aurei only!"

"I'll give you ten denarii for her hair," someone called. The auctioneer blinked. He turned to the slavers standing at the side. They looked at each other, then back to him. In unison, they shrugged.

"All right, then," the auctioneer said. "I have ten denarii for her hair. Would anyone else like to bid on her hair?"

The crowd snickered but there were no counter bids, and so the auctioneer beckoned the buyer forward. The man handed over the ten denarii and the two slavers walked up the block to the woman. They grabbed her roughly by her arms and tried to push her to her knees. She resisted.

"Little bitch!" one man snarled. He pulled a cane from his belt and hit the back of her knees hard. The knees gave way and the woman collapsed. The strain of controlling the pain showed on her face for only a moment before her expression of disdain returned. One slaver gathered up her thick auburn waves, tying it back with a strip of cloth he produced from a pouch at his back. The other removed a dagger. Taking the woman's hair, he pulled her head back, making her wince. She stared resolutely at the sky as the slaver sawed her hair off.

The slaver with the knife released the woman, pushing her forward so that she was forced to brace with her hands to prevent cracking her nose on the auction block. Adalbern kept his eyes on her as the slavers tossed the hair to the buyer and walk back to their position. Amidst the jeers of the mocking crowd, the woman took a deep breath and slowly rose to her feet. Lifting her chin, she stared out at the crowd, her expression returning to haughty disdain.

"How much for her skin?" a man yelled from the crowd.

The woman's eyes fell to him. She smirked. "Come, try and take it and find out, Roman," she sneered.

Even Adalbern, proud as he was and as angry as he was at Rome was taken aback by the woman's impudence.

"That does it," one of the slavers snapped. He marched forward, pulling out his cane again. But the woman was prepared for him. As he charged, his cane raised high, she spun and crouched in one fluid motion. It was too fast to see what she had done, but in the end, she was once again standing, and the slaver had been thrown some distance, landing hard on his back. The other slaver charged, and she raised her leg and delivered a powerful kick, lifting the man off his feet and backwards several steps.

The centurions leapt into action, drawing their weapons. Chained as she was, the woman still fought well, knocking down three centurions before one managed to deliver a blow that sent her sprawling. The guards were on her in and instant. It took a further three men to restrain her. They dragged her to the centre of the market place, where stood a short post with an iron loop attached to it. They chained her there and stepped back, now primarily concerned with crowd control. The first of the slavers stalked forward, his cane at the ready.

It landed with a crack on her back, splitting her flesh through her ragged clothes. The woman winced, but did not cry out.

"Scream, you bitch!" the slaver grated, hitting faster and harder.

"Stop," Ambrosius whispered from beside Adalbern. "Please stop."

Adalbern turned to him to find the youth's eyes fixed upon the woman, tears streaming down his cheeks.

"Enough! Enough!" a large man said, laughing. "Enough!" He strode forward, beaming. "Three aurei, you said? I'll give you one and ten denarii, since I will have to use the rest to hire a healer."

"Who is he?" Adalbern asked Ambrosius quietly.

"That is Vitus," Ambrosius replied. "He runs the ludus—the gladiatorial school here. The only slaves he buys from market are those he sacrifices to the games... and there is talk of a gladiator from Rome coming soon to fight. I fear she will number amongst the slain on that day."

"Two aurei," the slaver growled. "She's given enough trouble to warrant much more."

"The Hunt take you, Roman," the woman hissed. The slaver stepped forward and delivered a hard kick to her stomach. She curled into herself, coughing blood.

"Two it is!" Vitus said, his face splitting into a wide smile. "The spirited ones have the best deaths!" The man reached into his purse and withdrew two small gold coins. He handed them to the slaver, who in turn handed the man the key to the woman's shackles.

"Here," the slaver said, handing his bloodied cane. "You will need this."

"Oh no," Vitus replied. "My methods are far more effective." He unlocked the woman's shackles and she slumped to the ground. Lifting her by what remained of her hair, Vitus tossed the woman to two burly men. "Put her in the cart with the others." He snapped.

The men obliged, dragging her unceremoniously away.

Geraint watched Mederei as she was dragged away, bloodied and barely conscious. His eyes met hers only briefly, and the flash of recognition from her was so faint that he doubted he had seen it at all. His stomach had swallowed his heart at the sight of her brutalized form and his eyes stung with tears. He had searched for her all over Britain, finally catching wind of her purchase by slavers near Londinium. He had raced there, only to find that they had crossed the straight to Gaul. It took him a month to find her again.

He had not been prepared to see her as she was; gaunt, wounded, filthy. And still she had the fire that had so enchanted his lord Rhys.

It took a moment for the crowd to settle back down after the impromptu spectacle that had been Mederei's temper. Geraint took that time to observe the crowd. His gaze locked on the eyes of a foreign man standing near the back centre of the market place. Tall, broadly built with a ruddy complexion, the man was obviously not Roman; northern certainly, probably German. He wore a neat beard that was closely trimmed to his face, trousers and a tunic with a leather jerkin over it. A Roman man beside him moved, breaking the contact, and the German looked away.

Geraint left the market, seeking a place to sit and think.

Adalbern turned when Aetius angrily addressed his son, "Are you weeping?"

Ambrosius wiped his eyes hurriedly. "It's dusty," he muttered.

"What manner of son did my idiotic wife give me?" Aetius snapped. "Get out of my sight, you miserable worm of a child! Weeping? At what? The slave girl? Get out. Get away. Your pathetic mewling is irritating me. And take the Batavian with you. Jupiter knows you would not survive the walk home by yourself."

Ambrosius clenched his fists. "Yes, Father," he grated. He turned and marched away.

"See if you can't turn that limp fish into a man," Aetius said to Adalbern. He used a conspiratorial tone, as if Adalbern would understand his frustration with his son. Adalbern scowled at him and, without giving answer, turned to follow Ambrosius from the market place. As he turned, he scanned the crowd.

The Celt who had met his eye had vanished.

"Ambrosius," Adalbern called, striding to catch up to the boy who hurriedly walked through the city. "Ambrosius, wait!" Adalbern's long legs meant he did not have to try especially hard to catch up with the boy. He reached out and grabbed Ambrosius at the wrist. The youth spun, his eyes burning.

"What?" he spat. The heat was gone from him in an instant. The warmth in Adalbern's brown eyes had been the last thing he expected. He burst into tears, covering his face with his hands to try and hide it.

Adalbern looked around, noting the curious glances at the boy. He spied a quiet, cool alley, shaded by a tired-looking elm, and gently guided Ambrosius to it. "Here," he said, backing Ambrosius against the trunk of the tree. "Sit."

Without complaint, Ambrosius slid to the ground, still crying. "I hate him," Ambrosius wheezed between sobs. "I hate him so much."

Adalbern squatted beside Ambrosius in silence as the boy cried. "That girl," Ambrosius sobbed next. "That poor girl. I just... I couldn't... It's..." Ambrosius's heaving lungs made speech impossible.

"Hush now," Adalbern said. "Cry first. Talk second."

"I wish I could be more like him," Ambrosius admitted once he had calmed down enough to speak coherently. "I wish I could look at it all and not be hurt by what I see."

"A man who does not weep is not a man, but a beast," Adalbern answered.

"I bet you don't cry like a little girl all the time," Ambrosius spat.

Adalbern smiled sadly. "I have wept often, little Roman."

Ambrosius looked up at Adalbern and scoffed. "Oh yeah?" he said. "When?"

"Well," Adalbern moved and settled against the tree trunk beside Ambrosius. "I wept when I was a little boy and my sister's best friend punched me in the eye."

Ambrosius smiled.

"Don't laugh," Adalbern said. "She hit hard. It still hurts."

This drew a chuckle from Ambrosius and Adalbern smiled. He grew serious. "My first night away from home with the auxiliary, I wept."

"Really?"

"Yes. I missed my mother. I missed my sister. I had often fed a squirrel when I went swimming, and I missed that little bastard. I wanted to go home, and so I wept."

"Did the other men make fun of you?"

Adalbern shook his head. "No. They all knew what it was like, leaving home for the first time, being away from loved ones, knowing you would be fighting wars you had nothing to do with. They had all wept their first night. If I remember correctly, I was given an extra serving of soup and a ruffle of my locks."

Ambrosius smiled at the image. "How old were you when you left home?"

"I was sixteen."

"I'm sixteen."

"You look it."

"And you cried?"

"Yes, I cried. And it was not the last time I would, either."

"Do you… I mean… do you cry often?"

"More often of late," Adalbern answered. He leant back against the tree and gazed up at the canopy.

Ambrosius turned his gaze to the ground. "I'm sorry for what happened to your family," he said. "It's all right if you hate me, you know."

"Why would I hate you?"

"I'm Roman."

Adalbern smiled at this. "My father loved Rome. He thought the empire, and the men who ruled it, wise and learned. He was convinced they were all honourable and noble. It devastated him when he learnt otherwise. But as he had come to know that not all Romans were good, I have come to know that not all are evil, either. I do not hate you, Ambrosius. Nor could I bring myself to. You are a good Roman."

"My father would disagree."

Adalbern sighed. He had a few choice words to describe Ambrosius's father, though he decided it wiser not to share them.

"He's threatened to send me into the army. I don't want to be in the army."

"What do you want?"

Ambrosius shrugged. "I want to be a musician. Mother loves it when I play."

"What do you play?"

Ambrosius looked sidelong at Adalbern, as if deciding whether or not to tell him. "The Gaulish lyra," he said at last.

Adalbern laughed. "That must upset your father."

"It does. I only play it when he's gone away on business."

"I should like to see this instrument. We had Gaulish bards come play at Batavorum. I always enjoyed their music." He rose to his feet and offered Ambrosius a hand up. "Let's beat your father home so I can listen."

Grinning, Ambrosius took the man's hand and allowed himself to be pulled to his feet. Together they walked from the alley and wove their way through the streets of Lugdunum to Ambrosius's home, a pair of privately hired guards keeping pace.

Mederei could not move as the cart upon which she lay rumbled into the gladiator school. They called it a school, but the high walls and barred gates were unworthy of that name. It was a prison. Though made hazy by pain, her gaze swept the exercise yard where gladiators of every kind lounged in the sun. Many were Celts, she could see. Many more were not. Their skins were as dark as ebony. All of them were men.

"Ho Vitus!" a man called. Braving the pain, Mederei attempted to turn her head to spy the owner of the voice. "What haul from the market?"

"Slaves enough to look an army," Vitus answered back. "With some training."

"Let me see them."

Mederei decided it would be best if she feigned unconsciousness. She closed her eyes as the cart stopped, letting her body relax.

"Aye, from the province of Africa, I s... What is this mess?"

Mederei felt her bare leg being prod with a firm, rounded stick.

"A woman," Vitus said. "From northern Britain, if that shoulder tattoo is anything to go by."

"Gods, Vitus! What manner of idiocy compelled you to buy this lump?"

"Before you get mad," Vitus said. Mederei could hear that he was moments away from bursting into raucous laughter. "I have heard that female gladiators are quite fashionable in Rome. She will draw a crowd for the spectacle if nothing else. And, if we are to have an army of Britons for the big fight we're arranging, we will need women in the mix. British women are famous for it."

"We could have dressed up some of our male fighters. What the hell am I supposed to do with this heap of bloodied pulp?"

"We'll patch her up. I hear British women are particularly tough."

"And if she doesn't pull through?"

"She'll pull through," Vitus said. "You should have seen her in the market. She's got a belly full of fire, this one."

There was a silence before the other man sighed. "Fine. Take her to the infirmary. We'll patch her up." To someone else he called, "You four, get this butchered bird to the infirmary, would you? Move!"

Mederei remained still and relaxed as she felt two pairs of hands grab her ankles. Not bothering to be gentle, they yanked, pulling her half off the cart. Two more pairs of hands grabbed her wrists. They all yanked together and hauled her from the cart, carrying her with one person on each limb. She kept her eyes shut, even when the shade replaced the sun.

"This one's female," she heard one of the men say in a lilting accent she could not place. His Latin was not nearly as refined as the next one who spoke.

"Let's hope she gets put in my cell. I've a spare bed in mine… not that she'll be using it."

The men guffawed and Mederei held back the sharp words that leapt immediately to her tongue.

"On the count of three, then," one of them said. "One…"

Mederei felt them swing her.

"Two…"

Another swing.

"Three!"

An extra high swing and they let go. She landed hard on her side on a wooden table. Despite the sudden pain that flooded her, she kept quiet.

"Reckon the master would be mad if we had a little diddle?" someone asked.

"Best not," the lilting voice said. "What if he wants first go? We'll be beaten for sure."

"He doesn't need to know."

"Oi!" someone called outside. "You lot! Get back to the yard!"

"There goes that idea."

Mederei listened as four pairs of feet walked away from her. She sighed her relief, and rested her head against the table. Blessed unconsciousness swallowed her.

The air was thick with the smell of sweat, unwashed bodies, and the acrid smoke of rendered fat lamps. Mederei stirred, opening her eyes slowly. She lay on her stomach on a wooden slab covered in a ratty blanket that served as a bed. The walls were strongly built of undecorated stone and mortar. They surrounded her on three sides. The fourth wall was not a wall, but a row of iron bars. She was in a prison cell.

Only when a cool breeze touched her skin did she realize that she was naked, save for her ravaged back, which had been covered in a poultice and had a cloth thrown over. Mederei tried to lift her weight, but could not. Her body ached too much.

"Ah," someone said.

Mederei turned her head towards the sound. The man from the market, Vitus, stood at the edge of her cell, peering in.

"You're awake, then," he said.

Mederei scowled at him and Vitus smiled.

"You've been unconscious for two days now."

When Mederei's scowl did not abate, he added. "Don't worry. No one touched you. I wouldn't want you to fall pregnant before fighting. That would be a waste. You must be hungry. I have food coming, and we'll get that poultice replaced for you."

Vitus sighed. "You know why you're here, of course. You've hit rock bottom, I'm afraid. It is inevitable that you will die fighting for me, but that does not mean we cannot be civilized."

"Only a Roman would believe having people die for their entertainment is civilized," Mederei spat in British.

"I am a Gaul," Vitus answered in Gaulish. Mederei did not try to hide her surprise.

"My family were made citizens by Julius Caesar. We had the foresight not to engage in hostilities with Rome."

"Foresight? Your family was merely cowardly."

"Perhaps," Vitus said with a shrug. "But since I am on this side of the cell, I find I cannot regret it."

"That is the corruption of Rome," Mederei said. "It makes men revel in their own cowardice." She turned her head away from him.

Vitus chuckled. "Perhaps. Still, I eat well every night. My family is provided for. Times have always been uncertain. We must all do what we can to protect ourselves and those we love."

"Some of us are," Mederei whispered.

"Come now. Your food is here."

Mederei refused to move, though she heard the cell door's creak of protest as it opened. She smelled the food as it was brought in, and her stomach rumbled. Despite herself, she turned again, and watched as a fair-haired man set a tray down. On it sat a stew consisting largely of leeks and barley, a large cup of ale, a chunk of dark bread and a wedge of cheese.

She struggled to push herself upright.

"Gandwy, will you help her sit up?"

The fair-haired man nodded. Moving slowly and carefully, he lifted Mederei into a sitting position. She winced as the poultice on her back cracked, moving the wounds beneath enough to cause pain.

"Gandwy is a British name," Mederei murmured to the man. The man nodded. Saying nothing he lifted the tray carefully into Mederei's lap. She gratefully accepted it.

"Thank you."

Gandwy offered her a small smile. He stood up and back, making a noticeable effort not to look at Mederei's naked form.

"Gandwy is one of your countrymen," Vitus said. "So I thought he would be the best choice to help you. I'm afraid I have no eunuchs, who would, no doubt, be eminently more suitable for the task of attending a woman. Still, Gandwy knows not to become..." Vitus cocked his head and smirked. "Inappropriate."

Mederei looked briefly at Gandwy as she ate. He refused to meet her eye. Vitus, however, stood and carefully watched her eat. When she frowned at him he smiled. "I'm just making sure you're eating everything. Some arrive here so despondent they starve themselves to death. I swore to my brother-in-law that you would not, but he wants me to make sure all the same."

Beyond caring about anything more than food, Mederei continued to eat. She did not stop even when a large bucket of hot water was carried into the room. Chewing, she watched a dark-skinned man set the bucket down by her bed and leave. He also did not dare look on her naked form or meet her gaze.

When she swallowed the last morsel of food, Vitus nodded at Gandwy. "If you please," he said.

Gandwy nodded. He moved behind Mederei and began carefully removing the cloth and poultice.

"We're going to wash your wounds and apply more poultice," Vitus said. "I applied it last time, but if you prefer, Gandwy can do it. He knows how."

"What care you for my preference?" Mederei demanded.

Vitus smiled. "You will find that I am not a bad man," he said, "if you do as you are told and try hard. You might not live long, but while you do, I will try to make things as pleasant for you as I can."

Mederei scoffed.

"Just fight," Vitus replied. "Fight and try to live. If you live long enough, you may be able to win your freedom."

"I thought my purpose was to die."

"Death is what will come for you," Vitus answered. "But as much as you and I must expect it, you have the chance to escape it. Now would you like Gandwy to apply the poultice?"

Mederei straightened as the Briton began to wash away the poultice that remained stuck in her lash wounds with a cloth from the hot water bucket.

"Do you have a wife?" Mederei asked Vitus.

"I do."

"Then you do it, and spare your man the torment of touching flesh he cannot have."

Vitus grunted. "Ah. Good point. Gandwy, you are permitted to leave once you've finished washing her back."

Gandwy grunted his thanks as he worked. He tried to be gentle, though often failed as the poultice would not come loose easily.

"Forgive me," he murmured in British every time Mederei's body twitched in pain.

"This was not your doing," Mederei answered.

Done at last, Gandwy stood. He collected the bucket and walked quietly from the cell, not sparing one more glance for the naked woman sitting on her hard bed.

"Lie down on your stomach," Vitus said gently, entering the cell. "I'll try not to hurt you."

"Don't pretend you care," Mederei answered, though she did as she was told.

Vitus's skilled touch sent her back to sleep as he worked. She did not feel him leave her side, nor did she hear her cell door close and lock. For Mederei, there was only blissful nothing.

It took two days of silent care in her cell before Mederei was fitted for clothes—a sleeveless tunic and loose trousers—and taken outside to train. She followed Vitus through the bare, though well-kept, halls of the prison to the courtyard. Before her was a large open space, so trampled by feet that grass no longer grew. There were several machines intended to increase strength and speed, a large platform intended for unarmed sparring and the rest of the space was for weapons training. Every station was full of gladiators drilling, trying to make themselves better fighters that they may live another day.

They stopped and turned as she entered the yard. She was the first woman they had been in close proximity to in quite a while. Their gazes threatened a hunger that made her skin crawl. Mederei was a Briton, however, and daughter of that island's greatest queen. She drew herself up, squaring her shoulders and lifting her chin. Her hazel eyes met the gazes of the gladiators in the courtyard, daring them to test her mettle, and promising regret to any who did.

"Did I tell you to stop?" Vitus bellowed. "Get back to work!"

The gladiators returned to their training, now silent. Mederei knew that silence meant trouble.

"Izem," Vitus called. "Come here."

A tall, ebony-skinned man turned away from the partner he had been drilling sword play with and jogged to Mederei. Izem was impossibly tall, with strong, broad shoulders. A deep scar ran across his chest, cutting through the muscle and misshaping the curve of his pectorals.

"Woman," Vitus said. "This is Izem. He is the senior gladiator here, and responsible for training the rest. You will be trained by him. You will listen to everything he tells you, and you will do precisely what he says. Do you understand?"

"How do you expect me to train this woman?" Izem demanded, his Latin musically accented. "She is nothing."

Mederei bristled at the remark. She glared up at the man. "I am a daughter of Britain," she snapped. "That is not nothing."

Izem grinned, a slash of white in blackness. "Is that so? Well, 'daughter of Britain,' show me what you can do."

Izem indicated to his drill partner. The man walked forward with a smirk, adjusting his grip of his wooden gladius and round shield.

"Here," Izem said to Mederei, handing her his own wooden training tools.

Mederei took them, pursing her lips as she observed the approaching man. She detested his smirk. It told her all she needed to know of what this man thought of her. She would prove him wrong, as she had done Rhys's men. They had learnt to fear her. So too shall these men.

The man moved first, striking down swiftly. Mederei stepped out at an angle, bringing her wooden gladius across and striking him on the belly. The man was not wearing armour, and Mederei knew the objective was to prove herself, not kill him. Not yet. She struck only hard enough to knock the air from him. It came out with a loud grunt. She danced away, turning expertly to face him.

The grunt caught the attention of nearby gladiators who turned to watch. The man straightened, his smirk now gone. Mederei permitted herself the barest of satisfied smiles. Now he would take her seriously. He did. His next attack came suddenly and with considerable speed. Mederei had not expected it, and so found herself on her back foot, reeling around in an effort to escape the blows. She was grateful for the shield. It was the only thing that saved her.

The crack of wooden gladius against wooden shield attracted the attention of the rest of the gladiators. They approached, forming a make-shift ring, to watch the fight.

Mederei's training put her in good stead. She was fast and disciplined. Her injuries pulled, however, restricting her movement, the pain distracting her; and she was not as strong as her opponent.

They danced together until an ill-timed step resulted in the sharp crack of the gladius against the side of her knee. The knee buckled and hit the ground hard. Sparing no time to complain, Mederei pushed herself up, and her face met the edge of her opponent's shield. She fell on her side with a grunt, blood rushing from a large split in her lip.

She heard a deep laugh.

"That is good," Izem said, smiling broadly.

It was not good enough for her opponent, who levelled a hard kick into her stomach.

"Hey!" Izem shouted, moving swiftly between Mederei and the man who had bested her. "Get back! I said get back!"

Mederei saw none of what was happening right in front of her. Though her eyes were open, she could only see the blinding white of pain. She coughed as the sounds of a scuffle hit her ears.

"Go," Izem ordered, pointing to a corner of the courtyard. "Go away until you learn how to be a man."

Scoffing, the man threw down his equipment at Izem's feet and marched away, followed by two of his supporters. The rest of the gladiators drifted away.

"Come on then, daughter of Britain," Izem said, taking one of Mederei's arms. "Get up."

The touch pushed Mederei into action.

"Don't touch me!" she snapped, yanking her arm out of the man's grasp. She struggled to her feet and, not bothering to look at her new trainer, turned and marched as best as her wounded body would let her, to a bench in the shade. She sat and pressed her bleeding lip against the cloth on her shoulder in an effort to stem the flow of blood.

Izem's answering laugh was drowned out by the dull clanging of metal on metal. Mederei paid no heed as the gladiators gladly answered the bell and left their posts to eat the main meal of the day. She sat sideways on the bench, fighting tears of anger and humiliation. Her failure to win that fight would mean a difficult road ahead. Not only would she have to work twice as hard for a shred of respect, now she would likely have to fight off a horde of rapists as well.

"Here," a familiar voice said. A bowl of barley and leek pottage and black bread appeared under her nose.

Mederei looked up to find Gandwy standing beside her, offering a bowl of food. He also had two cups of ale pressed against his body with his other forearm. It took Mederei a moment before she accepted the food, followed by the cup of ale.

"Thank you," she murmured in her own language.

Gandwy nodded, but said nothing. He sat next to her in silence and ate. Despite the day's exertions, Mederei found she had little appetite. She lifted a spoonful of the slop in her bowl and tilted it, watching the food plop back into her bowl.

"You should eat," Gandwy said. "You will need to keep strong if you are going to survive this place."

Mederei stared down at her food, saying nothing.

A new presence arrived at the bench. Nothing was said, but Gandwy stood and left. Mederei did not look up as someone else took his place.

"Well, daughter of Britain," Izem said. "You are not nothing."

Mederei scoffed, put down her bowl and turned her back to him, clutching her ale cup and staring pointedly down at the ground.

"Your problem is that you are all fire. If you wish to live, you will have to become ice."

"Fire melts ice," Mederei said.

"Yes, but the melting ice becomes water and extinguishes the flame. If you are ice, you can become water. If you are fire, there is nothing for you. You can either be fire, or nothing."

Mederei turned to look at Izem. "Fire cannot become ice."

"I am a wizard," Izem said, his face splitting into another grin. "I can turn fire into ice, if you let me."

Mederei shook her head. She turned her gaze to the other gladiators. They sat in groups, talking and laughing amongst each other as if they were the best of friends.

"They will one day have to kill the man next to them," Mederei whispered. "How can they sit together like this?"

"We all must die sooner or later," Izem said. "Life is made easier if we have friends."

"They are not friends if you would kill them to save yourself," Mederei said.

"Perhaps. Then let me say that life is easier if we are friendly. Better?"

Mederei said nothing.

"You must eat, daughter of Britain, or you will be nothing."

"Well, we can't have that, can we?" Mederei replied. She picked up her bowl and attempted to eat. Humiliation and anger blocked the food, and it proved hard work to swallow past them. Izem kept a careful eye on her and made sure she finished her bowl of gruel.

"Come, I will show you where we clean the dishes."

It took Mederei a number of times before she could stand upright. Izem attempted to help once, but she roughly pushed his aid away. She limped after him, trying hard to control her wincing.

"You did well today," Izem said.

"I lost," Mederei replied.

"Not by much. Look, Amose is also limping."

Mederei looked across at the man she had fought. He glared at her, hobbling into the line that led to the washing troughs.

"Not enough," she muttered.

Izem laughed. "Are all British women like you?"

"Not enough," Mederei answered in a whisper. "All of Rome would not prevail if we were."

"A shame," Izem said. "A shame."

"Yes."

The barbed sting of homesickness struck Mederei in the chest. She blinked rapidly, forcing back the tears that threatened. She missed Britain; the rolling hills of the south and the jagged crags of the north, the cool green springs and the humid summers. Most of all she missed her sister; kind Modron, sweet even through the madness. And she missed Rhys, Lord of Caledonia. She saw in her mind's eye his tattooed arms, remembering their strength as they wrapped around her, the smell of him as he pulled her close. The memories of her lover brought a pain so sudden and so strong that Mederei had to turn her head away to hide her tears.

Her turn at the washing trough brought on a lesson in cleaning dishes, and she used that to distract herself from thoughts of home. Home was long gone, and she would die for Roman entertainment. That was the way of it. There was no use crying.

Geraint strummed his lyra as his mind wandered. Mederei had been sold to a lanista—a man responsible for housing and training gladiators. It was a death sentence, surely. The man, who Geraint learnt was named Vitus, had a relatively large ludus. The gladiator prison and training facility stood on the eastern edge of the city. Vitus earned enough from sending his slaves to die to keep it well guarded with private fighters. Geraint would not be able to simply break Mederei out of prison. He would be captured and killed, and he would fail his lord.

Geraint sighed. He watched the Gauls and Romans in the city go about their day, oblivious to the heartbreak of the lord of the Caledonii. Would they care if they knew? Did they care how the free peoples on the edge of the empire suffered?

Turning his thoughts away from that path, Geraint once again concentrated on the problem he now faced. There were a few things he knew to be true.

Gladiators rarely lived past their thirties, and not more than ten or so matches. Very few made it through to retirement, but those who did were famous. Very famous. They were freed, and often bestowed great gifts of land and riches that would make most people dizzy.

Mederei was headstrong. A more determined woman could not be found in all of Britain. That would not be enough to save her. And if she believed herself lost forever, what then? Would she die of the wasting sickness? Would heartbreak claim her?

It could not. It must not. Geraint would not carry a corpse back to his lord.

He had no idea how he was going to free Mederei, but he knew the first thing he must do.

He must ensure she had a reason to live.

Nodding to himself, he rose and fetched a stick. Standing in the shade, he scratched his markings on the stick and headed to the marketplace. He had a contact there that would be able to ferry his message to his lord. Rhys could rejoice; Mederei was alive.

For now.

Mederei sat in the garden, watching the birds as they flitted between the branches of the shrubs, shrieking. It was late afternoon, and time for the gladiators to relax. They were given time in the gardens to walk and talk. Mederei, being the only woman and brand new to the ludus, had no one to talk to, so she walked as far as the barred walls would allow her. It was not very far. She wrapped her hands around the iron rods that separated her from freedom and stared out at the city.

Lugdunum had grown of late, and small houses bridged the gap between the gladiatorial school and the city. Mederei could see children playing in the streets, while others, slightly older, ran their errands.

"A song for the melancholic lady?" someone said.

Mederei turned her gaze and scowled. It took her a moment to realize that she knew the voice's owner, and used every ounce of self-control not to scream. She checked the gardens to see who was watching. Izem and Gandwy were, though they did not seem concerned about the man with the lyra on the other side of the prison bars.

"And what songs do you know?"

"Have you heard 'The Weeping Lord'?" Geraint asked, smiling at Mederei's quick wit. She knew as well as he that any chance he had of helping her escape relied on stealth.

"I have not. What is it about?"

"A young lord of a faraway isle lost his lover, and weeps for the heartbreak."

Mederei's face fell. Geraint was speaking of Rhys.

"It is a good story," he assured her. "Very romantic."

"I would like to hear it," Mederei whispered.

"Then I shall oblige. Make yourself comfortable, gentle lady, and allow me to paint a scene."

Mederei settled herself on the grass, letting the bars support her weight. Geraint sat on the ground and positioned his lyra. He thrummed it gently before his skilled fingers began to work the strings.

"There once was a lord," he sang. "A handsome lord of green isles, and he loved his lady fair. She was strong and she was quick and thrice his match for wit."

Geraint winked at Mederei and she smiled.

"Greatly he loved his lady fair."

With his skill at the lyra and his warm, homey voice, it was not long before Geraint's song drew a crowd. He sang on, telling the tale of a lord in love, how wicked thieves had come to the lord's kingdom with the goal of stealing his throne.

"And they stole her away, his beloved lady fair," sang Geraint. He changed the pace of the song, becoming slower, sadder.

"And he wept, that handsome lord of green isles,

for he loved his lady fair.

And he rode the land, that lord of green isles,

to seek his lady fair.

He wept as he rode and ride did he, weeping,

Seeking his lady fair.

And he searched all his long life,

For his beloved lady fair.

And on cold nights it is said,

That his ghost may be seen,

Riding the land,

To seek his lady fair.

Oh there once was a lord,

A handsome lord of green isles,

And he loved his lady fair."

The song ended, and the gathered gladiators clapped. Geraint grinned and rose to his feet. He bowed low, ignoring the tears in Mederei's eyes, though he saw them. They let him know she understood. Rhys had sent Geraint to retrieve her. Her beloved waited for her return.

"That is a sad tale," Gandwy said from his position standing behind Mederei.

"It is indeed. But I have been to that isle, and I have spent many a cold night there. Ne'er once did I see the lord's ghost riding. Perhaps he has found her, and they have gone home together at last."

"You are a romantic," Gandwy said, his lips twisting into a smile.

"Thank you," Mederei said, "for the song, minstrel…?"

Before Geraint could introduce himself, he heard, "What is going on here?"

He straightened as the gladiators moved aside to permit a strongly built man through. Geraint recognized him from the market. He bowed low, giving himself time to reign in the expression of distaste that naturally twisted his features at the sight of him.

"Forgive me, Lanista!" he said, rising. "I am but a poor bard, newly come to Lugdunum in hopes of earning a living. I have not yet been successful, alas, and so asked permission to entertain these fine warriors so that I might keep in practice. I am Geraint."

"A British name. Where in Britain are you from, Geraint?"

"I am a man of the Silures," Geraint lied. "Born in the rolling hills of the southwest."

Vitus eyes him up and down, and seemingly satisfied said, "I will not pay for entertainment unasked for."

"No indeed," Geraint answered. "I never expected payment for this, good sir, merely a chance to practice. You do not know the balm to the soul that is performing for an audience."

Vitus raised his brows.

"By the by, my good man, do you happen to know if there are any lords of the city who may be in want of a minstrel? It has been long since I've had money enough for a full meal, and I crave a bed that is not beneath a roadside shrub."

The threat of a smile twitched at Vitus' lips. "There are none that I know of at present, Geraint of the Silures. However, I am currently dining with my brother-in-law and his wife. I invite you in to play for us. I can offer you a few denarii and some food for the trouble."

It was not acting that painted Geraint's face into the very image of relief.

"Good sir, you are surely descended from great nobility!"

Vitus grunted. "Come around to the gate. I'll let you in."

Geraint bowed low. Not sparing another glance at the woman he had come to rescue, he walked the length of the bars to the gate. It opened onto a walkway protected from the gladiators in the garden by the same bars that separated the prisoners from the city. The walkway led into the ludus. Geraint watched as Vitus moved up the long walkway. He smiled brightly in greeting when the man opened the gate.

"You will find we are modest," Vitus explained.

"Modesty is the mark of goodness," Geraint replied. "As hospitality is the mark of nobility."

"Aye, well, Roman citizens we may be, but I have not forgotten everything about being a Gaul."

"Oh?" Geraint said. "You are a Gaul?"

"I am. My family was granted citizenship by Julius Caesar all those years ago."

"How fortunate," Geraint murmured.

"It has spared us a great deal of grief," Vitus replied.

Geraint smiled. "Of that I am sure." He did not voice his opinion of Celts who turned against their own to curry Roman favour.

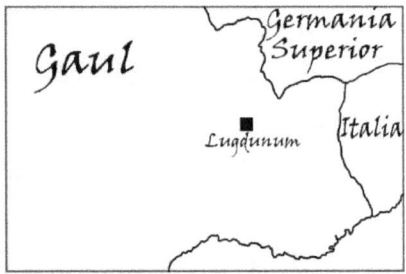

## 70 AD, WINTER, LUGDUNUM, PROVINCE OF GAUL

Lilius smiled as he stepped from the decorated wagon bearing his bulk into the courtyard of Aetius, the master merchant. The man waited with his family and his hostage at the entrance to the house, striding forward only when Lilius made an appearance.

"Governor!" he greeted, smiling broadly. "Welcome, welcome."

"Ah, thank you Aetius," Lilius said. "Once again I am honoured to partake of your hospitality. How fares things for you?"

The pair walked back to the house.

"The same, the same. How was Rome?"

"Stunningly beautiful, as always. How happy I would be to walk there forever. Instead, I live here amongst the savages. The things we do for political advancement, eh?"

Aetius smiled. "Indeed."

"Speaking of, how is your hostage?"

"You can see for yourself," Aetius said. He stood behind the governor wringing his hands as Lilius looked Adalbern over. "I am sure you will relay back to the emperor how well he looks?"

"Indeed," Lilius agreed. "He looks well. Are you well, Batavian?"

Adalbern shrugged, his arms folded across his broad chest and his expression unfriendly.

"Good enough," Lilius said. He turned to Aetius's wife. "Ah Maxima," he crooned. "You look lovely as ever."

"You are kind, Governor," the woman answered with a tight smile. She curtsied slightly.

Adalbern watched her closely. The woman looked like she had not smiled a day in her forty-two years of life. Lines of concern sat permanently around her lips, pulling the corners of her mouth down. A deep line had developed between her eyebrows, giving the impression that she was always frowning. In fact, Adalbern had only ever seen her smile when Ambrosius played his lyra for her. He had sat quietly away from the family and watched as Ambrosius played. His younger sister, Porcia, sat enraptured and always clapped excitedly when Ambrosius finished a song. Maxima simply smiled; a genuine, pure smile that proved her pride and her pleasure at her son's considerable musical talent. It was a talent Ambrosius hid from his father.

"Ambrosius," Lilius greeted the boy. "Still as skinny as ever. Do you eat?"

"More than he should," Aetius answered for his son, "to look at him."

"And Porcia," Lilius said, sighing out the girl's name. He snatched up her hand and kissed it. His attention on the girl's hand, Lilius missed the brief flash of revulsion that crossed her face. Adalbern did not. Nor did Ambrosius. He offered his sister a sympathetic look. "My dear, you grow more beautiful with every meeting."

"That cannot be possible," Porcia said, smiling at the governor to be polite.

"Oh but it is! What a delight to the eyes you are!"

Porcia offered another mirthless smile, and yanked her hand from Lilius's grasp.

"Come, come," Aetius said. "Let's in to eat!"

"Indeed!" Lilius went to Maxima's side and they followed her husband through the house to the dining room. Ambrosius went to his sister's side and offered her the crook of his elbow. "He could really stand to eat less," the boy murmured to his sister.

"Shh!" Porcia said, though she giggled. Then she added, "But when he isn't eating, he's talking, and I can't decide which is worse!"

Ambrosius giggled conspiratorially with his sister. Following slowly behind, Adalbern grinned.

They sat on the low lounges that lay around the dining room, eating and conversing. Aetius and Lilius did most of the talking. Maxima sat obediently with her husband, and did not utter a single word. She wore her usual miserable expression, her eyes downcast much of the time. Ambrosius entertained his sister with riddles and Adalbern sat on his own lounge, watching the scene.

The strangeness of this family's dynamic had him missing home. He could not imagine taking a wife that could not or would not participate in discussion, though Adalbern long ago observed that this was something Roman men seemed to prefer. Aetius had conditioned his wife to remain silent. Adalbern thought back to his own family. Their meals were generally full of conversation, and every voice was as important as the other. His father welcomed his wife's input, and often sought her advice on important matters. He would include his children, asking their opinions on everything. Adalbern's sister had been lively and opinionated during these discussions.

The atmosphere in this Roman dining room was one of quiet suffering, a misery too thick for Adalbern to ignore. Aetius and Lilius appeared oblivious, however.

"...And so it is I find I must take a wife," Lilius said.

The room's mood changed. The misery was gone, replaced by a sudden tension that had Adalbern's shoulders bunching together. He did not miss the panic in Maxima's eyes as her head snapped up to look at Lilius. Ambrosius's gaze flickered briefly to his sister, who had been halfway through biting into an olive. She held the olive between her teeth, frozen in wide-eyed fear.

"Tell me, Porcia," Lilius said, ignorant of the changes around him. "How old are you, girl?"

Slowly Porcia finished biting her olive. With some effort, she swallowed past her closed throat. "Fourteen," she said quietly.

Adalbern glanced briefly at Maxima. The woman had paled, and the misery that had been permanently writ across her face deepened.

"Fourteen, is it? A good age to be married, I'll warrant."

"A little young, don't you think?" Maxima asked. She was silently admonished by her husband's vicious glare.

"Lilius," Aetius said. "Am I to understand that you wish to propose marriage to my daughter?"

"It would be a fine match, don't you agree? The wife of a governor would surely be granted entry to some of the highest circles in society, giving you ample opportunity, Aetius, to expand your business."

Porcia stared at her father, her deep brown eyes pleading. She shook her head at him, a movement slight enough to be unseen by those not looking at her. Her eyes darted between her father and her mother, hoping her silent pleas would find purchase with one of her parents. In an effort to aid her daughter, Maxima placed her hand lightly on her husband's forearm.

Aetius ignored it all. He grinned widely at Lilius. "It is indeed a good match!" he proclaimed. "It is a great honour you bring to my family."

Lilius smiled, his round face shining with pleasure and relief. "I had hoped you would see it thusly."

"We must make arrangements!"

Adalbern heard the exchange between Aetius and his guest, but his eyes were transfixed by Porcia's face. She stared blankly at the floor, her bottom lip trembling with the effort of holding back tears. It was a battle she could not win. Before her grief could make its victory known, she rose abruptly to her feet and, mumbling her apologies, walked swiftly from the room. Ambrosius moved to follow her, but Aetius's glower had him settle back down upon the lounge.

"You must excuse her," Aetius told Lilius of his daughter. "She has been unwell and is still recovering."

"Of course," Lilius said, waving his hand dismissively. "Let her rest. I would want her to be well for my offspring. Now, let's say we celebrate this engagement!"

Ambrosius looked at Adalbern, who could do nothing but offer helpless sympathy.

Mederei sat quietly after having cleaned her dishes, and combed her short hair clean. The fine-toothed comb was all she had to clean her hair in between the baths the gladiators were permitted each week. The comb had been a gift from Vitus, part of a promise he made to ensure that she would be taken care of while she lived. So far, he had held true to that promise.

In her time at the ludus, there had been some difficulties with her femininity. Being the only woman many of these men had access to in a very long time, Mederei had been involved in several fights. Vitus had always arrived and, with the help of Izem and Gandwy, broken up the fight, saving her from certain rape.

Now, she was separated from the other gladiators when she was not training. She was left to wander the gardens that sat on the other side of the barred walkway from the lawn where the rest of the gladiators lounged.

Surrounded by flowers and stunted trees, Mederei need only turn her back on her fellow gladiators, and she could almost forget she was in a prison.

The food was wholesome, if lacking in meat, and the training kept her too busy to think overmuch on her situation. Geraint's regular visits to the ludus as a new friend of Vitus did much to give her hope. She was careful not to allow herself to be overly familiar with him, though she desperately wanted to hear news of home. Often, Geraint would be permitted to play for the gladiators under the guise of keeping in practice. He would sit on a stool on the walkway and play and sing. In this way, Mederei managed to glean some of what was happening in Britain. She knew from Geraint's songs that Rhys was continuing the fight against Rome.

That thought alone sustained her. Some part of Britain, at least, was still free. She mulled on this, smiling as she dragged the short comb through her hair. Her mind far away, it took her a moment to realize that there were visitors at the gate. Her smile changed as she saw a group of four men, one of whom was definitely not Roman, and a young, miserable-looking woman. She stopped combing to observe them. Judging by his build and his ruddy complexion, the non-Roman man was from the north; likely German as he did not look British. The tall man, wearing trousers and a tunic and a beard clipped close to his chin, met her gaze. His eyes were a deep, warm brown, and they observed her with interest. A powerful frame that matched his proud face indicated a strong man. Mederei wondered at his beard and clothes, both so un-Roman they had to be a statement. *I am with Romans, but I am not Roman.* Why would he make such a declaration?

The roundest man in the group rang the bell at the gate several times before Vitus made his appearance.

"Governor Lilius!" Vitus greeted with a broad smile. "What an honour!" He opened the gate wide. "Please, come in. What business brings you here?"

"Ah, Vitus," Lilius said. "Have you not heard? I am engaged to Aetius's daughter. It is a fine match, do you not agree?"

Vitus blinked, grinned and slapped the governor on the back. "It is indeed! A hearty congratulations to you! And this must be the future bride." Vitus took the miserable-looking girl's hand and kissed it. "Congratulations! You must be thrilled at such a fine match."

The girl smiled graciously at Vitus. The smile vanished the moment the man turned his back to her. Mederei felt her heart pull.

The girl was very young, and her soon-to-be husband was many years her senior. That in itself would not have been a problem, but it was clear she did not want to marry him. Her young face was permanently turned to the ground, her eyes downcast. The corners of her mouth followed her eyes, drooping down as if straining to touch the ground. The girl was desperately unhappy.

Roman or not, Mederei's heart went out to the tiny girl.

The sympathetic kindness in Mederei's gaze did not go unnoticed by the girl, who looked to her briefly before turning her eyes once again to the ground.

"I was hoping you might be able to help me plan the engagement celebrations, Vitus," Lilius said. "Perhaps a small games to honour my bride and her family?"

"That sounds like a marvellous idea," Vitus said. "Come in, and let's put our heads together to plan some fun!"

Adalbern did not care to hide his stare as he watched the only female gladiator in the ludus, alone in her garden. Clean of grime, and her hair, having grown, now reaching her shoulders in thick, dark auburn waves, her haughtiness looked earned. She watched the Romans converse with disdain, though Adalbern noted the softening of her features when she looked at

Porcia. She understood, as only a woman could, that Porcia was desperately unhappy.

The woman's soft face hardened once again as she turned her gaze to Adalbern. The Batavian did not miss the spark of curiosity in her eyes, however much her stony face gave the impression of contempt. It was a curiosity that was returned. Adalbern recognized her from the market, though her appearance now was more warrior queen than bloodied slave.

They held each other's eyes longer than strangers ought, each searching, trying to discern something about the other. The contact was broken as the group moved inside. Adalbern fought his desire to linger and speak with this proud woman. He offered her nothing as he broke his gaze and walked behind the group of Romans, shortening his naturally long stride to not overtake them.

Mederei's eyes followed the movements of the tall man trailing the group of Romans into the ludus proper. She did not know why she was so curious about him. She had not expected the mixture of warmth and sadness in his brown eyes. The Gauls in the city looked upon her with pity or guilt, the Romans with scorn. Neither, however, ever spared any warmth for her. The interest in the man's eyes had kindled her own curiosity. She wondered how he had come to accompany this family of Romans, and why he insisted on distinguishing himself from them.

Mulling on her thoughts, Mederei returned to combing her hair until Vitus called the gladiators into the training yard.

They stood in rows, eyes staring straight ahead as they were inspected by Lilius. The young woman at Lilius's arm paid little attention to the gladiators, who stood mostly shirtless and in fine form. The three others, including the tall non-Roman, stood to the side. The tall man leant one shoulder against a post holding up an overhang of the roof over the yard, his arms folded across his broad chest.

Though Mederei tried hard to ignore his presence, her eyes continually drifted back to him. His steady gaze never left her. Mederei found herself irritated by his gaze, though there was no malice in it.

"What's this?" Lilius pronounced once he reached Mederei. "A female gladiator! Oh, what luck! They were all the rage in Rome when last I was there. We must have one for our celebration, don't you agree, my dear?"

The young Roman woman at Lilius's side looked dully at her betrothed. "If you like," she intoned.

"Ah…" Vitus said, stepping forward and cocking his head apologetically. "Alas, she is my only female gladiator, and I was hoping to save her for the big fight we've been planning. You understand, of course. Being one of a kind, she is rather dear."

"I will pay double the fee if you'll put her in the arena!" Lilius said. "And we needn't have her fight anyone. Perhaps she can entertain us in a hunt? Boar, perhaps?"

"Boars are extremely dangerous," Vitus said.

"Precisely!" Lilius said, grinning. "No entertainment otherwise. Tell me woman," he asked of Mederei, "have you ever hunted boar?"

Mederei turned, brazenly meeting Lilius's gaze. "No," she said flatly.

"Ho!" Lilius exclaimed. "She is bold! I must have her for my games. I simply must! Name your price, Vitus!"

Mederei rolled her eyes as Lilius turned his bulk to face Vitus. The young woman accompanying her future husband caught the movement and hid a sudden smile behind her hand. Mederei offered her a smile in return, before turning her attention forward once more, her face falling into impassivity.

"Please!" whined Lilius.

Vitus sighed. He motioned to Izem, who broke rank and jogged to his side. "Tell me the truth, Izem," Vitus said. "You have worked closely with my woman. Can she fight a boar?"

"Anyone can fight a boar," Izem replied with an easy shrug. "But you are asking if she can win."

"I am."

Izem turned to regard Mederei, his expression thoughtful. "She is fast and clever. If she plays it right, she can win."

"All right," Vitus said. He turned to Lilius. "Twice the price of the others," he said. "And twelve denarii to procure a new female gladiator if she loses."

"Done!"

"And as per custom, I expect you to reward my champions for victory."

"Of course, of course," Lilius said, waving his hand dismissively. "And they will accompany you to the feast before and after. If your female gladiator kills the boar, we will roast and serve it in the evening."

"Very well," Vitus said. "Come inside again and we will tally the monies owing."

Lilius turned to follow Vitus back inside, and the miserable girl followed. "Oh no, my dear," Lilius said. "Let the men handle this. Go to your father."

The girl stared after her betrothed as he re-entered the building. She turned back to Mederei, who was watching her with unnerving forthrightness.

"I don't want to marry him," the girl explained, feeling she needed to clarify to the imposing, powerful woman standing before her.

"I imagine not," Mederei answered. She smiled gently at the girl. "If you're very lucky, his heart might give out soon," she said conspiratorially, making the girl giggle.

"I am Porcia," she said.

"A beautiful name. I am Mederei."

It did not escape her notice that at the mention of her name, Gandwy turned his head to look sharply at her, his eyes narrowed. Mederei ignored him.

Porcia opened her mouth, but was interrupted by, presumably, her father, who had come unexpectedly to the two women.

"Come, Porcia," he said sharply. "We do not talk to these savages. They are barely people."

Mederei's haughty expression returned as she watched the man drag Porcia away from the rows of gladiators, none of whom moved from their rank. Her top lip pursed slightly, giving her the appearance of someone who had just caught a foul stench. A deep chuckle turned her attention to the tall non-Roman, who remained leaning against the post. His eyes twinkled with mirth as he gazed at Mederei. Mederei reset her face, restoring her air of queenly disdain. This did nothing but add to the man's mirth. He grinned broadly and Mederei felt it a mockery. She turned her gaze away from him, determined to pay him no mind any longer.

Izem came to her side. "We will have to change your training, woman," he murmured to her. Mederei had never given anyone her name. They would not have used it. She had a different identifier, and it had marked her before anyone cared to learn her name. She was simply 'woman' to the others.

Mederei nodded. "Yes, we will." She could not care less about giving this city its entertainment. She needed to live to give Geraint a chance to help her find a way home.

Grinning, Izem clapped her shoulder. "You will go far if you can stay alive," he said.

Yes, thought Mederei. I will go far; far, far away from here.

"Hello," a meek voice said at the bars. Mederei looked up to find the young woman, Porcia, who had come to inspect the gladiators with her future husband the week prior, standing at the bars that separated the ludus gardens from the world. Mederei rose slowly to her feet and walked to the bars.

"Hello," she replied, guardedly. "Porcia, yes?"

The girl smiled and nodded. "You remembered."

"Very few Roman girls stop to give me their names," Mederei said.

Porcia's face fell slightly and she nodded. "I... I haven't got long, and I shouldn't even be here. Father would kill me if he found out."

Mederei cocked her head and regarded the girl. It was very possible that she was being utterly sincere in her description of her father's wrath.

"I just... well... I wanted to say hello."

Porcia played with the folds of her long tunic, losing the ability to look Mederei in the eye. "I should go," she breathed, turning away without looking up. She rushed away.

"Porcia," Mederei called. The girl turned. "Thank you for your visit."

The smile that crossed Porcia's features lit her face. For a moment, her melancholy vanished, replaced by a flash of happiness that beamed through like a sunburst. Then it was gone. Mederei watched as Porcia scurried away, head bowed for fear of being recognized.

"What did she want?" Izem asked from the gardens across the entrance to the gladiatorial school.

"I don't know," Mederei answered him. She turned back to the city, though Porcia was long out of sight. "A friend, perhaps," Mederei murmured. She shook her head and returned to her position beneath a short tree.

Training had taken a new turn for Mederei. Izem was determined that she live through the boar hunt, and so he taught her the hunting tactics his people used; the tactics he had himself used before he had been captured and sold into slavery. It was unlikely that Mederei would be granted more than a gladius for her hunt. She would not have the luxury of the uncertain safety of distance provided by a spear. It was the promise of blood and death that drew crowds to the arena, and these games would be no exception.

"They are big, but they move fast," Izem said as Mederei skipped and danced and spun in an exercise designed to work her speed and balance.

"Faster than that. Faster!"

Mederei swallowed back a retort as she trained.

"Faster!" Izem snapped.

Unable to keep track of her feet, Mederei misstepped and toppled to the ground. She pushed herself up, spitting mud. Izem laughed.

"It's not funny," Mederei snarled. Exhaustion dragged on her limbs and gnawed at her patience. Izem's mirth, however, could not be stemmed. He laughed harder.

"The Hunt take you," Mederei muttered beneath her breath. She forced herself upright, wiping the dust from her tunic. Her attempts to wipe the dust from her sweat-glossed chin resulted in a mud-smeared face. The sight made Izem double over laughing.

Mederei stared at him, her features a perfection of ire. She uttered not a word as she stood, staring at the gladiator as he laughed.

"Go wash up," Izem said, between peals of laughter. "Go. Go."

Grumbling beneath her breath, Mederei stalked to the large basin that held the washing water for the gladiators. She cleared the mud from her face and arms, Izem still chuckling behind her.

"It is time to eat," Izem said, waving Mederei away when she returned to him. "We will work on your balance tomorrow."

Exhausted, angry, and embarrassed, Mederei made no reply. Instead she turned to join the line forming near the building as the gladiators prepared for their main meal of the day.

Despite having washed herself, Mederei tasted dust with every mouthful of her barley stew.

Governor Lilius's grand plans for a three-day engagement celebration had since been whittled down to a single day of games. There were to be two feasts, however—one the evening before the games, and another following it. Aided by Vitus who, despite owning slaves who existed merely to die for entertainment, proved to be a jolly fellow, easy with laughter and as generous as any Gaul. Geraint managed to gain employment playing his lyra for both evenings. He would not be the only musician present, either. This was a boon, as it would provide him with time with Mederei, who he learnt would feature in the games; the only female gladiator in the city.

Geraint had not enjoyed the news. Mederei had proven herself a valuable member of the warriors of the Caledonii, but she had been fighting for a cause. He did not know how she might handle fighting for Roman entertainment. He prayed her belly of fire would burn just as hot in the arena as on the battlefield.

Plucking his strings on the evening of the first feast, Geraint launched into a song about a forest in Britain that swallowed men alive; a strange favourite for his audience. He snuck a glance at Lilius, who chatted amicably with Vitus and Aetius as he dined, happily ignoring his miserable bride-to-be. She sat on the lounge beside him. Her eyes downcast, she was a perfect copy of her mother, who sat silently in the same pose beside her own husband.

The German sat on his own, though near enough to Aetius's son, Ambrosius, to speak with him. The two kept their voices low, and could not be heard over the tune Geraint drew from his lyra. The conversation, however, looked intense.

"Father is wrong," Ambrosius said to his friend. "It is a terrible match."

"Not politically," Adalbern replied.

"Politics," Ambrosius spat. Feeling he had spoken too loudly, he glanced around to ensure no one had heard. There was no indication from the other guests that they had.

"Look at her. She is miserable."

Adalbern could find no argument for this. Porcia did indeed look miserable. Adalbern felt pity swell in his chest. He shook his head. There was nothing for it. This was the way it had always been for Roman girls. His mother, he felt certain, would be appalled. As much as her marriage to Adalhard had been political, it would not have gone forward had she refused.

"It seems to be the fate for all Roman girls," he said.

"It shouldn't be," Ambrosius snapped. His eyes lit suddenly. "And it needn't be. She cannot wed if she is nowhere to be found."

Cocking his head, Adalbern looked at the slender youth at his side. "Careful what you say, Ambrosius," he cautioned. "And most especially what you do. Your father does not take well to disobedience."

"I can't be punished if I'm nowhere to be found," Ambrosius murmured.

"You plan to run away?" Adalbern asked.

Ambrosius shrugged.

"Where would you go?" Adalbern asked. "How will you get there? There is nowhere that is safe from Rome. You will be discovered. What then?"

Sullenly, Ambrosius sat back. "I don't know. It's nothing. Just a foolish wish to spare my sister a lifetime of grief. Nothing more. Forget I said anything." Rising to his feet, Ambrosius went to his sister.

"Porcia," he said loudly, halting the conversation Lilius was having. "I'm bored. Come walk with me in the garden."

Porcia looked first to her father, who shrugged, and then to Lilius.

"Go on, my dear," Lilius said, rubbing her thigh. "I'm sure men's business must be fearfully dull for you."

Still mute, Porcia took her brother's offered hand and together they left the dining hall. Their departure was followed closely by the gaze of a grim-faced Adalbern.

Geraint observed the furrows that worry had carved into the German's brow as he watched the two children of Aetius leave the room. He noted it for future reference. There may come a time when the German would be useful. If Geraint could discern what had made him worry so, he may gain some leverage over the big man.

"You have a visitor," Vitus said, his happy voice booming in the closed space of Mederei's cell. Mederei sat up and frowned at him until a familiar, meek young face peeked around Vitus's bulk. Despite herself, Mederei smiled at the girl.

"Hello, Porcia."

"Come out to the garden," Vitus said. "It is far more pleasant for receiving visitors."

Mederei did not argue, she rose from her bed and followed Vitus from the cell block to the garden that had become reserved for Mederei. He smiled brightly at Porcia before leaving, locking the garden gate behind him.

"Thank you for taking the time to see me," Porcia said quietly after a long moment in which she and Mederei observed each other. Porcia only spoke when she could bear Mederei's observations no longer.

"Thank you for the visit. You have broken the monotony of the day."

Porcia flashed her rare smile, but turned her gaze to the ground.

"Why do you look to the ground?" Mederei asked. "What is there that is so fascinating?"

"It's not that…." Porcia's voice faded. She felt foolish and exposed here. Tears stung her eyes. "I feel unworthy to look upon you," she said at last, her high voice choked with tears. Mederei frowned. With one hand, she cupped the girl's chin and lifted it, so that she was forced to look Mederei in the eye. It surprised Mederei that tears flowed freely down the girl's cheeks. It surprised her more that she felt a swell of pity for this Roman.

"You?" Mederei asked, gently wiping the tears from Porcia's eyes. "Who is the daughter of a powerful merchant, and who will soon be wed to a governor?"

At this, Porcia burst into tears. She threw herself against Mederei, burying her head in Mederei's chest. Her sobbing was uncontrollable, wracking her entire body. Mederei wrapped her arms around the girl who, at the moment, seemed as fragile as a baby bird, and stroked her hair until she calmed.

"I am sorry," Porcia whispered once she had cried herself out. "Please forgive me."

"There is nothing to forgive," Mederei said gently. "Grief needs to be given a voice every so often, else it kill us."

Porcia nodded. She chanced a glance up at Mederei and sighed. "Do you know I envy you?" she asked.

Mederei did not care to stop the laugh that escaped her. "Envy me? I am a prisoner, sentenced to die for Roman entertainment."

Wincing, Porcia turned and began to wander slowly through the garden. "We are both prisoners," she said. "And your freedom will come sooner than mine."

Mederei said nothing as she followed the girl.

"I do not want to marry the governor. Sometimes I dream of running away, but where in the empire would I go? My father would hunt me down as if I was a hare and he a hawk. I would be captured and forced to marry." Porcia reached out to stroke the blackening leaf of a shrub. "Perhaps if I'm lucky, I will not survive childbirth. Then I will be free also."

"There are better ways to die."

"Are there? The men have battle. They will die and be given glories beyond measure. Women, we die in the bed, by our children or our husbands. There are no glories left for us."

Mederei scoffed. "Men bestow accolades upon themselves," she said, "because they are inadequate. Those who crow loudest are the least adequate."

Giggling, Porcia turned to face Mederei. "Your Latin is very good. I am surprised. I did not know the Britons of the north knew it."

Mederei cocked her head and smiled. "Can I tell you a secret, Porcia?"

Porcia nodded.

"I am from the south, originally. I fled north as a girl with my sister and there resolved to fight Rome or die trying." Mederei waved vaguely at the garden surrounded by bars. "I wish I had died. At least I would still be on my beloved island."

"Rome is not really so terrible," Porcia said. "There is much the empire gives us."

"Not terrible? Not terrible for those who know no better, perhaps. But I am British, raised by Britons under British law and custom. I value the freedoms I was born with; freedoms Rome seeks to take from me and my fellows. They call it civilization, but all I see are violent thugs who are entertained by bloodshed and tears. I weep at the thought that Britain will be ruled by men such as this. I cannot fathom it. I cannot permit it."

"They say you were found on a battlefield."

Mederei scowled. "Who says?"

"I have heard talk," Porcia replied vaguely. "My father is a well-connected merchant. They all speak with one another." Pausing, Porcia drew herself up. "Were you?"

With a sigh, Mederei walked past Porcia to stare out at the city. "Yes," she replied at length. "My king had resolved to aid his friend in fighting the traitor queen, Cartimandua, and taking back his city from Rome's puppet. I was part of an ambush, and we went south to waylay any escape attempt." Shaking her head, Mederei turned back to face Porcia. "But we were anticipated. Our ambush was ambushed. By German auxiliaries." She smiled ruefully. "For all its arrogance, Rome is nothing. It is the people who have aligned themselves with the empire that give it its glory."

"Don't let the Romans hear you say that."

"What have I to fear from them? They are nothing."

"I am Roman. Am I nothing?"

The word "yes" leapt to Mederei's tongue, and there it died. She watched the young Roman woman, so small and frail and miserable, a moment. "That is up to you," she said at last.

Porcia turned her eyes to the ground again, disappointed. "When I was a girl, I used to dream of being a hero," she said. "One they would write epic poetry about. I would be as Odysseus, or Heracles, fighting the enemy and winning the day!" Porcia moved to Mederei's side. "And then I would awaken and I would realize, I am just me; a good Roman girl. I do my needlework and I learn to manage a household. That is my place. It always was. I had almost forgotten my dreams of heroism. But then I saw you, standing so tall and proud. You looked at my future husband with all the strength of a warrior, and all the airs of a queen, and I wished… I wished in that moment I could be you."

Close to tears once more, Porcia bit her bottom lip. She reached out and grasped the bars that separated her from the city.

"You see, I am in prison too," she whispered. "The bars are invisible, but they are there, and they squeeze in at me from every angle, sometimes so hard I cannot breathe. What I wouldn't give just to breathe!" Blushing, Porcia released the bars and stared once more at the ground. "I have never spoken of this to anyone."

"I have spent my life hating Rome," Mederei said. She reached out and took one of Porcia's hands. "I imagined everyone in the empire were as cruel as the empire herself. I had thought that Rome hated British women especially. I never once spared a thought for Roman women. It seems that

Rome hates all women, even her own. I am so sorry you are so trapped. Perhaps, one day, you may find a way to freedom."

Porcia smiled sadly up at Mederei.

"Just promise me that if you find it, you will tell me," the Briton added.

"Will you be my friend?" Porcia asked suddenly. The words escaped her mouth in a rush of air. "Father doesn't let me speak with the natives here, and I have no friends at all. I have enjoyed speaking with you so much and... Will you?"

Mederei found that she had no defences against the wide, hopeful eyes of the girl before her. She laughed. "I would be honoured," she said.

Porcia smiled. "Oh, thank you!" She clapped her hands together before her.

"Begging your pardon," Vitus said from the gate, making both women jump. "But time's up. I have to be taking the woman to her training."

Porcia nodded. "Of course, Vitus," she said. She and Mederei walked slowly to the gate and there stopped.

"Thank you," Porcia said. "I very much enjoyed my visit. I will try to come again soon."

"Please do," Mederei said. "I do not get visitors, and you are good company."

Porcia smiled again and, thanking Vitus, made her way out of the garden, through the building and down the barred walkway to the ludus gate. There she waited patiently to be let out. Vitus obliged, wishing the girl well in his good-humoured manner. Before stepping from the ludus, Porcia turned and waved goodbye to Mederei, who watched from the garden gate. Smiling, Mederei waved back.

"A good move there," Vitus said as he arrived back at the garden gate.

"Oh?" Mederei said.

"That girl is soon to be a very influential woman. Sometimes gladiators will be patronized by interested families seeking to gain status. Play it right, and she may be able to buy you the best armour, and you will be invited to the best parties and eat the finest food."

"But always a prisoner," Mederei answered. "And always moments from death."

"True," Vitus said as they walked into the training courtyard. "But life can be very good until then." He clapped Mederei's shoulder before turning her over to Izem, who grinned broadly.

"You still do not move fast enough," he said. Mederei groaned.

"You what?" Ambrosius whispered as he walked in the central courtyard of his home with his sister. "Father would have a fit if he knew!"

"Then please take care to ensure he doesn't know," Porcia whispered back. She smiled. "She is all I imagined her to be, you know. Strong, clever, and she is also kind. I like her very much, Ambrosius."

Ambrosius shook his head. "No doubt she filled you full of ideas."

"Mostly she just listened to me. Really listened, Ambrosius. I was miserable when I went to see her, and I feel wonderful now."

"I cannot argue with that," Ambrosius said. "It is good to see you smile."

"You should come with me next time. Father cannot complain if I am chaperoned, can he? I'm sure you would love her too!"

"I think she would probably rip off my head. She's as tall as I, and twice my mass in muscle alone, I am sure!"

"Then we must bring Adalbern, too. For protection, you understand."

Laughing, Ambrosius said, "All right. Next time you wish to go, let me know. Adalbern and I will go with you."

"It will have to be after father leaves on business again."

Ambrosius nodded.

"What are you two plotting?" Adalbern asked as he entered the courtyard. He grinned at the pair.

"Adalbern!" Porcia said, rushing over to him. "I was just telling Ambrosius about an adventure I had today."

"An adventure, was it?"

"Yes, and I would tell you all about it, but you must swear to secrecy."

"She made the same demand of me," Ambrosius noted dryly.

"And did you?"

"Of course!" Ambrosius replied with a snort.

Smiling, Adalbern turned back to Porcia.

"All right then, little woman," he said, offering her the crook of his elbow. "What is this grand adventure?"

"I went to the ludus," she whispered, "and met with the woman."

"You did what?!"

"Shhhhhhh!" Ambrosius and Porcia admonished in unison.

"Sorry," Adalbern whispered. "You did what?"

"You should meet her, Adalbern," Porcia said. "She is as wonderful as you could imagine her to be. I am thinking I will convince Lilius to sponsor her. She is my friend, after all."

Exhausted, Mederei nonetheless could not sleep. She stared up at the ceiling, her conversation with Porcia running through her mind. Despite herself, she could do naught but like the girl. Pity made it easier to do so. The girl was not older than thirteen or fourteen, Mederei was certain; far too young to be marrying anyone, let alone a man surely thrice her senior. And Porcia clearly did not want the marriage, either.

How strange it was to be a woman in Rome. While it was usual in Britain for marriages to be negotiated between the parents of a woman and a suitor, the woman in question had the right by law to decline any proposal laid at her feet.

Anger on Porcia's behalf, and on behalf of the British women forced to live beneath an unjust law, flared in Mederei's breast.

"You best be fighting hard, Rhys," she whispered in the still air of the prison.

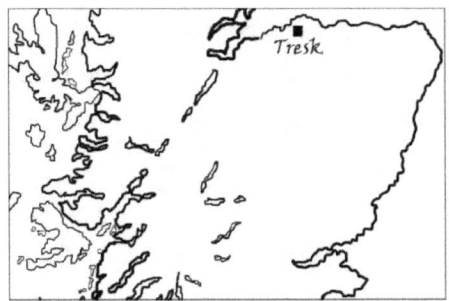

# 70 AD, AUTUMN, CITY OF TRESK, CALEDONIA, FREE BRITAIN

Rhys sat heavily on his seat, twirling a dagger unthinkingly on the arm-rest.

"Stop that," Calgacus said. "You'll drill a hole in that chair and let the wood worms in."

Rhys sighed and slid the dagger back into his boot.

"Word from Geraint, my Lord!" a man said as he ran into the large round house, waving a short stick in the air. He bowed low and handed the stick to Rhys. Rhys took it and stared down at the angular markings on the piece of wood. He looked up, to the old druid who sat near the fire staring into the flames.

"Cannot read it, young man?" the old man asked.

"No," Rhys said.

"Bring it here, then." Without looking, the druid stretched out a hand towards Rhys. The young chieftain rose and handed the stick to him.

The druid looked down, though his eyes long ago lost the ability to see. He ran his fingers over the stick, feeling the carved notches and lines, and grunted. "She has been found, Lord Rhys," he said. "And she is alive."

A faint smile appeared on the young chieftain's face as he breathed out a sigh of relief. "Is that all Geraint could say?"

"For now," the druid said.

"Well, for now it is enough. She is alive."

The druid smiled, cloudy eyes fixed upon the flames of the hearth. He tossed the stick into the fire and closed his eyes. Outside, an owl that had been perched upon the roof took wing, gliding on the cooling dusk air, turning its far gaze to Gaul.

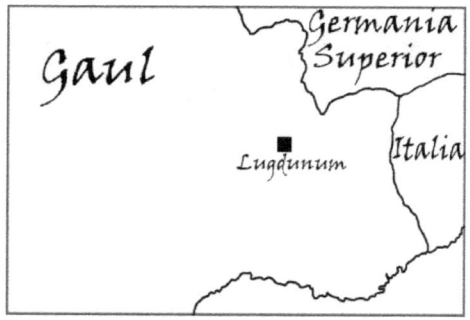

## 70 AD, AUTUMN, LUGDUNUM, PROVINCE OF GAUL

Mederei breathed deep and closed her eyes briefly. She stood in the small antechamber that marked the gladiators entrance into the arena, a gladius held loosely in her hand, as the dramatists did their best to quell the rancour of the audience. A great deal of shushing later, the dramatists began their introduction.

"The savages of Britain," they began.

"Savages," Mederei muttered under her breath.

A guard, one of a pair of Gaulish city guards used to ensure Mederei did not try and escape the antechamber, scoffed. His face immediately became impassive when Mederei glanced his way.

"They have no law! The live by no rule! And they, being men of weak wills, are ruled by women!" said one dramatist.

"In their defence," said another. "Their women are so mannish, it can be difficult to tell which gender is bellowing the orders!"

This seemed to please the crowd. A great roar of laughter echoed into the antechamber. Mederei growled.

"We bring you one such woman," the dramatists said in unison. "From the mysterious misted lands of northern Britain, welcome our champion!"

Mederei prepared to step forward, but the gates of the antechamber did not open. Moments later, she heard the awful squeals of an upset pig.

"Our mistake!" a dramatist said over the laughter of the crowd.

"No," said another. "That is her."

"That is a pig," said the first.

"Same thing," the second replied.

There was more laughter.

"But no!" the dramatists said in practiced unison. "Please stand and cheer your champion, from the crags of northern Britain, the Woman!"

This time the gates did open. Mederei walked forward to the deafening roar of a crowd that could not decide if it was amused, impressed or excited. A cacophony of laughter, booing, and cheers greeted Mederei as she stepped into the light.

Ignoring the tumult, Mederei took the chance to look around herself. The walls were high, made not of stone, but wood. One wall was higher than the others and contained a small pavilion. There sat the city dignitaries. Mederei met the gaze of Porcia, who stood pale-faced and tiny next to her future husband. She offered the girl a smile, and received the barest of smiles in return. On Porcia's other side stood her father, who glowered down in disapproval of the exchange between her daughter and Mederei. Beside him stood his son. Behind the pair was the tall German who had spent his entire visit to the ludus staring at Mederei.

Standing on the other side of Lilius was Vitus, accompanied by his smiling wife and their two young children.

Three flags hanging from iron poles stuck out from the wall just below the pavilion. Mederei could identify none of the symbols on any of the flags, save for the centre one, which bore the eagle of Rome. She desperately wished for some fire. It would be entertaining to watch that flag burn to ash—for her at least.

Mederei turned her attention to the arena floor. It remained a bare landscape of sand; not especially large, though large enough to house a small melee. There, trotting back and forth before the far gate, was a wild boar. The beast could bear no other description but one: massive. Its reddish-brown coat was shaggy, the wiry hair providing a thick mat that only added to the armour of impossibly tough hide. Upon its back stretched a crest of bristling black hair, sticking straight up into the sky. Two tall, sharp tusks graced each side of its snout, the ends jagged, indicating someone had taken blades to them to make them sharper than they already were.

Mederei glanced down at her gladius. The short blade was not long enough to reach the boar's heart from any angle but dead on. Facing such a beast in such a manner was the strategy of the dead. Yet there were few other options available to her. Her gladius would not pierce the thick skull of the animal. The blade was far too wide to attempt to brain the animal through the eye. The edges would get trapped in the sides of the socket.

"Damn everything," Mederei hissed. Crouching, she moved forward. If she was to die today, she would do so courageously. Let no Roman ever mock a daughter of Britain again.

Porcia bit her bottom lip as she watched the Briton move towards the enormous boar at the far end of the arena. She had been to visit Mederei several times. Ambrosius and Adalbern had accompanied her, but sat and spoke with Vitus, permitting Porcia some privacy with her new friend. Alone in the ludus garden, Portia had opened her heart to Mederei, pouring out her soul.

In return, Mederei would tell her wonderful stories of her life before her capture. Though much of it was laden with sadness, and Porcia sensed a weight of bitterness pressing on her friend's shoulders, there was much that Mederei remembered fondly.

There could be no mistaking the love Mederei had for her country and countrymen. The tender manner in which she described the rolling green of the south and the ancient crags of the north, the pride in her expression when she spoke of her adoptive tribe, the northern Caledonii and her king, a man named Rhys, filled Porcia with a deep longing for a world she would never know; a world where women were respected almost as equals, and men did not feel their manliness impeached by the strength of the women they lived alongside.

It seemed to Porcia heaven on earth. To think, had she been born a Briton, she may have been betrothed to a man she genuinely loved, instead of this political alliance with a man who made her skin crawl.

Anxiety gnawed at Porcia's stomach as she watched Mederei face the boar. Mederei had become important to her sanity, a rock to cleave to when the weight of Porcia's own woes grew too great to carry alone. It might all be taken away this very afternoon.

Placing her hand on the carved wood of the bannister before her, Porcia whispered a fierce prayer.

"Gods of Britain, your daughter needs you now. See her safely through and I shall abandon the gods of Rome. Keep my friend safe, I beg you."

A wave of guilt washed over her briefly. Then the boar attacked, and Porcia forgot all else.

Swearing, Mederei dove to the side. The boar had appeared disinterested. It had been a feint. With a terrible squeal it rounded and charged, faster than a beast that size had any right to move.

*You still do not move fast enough,* Izem's voice echoed in her head.

Mederei rolled to her feet only to find the boar almost on top of her. She lashed out with her gladius as she danced aside, slicing the boar's snout. It only made the thing angrier. Squealing its displeasure, the pig rounded again, charging. Mederei danced the other way, but with a swift flick of its head, the boar plunged one ragged tusk into Mederei's leg.

Grunting in pain, Mederei lost her balance. Falling backwards meant death. Instead, she thrust her weight forward so that she would land atop the beast. She raised her gladius high as she did so. She fell, plunging the blade into the pig's shoulder.

The boar squealed again, a sound closer to a scream, and opened its maw to bite Mederei's bleeding leg. The pig's shoulder blade had stopped the gladius. Mederei could plunge it no further. Swearing, she used the sword as a pole and vaulted over the boar, hearing the creature's teeth clack as they narrowly missed her leg. It turned quickly, and Mederei lost her grip on the hilt of her blade. She hit the ground running, the incensed boar fast at her heels.

The crowd laughed at the spectacle. Mederei could hear them through her panic. Pain ripped through her leg, but she did not have time to stop and examine the wound. The pig's splayed feet were too close for her to even turn and check the distance. It was almost upon her. In desperation, Mederei leapt sideways, tucking in to roll to her feet, and resume running. The move bought her a little distance. She checked behind. The boar was chasing again.

Turning forward, she saw the last of three crows land on the flag poles at the podium. One crow sat on one pole each, as if loath to share their perches. They made no noise, but watched the performance.

"Bastards," Mederei hissed from aching lungs. "Come to witness my demise. Have you no love for me, my Lady? Have I not fed your crows enough with my blade?"

A realization hit Mederei as she ran. Changing direction again, Mederei sprinted for the tall podium below which sat the flags. Aiming for the centre pole, Mederei pumped her legs, climbing the wall at a run. Feeling gravity begin to win her over, she leapt up, grabbing the central pole. The crows, disturbed or satisfied, took off, cawing.

Mederei's leap came just in time. The boar had reached her, and it screamed from below, pawing at the wall in an effort to reach Mederei. She looked down. That was a mistake.

The shift in her weight as she turned her head downward proved too much for the wood supporting the flagpole. The brittle board cracked, tilting the pole. Mederei dropped two inches. Above her, she could hear Porcia scream, a sound she would have matched if she had but opened her mouth in that moment.

Taking a deep breath to calm herself, Mederei reached for the pole on her right. The central pole dropped again, accompanied by another cracking of the dry wood.

The audience was now silent, staring as Mederei desperately clung to life. She could feel the hot breath of the boar beneath her feet. Her leg throbbed wildly and blood flowed freely from the wound.

"One more," Mederei whispered to herself. Pulling herself in, Mederei kicked the wall to give her extra lift, and swung up, reaching once more with her right hand. She felt her fingers close over the second flagpole just as the first came fully away from the wall. Porcia screamed again, and the audience gasped. The boar squealed in frustration as splintered wood rained down upon it.

Mederei tested her weight against the new flagpole. It did not budge. With the aid of her uninjured leg, she hauled herself up, struggling onto the pole. Balancing carefully with the middle pole still in her hand, she granted herself a moment to rest and consider her options. She looked upwards. The three crows she had disturbed circled the arena.

Mederei smiled. "Thank you, Lady War," she said. One by one the crows wheeled away, cawing. The world shifted for the gladiator. Mederei was no longer in this fight alone. Somehow, the gods of Britain had found her in Gaul. They were at her side. She could yet win this fight.

Turning her eyes downward, Mederei knew what she must do. Grimacing against pain not yet felt, she stood on the pole, and jumped.

The audience gasped. They held their collective breath as Mederei dropped. It was but a brief moment, but it seemed an age. Then the fight was on again.

Mederei landed on the boar's back, the sharp bristles scraping her leg, creating deep cuts. As she landed, she plunged the end of the flagpole down, hoping to break the spine. She missed. The spear instead plunged through the boar's neck.

Bucking, the boar tossed Mederei from its back as if she was nothing, as if it felt nothing. This time, however, Mederei did not lose her weapon. She was prepared when the boar rounded on her.

*A boar does not feel pain as we do,* Izem's voice reminded her as she recalled their earlier talk of strategy. *It will run the length of a spear just to get a chance at injuring its attacker. You must be prepared for that.*

Mederei danced to the side, using her left arm as bait. The boar's powerful jaws closed over her forearm and it violently shook its great head from side to side. Mederei cried out in pain. Finding her balance as the boar prepared to shake again, she plunged the pole into the pig's beady eye. The creature squealed a moment, before keeling over, its shoulder crashing into Mederei. She toppled backwards, pinned beneath the boar's dead weight.

It took Mederei a moment to understand that the fight was over. The boar was dead. Mederei opened her eyes. She was alive. Taking a deep breath, she reached over and attempted to work her arm free of the boar's mouth.

When the silent audience perceived movement beneath the boar, they erupted into bellowing cheers. Mederei was slow to hear their din, realizing that they cheered only when she staggered to her feet, free of the boar at last. She looked around her, her expression one of wide-eyed shock.

The sound of marching brought her from the shock. She turned to see a troop of twelve heavily armoured guards march into the arena; an escort to march her back to the ludus. Mederei limped obediently forward a few steps before turning to glance up at the podium.

Porcia clapped hard, smiling through her tears. Vitus caught her eye. He beamed down at her, wearing an expression of fierce pride as he clapped. Lilius, however, was not clapping.

Eager to be away from the crowd, Mederei turned once more and limped from the arena, flanked by Vitus's private armed force.

"Lilius," Vitus said, grinning at the governor. "I believe you owe me a considerable sum."

"It seems I do, Vitus," the round man answered. He beckoned a young lad forward. The boy moved quickly, producing a small bag made of worked horse hide. Lilius silently waved at Vitus.

"The bet was one aureus and three denarii, lad," Vitus said. The boy produced the appropriate coins and handed them to Vitus.

"There's a good lad," Vitus said grinning. He slipped the coins into a small pocket on the inside of his tunic. "Now, if you'll excuse me, I must make arrangements for a healer for the woman. I have a feeling she shall be a crowd favourite. I wish to have her around for a while yet."

"I can help," Adalbern said, his sudden words garnering the attention of everyone present. "I assisted the healers on campaign in my time with the Roman army, and my sister at home. I know many cures, particularly for wounds."

Vitus looked to Aetius, who shrugged. "He is dour company," Aetius said. "You're welcome to him for the afternoon."

"Very well, German," Vitus said. "I can pay you three denarii. Come with me."

Adalbern patted Ambrosius on the back as he moved away to follow Vitus out of the arena. Ambrosius sighed longingly. There was nothing he would rather do than to leave the podium and its view of death and gore far behind him. As it was, he knew he must stay and watch, or his father would lose face. He glumly swallowed back the bile that had risen from the last fight and slouched deeper into his chair.

Vitus looked at his companion as they walked from the arena. He was unused to feeling small. This German made him feel small.

"You take after your father," Vitus noted. He smiled when Adalbern shot him a glower. "I had the privilege of seeing him ride when I was a younger man. He was with some regiment or other on his way to somewhere else. Everyone deferred to him, whether they knew him or no. He was a commanding presence."

Adalbern said nothing.

"His treason was a surprise."

"It was Rome who betrayed him," Adalbern growled.

Vitus sighed. The man did indeed take after his father. "Rome tells it differently," he noted instead, finding it easier than starting an argument.

"Rome would," Adalbern replied. "For all their philosophers, they know nothing of truth."

The pair arrived at the entrance to the arena where two servants awaited them.

"Lads, this is Adalbern. I have hired him to tend to the Woman's wounds. Would you be so kind as to escort him to the ludus and show him into the infirmary? You are to fetch him anything he requires. Once he is finished, give him three denarii and ensure he has every comfort he requires until he is collected by either myself or one of Aetius's house."

One of the servants nodded, looking briefly up at Adalbern, before they both turned away and marched wordlessly from the men.

The servants said nothing as they walked, Adalbern striding easily between them. One of the boys kept glancing up at Adalbern, so the Batavian turned his head and stared at him. When his brown eyes met the curious glance the next time, the embarrassed servant turned smartly forward and did not again look Adalbern's way.

"The infirmary is this way," the other servant said, once they had opened the ludus gate and stepped inside. The gladiatorial school proved eerily silent, the gladiators having been sent to the arena. Those that were not fighting this day were spectating.

Adalbern nodded and followed the youths into the building proper, to a large room guarded by no less than six heavily armed men.

"Is this really necessary?" he asked one of the servants.

"You do not know the Woman," the elder one said, smirking. "We, however, have watched her train. Trust me when I tell you that even wounded, this one could almost be a match for her guard." The boy pushed open the door and indicated for Adalbern to enter. He walked in.

Mederei lay on a stone bench, her back to the door. A trail of blood flowed from the end of her feet onto the glazed tile floor, draining into a small opening near the bench. She had not yet removed the thin leather breastplate that served as her armour. She did not feel inclined. All she really wanted to do was go to sleep. Upon hearing the door open, Mederei struggled to sit up. She turned and paused.

"You are not the healer," she said in Latin, her eye narrowing.

"I am a healer," the man at the door replied in kind. He switched to Gaulish when he next spoke. "I am Adalbern."

"A German name." Mederei's lips twisted as if she had something sour in her mouth. "You speak Gaulish well."

"As do you."

"I'm supposed to," Mederei said. "They are kin to the British."

"They are kin to the Germans," Adalbern answered. "Some of us at least. My grandmother was a Gaul."

"What tribe?"

"Eburones."

Mederei twitched. "Eburones? You are Batavian?"

Adalbern raised his eyebrows. "Your knowledge of the events on the continent is surprising."

"I know the Batavi live on stolen land. Your grandmother must have been a very unwilling bride."

"It is never so black and white," Adalbern replied, smiling softly. "She loved my grandfather." He turned to the men and spoke in Latin.

"Bring in a large vat of freshly boiled water, a kettle of water, and the following herbs: camomile, comfrey, witch hazel bark, and meadowsweet. I'll take willow bark also if you have some, but that is not a necessity."

"That is quite a list," one of the servants noted, his eyebrows raised.

"Does your master want her healed or no?"

The servants exchanged a glance, shrugged at one another, and left to do as they were bid. Adalbern turned back to Mederei, switching once more to Gaulish. "Will you let me take a look at your wounds?"

"The Batavi fought for Rome when the empire came seeking our sacred isle. You slew the chariot horses in a night raid."

"I did not," Adalbern replied. "I was but a babe when that battle was fought."

Mederei stared at him. "The Batavi fought against the queen of Britain. You burned her city to ash and slew her subjects, down to the last child." The words brought tears with them. "You are an enemy of our island. How can I trust you to care for my wound?"

Sighing, Adalbern leant back against the wall and folded his arms across his chest. He regarded Mederei carefully. There was no ill intent in his gaze, and his warm brown eyes appeared sad. Mederei scowled at him.

"It is true our parent legion raided the city. We, as victors, were entitled to the spoils of war. But when *Gemina* began slaying the citizens, we withdrew. There was an argument about those actions, I am told."

"You are told?"

"My father fought that battle. He led the Batavi."

"This is supposed to make me trust you?"

"He did not speak much about that war. He did not like to recall it. It was the evil deeds of the Legion *XIV Gemina* which began the rift between the legion and her auxiliaries. It did not sit well with us, and memory of it brought tears to my father's eyes at every recollection." Adalbern looked at Mederei, pulling his gaze back from the past. "I did not fight that battle, but I did spend some time in Britannia after the fight was over. I have heard other stories of the horrors masterminded by both sides."

"Both sides?" Mederei spat, standing up. "You raped us!" The force of her words took all the strength from her. Swooning from blood loss, Mederei slumped, the world fading black. When it returned to her, she felt strong arms around her.

"Let me go, you bastard!" she spat.

The arms tightened slightly, though nowhere near enough to hurt. "You fainted," Adalbern said, his deep voice rumbling in his chest. "I barely caught you in time."

"I don't faint," Mederei answered. She wanted to struggle, but her arms felt like lead, and disobeyed her mind's commands.

"Not for long, in any case," Adalbern said. Mederei could hear the amusement in his voice and railed against it; ineffectually.

"The Hunt take you," she whispered. Tears of misery and rage, strengthened by the physical pain that wracked her body threatened to break free from her control. It took all of her effort now to fight them back.

"They probably will," Adalbern answered softly. "One day."

Mederei closed her eyes to guard against her grief and slumped in Adalbern's embrace. He held her a moment, not moving, before lifting her and laying her gently back onto the stone table. The sound of boots on tile and the pouring of water reached Mederei's ears. She turned her head and opened her eyes to find a large wooden tub being filled with steaming water by Vitus's servants. Another servant entered, carrying a large sack.

"These are the herbs you requested," the lad said, hauling the sack onto a nearby bench. He let his curious gaze flicker to Mederei briefly before Adalbern's soft thanks sent him on his way. Unable to sit up, Mederei rolled on her side and watched as Adalbern rummaged through the sack.

"Is there a mortar and pestle?" he asked one of the servants filling the tub. The servant wordlessly put down his bucket and went to the far shelves. He pushed aside a pile of linen strips and withdrew a wooden mortar and pestle. Bringing it to Adalbern, the servant placed the tools on the bench with the sack of herbs, and returned to filling the tub. Adalbern set to work, taking large strips of willow bark, and witch hazel and crushing them finely. He took a large bunch of camomile and tossed them into the tub of steaming water. The air filled with a gentle scent of grass and blossoms. Taking several larger pieces of the witch hazel, Adalbern threw those into the tub as well, and returned to the mortar and pestle, working all the ingredients he asked for into a powder.

The servants finished filling the tub and took their leave. After a moment of silence, Adalbern asked, "Are you able to enter the tub, or will you need aid?"

"I can do it," Mederei answered. She did not move, her eyes fixed on the broad back of the German as he worked the ingredients into powder. The heat from the water filled the room, the steam glistening on his skin. Mederei's eyes were drawn to the changing lines of muscle on his forearm, moving visibly as he ground his ingredients.

"Good," he answered, not looking at her. "Rest first, though. The water will be too hot yet."

Despite herself, the gentle tones of Adalbern's deep voice lulled her. She let her eyelids droop, then close. The only sounds she could hear in the room was the rhythmic grinding from Adalbern's mixing, her breathing and the distant birdsong from somewhere beyond the room.

It was Adalbern's touch that woke Mederei. She gasped and tried to sit upright. The effort achieved nothing but cost her her balance. The room spun wildly.

"Easy now," Adalbern said. "Easy. It's just me."

Mederei grunted.

"The bath water should be cool enough now. Come, let me help you."

"I can manage," Mederei said. At least, that was what she intended to say. The sounds that reached her ears were little more than garbled attempts at speech.

Adalbern chuckled and Mederei glared. Her glare only brought a wider smile to Adalbern's lips. Mederei struggled to push herself into a sitting position. It took longer and required more effort than she wanted. Demanding some recovery time before she attempted to stand, Mederei closed her eyes a moment as she sat.

Experienced with his share of proud patients, Adalbern merely waited, standing by the stone bench with kindly patience. He took this opportunity to observe Mederei's face. Even as contrary as she was at present, Adalbern felt certain he had never seen anything more pleasing to his eyes. Her alabaster skin bore barely a mark; a small scar on her top lip, and one at her jaw near her left ear were all the marks on her face. This was no small feat for a warrior. Even closed, her eyes were large, evenly set, and framed by shapely eyebrows. Her lips, though they had lost the pinkish hue of good health, were full and shapely.

It occurred to Adalbern that it had been long since his lips last met another's. The temptation to kiss Mederei swelled suddenly, and Adalbern forced himself to step away, walking to the tub to test the temperature of the herb-strewn water. It was unnecessary. He had checked but moments before. He just needed the distance.

Feeling the man's withdrawal from her side, Mederei opened her eyes and watched him as he checked the water. Sighing, she swung her legs over the edge of the table and slowly lowered herself to the ground. The resulting head spin forced her to lean heavily against the cool stone table. She looked to the tub. The distance suddenly seemed impossible to cross.

Taking a deep breath, Mederei took her first step towards the bath.

Her progress was achingly slow, but she refused to ask for aid. Even when Adalbern turned and his eyes softened at her struggle, Mederei refused to ask. She was Mederei, a daughter of Britain, and she needed no one, especially not a Batavian. Pain shot through her wounded leg as she hobbled slowly to the tub. It made her sweat, and stumble. She caught herself on the edge of the tub, and by some miracle of remaining strength, she kept herself from collapsing.

It took Mederei some time to relax her grip on the tub's edge. It took longer for her to regain control of her breath.

Mederei looked down at the water. The tub was too tall. She would not be able to get in without help, unless she toppled in head first. The image of her doing so brought a twisted smile to her lips.

"You will need to remove your armour and clothes before you bathe," Adalbern said softly, drawing Mederei's attention. She scowled at him.

"Turn around, then," she demanded.

Adalbern raised his brows and smiled. Still he turned his back. "Since when is a woman of the green isle so ashamed of her own form?"

"I'm not," Mederei snapped. "But I judge you unworthy to gaze upon it."

The answering soft laugh of the Batavian only deepened Mederei's ire. She straightened and attempted to reach to her side to unlace the breastplate. She found her body unwilling. Pain shot up her side when she moved, matched by the stabbing pain in her leg from the gore wound. After several attempts that served only to bring tears to her eyes, Mederei sighed.

"I can't do it," she whispered.

"So I am worthy to gaze upon you," Adalbern said as he turned. The tears on Mederei's cheeks wiped away his smirk. "Forgive me," he murmured. "I spoke unkindly."

Mederei refused to meet his gaze. She clung to the side of the tub and stared hard at the wall behind it. Adalbern moved to her side. He lifted her arm to rest it on his shoulder and worked on the laces of the breastplate. He could feel her tremble, a combination of fatigue, blood loss, pain, and the desperate clinging to what little pride she had left. Moved to pity, Adalbern refrained from speaking.

The breastplate took some prying to remove it from Mederei's body. Sweat and dust had cemented it to her tunic, which was in turn cemented to her body. Adalbern could not help but take a moment to observe Mederei now that her armour was removed. Her undyed muslin tunic clung enticingly at her waist, thighs, and buttocks. Beneath the thin fabric, he could see the layers of linen that bound her chest tightly; a fix Batavian women often used when they expected to do a lot of physical exertion.

"By your leave?" Adalbern said.

Mederei took a shaky breath and nodded once. Adalbern took the hem of her tunic and raised it up. Mederei did what she could to make her undressing easier, but pain greatly limited her movements.

Now naked save her chest binds, Adalbern could see why. A vast bruise, darkening even as he gazed upon it, covered her right side from her ribs to halfway down her thigh. An equally large bruise covered her right shoulder, with another smaller one at her right elbow. In addition to the larger cuts, her legs bore small scrapes caused by the sand in the arena. Adalbern checked over each wound carefully. Mederei flinched at his touch, but remained mostly still, even when Adalbern removed her chest binds.

The silence stretched on, though Adalbern was done undressing Mederei. She stood, bathed in the afternoon light that streamed in from the windows, staring down at the still steaming water in the tub. Her face might have been unmarred, but her body was not. An old wound cut across her left thigh, the scar barely visible. Across her back wound a jagged lattice of scars from a lashing, perhaps many, judging by their number.

Adalbern reached out, touching her scarred back. "These were not tended properly," he said.

"Why would they be?" Mederei replied. Though no more than a whisper, her voice still sounded thick; constrained by terrible memories and unshed tears. "I am a mere slave."

Adalbern lowered his hand and his gaze. Silence settled into the room once again.

Mederei did not move. She found she could not. She could feel Adalbern's gaze on her naked body. She liked it, and felt pangs of guilt for liking it. Rhys was her lover, a good, British man. How could she find pleasure in the gaze of another, and a Batavian as well? Her pleasure conflicted with how small and vulnerable she now felt, clinging weakly to the edge of the tub and unable to move, rocked by the memory of the violations done to her at the hands of

Rome and its allies. A storm of conflict raged through her, though her stillness gave no clue to it.

The storm blew into a silent howl when Adalbern placed a hand on her back, tracing the scars left there by Roman lashes. His hands were warm and strong and calloused; hands that knew toil. Yet the touch was gentle, tender. Mederei had not been touched tenderly for a long time, and it awoke in her supressed memories, buried desires.

The loss of the Batavian's touch brought a strange ache in her chest. She fought against it. Rhys was her man, not this Batavian.

Tense silence reigned over the room.

For a long time, Mederei simply stood at the edge of the tub, her eyes closed. When she felt controlled enough, she opened them.

"I cannot move," she whispered. It was not a lie. Mederei ordered her limbs to take her into the tub, but they instead remained still, taut, and trembling. She felt Adalbern's warmth at her back and her muscles clenched tighter still. Her trembling became violent.

"I'm not going to hurt you," he whispered.

The kindness in his voice tore her rage from her. Without it, she felt lost. She felt his hand wrap around one wrist. He lifted gently, but her fingers had curled hard around the edge of the tub and would not budge.

Adalbern released her wrist and closed his hand over the top of hers. He snaked his other arm around Mederei's waist, pulling her close until her back pressed wholly against his body.

"I have you," Adalbern's deep voice said softly in her ear. "I promise I will not let you fail. Trust me. Let go."

Panic bubbled in Mederei's blood. She gripped the edge of the tub harder, her mind falling blank save for the terror that flashed through her. Her lungs failed her, drawing breath in ragged stops and starts as she fought back sobs.

"Let go," Adalbern said again, his voice as tender as his touch. "I have you."

Mederei felt Adalbern's strong fingers work hers free from the edge of the tub. She fought it, gripping harder yet. But she was no match for his strength, and would not be even if she was not so wounded. Her hand came free, and when it did, the dam inside her broke.

Mederei's knees buckled. She cried out as she fell to the floor. But she did not land on the stone. Adalbern had gone down with her, pulling her closer so that instead of falling backwards, she landed softly in his lap. Mederei cried out again, a long, low keen as grief and shock found their escape. Sobs took over, tormenting her lungs with each wracking breath. Curled into herself, Mederei twisted so that she could lean into Adalbern's strong, broad chest.

In this moment, it mattered not that he was Batavian, that they were enemies. In this moment, Mederei was as a child, lost, hurt, and afraid. She needed another's strength. She needed comfort. She found both in the man who held her now. He wrapped both arms around her and she clung to him, weeping savagely into his chest. All this time away from her home, away from those she loved, all this time hidden behind a wall of strength she had conjured for herself, all this time under constant threat of beatings, the time spent training to die, her rape and all those long months of repeated rape attempts in captivity, all those years she had denied herself the luxury of tears bubbled to the surface demanding release.

Mederei wept until she had no more strength for tears. She let herself be rocked gently, slowly returning to herself. A strange calm flooded over her.

After a while, Adalbern, still holding her close, asked, "Will you let me tend to you?"

Mederei nodded, too exhausted to fight him on this. She closed her eyes and let her head rest on his chest as he rose from the ground, lifting her easily in his arms. She clung to him even as he gently lowered her into the tub.

Warm water flowed over her. Mederei felt her body relax and she let it. She opened her eyes as Adalbern lifted her injured leg clear of the water, and placed it on a thick linen on the edge of the tub. He fetched a second linen and placed it beneath her head so that she might rest comfortably.

Reaching up, Mederei stroked his cheek before he had time to move away. The touch froze him in place, and their eyes locked.

"Why do you aid me?" Mederei asked.

"I do not know," Adalbern answered. It was the truth. He did not know why he had volunteered his services as a healer, save that he felt compelled to, save for the fact that he wanted to be near this proud Briton. He added, "Perhaps it is to make amends. Rome has wronged us both."

Mederei let her hand drop into the tub. She gave him a sad smile and closed her eyes.

"Sleep," Adalbern said. "You are safe here with me."

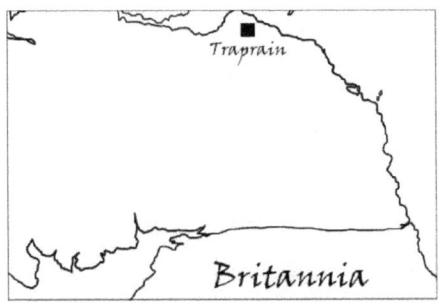

# 71 AD, EARLY SPRING, TRAPRAIN, VOTADINI TERRITORY, FREE BRITAIN

"My Lord! My Lord!"

Rhys groaned in the still predawn air. The boy shook him hard again. "My Lord!"

"What?" Rhys demanded, sleep slurring his words.

"Modron has gone missing!"

This brought the lord Rhys upright immediately. He sat up so swiftly the boy had to jump backwards to avoid a hard head collision.

"What?" Rhys said.

"Modron is gone," the boy said, his voice breathy with panic.

Rhys swore. He swung his legs over the bed, still cursing. "Wake my brother and tell him to form a search party."

The boy nodded and raced out of the large round residence in which the Caledonian prince was staying during his visit to the Votadini. Rhys pushed himself off the bed and ran to gather his clothing. He silently chastised himself as he dressed. How could he have let this happen? Modron was not well. Her mind had been poisoned by Rome. He knew. Everyone knew. He should have been more careful. Mederei had always taken care of her sister, but with her gone, that task fell to him. After all, they were family. Or would be. One day.

Rhys forced his mind away from Mederei's impossible demands before marriage and on to his current problem. He did not know Modron as well as Mederei did. He could not guess as to where the girl would go or why. The clan druid had often expressed sadness at Modron's condition. The girl had the gift, he had said. It was wasted on a mind so thoroughly lost. Perhaps Modron had received some sort of premonition, or a call from one of the Fae, and she was now led by one or the other to some unknown fate. For his part, Rhys hoped it was the former rather than the latter. He had heard of the things the Fae could do. He did not want to cross blades with any denizen of the Otherworld at present.

Rhys's imagination ran wild with guesses as to where Modron might have gone or why. They occupied his mind as he dressed. He was pulling on his boots when Calgacus walked through the door.

"We're ready," Calgacus said.

Rhys nodded at his younger brother. "Lead on, then," he said standing.

Calgacus nodded and left, Rhys following closely behind. Calgacus had changed a great deal since Mederei's capture. Gone was the carefree lad who plagued Rhys's days with jokes and an endless cascade of taunts. In his place stood a sombre young man, who took his duty as shield-bearer to the chieftain very seriously. His once bright smiles were all too rare, and dulled now with the weight of guilt and sadness.

Rhys missed the man his brother had been. As infuriating as he had been at the time, Calgacus nevertheless provided something of immeasurable value in these troubled times—a reason to laugh.

"Have you located any tracks?" Calgacus demanded of the group of men waiting by a small group of saddled horses.

"South," the man replied. "I think."

"You think?"

"Aye, well she is a small girl. I'm surprised to have found any tracks whatsoever, so light her step must be."

Calgacus grunted. "South it is," he said. "Mount up. We'll ride to the first hill and see what we can see."

"I can aid you," the young prince of the Votadini said, arriving late to the party.

"Thank you, my Lord," Rhys said. "But this is a family affair. Please excuse my absence from breakfast on the morrow."

The prince smiled. "No insult shall be dealt, Lord Rhys. Take care in the mountains. I pray you find the girl swiftly."

"Aye," Rhys answered. "So do I. We will return soon."

The prince nodded and stood aside, permitting the small group of Caledonian dignitaries to pass. They left the city at a gallop, desperate to find a mad girl lost in the wilds.

The search lasted most of the night. Modron had indeed gone south, near as they could tell. Though they lost her tracks, a little searching recovered them once again.

"She is a light little thing," the tracker grumbled as he squatted on the ground. "Look here. She has barely pressed the grass upon which she walked."

"Over the next rise then?" Rhys said hopefully.

"I mean, she is on foot," another man added. "How far could she have gotten?"

"A day's ride, clearly," Calgacus noted. He nodded at the horizon, which lightened rapidly.

"That should be impossible," Rhys muttered. "Let's go." He pushed his tired horse into a trot. At the top of the hill, Rhys stopped. Down at the base of the slope, a young girl walked as if in a dream, her fiery red hair shining even in the dull grey light of predawn. She wore nothing more than a white linen shift. Rhys scowled. She must be freezing.

He kicked his horse and the beast snorted, pushed into an unwilling trot. Behind him came Calgacus, who smiled in relief upon seeing the girl. "Thank the gods," he breathed, pushing his horse on.

Rhys had almost caught up to Modron by the time the search party had all reached the base of the mountain.

"Modron!" he called.

The girl continued walking, ignoring him as if deaf to all sound. Rhys slowed his horse. It walked half a step behind Modron.

"Modron," he said again.

Again, it was as if the girl was deaf. She did not stop. Her step did not falter, nor did it slow. She did not turn her head. There was not even so much as a twitch to indicate that she had heard him call her name. Sighing, Rhys dismounted. He walked by Modron's side a moment, enjoying the soft beginning of morning.

"Modron," he said gently. He reached out and took the girl's wrist in his hand. His touch brought her sharply around, her eyes wide with shock and fear.

"Modron, it's all right," Rhys said immediately. "It's just me. It's Rhys. You remember me, don't you?"

The fear faded from her expression, replaced by her usual, mindless smile. She stared up at him, her blue eyes distant; the eyes of a woman who lived in one world, but walked in another. Her eyes widened and tears welled in them.

She reached up one frail hand and placed it on Rhys's cheek. Tears spilled over, sliding down her cheeks.

Rhys frowned at her, confused.

"White is the colour of death," Modron whispered.

The frown marring Rhys's forehead deepened. A low, long whistle turned his head. His lips parted in surprise.

Arching through the air with deadly grace flew a javelin, a low whistle accompanying its flight.

"Rhys!" Calgacus bellowed as he saw the javelin descend. It flew, not towards his brother, but the young woman beside him. Rhys had grabbed her, pulling her into him as he sought to shield her with his own body. The impact of the javelin as it struck the chieftain echoed around the valley. Rhys uttered no cry. He stood a moment, then tumbled onto his side, leaving Modron standing, curled into herself and screaming.

Calgacus stared in shock a moment.

A small band of horsemen broke from a copse of trees nearby, galloping at the remaining search party, weapons out.

"Romans," Calgacus whispered. Then louder, "Romans!" He kicked his horse's flanks hard. The noble beast darted forward, stretching its neck as Calgacus loosened his reins. It mattered not that the party numbered just four, now. It mattered not that the Roman party had ten men. All that mattered was that there were Romans within the borders of the Caledonian Federation, and that Calgacus had seen his brother slain. He loosened his sword, not caring whether his men rode behind him or not. Raising it high, he bellowed, "Britain forever!"

In a valley watched over by silent mountains and the rising sun, Calgacus crossed blades with the Roman cavalry.

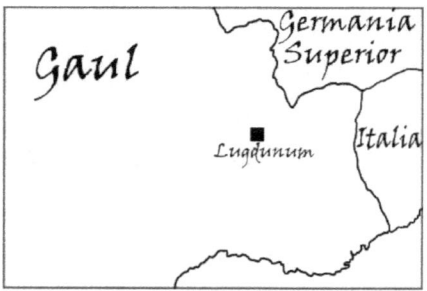

## 71 AD, EARLY SPRING, LUGDUNUM, PROVINCE OF GAUL

"Hello," Vitus said as Mederei's eyes flickered open. He smiled at her as she frowned up at him.

"How are you feeling?" he asked.

"Groggy," Mederei answered truthfully. "Exhausted." She struggled up, lifting herself on her elbows. "Hungry."

Vitus chuckled. "How is the leg?"

Mederei looked down at her injured leg. Only when she saw the bindings and the memory of the day's events returned did her leg begin to throb painfully. Another fight. This time against a pair of dogs. It was the same leg as the boar before that. At least, she mused, she might have one unmarked leg, still.

"Throbbing. But it could be worse."

"That it could. You impressed the crowd during your fight today. If you manage to keep displaying such courage and cunning, you might well become the city favourite. Perhaps you shall get to go to Rome and fight before the emperor."

Mederei stared at Vitus.

"It is a great honour," he assured her.

"A greater honour would be embalming the emperor's head in a jar of pine oil," Mederei answered.

Vitus raised his brows. He shook his head and entered Mederei's cell, sitting on the edge of her bed. Mederei sat up, giving him room.

"Rome is not the villain you believe Her to be, Woman."

"Not to you," Mederei answered. "You betrayed your own in favour of them. Tell me, how do the emperor's boots taste?"

Vitus shook his head. "Betrayed my own? Many of the tribes of Gaul thrive today, still intact. Mine included."

"That justifies leaving other Gauls to murder and worse at the hands of Rome, does it?"

"The Averni are not the Aedui. The Aedui are not the Ligones. We Gauls were never one people. Neither were the Britons, for that matter, yet you act as if we were, as if we didn't wage war between the tribes in search for land, and power, and glory."

"You could have been one people," Mederei replied. She drew her knees up and wrapped her arms around them. "Vercingetorix could have kept Gaul free. He sought to unite Gaul against Rome. If Gaul had but listened…"

"We would have all laboured under a different emperor."

"You would have been ruled by a Gaul, according to Gaulish law, and you would have been free to live as Gauls, instead of being forced to live as Romans, under Roman law. Have you no pride in your own people and your own traditions?"

Vitus shook his head. "Things are better for us under Roman rule, Woman. We do not battle one another now. Trade has made many of us wealthy—"

"And cowards."

Sighing, Vitus smiled slightly. "Prudence is not the same thing as cowardice." He looked over at the young warrior. "You know a great deal of Gaulish history, for a mere northern Briton."

"All know the story of Vercingetorix. The free peoples of Briton consider him the last good Gaul."

"He was as power-mad as the emperor," Vitus said. "You do not think he would have given the tribes their lands back after defeating Rome, do you? No, he would not. He would embark on his own conquests, build his own empire, using the support he gained to force young Gauls into wars that were not their own. It is as I said, Woman. What is one tyrant over another?"

"Rome murdered my mother," Mederei whispered, her eyes distant as she stared at the floor. They filled with tears that spilled unnoticed down her cheeks. "They razed my home to ash, and slaughtered everyone in the city. I was two days' ride away, and I could hear them screaming. Do not tell me Rome is not evil, while you sit there protected for your cowardice. I have seen what Rome is."

"Well," Vitus said, rising. "A Roman has sent you some gifts."

Mederei looked up and scowled at Vitus as the man beckoned his servants forward. They entered, one carrying a pair of fine new sandals, the other fabric folded neatly in his arms, a small pair of earrings in gold with pale blue gems hanging from the bottom. A carved wooden hair pin sat next to the earrings.

"You should change into them," Vitus said. "You are expected at dinner shortly. These games were very well-received, and dinner is bound to be sumptuous tonight. Now dress."

"Games," Mederei whispered. "*Games*."

"Be still," Vitus said. "I believe the Roman who gifted these to you is very attached to you."

Mederei scowled. "Who?"

"How can you not know? She has only been to visit with you often."

Mederei swallowed. Porcia. She turned to the clothes, which had been placed carefully on her bed.

"You see?" Vitus said. "They are not the villains you believe them to be." When Mederei did not answer, Vitus smiled and added. "I will await you in the main hall."

Nodding absently, Mederei did not look up as Vitus left. She reached out and touched the soft, light linen of the clothing brought to her. Sighing, she let her bed sheets fall to the floor and lifted the clothes. The cloth, a pale blue that appeared almost green in the light of the torches, was, in fact, two pieces of cloth with two ends sewn together. The top was almost identical to the bottom. The head hole was marked by two ornate brass buttons, one at either side of the hole.

It resulted in a sleeveless dress, a fact made obvious only when Mederei pulled the dress on. It hung low to the floor, far too long for walking. Scowling, Mederei turned, trying to understand how the fabric worked.

It was when she tripped, falling forward onto the bed, that she noticed a deep blue belt hanging from the edge of the bed, near the earrings. She cursed to herself, snatched up the belt and lifted the fabric enough that she could walk comfortably. Holding the excess fabric with her chin, she wound the long belt around her waist. She released the extra fabric and arranged it evenly around her. It covered her belt. She slipped on her sandals, noticing that pale blue gems matching those in her earrings were on them. She put on those earrings, their weight tugging oddly at her lobes. It had been a long time since she had worn jewellery of any sort.

Finally, Mederei struggled to tame her thick waves. She pulled her hair loosely back, wrapping it around itself and looping it through to create a large, loose knot. Thick waves of auburn hair pulled through the knot and hung over one shoulder. It was a style Mederei had much admired her mother wearing when she was a child. She slipped the pin through the knot to keep it in place and straightened. She had no mirror to view herself, and could only trust that she had done everything well enough not to shame her heritage.

It was not for Rome that she wished to dress well. It was for her mother, who had always faced Rome's messengers, threatening generals, and false traders with a quiet but fierce dignity. Mederei would match her mother's pride tonight. Dignity, however, required her to control her tears at the sharp memories of her mother in queenly attire, which threatened to take away her composure. So, for a time, Mederei paced her cell, fighting the tears, and preparing her mask of disinterest and disdain. Once she felt prepared, she squared her shoulders and walked from her cell.

The presence of jewellery and the wearing of fine fabric aided Mederei in her pride. Despite her wounded leg, she appeared to glide as she entered the main hall. Vitus spoke quietly to his wife. Izem, Gandwy, and another gladiator Mederei did not know well stood to the side, surrounded by Vitus's private guard.

Silence descended as Mederei approached. She paused. "Did I dress correctly?" she asked Vitus, holding his gaze boldly.

"My dear," Vitus's wife said. "Who knew how beautiful you would look? Come here. You need a little fixing."

Mederei looked at her a moment before gliding forward. Vitus's wife adjusted her dress a little and tucked in a few wayward strands of hair.

"There," she said. "Much better."

"You will be escorted by the guard," Vitus said, reaching out to take his wife's hand as she returned to him. "I will see you there." He kissed his wife on her smooth cheek. "Come," he told her. "Let us go now."

Mederei watched Vitus and his wife leave, before a rough voice announced in Latin, "This way."

Turning, Mederei joined the gladiators encircled by the heavily armed guards. Izem grinned broadly when Mederei came to stand before him.

"You are truly the jewel in Vitus's crown," he said, his white teeth flashing in the dim light. "You did very well today, and now I find, to my surprise, you are beautiful as well."

"To your surprise?" Mederei asked, arching one brow at him.

Izem laughed. "You are not so pretty covered in the grime of work," he said.

Mederei could not help the smile that sprang to her lips. "Strange," she murmured. "That is when men are the most beautiful."

"I will never understand the women of your country!" he declared.

"All right," one of the guards barked. "Let's go."

The guard turned sharply and began to march. Surrounded on all sides, the gladiators had no choice but to move.

As they exited the ludus building, a great roar went up. Mederei blinked in surprise as the sudden light of the setting sun revealed a great gathering. It seemed the whole city had come to the streets to cheer the gladiators as they moved to their feast.

"Smile," Izem said to Mederei, who had scowled the instant the surprise had worn thin. "These people crave a hero. Smile at them and let their hearts be glad."

"They can seek their heroes elsewhere," Mederei hissed. "I cannot save them from their fate."

"No," Izem answered. "But they need an example to prove they can save themselves. So smile, and show them the strength they need to mimic."

Mederei looked back at the crowd. One woman stood at the edge of the crowd, holding an infant child to her. The woman's gaunt face made her eyes seem too large. Those eyes stared up at Mederei, shining with hope. What hope the woman found in her was something Mederei could not fathom. She slowed in her walking, meeting the young woman's gaze with a soft expression. The woman smiled shyly at Mederei, who replied with a small smile of her own.

The woman began to weep, pulling her child to her. She continued to weep as Mederei passed her by. Incapable of taking her eyes from the woman, Mederei turned. The girl stood there still, staring at Mederei with wide, adoring eyes, weeping openly.

Unable to walk forward with her head craned so, Mederei turned away. "What do they hope for? What do they see in me to give them such hope?"

"They see a Briton sentenced to death," Izem replied. "Who lives still. They see defiance in the face of oppression. It is a powerful thing for the hopeless to witness."

"They will be disappointed," Mederei whispered.

"Perhaps, perhaps not. That, Woman, is up to you."

Mederei said nothing else in the long walk to Lilius's home where the feast was set to take place. The entire journey, citizens of Lugdunum crowded the streets, cheering the gladiators as if they were returning from battle, victorious. Children ran alongside the marching guards, calling out for blessings. More children wove through the crowd, small knives hidden in their palms, using the parade for a distraction as they cut purses and stole jewels.

Hungry children begged, ignoring the parade altogether. Watching was for the fortunate, for those who had eaten that day.

Even the regular Roman citizenry appeared excited by the parade, though not one gladiator walking was Roman. They cheered and watched on in adoration with the rest of the crowd.

So great was the din, and the strain of walking tall beneath the weight of the crowd's expectations, that Mederei found herself relieved upon entering the private home of Lilius. The applause that greeted the gladiators jolted Mederei from her thoughts. Izem greeted the crowd gathered in the dining room with a bright smile. Mederei saw the white flash of his teeth from the corner of her eye. She answered the applause with a deep scowl. Those who appreciated her presence now would cheer equally as well watching her choke on her own blood.

"Welcome, welcome!" Lilius greeted, spreading his arms wide and striding forward to clasp hands and touch cheeks with Vitus and his wife. "Welcome to my home, to you and your warriors!"

Mederei rolled her eyes and turned her head away as the large man approached, wearing a smile that appeared painted on. She did not care to disguise her disdain from the gathered guests. It vanished momentarily, replaced by the smallest hint of a smile, when Porcia clasped her hands over her mouth to stop herself laughing aloud at Mederei.

"We are honoured, Lilius," Vitus said, grinning.

However distasteful Mederei found the man and his position, there was none of the falsehood in Vitus that was easily discernible in Lilius. Though he held in his hand the earnings made on the backs of the maimed and dying, Vitus's warmth felt genuine. Mederei pondered briefly how the two aspects could reconcile themselves in one person. It was almost as absurd as the thought of a good Roman, and yet there stood Porcia, sweet and sad; a good Roman. Melancholy settled over Mederei as she vanished within her own mind.

"Make yourselves comfortable," Lilius said. "There is plenty of food and drink to be had."

Mederei and the other gladiators were ushered to the back of the room, where a table awaited them. They sat, their escort of guardsmen taking positions behind their table, close enough to react quickly should any of the gladiators be in a homicidal mood.

Mederei watched the spectacle before her. Romans of high station wandered around the room, dressed in gowns not dissimilar to Mederei's own, though their jewellery was considerably more ornate.

A young serving boy, Gaulish by the look of him, approached the table with a large vessel of wine. He poured the drink for each of the gladiators into the terracotta cups.

"Thank you," Mederei said in perfect Gaulish.

The boy looked up at her in surprise and smiled shyly. He bowed before her slightly before retreating to continue his duties for the evening.

Mederei picked up her cup and stared down into it. The sharp smell of spices emanated from the cup, tickling her nose.

"The Romans know finery," Izem said with satisfaction as he drank deep.

"They know greed," Mederei answered quietly, still staring down at her cup.

"Come now, Woman," Izem said, grinning. "You are a guest of honour at a feast! Enjoy yourself."

"I am as a beast in a menagerie," Mederei answered. "Here to satisfy morbid curiosity and nothing more."

"You have escaped a fight alive! You should not be so gloomy! Who knows when our ancestors will welcome us into death? Enjoy what entertainment there is to be had until then, or what is the point of living?"

"Without freedom," Mederei said, "there can be no living."

Izem grunted. He shook his head, and turned instead to Gandwy.

"Who do you think will bid for me first, Briton?" he demanded.

Upon hearing those words, Mederei turned to Gandwy, her eyebrows raised.

"Romans will pay good money to take a gladiator of their choice to their beds," he explained. "Izem is considered exotic by them, and is therefore highly popular."

"It is a good thing," Izem said. "Not a hard duty to undertake."

"Perhaps not for you," Gandwy whispered. He nodded his head at Mederei, who sat, suddenly tense, wearing an expression of horror.

Izem frowned at her. He nodded. "Ah yes. But it is different for women. I forgot."

"Any man who tries," Mederei hissed, "will find himself quickly unmanned."

Gandwy smiled. "Good," he said.

Mederei smirked at him. It was a wicked smile that promised hell. If wildcats could smile, they would look like Mederei did in that moment. Gandwy chuckled. "I almost pity them," he said.

"How is your leg?" a deep voice broke in, drawing Mederei's attention away from her countryman. She looked sharply up to find Adalbern standing by the table. He wore a tunic and trousers, contrasting sharply with the flowing robes of the men of Rome. Had that been a deliberate rebuke of his allies? Kindly brown eyes watched Mederei, uncomfortable in their intensity. The greatest part of the discomfort was Mederei's reaction to those eyes.

Swallowing back her unease and fighting to quell the fluttering in her stomach, Mederei put down her wine.

"It throbs," she answered. "But that is to be expected."

Adalbern smiled slightly. "Will you permit me to see it? I wish only to inspect my binds and ensure they will hold the night."

Mederei nodded, unsure. She turned in her seat and lifted the hem of her dress until the bandaged wound was exposed. Adalbern knelt. Mederei's body gave an involuntary twitch when the German's calloused hand gently took her leg by the ankle and lifted it closer.

Porcia stood impatiently by her betrothed's side. She smiled benignly at the woman with whom he was speaking, though she desperately wanted to slip away and go to Mederei's side. Mederei was infinitely more fascinating. Porcia snuck a glance at the Briton. She paused.

Adalbern knelt before the woman, his hands upon her leg. Ostensibly, it looked as though he was doing little more than inspecting his work, but Porcia could see in his gentle touch and in his face that there was more to his attention than medical ministrations. Porcia could not contain her smile. She straightened and scanned the room, looking for her brother in whom she confided everything.

He stood next to their father, looking as bored and miserable as she felt. Their eyes met, and Porcia bobbed her head twice in Mederei's direction. Ambrosius looked over and spied Adalbern and Mederei. His expression changed, moving from intense boredom to comical understanding, to mischief. He grinned at Porcia and nodded, and she turned back to the conversation her betrothed was having.

Ambrosius watched Adalbern and Mederei a moment, smiling to himself. It was painfully obvious to anyone who observed that Adalbern's intentions were amorous, even if he did not yet understand that himself. He turned and grinned at his sister. Adalbern was sure to get cornered later in the night.

"Well, the bandages will hold," Adalbern said at last, gently releasing her leg. "As for the wound, I will have to visit again to ensure it is healing properly."

Mederei shrugged. "As you must." She immediately regretted the hurt that flashed across Adalbern's face at her uncaring. "I live to die," she said quietly, by way of explaining. "Your efforts will be wasted."

"We all die," Adalbern answered. "Some of us are lucky enough to die well."

Mederei looked up at Adalbern, caught by the sadness in his features. She opened her mouth to reply, but found her tongue had gone dry. She had no words to utter. So she simply stared up at him.

Her gaze was broken before it could get uncomfortable by the bawdy first strains of a loud Gaulish drinking song. Recognizing the voice, Mederei turned her head and immediately smiled.

Geraint stood upon the stairs, having arrived moments ago, his Gaulish lyra in his hand, singing outlandishly. The song, heavy on mentions of drinking and willing Gaulish women, served to bring smiles and elicit chuckles from those who could understand the words. As he sang, Geraint descended the stairs and walked through the crowd, winking broadly at the various women in the room, making them giggle. Mederei could not help but smile when he threw a particularly cheeky wink in her direction.

His song ended to guffaws and applause. Some pretended they were above such boorish humour, clapping politely with their faces twisted in distain. Others, already quite drunk, demanded more songs in a similar vein.

Geraint sang eight songs before he retired for a time, other musicians coming in where he left off. He spent his time moving through the crowd, doing all he could to charm his company.

"Ah!" he said loudly, when he arrived at Mederei's table. "The fearsome boar-killer! How pleased I am to see you alive and well."

"I am alive, in any case," Mederei answered, fighting to keep herself from smiling.

"But not well? Tell me, what ails the beautiful murderess of mongrels?"

Mederei declined to answer, so continuing his theatrics, Geraint said, "Ah! But it must be for want of food! Yes! That must be it! Surely they will feed the great slayer of beasts?"

"The food will be coming shortly," Lilius said from behind Geraint.

Izem, Gandwy, and the other gladiator all stood, so Mederei followed suit. Geraint bowed low before Lilius. "Good sir!" he said. "I must commend you on your fine gathering!"

"Vitus was not wrong about you," Lilius said, smiling a smile that spoke more of contempt than mirth. "You are indeed a lively fellow."

"I suppose I must be," Geraint said, grinning, "if Vitus said so. And would you blame me? Life is too short to wallow in sorrows."

"Woman," Lilius said, having grown bored of Geraint. "My betrothed has requested some time with you. Would you walk with her in the garden a while?"

"Of course," Mederei answered. "I would be honoured to accompany such a lady."

Lilius's lips twisted again, signalling his discontent, but he nevertheless permitted Porcia to leave his side and move to Mederei's.

"The garden is this way," Porcia murmured. She began to walk and Mederei followed, ensuring to keep a step behind until they were well away from Lilius's hostile gaze. Once they had entered the central courtyard, Porcia turned and threw her arms around Mederei. "I am so glad you're all right," she breathed. "I was so worried, I thought I was going to be ill."

Mederei smiled. "Give me some credit. I am harder to kill than that."

Porcia smiled. "I'm sorry. I should not have doubted but… Still, I was worried." She looked down at her hands, playing with her fingertips. Mederei took those hands and Porcia looked up at her in surprise.

"Never apologize for your goodness," Mederei said. "There are so few who still possess any, I fear it has come to be viewed in a poor light."

"I'm sorry," Porcia apologized again, before frowning. "Or is that something I should not apologize for also?"

Mederei laughed. "I am glad we have time to talk. I have missed you."

"It must be awful in the company of nothing but men." Porcia turned and, still holding one of Mederei's hands, began to walk through the small garden that sat in the centre of Lilius's villa.

Mederei shrugged, keeping to Porcia's slow pace. "I travelled with an army of men," she said, "for most of my life. I'm used to it. These men are not so unlike the men of my country. A little more hopeless, I suppose. A little more hostile. I do miss my sister, though."

"You have a sister?"

"I do. She is three years my junior."

"Is she a warrior, like you?"

Mederei looked away from Porcia a moment before shaking her head. "No. When Rome came to our city, they slaughtered everyone. My sister and I were… we were raped. Our mother was murdered. Modron was too young to face such terror and pain. It drove her mad."

"I'm so sorry," Porcia breathed.

Again, Mederei shrugged. "There is nothing that can be done about it now," she said. "And, in truth, I sometimes envy her. She does not know reality any longer, and so it cannot wound her. Her mind is gone, and her spirit is made safer for it."

"How you must hate Rome," Porcia whispered.

"The empire is evil," Mederei agreed. She stopped walking and turned to the young Roman. "But I am learning that her people are less so. I wonder at how such a strange opposition could be."

Porcia looked down at the ground. "You are more generous than I. Sometimes I feel my brother is the only good Roman left in the world."

Mederei said nothing, instead she turned to the moon and stared at it a while.

"I wish I could see your country," Porcia said, finding a dry patch of grass to sit on. "I imagine all the women must be as tall and beautiful as you, and as fierce. And if British women are all so brave, how incredible must your men be? Gods, surely."

"Hardly gods," Mederei said. "But they are good men. Bold and brave, worthy of their women."

Porcia smiled. "I love the way you say that... 'Worthy of their women.' It makes women sound valued."

"Women are valuable."

Tears struck Porcia's eyes. "Not in Rome," she whispered.

## 71 AD, EARLY SPRING, NEAR TRAPRAIN, VOTADINI TERRITORY, FREE BRITAIN

"Here!" a tracker of the Votadini called, his voice carrying down through the mountain pass. He stood atop the crest, staring down into a valley where recently a slaughter took place. Seven men and three horses lay in the valley, javelins sticking out of them; death's flagless sigil.

"Gods above and below," the prince of the Votadini breathed as he crested the pass. "Please let that not be them."

"Romans," the tracker spat. "I can see their eagle near the trees."

"Impossible!" the prince snapped. "I would know if one of their legions had come through my lands."

"Probably not a legion," the tracker said. He leapt from the rock that was the summit back onto the path. "Seven men, my Lord. It's them."

"Pray it is not."

The prince's search party of ten made their slow way down the mountain, their small, sturdy northern horses picking their way carefully over ground slick with the day's rain. The prince's heart sank as he reached the bottom. He recognized the horse nearest him. Rhys's horse, killed in its flight from the battle.

"Search for survivors," he whispered.

Three men moved forward, their weapons drawn. They would be the guard. The rest moved to each man, hopelessly searching for signs of life.

"My Lord!" a man called near the middle of the valley. "Here! It's Lord Calgacus! He's alive!"

The prince kicked his horse into a run, dismounting on the fly to Calgacus's side. The young Caledonian prince breathed slowly, the air forcing its way past something thick and liquid caught in his throat.

"Send for a healer!" the prince demanded, kneeling by Calgacus's body and touching his cold face. "Hang in there, my Lord. Stay with me. We will have you safe soon."

Calgacus's only answer was a short sighing breath.

Calgacus awoke three days after being found. He frowned as he stared up at the wooden roof that swung in his vision. He closed his eyes again and waited for the dizzy spell to pass.

"My Lord," the prince of the Votadini said quietly.

Calgacus opened his eyes again and turned his head. This time it was the Votadini prince who swung wildly in his vision. He closed his eyes once more and fell unconscious.

Two days later, Calgacus once again opened his eyes. His vision no longer swam, and his stomach ached with hunger. Struggling against protesting muscles, Calgacus hauled himself to a sitting position.

A young face peeked into the room, squeaked and vanished. Calgacus smiled slightly at the sound of someone running. Moments later, Prince Cynbel of the Votadini entered. His sombre expression broke momentarily for a smile.

"My Lord," he said. "I am glad to see your eyes open."

"I am glad that they are no longer betraying my stomach," Calgacus said. "May I impose upon your hospitality for some bread and cheese?"

Prince Cynbel nodded. He went to the door to relay the request. Once the food was delivered, he watched Calgacus eat a moment before sitting on the stool by the bed.

"What happened?" Calgacus asked. "There were Romans…" His face paled. "Where is my brother?"

"My Lord," Prince Cynbel began.

Calgacus dropped his food and pushed his plate away.

"Where is my brother?" he repeated.

"Forgive me, my Lord," the prince said. "Your brother is dead."

The food forgotten, Calgacus leant back against the head of the bed and closed his eyes, grief robbing him of his breath. He opened his eyes again.

"Where is Modron?" he whispered.

Prince Cynbel stared at him helplessly before answering.

"Rome has her."

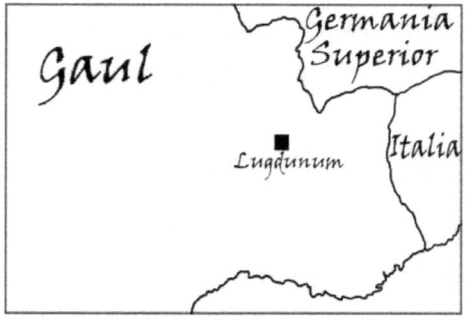

## 71 AD, SPRING, LUGDUNUM, PROVINCE OF GAUL

Geraint trembled as he sat by the stockyards in the market and stared into nothingness. In his hand he held a short twig carved with lines and hatching that would look like nothing more than the decorations of a bored child with a knife if one did not know what to look for. Geraint knew, and he cursed that knowledge. In the message carved upon that twig was written his lord's murder.

Rhys was dead.

The grief hit him suddenly, taking his breath from him in a single blow to his gut. Closing his eyes to guard against tears, he forced his burning lungs to work, drawing in a deep breath.

His mind turned to Mederei. What now? The resistance was her reason for existing. What would this news do to her?

"Excuse me, mister," a young Gaulish boy said.

Geraint opened his eyes to look at the child. The boy's mop of blond hair was filthy, though not nearly as filthy as his starved face.

"My sister forgot to give you this." The boy held out his hand, another twig grasped in his grubby fist.

Slowly, Geraint reached for it. He smiled shakily at the boy, who offered a bright smile in return. He turned and began to scurry away.

"Wait," Geraint croaked, his voice cracking with a grief struggling for expression.

The boy turned, large blue eyes hopeful. Geraint withdrew a large coin from his purse. "Here. Buy something sweet for you and your sister."

The boy's eyes grew wide.

"Thank you, mister!" he breathed before snatching the coin and running away, as if frightened that Geraint may change his mind. The bard watched him disappear into the crowd before turning his attention down to the twig. He smiled slightly as he read the message. He wrapped one large hand around the carved wood.

"I swear it," he whispered to no one in particular before rising from his place and leaving the market.

Mederei watched the Batavian as he carefully unwrapped the bandages that bound her wounded leg. He kept his gaze on his work, deliberately avoiding her eyes so much it made things tense.

"Why are you here, German?" she asked softly.

"To tend to you," Adalbern answered, his deep voice equally soft.

"And for that I thank you," Mederei answered. "But why are you in Lugdunum?"

The pause in his working hands would have gone unnoticed, but Mederei was watching for it. What Porcia had told her about the Batavian was true. There was a story behind his presence here, and his defiance of Roman dress and custom.

"Beg your pardon," Vitus said from the door of the infirmary, drawing the attention of its occupants.

Mederei's lips pursed as she spied the man's expression. Vitus, though a master of slaves, was not good at masking his emotions. His grey-eyed gaze filled with sadness when it fell to Mederei.

"What is it?" Mederei asked.

It had been three weeks since the fight with the dogs. Adalbern had come by the ludus every day for the first week to ensure Mederei's wounds were not festering. Then it was once a week after. This week promised to be the last that the bandages were necessary. Vitus had showered Mederei with favourable treatment, pleased that her renown had made him a celebrity of sorts. People had come to the ludus bearing gifts for him and his female gladiator. The pair had been invited to many a public function and were always treated with honour.

Mederei had not missed the evils in these appearances, however. Many high-ranking men leered at her, their gazes hungrily tracking her like wolves about to strike. They served always to remind her that she was not a guest, she was an attraction, no better than the exotic animals brought in from the Province of Africa. She existed only to amuse and entertain.

At least here in the ludus, she was amongst peers. Strangely, she felt safer surrounded by criminals and trained killers than the Romans of Lugdunum.

Vitus cleared his throat. "I am given to understand that the empire is celebrating this evening. There are parties in all the major cities."

"Oh? And what is Rome celebrating?"

"I understand that the empire has made some progress in Britain."

Mederei's demeanour changed immediately. Every fibre in her body became tense and her frown vanished, replaced by a flash of panic. Still, she kept her voice calm even when she asked, softly, "What progress?"

"I do not know," Vitus said with a shrug. "But we have both been invited to celebrate at the residence of Governor Lilius."

Mederei stared incredulously at Vitus. "You expect me to celebrate Roman success against my own people?" she demanded, a dangerous flash in her eyes.

"I do not, no. The governor, however—"

"The governor can dine on poison!" Mederei spat.

Her heart raced. What could Roman progress in Britain mean? Surely the island had not been conquered? Surely Rhys would not have permitted it? Questions and scenarios raced through her mind with nauseating speed.

"This is not optional, Woman," Vitus said patiently. "You cannot turn down this honour to dine with your patron."

"And what if I do?"

Vitus sighed. "You will be dragged there in chains," he said. "And their entertainment this evening will be less savoury than the bawdy Gaulish tales that bard Geraint is so fond of."

Mederei scowled at Vitus. A gentle touch on her calf drew her attention away to Adalbern, who met her gaze briefly. As Aetius's hostage, and thus connected to Lilius's fiancée, he would be present at the celebration. She would have at least one friend there.

"You will come," Vitus said. "I expect you to be prepared before sundown."

With little else to say, Vitus turned and marched from the room. Mederei's gaze followed him, her dun eyes like stone. Out of sight of the slave master, she began to tremble. What news from home awaited her at this celebration?

"It will be all right," Adalbern murmured, resuming his work.

Mederei turned to him and found she had no words. The rest of the afternoon passed in silence.

Pacing in the courtyard provided no relief for Mederei, though she could not stop herself from so doing. She gnawed on the side of her thumbnail as she paced, not caring about the taste of blood in her mouth.

"Ready?" Vitus asked as he approached Mederei, the gladiator Gandwy at his side, looking despondent. Vitus smiled slightly. "It never ceases to amaze me how well you look in your finery."

Mederei said nothing to him. "What news?" she demanded. "What news of Britain?"

Vitus shrugged. "I swear I do not know. Lilius has kept the information to himself."

"Do you know?" Mederei demanded of her fellow Briton. Gandwy shook his head.

"I do not," he confessed. "But it bodes ill whenever Rome celebrates."

Mederei nodded. Gandwy had spoken true. She bit her lip and turned away from the two men.

"We'll be late. Into the wagon," Vitus said.

Mederei did not move until she felt Gandwy's hand upon her shoulder. She walked with him to the wagon and permitted him to help her up. Vitus sat at the front of the wagon with the driver, and they made their unsteady way out of the compound and into the city.

"You are from the north," Gandwy said to Mederei in their mother tongue.

Mederei looked at him and nodded. It was not so much a lie. She had spent the majority of her life in the north.

"Is it true that they drove Rome from there?"

"It is true that we drove Rome from the southern reaches of the Caledonii Federation," Mederei replied. "We restored Venutius to the Brigantian throne and drove out the traitor queen, Cartimandua."

Gandwy smiled a little. "Perhaps their celebration is only that they have retaken Brigantia."

"The gods forgive me," Mederei whispered. "I wish it so. The alternative is too much to bear."

Gandwy watched Mederei as she struggled to hold back the tears which threatened to escape her eyes. "What alternative is that?"

Unable to bring to voice her deepest fears, Mederei shook her head and turned away. Gandwy knew better than to force the subject. There was someone the Woman had left behind who was dear to her; a man, perhaps, who fought with the northern rebels. If Rome had not retaken Brigantia, then they had claimed the rebels, and this man of hers was dead. Or worse.

The cart rolled up to the expansive house of the governor Lilius and stopped abruptly. Lost in her thoughts, Mederei was unprepared for the lurch and very nearly tumbled off her seat.

"Out," Vitus said, his cheery voice doing nothing to lift the fog of fear and melancholy that surrounded his British gladiators.

Gandwy and Mederei did as they were bid and Vitus started up the stairs. He paused, turned around, and returned to his gladiators.

"Whatever news you hear in there," he said, his voice and expression kindly, "stand strong. Rome does what she must."

"Rome does what her lust dictates," Mederei answered. She glared at Vitus with eyes of burning coals. "You needn't concern yourself with the fate of the peoples you abandoned in your own greed."

Vitus shook his head. "One day you will understand the good Rome has done in the world."

"Only when I am blinded to all the evil she has wrought."

"Inside then." The warmth left his voice.

It was a small victory for Mederei, and she smirked at Vitus as she passed, gliding up the stairs like a queen.

"Mederei," a familiar voice hissed from the shadows as she passed beneath the lintel of the door. Mederei turned her head to spy Geraint hiding in the shadows there. "I need to speak with you."

Before the bard could say more, Vitus stepped through the door, and Geraint's chance was lost. He leant back, deeper into the shadow, and disappeared. He would find another way to speak to her in private.

"Ah!" Lilius said, brightening at the arrival of his honoured guests. "The British animals and their handler!"

Mederei ignored him, her focus on Porcia. The girl tried to meet her gaze, but welling tears forced her to turn her head whenever she tried. A slight frown touched Mederei's brow. What had the girl so upset?

"Come, come!" Lilius said, approaching Vitus in a friendly greeting. "Avail yourselves of my food and my drink. Today is a good day for Rome."

"What is going on?" Adalbern murmured into Ambrosius's ear as he watched the Britons be escorted to their seats.

"I don't know," Ambrosius said. "Whatever it is, it cannot be good. I have never seen Lilius so filled with malicious glee."

"Have you had a chance to speak with your sister?"

Ambrosius shook his head. "No. I'll try and tear her away from her betrothed before long, though. She does not look happy."

"No," Adalbern replied. "She does not."

"So, Lilius," Vitus said, grinning at his giddy host. "Shall you tell us why Rome celebrates, or must we guess?"

"In time, in time, Vitus! Drink first and enjoy this night. I shall get to the announcements presently."

Vitus shrugged, accepted the Roman wine and accompanied his host in entertaining the gathered guests.

Geraint took his position on the stairs of the room and tested his lyra. Now a favourite of the elite of Lugdunum, he had been hired to provide the entertainment this evening. He had worked hard to be the man in demand. It put him in near constant contact with Mederei and access to all manner of information gleaned from overheard conversations and careful investigation. Still, after all this time, he was no nearer to a plan that would save Rhys's beloved.

He played absently, resorting to wordless tunes from his home, rather than the raucous tales designed to titillate that he usually sang. He missed home this night; the craggy mountains and deep valleys, the long lakes and ancient forests. He missed the moon over the moors in the south and the sound of waves against the firm rock in the north.

"Come now!" Lilius called from the table, pulling Geraint from his musing. "This is a celebration, Bard. Play something lively!"

Geraint smiled and tilted his head. "Of course. Forgive me. My mind had gone a-wandering." In obliging pretence, Geraint's fingers plucked a faster tune. He briefly caught Mederei's gaze. She stared at him, pale and miserable, a thousand questions writ across her melancholic features.

Geraint swallowed past his discomfort and broke into song, singing about a wench stronger than her brothers brought low and conquered by love. It was a favourite amongst this particular crowd. He played for two hours before laying aside his lyra. The guests were all quite drunk now, eagerly awaiting the first course. Mederei had not moved from her seat. Now may be the only time Geraint had to relay the news.

"Bard!" Lilius said loudly as Geraint passed the table.

"Governor!" Geraint replied in kind, bowing in preposterous fashion in order to elicit guffaws from the crowd.

"Have you heard the news?"

Geraint tensed slightly. "I have," he said, letting himself become sombre. In his peripheral vision, he saw Mederei straighten. He offered the governor a small, apologetic smile. "News travels fast between Britons."

"Why then," Lilius said, grinning viciously. "You must be the one to announce it!"

"Pardon?" Geraint blinked.

"Come now, who better to announce than a bard? Announce the news! No doubt our British guests are dying to know."

Geraint swallowed. His gaze flickered to Mederei, who watched him, unblinking. The dining hall fell silent.

"Come on now," one Roman said loudly. "Do not keep us in suspense!"

Geraint took a deep breath. "Surely, as governor—"

"Announce!" Lilius roared.

"Governor, I'm afraid I know none of the details."

"Ah! Then permit me to fill you in!" Lilius stood. "The northern rebels are no more!"

The words hung in the air. Mederei stared at the governor.

"Lies," she whispered. In the silence, it rang across the room. Lilius spun to meet her gaze. He smiled. "Bard!" he barked. "Tell this northern witch what happened!"

"I do not know much," Geraint said softly. "But, as I understand it, Rome made an incursion into the southern edge of the Caledonian Federation."

Mederei stared at him.

"Tell her who they got!" Lilius demanded.

"Lilius," Porcia whispered, her small voice strained. "Please."

"Shut up, girl," Lilius snapped. He smiled at Geraint. "Go on, Bard."

"As I understand it," Geraint said slowly, "Lord Rhys, Prince of the Caledonii and leader of the rebellion, was slain in combat."

Mederei's face paled more as she searched Geraint's eyes, seeking the sparkle of jest. "You're lying," she whispered.

"No," Geraint replied, his voice cracking. "I am not."

"Hah! Hah!" Lilius said, raising his cup of wine. "Cut the head off the snake, and the beast dies! The rebellion is crushed! Rome shall have all of Britain before the month is out, mark my words!" Turning away from Mederei, who still stared at Geraint, he addressed the gathered Romans. "And so this is a night for celebration! The war in Britain is at last ended and Rome is victorious. A toast!"

The Romans in the room raised their cups. Porcia responded only when her father elbowed her sharply, her hand trembling as she lifted her cup. Ambrosius, sitting with Adalbern, did not raise his glass, following the Batavian's lead.

"To Rome, the greatest nation on earth!" Lilius said.

"To Rome!" the revellers answered, and they cheered.

The party resumed, excited chatter filling the room, most of it about the wild highlands of the island of the Britons.

There was no deceit in Geraint's eyes. His words, though spoken gently, cut through her. A single sentence robbed Mederei of her breath. Tears stung her eyes and grief gored her heart. She sat frozen in her chair, staring at Rhys's shield-bearer, hoping for some sign that would ease the sudden pain. No sign came forth and Mederei's world crumbled.

Though she stared at him, Geraint was no longer in her vision. Though the people around her spoke, she heard no words. There was no sound in her ears but the long, high ringing of anguish. Her mind recalled a thousand happy memories of Rhys; his smile, the strength of his embrace, his kind words and passionate kisses. Over these memories lay her imaginings of the walls around her crumbling, revealing a gaping chasm of nothing. Blackness yawned from the void, clawing at her throat with burning talons.

The thunk of the platters of food arriving at her table shattered the images, slamming her back into reality with a start. Unable to cope with the rush of voices and the pressing sorrow, Mederei stood abruptly, turned and fled the dining hall.

Vitus noticed the gladiator's departure and motioned for two guards to follow her. She was still a gladiator and his highest earner, however aggrieved, and he had no intentions of letting her escape.

"Bard!" Lilius, now quite drunk, barked from beside Vitus. "We have need of entertainment! Sing for us!"

Geraint, now free of Mederei's despairing regard, turned slowly to the governor. "Of course," he said softly, grappling with the grief that threatened to rob him of his voice. He walked stiffly to his place on the stairs and sat down. After some adjustments on his lyra strings, he began to play. No one hearing his music that night could guess at the agony of his breaking heart.

Adalbern could not take his eyes off the Woman. She sat stiffly in her chair, staring at the bard, her ashen face a twisted tapestry of denial, grief, and shock. He watched, his heart breaking, as two tears escaped her eyes and made their slow way down her cheeks, unheeded.

The arrival of the food awoke the Briton, and she started. It was not long before sobs threatened to overtake her entirely. She rose and left the room, walking quickly. Downing his drink, Adalbern stood. Unnoticed by anyone save Ambrosius, he followed the guards that had been sent after the gladiator.

It was quieter here. Though the sounds of the night's revels could not be completely shut out, here at least they were reduced to a low hum. Mederei stopped her flight, stepping into the room as if in a dream. She heard her breath come in ragged starts, but felt nothing—not her heartbeat, not her breath, not the feel of fabric against her skin, or the cool of the night through the open windows. There was nothing.

Unaware of her surrounds, Mederei sank slowly onto a lounge, staring numbly at the floor as tears continued their trickle down her cheeks.

She sat in silence a long time, staring into her own thoughts, unknowingly weeping before a soft voice dragged her back into the room.

"Mederei."

Frowning, feeling the voice familiar, yet not recognizing it, Mederei lifted her head. Her gaze met eyes of warm brown, eyes she felt she should know but could not place.

"He is dead," Mederei whispered to those eyes. "He's dead."

The admission destroyed her tenuous grasp on her control. She collapsed inwards, sobs wracking her chest as they fought to free themselves of her torment.

Arms wrapped around her. They were strong and warm, enveloping her in safety. There, shielded from the world for a time, she let her grief take her.

Adalbern said nothing as he held the distraught woman against his chest. She leant into him, pulling herself tightly against him, as if she was trying to bury herself in his chest. He tightened his hold and closed his eyes.

She wept almost an hour before exhaustion claimed her. She relaxed in his embrace as her breathing grew more even. Adalbern held her until he was certain that she was asleep before he laid her gently down on the lounge. Adalbern's tunic was wet with her tears.

"Here," someone said as Adalbern finished fixing Mederei's clothes. He looked up to find the bard holding a blanket out to him.

"Thank you," Adalbern said. He took the blanket and spread it over Mederei. Satisfied that the night chill would not harm her, he stepped away and regarded the bard more fully.

"I am Adalbern," he said, extending his hand to the man. "I have seen you play often."

"Aetius and my patron are good friends, it seems."

Shrugging, Adalbern said, "I doubt Aetius has friends. He has connections; a different animal altogether."

The bard smiled. "I suspect you are correct. My name is Geraint."

"British then?"

Geraint nodded. His eyes drifted to the sleeping form of Mederei on the lounge. "From the south," he said absently. He returned his attention to the Batavian standing before him. "Aetius sent me to fetch you. His children, as I understand it, are being unruly and he thinks you can set them right."

"It's not his children that are wrong," Adalbern growled. He looked down at Mederei.

"I will watch her," Geraint said. "There are other entertainers at present, and I have the time. There are guards at the door," he added. "And Vitus is protective of his only female gladiator. Were I inclined to harm her, I could not."

Adalbern nodded. "Thank you," he said simply before moving off.

Geraint watched his retreating back thoughtfully before turning to Mederei. He walked to a chair, pulled it close to Mederei's side, and sat down.

The dining room was raucous with rough laughter and loud chatter when Adalbern returned. Ambrosius and Porcia, however, were nowhere in the room.

"Ah! Batavian!" Aetius said, beckoning Adalbern to him with wide, slightly wild motions. Adalbern obliged, crossing the distance in a few easy strides of his long legs.

"Aetius," he said by way of greeting as he arrived at the table.

"My daughter and her brother have left dinner. Find them and bring them back, will you?"

"Why did they leave?" Adalbern asked.

"You know how women get," Lilius interjected. "Hysterical creatures. It was a cruel joke indeed that they were made necessary for breeding."

Adalbern turned to the portly governor, his brown eyes growing hard. He pursed his lips in distaste before turning and stalking from the room in search of Aetius's children.

It did not take much searching. Sobbing from the gardens drew Adalbern outside. He found Porcia and Ambrosius under a struggling poplar, Porcia's face in her hands as she sobbed. Ambrosius looked up from his sister with a frown, his expression relaxing when he recognized the interloper.

"What happened?" Adalbern asked softly, coming to kneel before Porcia. At the question, the distraught girl let out a soft wail and sobbed harder.

"Lilius has arranged a games to celebrate Rome's recent victory in Britain. A re-enactment."

"Of the defeat in the north." It was not a question. Adalbern knew it immediately.

Ambrosius nodded. "Lilius means for the Woman to fight." He grimaced and said, "The British forces were slain to the last man."

Understanding flooded Adalbern and he closed his eyes and gritted his teeth in an effort to control the sudden swelling of grief and anger.

"Mederei will be killed," Porcia wailed from behind her hands.

Adalbern looked at her. "We don't know that," he said softly.

"How could it be otherwise?" Porcia demanded, taking her hands away from her face to hiss her words in anger.

"Mederei is a strong woman," Adalbern said. "And she is clever. Things do not always go as they plan in the arena, even if Rome plans them."

"And what if she does?" Porcia whispered. "There are so few joys in this life for a woman. Lilius would take away the one I have found." She shuddered and started sobbing again. "I cannot marry that man," she said between breaths, burrowing her face in her hands once more. Ambrosius wrapped his arms around his sister.

"You won't have to," he whispered fiercely. "We'll find a way to free you from him." Tears slid down his face. "I promise."

Adalbern's heart sank. He could not fathom a way for Porcia to avoid her coming marriage. Rome left no room for its women to do anything but obey. There was no escaping her fate. Not for Porcia. Not for Mederei.

"Rome swallows all light," Adalbern mused aloud. He sighed and settled on the grass beside the grieving siblings.

"I'll find a way," Ambrosius whispered to his sister.

"How?" Porcia wailed.

"We could run away," Ambrosius said. "Together. Flee Rome."

"Where would you go?" Adalbern asked, repeating the question he had asked some months ago. "Where can you go that Rome will not find you?"

Ambrosius scowled at him. "Britain," he said suddenly. Porcia stopped crying and looked up at her brother, her sad eyes now lit with curiosity.

"You are Roman," Adalbern said. "You will be killed on sight, if you make it at all."

"Rome has conquered Britain," Porcia whispered.

"Not all of it," Ambrosius said. "Not the north. Not yet."

"You heard Lilius," Porcia said. "The resistance is dead."

"You don't really believe that, do you?" Ambrosius asked his sister. "One man is dead. How many men has the north lost, and yet they still fought. You know a Briton. Do you think she would stop fighting Rome?"

"She is a captive of Rome," Porcia said.

"And yet she walks as a queen," Ambrosius answered. "I don't believe Britain will ever be conquered. And I've heard stories of their women. I've heard that they can choose their own husbands. And they can divorce them, too."

"Those are just stories, Ambrosius."

"They're not," Adalbern said. The siblings turned to him. "The same laws were true of northern Gaul. The Belgians still cleave to the old laws."

Porcia's tears ceased their flow as she stared at Adalbern, hope widening her eyes and lifting the corners of her mouth.

"That's right," Ambrosius said, nodding. "We can flee to northern Britain."

Porcia turned to her brother. "How?"

"We can figure that out later," he answered. "Right now, we must resolve to do it. Will you, Porcia? Will you run away with me?"

"What if father finds out? What if we are caught?"

"What if he doesn't? What if we aren't?"

Porcia smiled. She reached out and touched her brother's cheek. "You are a good brother, Ambrosius," she said. "I have one stipulation."

Ambrosius raised his brows at his sister.

"We take Mederei with us."

Adalbern, sitting on the edge of the conversation, blinked, looking sharply at Porcia.

"She is my friend, Am," she said. "I cannot flee to her home and leave her behind."

Ambrosius smiled and nodded. "You ask the impossible, Porcia. But we'll find a way."

Porcia threw herself around her brother, hugging him close. "Thank you," she whispered.

"Your father expects you both back at dinner," Adalbern said.

Porcia turned to him and nodded. She wiped the tears from her eyes. Still cleaving to her brother, she rose to her feet and tried to make herself presentable. Together, the three of them walked slowly back towards the dining room. Adalbern wandered unhurriedly behind the siblings, his eyes downcast as his mind fluttered with strange ideas.

"Adalbern," Ambrosius said as they reached the edge of the garden. "Swear you will utter not one word of this to anyone. Please."

Adalbern raised his eyes to meet those of the Roman youth before him. Ambrosius's face was earnest, his eyes fierce with resolve. Adalbern scowled.

"Please," Ambrosius repeated.

"Not a word," Adalbern answered. "I swear." He paused. "I hope you succeed, Ambrosius," he said quietly. "I truly do."

Ambrosius smiled tightly at Adalbern before turning and escorting his sister back to their table. Adalbern paused at the threshold, staring into the loud room as if it wasn't quite real. His mind whirled.

Mederei free.

He could see it in his mind's eye; her, standing on the edge of a craggy hill, a sword in her hand. In his heart, he wished he could stand beside her.

Mederei sat quietly in her garden in front of the ludus, staring blankly at the bars that kept her in. Beside her, untouched, sat a bowl of barley gruel, and a large hunk of pork. As Vitus's most prized attraction, she was well fed. Today, however, she found she could not eat. Her stomach sat low in her gut, kept down by a heavy heart.

Rhys was dead. Her betrothed. Leader of the British resistance.

It was all she could think about since hearing the news two nights ago. She found, however, after the initial shock of the news, she could shed no tears. Should she not be distraught? Instead, she felt nothing.

"Eat your food, Woman," Izem said from his side of the ludus gardens.

"Why?" Mederei answered. She did not speak loudly. She did not need to.

"You must keep strong."

"Why?"

Izem grumbled and walked away from the bars. He did not have a good answer. He had been trying to convince her for a day and a half to eat. Always she answered with "Why?" And what did Izem have in reply? "Or else you will die." But that was the only reason she now lived. She was a gladiator, sentenced to death. What did it matter if she died in the arena from a sword in her guts or in the ludus from starvation?

"Because you will need it for the upcoming games," Vitus growled from behind Mederei.

Mederei turned dull eyes to him. She did not rise. She remained on the ground, staring up at Vitus with a lifeless gaze. She frowned slightly.

"Eat. I have something to discuss with my Britons."

Mederei did not move.

"Eat, or I will shove this food down your gullet," Vitus snapped.

Very slowly, Mederei reached for the bowl of food. She pulled it into her lap and stared down at it. Painfully languid, she lifted the pork to her lips and took a small bite. It took some work to get the meat past her closed throat. Forcing herself, despite her protesting body, Mederei ate everything. Vitus stood guard over her, ensuring her bowl was empty before stomping away. Still moving slowly, Mederei rose and floated behind him, walking without paying any mind to anything but the heavy emptiness that filled her.

They did not walk long. Vitus stopped in the shade near the fighting platform. Gandwy was there already, patiently waiting as he had been told to do.

"Britons," Vitus said curtly. "There is to be a games to celebrate the recent Roman victory." Vitus glanced briefly at Mederei, but she did not appear to have heard.

"Lilius has commissioned me to design a games re-enacting the events in northern Britain." Again, Vitus looked to Mederei.

"He and I are leaving for Juliobona to acquire more British slaves. As my most senior British gladiators, you will be in charge of the fight in the arena. Gandwy, you are to play the part of the slain resistance leader." Another glance at Mederei revealed nothing. Gandwy, however, quailed momentarily before drawing himself up.

"Rhys," Mederei said.

Vitus looked at her. "Pardon?"

"His name was Rhys ap Brennus, Chieftain of the Caledonii, Lord of the Federation." Mederei turned to Vitus, her eyes blazing so fiercely he found himself rooted to the spot, robbed of his voice. Mederei turned away again, resuming her air of dreamy disinterest.

Vitus looked down at the ground briefly before sighing and lifting his head. "This is not how I might have chosen to end it, but we all must die someday. Play your parts well and honour those you portray. I will be back in a month or so."

With little left to say, Vitus turned and walked from the training ground. Mederei did not acknowledge his departure. She stood, her head turned towards the grounds where gladiators wandered. Gandwy stepped forward, coming to her side.

"You knew him? The leader of the resistance?"

"Yes," Mederei said softly. "I knew him very well indeed." She turned and faced Gandwy. "I will not let you die this fight," she said. "If it is Rhys you are to play, the lord of free Britain you shall be. I could not save him. I will not fail you."

Gandwy could find no answer. He watched Mederei as she walked back to her garden. In voice and bearing, she seemed not a slave from the north, but a queen of the south. The queen of the south. Gandwy's eyes narrowed as the sun caught her hair and, for a brief moment, it flamed red.

"Hello, Bard."

Geraint looked up in surprise to find a familiar-looking Roman youth addressing him as he sat by the well near the marketplace. He frowned. "Ambrosius, correct? The son of Aetius the merchant."

"The same," Ambrosius said, giving a small, mocking bow. Geraint stood from his seat at the edge of the well. He laid aside his lyra, which he had been practicing, and extended a hand to the youth.

Taking it, Ambrosius smiled slightly. "May I ask you a personal question, Bard?"

"Only if you promise to refer to me by name, master Ambrosius. I am Geraint."

"What are your feelings towards the Woman, Geraint?"

Geraint blinked. "The female gladiator?"

"Yes."

"That is an unusual question. I like her well enough. She is clever and brave, and I have spoken to her some. When she is in a good mood, she can be very agreeable. Why do you want to know?"

Ambrosius shrugged. "Do you believe Lilius, Geraint? Do you believe the British resistance has been quashed? Has the north been subdued?"

Unsure what to make of these questions, Geraint rubbed the side of his jaw. He sighed. "I think you know your answer already," he said. "Have you ever been to the highlands of Britain?"

"No."

"It is a craggy place, filled with rocky mountains and deep valleys. It has lakes that would take a day to travel the length of, and much of it is covered in ancient forests. It is a wild place. Its people are just as wild. No, master Ambrosius. I do not believe the governor. Rome could slay every man there, and its women would throw them down. So long as there lives but one Briton in that place, the north will never be subdued."

"Are there many places to hide?"

"To what do these questions tend?"

"Nothing," Ambrosius said with a shrug. "So, are there?"

"Places to hide? Certainly. There are many caves. Some are even in use. And there are tribes there who have made the forests their home, eschewing towns and cities entirely. No Roman legion marching through the northern woods would make it out again." Geraint watched the boy carefully, noting the slight tics that indicated the boy was pleased by this information. What was he planning?

"Ambrosius!" the younger of Aetius's two children called, her voice high and sweet. "Father is looking for you!"

Her voice turned the heads of both Geraint and Ambrosius. Geraint noted the large Batavian hostage standing a few steps behind her, and the private guards who accompanied both him and the girl. A small seed of suspicion formed in the back of Geraint's mind, a hint at the boy's plans. Geraint made note of it and filed it away. He would find out more about this boy and his sister. And the Batavian for that matter. Perhaps he could learn something that could leverage their aid. Geraint was sore over the death of his beloved lord, and was not above blackmail.

In Vitus's absence, Izem took on the responsibility of training the gladiators. He took this charge very seriously.

"You must move your feet!" he called as Mederei and Gandwy circled each other with their wooden weapons. "Do you want to die?"

Gandwy's lips twisted in a dry smile, matched by his opponent. "We aren't supposed to live," Gandwy muttered.

Mederei lunged forward, forcing Gandwy back and to the side. Recovered from the onslaught, he returned the blows and soon they were sparring. Izem shook his head. They were not truly fighting, but playing, none of their strikes aiming to hit the right places.

"This is not a game!" Izem snapped.

The pair stopped. "They call it 'the games'," Mederei pointed out, making Gandwy grin.

Izem stared at her a moment before his temper bested him. He leapt up on the platform, snatched Gandwy's training sword from him and attacked Mederei. The playfulness in Mederei vanished under Izem's onslaught. His intent was clear—to hurt. Mederei skipped sideways to escape and struck down. Her sword missed by quite a margin as his fast feet carried him far from harm.

The fight lasted only fifteen minutes. Mederei's eyes flashed dangerously as she pressed the wooden sword edge against Izem's throat.

"Look down," he demanded.

Mederei did, and found his sword pressed lightly against her hard leather breastplate.

"You fight well," Izem said. "But you must keep your mind on the task, or you will die."

"We are supposed to die," Mederei answered. "The British hunting party was slain to the last man."

Izem straightened and let his sword drop. Mederei followed suit.

"But you have a plan, yes?" he asked.

Mederei smiled slightly. "Yes," she said quietly. "We have a plan."

"Good. Now it's time for food. Go."

Mederei and Gandwy jumped down from the platform and made their slow way to the already-forming line for food.

## 71 AD, SPRING, LUGDUNUM, PROVINCE OF GAUL

Mederei turned her gaze up to the rough stone ceiling of the holding cell where the contingent of British gladiators waited. The dull drone of an excited crowd echoed in the small space. Beside her, Gandwy sat still as a stone, pale and grim. This was to be his moment; his gory death for the purposes of Roman entertainment.

"Hello," a soft voice said from the barred door. Mederei turned. Geraint stood at the bars, looking miserable. Mederei lifted herself away from the wall against which she leant and walked to him.

"Hello, Bard," she said softly, offering him a smile. Geraint tried to return it, but failed.

"Forgive the lateness of this visit," he murmured. "Though I tried, I could not come sooner."

"It's all right, Geraint," Mederei answered. "It's all right."

Geraint took a deep breath. "There is something you should know before you go to this fight."

Outside, the crowd exploded into loud cheers, distracting Geraint momentarily.

"You'll be headed to the arena soon," one of the guards at the barred door said gruffly. Mederei nodded at him. She turned back to Geraint.

"Say it quickly, Bard."

Geraint flickered a small smile. Even now, though certain death lay only a few moments away, Mederei continued her pretence of knowing him only as a southern British bard she met here in Lugdunum.

"I have heard it said," Geraint said, trying to sound as if he did not know it for fact, "that British resistance is not dead. Calgacus lives, and he has taken his brother's mantle as lord of the Caledonii—"

"All right," the guard said. "Time to go."

"The north is still free," Geraint blurted as one guard pushed him aside to unlock the cell holding the gladiators, and another grabbed his shoulder.

"Come on then," the guard said in a kindly voice. "Visiting time is over."

Geraint obliged. He stepped back to permit room for the gladiators to exit the cell. He watched, helpless to act, as Mederei led the Britons to the arena doors. He closed his eyes, sending a forceful prayer to whatever god may hear.

*Keep your daughter safe.*

Mederei stopped at the large doors to the arena. They remained resolutely shut, but did nothing to dull the sound of the crowds outside.

"Mederei," Gandwy whispered from behind her. "I must ask you something."

"After the fight," Mederei answered.

"There will not be an after," Gandwy said. "We both know that."

"I swore I would keep you safe, Gandwy," Mederei replied. "And I will. Ask me after the fight."

"Now you have to live," a short man said from beside Gandwy. "If only to have the chance to ask. Typical woman." He sniffed. "Spitefully giving you reason to live."

Mederei smiled. "Hush," she chided the man. "Don't give away all our secrets."

Grunting a small laugh, the man said, "For the record, I am a farmer. I cannot fight."

"You are British," Mederei murmured. "Trust that if nothing else."

The man grunted.

"What is your name, farmer?"

"Pertacus."

"Pertacus," Mederei said. "I have a plan, which I will share when I get a feel for how they've made the arena. I need you to swear you will follow it to the letter."

Pertacus shrugged. "I have no plan, so I will follow yours."

"I thank you for your courage," she said, turning to him. She smiled at the grey-haired man with thick forearms.

"I am British," he answered. "Anything I can do to embarrass these Roman dogs, I will do."

"Good."

The crowd roared again, this time in response to the dramatists' introduction. The doors swung open and Mederei walked boldly forward, Gandwy at her side.

Adalbern straightened in his seat behind Aetius's children as Mederei and the small contingent of newly acquired Britons walked into the arena. Most of those in the small group were not fighters, he knew. This was designed to be a slaughter. The only reason real fighters were included was to make it a least a little interesting to the roaring crowd.

Mederei walked tall, her head held high. She paused briefly and surveyed the arena. A large number of small trees and shrubs stood in pots to one side, meant to represent the forests of the highland, no doubt.

Large rocks had also been brought in. They looked constructed rather than natural boulders.

From his seat, Adalbern could see the twenty hidden gladiators awaiting the hapless six Britons. They were dressed as Roman soldiers, and were as disciplined. Fighters, every one. His skin pimpled as fear coated it in sweat, the sweat turned cold by the still chilly spring breeze. A small movement from Ambrosius in the seat in front of him drew his attention away momentarily. The Roman youth had reached out to take his sister's violently trembling hand.

The Batavian swallowed hard and turned his attention back to the arena, hoping that by the sheer force of his faith, Mederei would survive the coming slaughter.

Mederei took stock of the layout quickly.

"All right," she said, turning back to the group. Of the five who stood before her, only Gandwy and the farmer Pertacus stood tall. "This is what we do."

The crowd fell silent. Tense anticipation of the coming ambush clamped their mouths shut as it beat a frantic rhythm in their chests. Adalbern was not immune to this anticipation, but he did not find it entertaining. In his hand, he gripped a strip of white cloth. So tightly did he clench that fabric that his fingernails dug into his palms. He did not feel the pain.

Ignoring the whispered prayers of the Britons behind her, Mederei walked carefully before the group. The enemy would likely come at the Britons from either side of the arena; from both the rocks and the potted trees. Behind her, Gandwy matched her step.

A chance glance down stopped Mederei's next step from landing. Buried in the sand just beneath her foot was a rope lasso. She followed the slight rise in the sand that snaked its way back to the line of trees.

"Gandwy?"

"Yes?"

"Ready your sword. I'm about to fish."

Before Gandwy had a chance to ask what she meant, Mederei bent down and snatched up the rope. In a swift move, she wrapped a portion of the rope around her arm and yanked hard.

A young gladiator in a Roman uniform flew forward, knocking over two potted shrubs as he did. Before the rest of the opposing gladiators had a chance to react, Gandwy ran forward, gladius in hand. The youth's throat was slit and Gandwy was back with the rest of the Britons before anyone had moved.

He smiled slightly at Mederei as he resumed his position.

"Your ambush has been discovered," Mederei said in Latin.

Porcia gasped as Mederei, swift as a serpent, flushed one gladiator out of hiding and her fellow Briton slit his throat. The crowd around the arena remained dead silent, their anticipation now mixed with shock. The gladiators dressed as Roman soldiers shuffled in their hiding places, unsure of what to do now.

"Clever little witch," Porcia heard Lilius mutter.

She smiled, her aching heart thrilling with a glimmer of hope. She tightened her grip on her brother's hand.

Waiting patiently, Mederei scanned the sandy floor of the arena for more traps. She could see none, but did hear, in the aching silence of the arena the snort and stamp of an impatient horse behind the other door.

"They have a charioteer waiting," Mederei whispered to Gandwy.

Gandwy nodded, but did not reply.

"Stand and be counted, Roman cowards," Mederei said, loudly this time so that those sitting in the podium would be able to hear her clearly. "And learn why you will never rule Britain."

Slowly, unsure, one hiding gladiator stood. "Might as well," he said so his fellows could hear. "We outnumber them some three to one."

Another stood. Then another. Then another. Then, as if commanded, they all stood.

Mederei swept the arena with her sharp gaze. They faced a force of nineteen gladiators, all of them fighters.

"Gods," one Briton quailed.

"Hush!" Mederei snapped at him. "Do as I say and you may live."

"So," Pertacus said, his grim expression contrasting with the cheer in his voice. "Four to one."

"They need it," Mederei answered. Pertacus burst out laughing.

The crowd stared at the laughing Briton, their expressions almost identical in their surprise. In the silence of the arena, his laughter sounded like a madman's glee. Many of the Gauls could not contain their chuckle when the man said loudly for all to hear, "I like you, Woman." Those in the audience who did not speak Gaulish, or its sister tongue—British—stared at their companions, uncomprehending.

The Briton resumed his raucous laughter, even doubling over with the force of his mirth. Then, he walked boldly forward and addressed the rival gladiators.

"Are you going to fight or not?"

This woke the crowd out of their stunned stupor. In a sudden roar, they leapt to life, bellowing their support for the Britons.

How quickly a crowd could turn, Adalbern mused. Before the speeches of the dramatists that preceded this fight, they had booed the Britons, condemning them as slovenly cowards who hid in the northern reaches of the island, too scared to confront Rome. Now, they screamed their support for them.

Adalbern leant forward, resting his lips against his knuckles in an attempt to hide his mirthless smile. Now, should the fight go to a decision, Lilius would have to let the Britons live, lest the crowd riot. His smile vanished as the opposing gladiators rushed forward.

"Now!" Mederei screamed. The cluster of Britons split, each sprinting in a different direction. The rushing gladiators unthinkingly followed suit. Of the six, only Mederei, Gandwy, and the laughing madman engaged their opponents. Mederei hacked off the sword arm of her first gladiator, spun around over his back to kick another in the face. The man dropped to the ground, his helmet flying. She was fighting her third gladiator before her feet even touched the ground.

Gandwy knocked the first gladiator he encountered back several steps. They clashed shields. Gandwy was larger and stronger, and the man slid backwards. His right leg was gone below the knee before he had a chance to recover. He screamed and toppled over as Gandwy slid past the second gladiator, sliding in the loose sand and slashing out with his gladius as he did so. His opponent jumped just in time to avoid having his foot taken off, spinning as he leapt. He landed on his feet and regained his balance. By that time, however, Gandwy had sprinted well out of reach and was dancing around his third gladiator.

Pertacus was nowhere near as skilled, yet he managed to hold off. Though none of the gladiators he had encountered had suffered any harm, they were unable to harm him. His instinct with a shield was good, even if his skills with a sword were not. And he was clever, using the terrain to his advantage to evade the gladiators trying to strike him down.

The other three were far less methodical than Pertacus. They ran blindly, sheer luck or animal instinct the only reason they yet lived.

Adalbern's eyes remained fixed on Mederei. She had elected not to use a shield at all, instead opting for two gladii. The swords flashed faster than Adalbern had ever seen as she danced around her opponents. Like Pertacus, she used the terrain well, vanishing amongst the potted shrubs and luring her two remaining attackers in. They did not live long after that. She emerged again, pausing only a moment to find Gandwy. Hard pressed against two gladiators simultaneously, Gandwy had no way to escape to the boulders as had been the plan. Mederei sprinted forward.

The crowd roared as she leapt, driving one gladius straight through the neck of one of Gandwy's attackers. The momentum slammed them both into Gandwy's other opponent, knocking him off his feet. Gandwy dispatched him and the man's head rolled in the sand. Now free, both Mederei and Gandwy ran to the aid of Pertacus, who was cornered.

The fight became four on three, and Pertacus was free to run again as Gandwy and Mederei drew off three of the attackers. Again splitting up to force the three they faced to divide, Gandwy and Mederei sprinted to the other end of the arena, taking some of the gladiators there by surprise, and relieving the other Britons some.

Their fight looked little more than the frantic flight of hares. They darted this way and that, engaging their opponents briefly. If their opponents could not be killed in three or four moves, they took off running again.

The frustration of the gladiators the Britons fought was palpable. And they were tiring fast.

The armour of the Roman soldier was designed to keep them safe, but it was heavy and hot. Vitus, in accordance with Lilius's wishes, had not equipped his Britons with anything more than leather breastplates.

The British had managed to use this to their advantage, falling to quick strikes and much running. Their opponents were necessarily slower, the weight of their protection proving to be a disadvantage. Adalbern's smile widened, though he kept it behind his knuckles.

The crowd bellowed its approval as Gandwy lopped the head of the last standing gladiator. The fight, however, was not over.

"With me!" Mederei screamed. She ran over to a boulder and threw her shoulder against it. Realizing immediately what she hoped to achieve,

Gandwy ran to her aid. He ignored the fiery pain in his wounded shoulder as he slid his sword in his belt and pressed both palms against the rock.

The rest of the Britons followed suit, save for one, who collapsed under the gravity of her wounds. She would not rise again.

"Wait for it," Mederei said. The sound of a heavy bar sliding from the inside of the second door to the arena echoed surprisingly loud. "Now!"

As one, the Britons pushed against the fake rock. It slid across the ground. They pushed at a run, straight for the doors. They swung open, and a charioteer urged his horses forward. They left at a gallop, and were met with boulder at their hooves. Unable to pull away from their yoke, the horses leapt. The chariot's axle hit the rock, and the whole thing flipped sideways, throwing the charioteer and the archer from the carriage. Stuck in their harnesses, both horses fell. One broke its leg and squealed horrifically.

Mederei and Pertacus were on the charioteers in a flash. Mederei slew the archer and snatched up the bow and quiver. Pertacus took up what javelins he could before more gladiators dressed as Roman soldiers poured through the open door.

They were met with death and chaos. Mederei expertly picked off the soldiers from the left as they ran forward, and Pertacus's aim was true with his javelins. He skewered four before he ran out of ammunition and retreated to collect his sword and shield.

"Into the woods!" Mederei barked. The five remaining Britons ran into the mock forest that had been set up to conceal the ambush, Mederei retreating more slowly, firing arrows as she did.

Twenty more soldiers had rushed through the door. Of them, there remained only eight by the time Mederei entered the faux woods.

The crowd cheered as the new gladiators fanned out, straining to see where the Britons had hidden themselves. Elevated as they were, the spectators could see precisely where the Britons were. They were far closer to the edge of the potted plants than their opponents could guess.

Mederei looked over at Gandwy. His arm bled heavily and his face had turned ashen. Nevertheless, the resolve in his steely eyes remained firm. He nodded back at her. She mouthed her count. On three, the pair rushed forward, crashing bodily into two of the gladiators, who had lifted their shields to protect themselves. Mederei crashed into her target at an angle, spinning the poor man sideways with the force of the blow, then sliding her sword edge across his newly exposed throat. Gandwy had lifted his opponent, throwing him over, and stabbing down as the man fell face first onto the ground.

Then they were gone, sprinting for the boulders and finding new places to hide. The movement had distracted the other gladiators. They turned to try and see what was happening and a third one had his head lopped off by Pertacus as he sprinted past to join Gandwy and Mederei hiding in the boulders.

They were now five on five.

Scared, the remaining gladiators playing the part of Roman soldiers clustered together in a circle so as to keep watch over both sides of the arena. For a while, nothing happened as Mederei considered how to break their circle. Above her head, the crowd bellowed. She turned to look up at them and smiled. Turning back to the waiting circle of gladiators, Mederei stood.

Adalbern swallowed past the sudden lump in his throat as he watched Mederei stand to face the five fighters in the centre of the arena. The crowd's volume rose to impossible levels as she strode forward.

The five men shuffled back slightly as she approached. She stopped at the edge of the rocks and lifted one gladius to point at one of the five. A challenge. The crowd reached a new volume. Adalbern winced.

"Yield," Mederei demanded of the man at whom she pointed.

"Die!" the man spat. He broke the circle, sprinting forward.

The engagement proved longer than optimal for Mederei. The gladiator was skilled and relatively fresh. Mederei's arms ached with the effort of gripping her swords. They slipped regardless, the hilts slick with blood. The combatants paused in fighting a moment.

The crowd had quietened again, watching the fight with baited breath. Apparently having forgotten their task, the remaining gladiators also watched the fight.

"Should we not go to her aid?" Pertacus whispered to Gandwy.

Gandwy shook his head. "Only if she gets into trouble. She can hold her own, and her pride is fearsome. I would not want to earn her ire."

Pertacus grinned at Gandwy and shifted his weight.

"Do you know why I became a gladiator?" Mederei's opponent demanded, his Latin perfect. "I raped a girl. She looked just like you."

His intent had been to unsettle Mederei. Instead, ice cold control flooded her and she prepared to engage him again, her lips twisting upwards in a mirthless smile. "Do you know why I was made a gladiator?" she answered before leaping forward.

They clashed again, the force of Mederei's advance catching her opponent unprepared. He never quite recovered. Mederei's speed had him on the defensive. He did not turn in time as she danced around him. A quick stab and Mederei buried her gladius to the hilt in the man's back, square between his shoulder blades. He looked down in surprise at the blade sticking out of his chest.

Mederei leant in and whispered in his ear, "I killed Romans." She twisted the blade and withdrew it. The man fell forward.

The four remaining Roman gladiators stared wide-eyed as the man fell. Their gazes shifted up to Mederei, who glared fiercely at them. They took a collective breath and charged, screaming.

"Now we help her," Gandwy said. Despite his wounds, he launched himself upright, sprinting for the back of the group, Pertacus following suit.

Mederei noted with satisfaction that Gandwy and Pertacus had rejoined the fray. They had understood the need to break the circle in order to finish the fight, and were patient enough to permit her to do it. Gandwy slew one gladiator, who had not seen the Briton run up behind him. The others were not so easily caught unaware. Two gladiators disengaged from Mederei to meet Gandwy and Pertacus.

Mederei's lungs burned as she forced her feet to move. She was quickly losing steam, and her opponent could see it. He pressed his attack, forcing Mederei backwards. Her muscles ceased to respond properly to her commands, and her sword swings became wild. She needed some space. She dove sideways before her back could hit the arena wall, tumbling and rising to her feet. Shaking the stiffness from her arms she crouched low, prepared for the oncoming attack mere seconds before it came. Once again, the two fought, circling around each other like wolves.

There was little Mederei could do. She was too tired now for aggression, so she adopted a different strategy. The gladiator before her would tire, or get frustrated. Either way, he would err. Frustration took the gladiator first. He tried to rush and slash at the same time, opening his throat to the edge of Mederei's blade. Like a snake, she stepped under his slashing arm and drove the point of one of her blades up into his jaw, piercing his brain through. She yanked hard, drawing her sword free and forcing the body to fly forward a little.

Rising and turning, Mederei straightened in time to see Pertacus pierced through.

"No!" she screamed. She sprinted forward and leapt.

The gladiator smirked as he watched the Briton slide off his gladius. The smile vanished as the sinking of one British body revealed the flying of another. The gladiator had no time to react as the points of two blades plunged into his chest. Surprisingly, he felt the force of the British woman's knees more as they struck his stomach. He flew backwards, the twisted features of the fearsome woman the last thing he saw before his body hit the ground.

Gandwy watched dispassionately as the head of his opponent went flying. How many heads was that now? If he was back home in Britain, he'd need a great deal of pine oil for his trophies. The thought made him smirk. He turned to find Mederei kneeling, holding the farmer, Pertacus.

A thick cough sent pain shivering through his entire being. He felt gentle hands lift his head, strong arms cradling him. He smiled and opened his eyes. Mederei stared down at him, tears threatening to break free from the prison of her lashes.

"Shhhh," Pertacus soothed. "It's all right. It will be all right."

"Brave Pertacus," Mederei answered, offering him a small smile. "Forgive me. I was too slow to save you."

"Do not fret." Pertacus felt himself fading fast. "I die today fighting for my queen. There is no greater honour for a man of the Magni Ceni."

He noted the surprise on Mederei's face and laughed, regretting the pain that wracked his being even as his shoulders jumped with mirth. "Did you think you could fool me, hm?" he rasped. He reached up, feebly wiping away a tear that now made its way down Mederei's blood-splattered cheek.

He smiled. "You look just like her."

Then there was nothing.

Mederei lowered Pertacus's limp body to the ground. Working slowly, she laid his body out.

"Gandwy," she whispered. "His sword."

Moved to action, Gandwy turned and scanned the sand around Pertacus and Mederei, searching for the man's sword. He retrieved it and walked over. "Here," he said gently, offering the blade hilt first.

"Thank you," Mederei answered. She laid the weapon on the dead man's chest, moving his hands so that they clasped it there. Closing his eyes with one hand, Mederei leant over and kissed his brow.

"You will find your rest on the Island of Champions," she whispered to him. "My brave countryman."

Then she stood, snatching up one of her blades as she did so. She walked forward and leapt onto one of the constructed boulders, facing the podium, where sat Governor Lilius. Looking at him, she spoke boldly in Latin so that the entire arena would hear.

"Rome does not have the north," she said. "Rome will never have the north." She switched to her native tongue. Raising her bloodied blade high she roared, "Britain forever!"

Governor Lilius stared in disbelief at the arena. Forty gladiators, and one charioteer and chariot archer had been slain. Forty-two trained warriors taken down by the band of six Britons that should have died this day. The rest of the audience were similarly struck. Silence louder than thunder echoed in the arena as Lilius's eyes followed the figure of the Woman, the Briton he increasingly detested, as she rose from beside her dead companion, strode forward and leapt onto one of the carefully crafted boulders.

"Rome does not have the north," she barked. "Rome will never have the north." Then, "Prydein am byth!"

Adalbern leant back in his chair, relief so profound it made his head spin and threatened a fainting spell as the crowd erupted at the Woman's declaration of British defiance. The Gauls especially seemed to approve her direct challenge to the governor of their city. They repeated various versions of the Briton's sentiment; Gaul forever! The Parisii forever! The Sequani forever! They chanted, pounding their feet on the stone ground, and clapping their hands in rhythm.

The noise barely reached Adalbern's ears. Numbed by the protracted stress of the fight and its sudden release, the Batavian had only eyes for the woman standing boldly on the rock, challenging all of Rome.

His singular focus changed as Lilius lifted himself from his seat, drawing everyone's attention. Adalbern held his breath. Lilius would decide on the fate of the Britons now.

Mederei let her sword arm drop as the sudden cheering flooded the arena. She remained standing on the rock, her blazing eyes fixed upon the governor, mocking in their audacity. She heard the arena doors open and the rhythmic march of a Roman guard enter. Her eyes did not waver from the governor's face as the chanting in the crowd began to coalesce into an organized demand.

"Live! Live! Live!" the crowd chanted. Their chanting did not abate when the governor stuck out his hand, his fingers curled into a fist, his thumb sticking out.

Adrenaline rushed through her as the governor held out his hand. It felt to her like an age before he gave the signal. He turned his thumb down.

Swords down.

Mederei would live another day.

The crowd cheered wildly.

Permitting herself the barest of smiles, Mederei tossed her sword onto the sand at the foot of the podium and leapt from the rock. Only when she landed did she realize the extent of her wounds. A deep cut at her hip made movement awkward. She had two gashes on her left arm, the one at her shoulder still bleeding. A cut cheek, the skin split by the impact of a shield, started throbbing wildly now the fight was over. A turn of her head revealed a painful sword slice across the back of her neck. She winced as she hobbled past Gandwy. Nevertheless, she led the Britons out just as she had led them in, her head held high.

Porcia could not contain her glee as she watched Mederei escorted out of the arena by the guard. She grinned over at her brother, who smiled gladly in return.

"Forty-two!" Didacus of Alesia exclaimed. Porcia looked over at the man as he blustered.

"Forty-two of my prized fighters!"

"Don't be dramatic," Vitus replied to his fellow master. "Hardly your prized fighters. Perhaps next time, you won't be so swift to dismiss my woman."

"Indeed," Didacus muttered. "This has been a costly fight. I have made barely enough in their price to replace them all."

"Ah," Vitus said. "But you have made enough. I also expect you to honour our bet."

"You bet the Woman would win?" Porcia asked before a stern glance by both Lilius and Aetius clamped her mouth shut.

"Only a small amount," Vitus replied with a broad smile. "I did not expect to do anything but lose today."

Didacus continued his spluttering.

"Come now," Vitus said, clapping the man on his shoulder with a good-natured smile. "Just think. Fewer mouths to feed on the long march home."

"It seems, Vitus," Lilius mused, "that we have all underestimated your British woman."

Vitus merely grinned.

"We shall have to do something spectacular when Creon arrives from Rome to fight next year."

"I have no doubt, Governor," Vitus said, "that your prodigious imagination will conceive something appropriate." He turned to Aetius. "I would borrow your Batavian hostage again, if you'll permit it Aetius."

Aetius grunted. "Why?"

"He's a fine healer, familiar with the barbaric remedies that the Woman seems to prefer. Naturally, the work will be compensated."

"Very well," Aetius said, waving dismissively at Adalbern without so much as turning around to face him. "Ensure he's under guard at all times."

"Come now, Aetius," Vitus said with a smile. "He has been nothing but an ideal hostage, by all accounts."

Aetius merely grunted a second time.

"May I also go, Father?" Porcia asked.

"No," he and Lilius replied sharply and in perfect unison. Porcia slumped back in her chair.

"You will see her at the party tomorrow evening," Lilius said smoothly, though he found it impossible to hide his disdain.

"Of course," Porcia whispered.

Adalbern clasped Porcia's shoulder in sympathy as he stood. Nodding to Aetius, he turned and followed Vitus's guard from the podium.

Mederei sat in silence with Gandwy, awaiting whatever healer Vitus would send. The ludus was empty, their fellow slaves seated amongst the audience at the arena.

"Why did you not tell me?" Gandwy asked, breaking the quiet of the campus.

"Tell you what?" Mederei asked. She leant against a wall, her eyes closed.

"You know what."

Opening her eyes, Mederei turned to frown at Gandwy. He met her gaze squarely.

"You're not from the north, are you?" he asked.

Mederei closed her eyes again and resumed her lean. "No," she answered at length. "But I have lived there since I was a girl. I might as well be from the north."

Gandwy nodded, examining Mederei's face. "Your mother—"

"Is dead," Mederei said curtly, opening her eyes again to look at Gandwy.

"You are a queen," Gandwy whispered.

"The Magni Ceni are no more, Gandwy," Mederei answered softly. "The queen of nothing is not a queen."

"I am Magni Ceni!" Gandwy hissed. "And so are my brothers. My cousins survived the slaughter. So many of us live. We may be in hiding, but the Magni Ceni live still. If they knew you—"

"They would be sorely disappointed," Mederei answered. "I am not my mother."

"You are her almost exactly!" Gandwy answered. "It was as if I was upon the downs again, facing the druid-killer when you stood upon that rock and declared Britain free."

Mederei cocked her head at Gandwy. "I did not know you were in that fight."

"I was just a lad," Gandwy answered. "Just one of hundreds. We had only old swords and what armour we could scrounge or make ourselves. I remember the first time I saw your mother." Gandwy smiled wistfully. "It was as if Andrasta herself had graced us with her presence. She was so fierce and so beautiful…" He shook his head. "I thought myself in love."

Mederei smiled at Gandwy. It was rare her mother was ever discussed in front of her, and rarer still that she was remembered with any warmth. Few in the north had met her, and knew her only by name or deed. Those who had so much as seen her were mostly Roman, and they did not speak kindly of her.

"Not since our defeat have I felt so much shame," Gandwy said. He did not bother holding back the tears that struck his eyes, making him suddenly blind. "I should have been protecting you this fight. I failed defending her. I broke rank and fled. And now I have failed you, too. I should have been defending my queen."

At this, Gandwy broke down. His shame and grief brought him to his knees. Moved, Mederei lifted herself from the wall and went to him. Despite the pain of her wounds, she knelt by Gandwy and wrapped him in a close embrace.

"You did what you were told, and that is right. There is no shame in that. As for facing the druid-killer, you did more than most anyone. It was Britain that failed my mother. Not you. Had the islanders but risen, we would have been rid of Rome and living in a free country. You had great courage to stand and be counted, Gandwy. Too few British men can claim the same."

Gandwy was beyond answering. The sudden decline in adrenaline and the realization of Mederei's identity rendered all thought impossible. He simply knelt and sobbed, and so Mederei simply held him.

Adalbern paused at the door. One of the Britons was on his knees, sobbing hysterically. Mederei held him as if he were a child. Adalbern knocked on the open door, drawing Mederei's attention. He smiled apologetically at her.

"Gandwy," Mederei murmured. "The healer is here."

The sobbing man nodded, and struggled to bring his weeping under control. The resulting hiccoughs made Mederei laugh, bringing a smile to Gandwy's lips. He wiped his eyes and tried to stand. Mederei tried to help. They were both too tired and the effort was wasted.

Adalbern smiled and stepped into the room, his perpetual shadow of guards taking their positions outside the door. A servant scurried in, saw Adalbern, and left again. The Batavian had become the healer of choice for all the gladiators in Vitus's ludus. Izem said there was magic in his touch. The servant, the same boy who always accompanied Adalbern while he visited the ludus, knew precisely what Adalbern would request and so set about it without needing to be asked.

"Come on, then," Adalbern said gently. He hauled Gandwy to his feet, then Mederei. He checked their wounds.

"Gandwy first," Mederei said. She nodded her head over to the man, who swayed dangerously.

"No," Gandwy slurred. "No. You first."

Mederei smiled. "Gandwy first," she said again.

Adalbern was inclined to agree. Gandwy's wounds were worse by far, as was his exhaustion. He needed to be treated and taken to bed.

"Can you get to the bench?" Adalbern asked Mederei. She nodded at him and began to move towards the bench at the far end of the room. Her vision was swimming by the time she reached it. It took her several attempts to turn herself around and sit. She watched a moment as Adalbern guided Gandwy to the side of the bath and helped him undress. In this time, the servant, a Gaulish boy named Gaius, returned with help to pour cold water in the tub. They left again to fetch the hot water.

Mederei watched Adalbern as he worked, checking over the worst of Gandwy's wounds, cleaning them with water he had fetched from the tub, and making mental notes as to which wound would require which poultice.

Unable to keep her eyes open, Mederei lowered herself onto her side and, surrounded by the restful silence of the empty ludus, fell to sleep.

She woke gently, opening her eyes to find Adalbern kneeling before her, checking her wounds. She smiled at him slightly. He returned the smile.

The sun lit the room orange, streaming in slantwise from the windows. Behind Adalbern, the bath steamed with fresh water, into which rose petals and witch hazel had been thrown. Mederei breathed in the fragrant steam.

"How is Gandwy?" she asked softly.

"He is asleep," Adalbern replied, matching his volume to hers. "He had to be carried out. He will sleep long, I think."

Mederei nodded. "He was supposed to die this day."

"So were you."

Smiling, Mederei nodded again.

"Forty-two," Adalbern said. "You were six against forty-two, and only two of you were killed. Rome is right to fear British women."

"Yes. They are."

Adalbern laughed a deep, quiet rumble. Feeling strangely relaxed and content, Mederei closed her eyes briefly. Lulled by Adalbern's gentle touch and her own fatigue, she fell asleep again.

Hot water touching her toes woke her. She was naked, cradled in Adalbern's strong arms as he lowered her into the water. Mederei did not fight. The Batavian had seen her naked many times before now and never once had she been forced to fight him off. He had not noticed that she was awake yet, so she took some time to observe him. He was tall and obviously strong, the breadth of his shoulders and size of his hands formidable. Yet he was as gentle as a doe. Though his features were handsome and fierce, he often looked melancholic. His eyes were never anything but warm when he looked at Mederei, reminding her of thickened honey. Behind them sat a heavy sadness that even his smiles could not touch.

He turned to make sure Mederei's head did not go under the water and paused briefly when he spied her watching him. Half-drunk in her post-battle haze, Mederei reached out and touched his cheek.

"There are tears unshed in your eyes, Adalbern of Batavia," she murmured. "They are as pools of memory and melancholy."

Adalbern had no answer to give. He stared into Mederei's hazel eyes, lost in them momentarily. He covered her hand with his, pressing her palm against his face. "I feared I would be digging your grave this night, Mederei," he whispered.

"And would you have wept?" Mederei asked.

Adalbern nodded. "It would have broken my heart."

The answered pleased Mederei. She smiled at him and let her hand drop. To her surprise, Adalbern did not release her hand. Instead, he curled his long fingers around hers and brought her hand lower. He kissed her palm before lowering her hand back down in the water. Mederei watched him, her expression difficult to read.

"Rest now," Adalbern said. "Let the water work your muscles. I have to mix the poultices."

Mederei nodded. She relaxed into the tub, but she did not take her gaze from him. She watched him even as he rose and turned away. Only when he stood at the high workbench, his back to her, did Mederei close her eyes.

Adalbern's hands shook as he measured the ingredients. He had to throw his first attempt out, so distracted was he by the heat that had flooded his body when Mederei touched his cheek. The site of the contact tingled, as did his lips, even now. Adalbern put down his mortar and pestle and leant his hands on top of the workbench for a moment, struggling against his imagination, which had him lowering himself naked into the bath with Mederei. He closed his eyes, berating himself briefly before he forced thoughts of the woman aside. It took considerable effort to focus on his work, but he managed it.

When he felt he could face her again without losing himself, Adalbern turned and walked to the bath. He touched Mederei on the shoulder and her eyes opened. They stared up at him.

"You can get out now," he said quietly. "Do you need help?"

Mederei shook her head. She attempted to rise from the water and found her body unwilling. "Yes," she whispered to Adalbern.

The Batavian nodded. He leant forward and wrapped a strong arm around Mederei's waist. She wrapped both her arms around his neck. Adalbern paused briefly, distracted by the feeling of her rose-water soaked breasts pressed against his chest.

"Ready?" he murmured in her ear. Mederei nodded, and Adalbern easily pulled her out of the water. He lowered her to a sitting position on the edge of the bath and pulled away.

Mederei resisted, grabbing his tunic, and pulling him back so that they remained pressed together.

Confusion was the first emotion Adalbern felt. Heat raced through his body and his pulse quickened. His breathing shortened. He felt Mederei's lips brush against his clavicle and his body tensed. Had that happened? Was this happening?

The questions were answered when Mederei kissed Adalbern's neck. His lips parted as he felt her press hers against his flesh. His head tilted back unconsciously and closed his eyes. He wanted to speak, but all that escaped his lips was a soft sigh.

As if of their own volition, Adalbern's hands began to move. The one at her waist moved lower, marking the curve of her hip and sliding around to her buttocks. His other hand slid up to cup her face near her ear as her lips left a trail of kisses, slowly moving upwards. Thought vanished momentarily, returning suddenly when he felt his belt removed.

"No," he gasped, pulling away. Again, Mederei resisted, grabbing his tunic and pulling him back to her. "Mederei…" He looked down at her and lost his thoughts. They vanished in a jumble of conflicting desires as he looked into her eyes. They were enlivened now, unclouded, and direct. British women were famous for being open about their yearnings, and so confronted by her desirous eyes, Adalbern found he had no defences.

"I almost died today," Mederei murmured. "Bring me to life."

Adalbern did not resist when Mederei lifted herself to take his lips in her own. His response was immediate, and hungry.

It had been too long since he last had a woman, too long since he had felt such rushing desire. He was overcome. He pulled her tightly to him, returning the kiss with force. She trembled against him, and Adalbern was thoroughly lost. He let her remove his tunic and undershirt. He relished the feeling of her fingers running down his torso to his trousers, the taste of her lips on his mouth, the soft skin stretched over the strong frame beneath his exploring hands.

He was thrown off balance slightly when Mederei touched his penis, the sensation of her fingers there robbing him of breath momentarily. He grabbed her hand and pulled it away. "Not yet. Not yet."

Adalbern wanted to bring her to orgasm first. He knelt before her, his fingers tracing a lazy line on her inner thigh. Her legs opened, allowing him access. Adalbern's kisses travelled there. Satisfaction flooded him as she whispered her first moan. It was not long before she pushed his head away with a whispered, "Stop!"

Adalbern looked up at her. Her face was flushed, making her eyes appear bright green. He searched those eyes before she leant down and kissed him, pulling him up to her level. Gladly, Adalbern let her guide him. He let his lips wander over her skin as she turned, drawing him around, and leant back, lying on the side of the bath.

Adalbern barely even noticed the changes. Everything was automatic, his desires controlling his body. His mind had abandoned him, choosing refuge in the untouched recesses of his consciousness. The woman beneath him had complete control over him, and he wished for nothing else.

New sensations flooded him and he thrust instinctively. Mederei arched her back with a gasp and Adalbern felt her strong legs wrap around his hips.

This was not merely love-making to Adalbern. It was not a shallow capitulation to animal lust. This was worship. Adalbern gave himself over fully, losing and finding himself in Mederei, knowing this would forever change him. He did not care. He needed her. He needed her strength, her certainty of purpose. He needed to be hers.

The orgasm that rocked him was like stars exploding in his head. His body convulsed, then lost all strength. He fell on top of her, out of breath. He remained there, his muscles trembling, twitching from the strain that had just ripped through them. It took him some time to regain his breath and recover his mind.

Mederei, in that time, did not move. She remained, her arms around his shoulders, breathing him in. Only reluctantly did she loosen her hold as he pulled himself upright. She smiled at him as he gently brushed hair away from her cheek, closing her eyes when he kissed her forehead.

Nothing was said for a moment as Adalbern held her close. Steeling himself, he pulled away. The absence of her warmth sent a rash of bumps all over his body. In silence, he recovered his clothes, and quickly dressed himself. A quick glance revealed that Mederei was watching him, her face still pleasantly flushed. The rise and fall of her breasts as she lay languidly on the side of the bath threatened to cloud his mind again, so he turned to gather his various medicines and poultices.

Her eyes were closed when he turned back. He went to her and knelt. She was asleep. Sighing, Adalbern set to work.

Vitus paced the ludus training ground. He looked up sharply when the door to the adjoined infirmary opened and Adalbern stepped out. Vitus went to him immediately.

"Is she all right?" he demanded.

"She is a slave sentenced to death," Adalbern answered. "No. She is not all right. If you are referring to her wounds, however, I believe she will heal. She has done well up until this point."

Vitus nodded. He observed the tall, sombre man in front of him. "You probably don't think much of what I do—"

"No," Adalbern interrupted. His voice was as soft as ever, but he spoke sharply. "I don't."

Taken aback by the bluntly spoken admission, Vitus forgot what it was he had intended to say. He frowned at the Batavian.

"For what it's worth, German," he said, "I care for her."

"Forgive me, master Vitus, if I don't believe you."

"If I didn't, would I treat her so well?"

"Only because she is worth more to your treasury alive," Adalbern answered. Again, he spoke softly, but decisively. Turning his attention momentarily away from Vitus, Adalbern addressed one of the serving girls who attended Vitus this evening. "Please fetch some clean clothes for the Woman. I will not dress her in her filthy fighting rags."

The serving girl looked to Vitus for permission. Vitus dismissed her to do as Adalbern asked without so much as looking at her. She scurried away.

"She might yet earn her freedom," Vitus murmured to Adalbern.

"Forty-two," Adalbern rumbled, "against six and only two of them fighters."

"Those odds were not of my choosing."

Adalbern scoffed, but declined to comment further. He stood at the door of the infirmary, leaning on the lintel, and watching Vitus with eyes like flint.

"You are oddly concerned, Adalbern," Vitus noted.

"I am a healer, master Vitus," Adalbern replied. "Of course I am concerned. It is my job to be concerned. If it makes you uncomfortable, find a healer that doesn't care."

"I did not mean to imply…" Vitus stopped himself. He rubbed the side of his face and moved to lean against the wall next to the door. He pressed his back to it and watched the moon rise over the ludus walls. He folded his arms across his chest.

"Strange," he said after a long silence. "I find I like you, Batavian, despite your impertinence."

"Honesty is often mistaken for impertinence, Roman."

The servant returned with a long, sleeveless dress which she handed over to Adalbern with a short curtsey.

"I am a Gaul," Vitus corrected.

Adalbern took the dress. He smirked at Vitus. "No, you're not." He disappeared into the room and left Vitus to ponder his words.

Inside, Adalbern dressed Mederei, pulling her from sleep.

"I'm sorry," he said softly. "I did not mean to wake you."

Mederei mumbled something incomprehensible in return and a soft smile touched Adalbern's lips.

"Vitus is outside," he said. "Asking after you."

"He can drown," Mederei mumbled. Her words were slurred, but understandable this time. Adalbern grinned quickly at her. Finished dressing her, he scooped her easily into his arms. Mederei wrapped her arms around his neck and rested her head on his shoulder. Adalbern pulled her closer momentarily before turning around and walking from the infirmary.

"I can get a stretcher if you like," Vitus offered when Adalbern reappeared, Mederei in his arms. The woman was not a tiny creature, but she looked it against the broadly built German.

"That is unnecessary. I can carry her. But I do not know which chamber is hers."

"Follow me." Vitus pushed himself away from the wall and led Adalbern into the living quarters of the gladiatorial school. He retrieved a key from his belt when they arrived at Mederei's chamber. There were three locks, all using the same key, required to open the barred door.

Vitus pushed the door and stood aside, permitting Adalbern in first. The chamber was relatively large, with a barred window that looked out over the outer gardens and the bars beyond. The bed was large and looked soft and warm. The chamber itself was richly decorated—a beautiful embroidery hung on one wall. On the opposite wall sat a shelf with various trinkets—a small silver water jug, various small clay amphorae of expensive perfumed oils, a carved wooden horse statuette and various other offerings.

Against the wall, opposite the bed, sat a large wardrobe, one door hanging open slightly. Adalbern caught sight of richly dyed dresses. On a table beside the wardrobe sat a bronze bowl filled with jewellery of all kinds.

"Surprised?" Vitus asked when he noticed Adalbern's gaze.

"Aye," Adalbern answered, returning to the task at hand. He walked to the bed. Vitus rushed forward and pulled back the furs and blankets there.

"Thank you," Adalbern said.

Vitus nodded at him. "Gladiators have ever been honoured with gifts from their admirers. Many have gone on to live in great prosperity and die in their old age. The Woman has been good for this school, and so she is also thusly honoured by me."

"That is how you justify it, is it? Prospering from slaughter?"

"Do you honestly think her life would have been better if I had left her to bleed in the marketplace?"

Adalbern had no answer to this. It was very likely that it would not have been. Vitus was not a cruel master, Adalbern was certain. He had observed Vitus enough to know this. Still, Mederei was a caged lion; beautiful to look at, but a sad sight when viewed through bars. Adalbern covered Mederei in the furs and straightened.

"No, master Vitus," he said at length. "I do not think so. But you should ask her which she prefers; to live in captivity, or die free."

"I would probably find her answer ungrateful."

Adalbern flashed a smile. "Probably," he said.

Vitus smiled in return. "Come, then. You are overdue at Aetius's house. I will send you home in the carriage."

"That is not necessary. It is a clear night. I can walk."

"Your guard may not appreciate the walking."

Adalbern shrugged. "That is not my problem."

Vitus laughed. He extended his hand to the German. "Thank you," he said. "For once again taking such good care of my best fighter."

Hesitating only briefly, Adalbern returned the handshake. "Aetius is grateful for the money, I am sure."

Vitus grinned. "I'm sure. You will find your guard waiting at the entrance of the ludus. I sent them there after I returned from the post-fight celebrations. I shall see you at the official celebration tomorrow night."

"Until tomorrow, then," Adalbern replied. He left Mederei's chamber, never giving a sign that he feared Vitus may have discovered their love-making earlier in the afternoon.

Vitus fussed a little over Mederei's blankets, ensuring she was well guarded against the increasingly chilly night before turning around and, taking care to lock the door firmly behind him, retiring to his own home.

In the still, moonlit room, Mederei opened her eyes and stared blankly at the ceiling. Her body was still, but her mind roared with a maelstrom of thoughts and emotions. Despite herself, she had loved the sensation of being held by the Batavian healer. She had pretended to fall asleep in his arms as he walked with her to her chamber. In truth, she had felt so warm and safe in those strong arms that she very nearly did fall asleep.

Confusion and guilt waged violent battle with this new-found realization. Adalbern was a Batavian. They had been instrumental in the conquest of Britain. He was one of the enemy. And yet… and yet… she had desired him, did desire him. She had caved to those desires and lain with him. She had never craved another the way she did him, not even Rhys, the man to whom she had given a promise to marry.

Had she not loved Rhys? Guilt wracked her tired body, shaking her very bones as the answer came to her; no, she had not.

Rhys was a man of Britain, and the Batavian was her enemy. How could her heart have betrayed her country so? How could she have abandoned Rhys's memory so soon after his death?

Plagued though she was, Mederei did not have the strength for tears. She turned onto her side, curled into her grief, and fell to sleep.

## 71 AD, SPRING, LUGDUNUM, PROVINCE OF GAUL

The party grew in volume as the gathered dignitaries drank. Their bellies full of food, and the whole city still feeling festive after the unexpected turn of events in the arena the day before, the Romans of Lugdunum were in fine spirits.

Mederei sat alone at the table reserved for the gladiators. Gandwy had been rented out fairly early after dinner to please an elderly woman. Many offers were made on Mederei, but Vitus had a firm policy of not renting out unwilling gladiators. Most of the time, that proved unproblematic. The gladiators were most usually happy for a night of pleasure. Life was short and pleasures too few and far in between. Mederei was different. Vitus ascribed that to her womanhood, despite many a Roman man trying to convince him that British women had manly appetites. Mederei was grateful for this one small kindness from Vitus. Even so, even though she was not expected to grace the beds of any Roman man, Mederei despised this evening, and all the celebrators attending. They would feast and be just as merry had she died yesterday. She stared down at her hands, unmoving as the party raged around her.

Geraint walked around the room, strumming his lyra and singing beautiful ballads and hilarious ribaldries. He continually looked around, soaking in every detail, searching for some clue that might help him find a way to escape with Mederei. He noticed one odd detail. Mederei sat with her head bowed slightly, staring down as if her hands were the most interesting thing in the known world. On the other side of the room sat the Batavian hostage. He barely took his eyes off her, ignoring the family entrusted with his care. There was longing in those brown eyes.

A faint smile touched Geraint's lips. That was something he could use. He turned away to address a small cluster of young women and began a song about a Gaulish warrior outwitted by an Otherworldly woman. The song was humorous in its portrayal of the buffoonish Gaul as he fell haplessly in love with a woman he had no hope of ever wooing.

Adalbern listened half-heartedly to the conversations happening beside him. His mind was on Mederei. He had been worried about this night, nervous that, despite all that transpired between them, the Briton would reject him after all. When she had caught sight of him watching her, she turned away. Some hours later, and she still refused to meet his eye.

Bitterness crept into his throat, and Adalbern found food impossible to stomach. Around him, Roman dignitaries laughed loudly, alcohol diminishing their usually rigorous control. The mirth surrounding him pressed heavily on him. His shoulders bunched in response, and he felt his agitation grow.

Mederei's sudden departure from the room made him forget his growing tension a moment. He watched her as she glided away from the noise, hindered not one bit by her wounds. He waited for as long as he could before he excused himself from Aetius's table. They barely noticed.

He found Mederei without difficulty. She was in the first place he thought to look; a small nook in the garden near the wall, shielded by a row of well-groomed shrubs and vine-covered walls. There was a small bench upon which

Mederei sat, her back to the opening. Adalbern watched her a moment before clearing his throat.

Mederei did not have the strength to face Adalbern this evening. She had slept poorly, plagued by guilt and bad dreams. Her whirling mind had done nothing but confuse her further.

"Are you well?" the Batavian asked from a respectful distance.

"Tired," Mederei answered. She could not keep the misery from her voice.

She closed her eyes as she felt Adalbern come to stand at her back. She wanted nothing more than to lean against him, to rest a moment in his strength. She could not, must not. The Batavi were the enemy. He was the enemy. Rousing herself, Mederei jerked upright and walked further into the alcove, pausing by a still-blossoming elder shrub. She reached out and touched the small white blossoms, only to see them crumble to the ground. She withdrew her hand.

"Mederei," Adalbern said. "Look at me."

Mederei almost did. She wanted the warmth of his gaze, promised by the gentleness of his voice. Instead she shook her head and turned away.

"Mederei."

His hand touched her wrist and she pulled away, turning to face him. "Please leave," she whispered.

Adalbern frowned. He opened his mouth to respond, and shut it again. He watched her, his confusion plainly written across his features.

"Please," Mederei whispered.

"Have I upset you?" Adalbern asked at length. "If so I—"

"No," Mederei said. "But please leave."

Again, Adalbern scowled at Mederei, his mouth begging for words that would not come. Mederei turned away, unable to stand his gaze any longer. "This shouldn't hurt," she whispered.

Immediately, Adalbern was at her side. "What hurts?" he asked, slipping into his role as healer. "There may be an infection. Show me."

Mederei turned to look at him. She took his hand and placed it on her chest. Her heart beat wildly beneath his palm. "This hurts," she said.

Adalbern swallowed. Mederei dropped her hand, but Adalbern could not withdraw his. His thumb stroked her exposed clavicle gently.

"My heart is breaking."

"Why?" Adalbern whispered.

Mederei stepped away from him and turned around, this time stopping to examine a rose bush. Adalbern remained unmoving, watching her, dreading the words that were to come.

"Rhys ap Brennus was the chieftain of the Caledonii and leader of the resistance against Rome in the north," Mederei said. "And he was my betrothed."

Adalbern nodded. This he knew.

"I—" Mederei stopped, struggling to find the right words. What were the right words? She could not both honour her betrothed's memory and lie each night with one of the enemy.

"I gave myself to you," Adalbern said quietly. "Whatever transpired between us, you have all of me now."

"I don't want you." It was a lie, and it hurt her to say it. She did want him. She turned away. "You are a Batavian man. You fought for Rome in the subjugation and oppression of Britain. I will not be a traitor to my people."

Adalbern stepped back. Mederei closed her eyes to guard from the tears the absence of his heat pulled from her.

"I see," Adalbern said. Mederei neither responded nor looked at him. "I see," he said again. His chest crushed inwards, squeezing at his heart and making it difficult to breath. Adalbern turned and, as if stunned, began to walk away.

A stone flew past his shoulder and slashed the trunk of the elderberry. Adalbern turned to find Mederei staring at him, her eyes blazing.

"Don't you dare turn your back to me," she hissed.

Adalbern scowled, pursing his lips. "What do you want, Mederei?" he demanded.

Mederei trembled with rage. She knew it was not Adalbern she railed against. The moment his brown eyes, filled with confusion and aching loneliness, locked with hers, Mederei's knees collapsed. She fell to the ground, dropping like a stone to sit on the grass. She covered her face as tears escaped. She turned around and hugged her knees to her chest.

Adalbern did not speak. He did not move. He simply stood, a pillar of patience, awaiting Mederei's answer.

It came in a whisper. "I want to hate you."

The frantically beating heart in Adalbern's chest skipped painfully; signalling a small hope. She wanted to hate him. Did that mean she could not?

Adalbern moved forward slowly. He sat himself down on the grass beside Mederei, but facing the other way. "You asked me once what I was doing in Lugdunum."

"Yes," Mederei answered, her voice distant.

"I am a hostage," he said. "My father had loved Rome almost as much as he loved Batavia. He thought Rome was a force for good. He thought they would bring stability and peace to the warring peoples of the north. Rome had, after all, saved our people as we fled incursions from the tribes in the east and gave us our home. He loved Rome for this. Rome, however, seems to have forgotten what love is."

Adalbern paused a moment to collect his thoughts and brace himself against the misery his remembrances brought. "Two years ago, Rome broke its treaty with our people. In an effort to raise an army to defeat the man who would become emperor, Rome stole our children away too young, and in numbers far greater than agreed upon in our pact. They tried to take my nephew, then a lad of just eight. My sister resisted, and the Romans slew her." Adalbern swallowed. "Father's heart broke that day. Betrayed and aggrieved, we revolted. We had almost won back Germania Inferior from Rome, but the war in the east had been won, and Rome would no doubt turn her armies on us. My father sued for peace, and so it was granted. But the price was high."

Again, Adalbern was forced to pause, this time to swallow back the tears that threatened to close his throat and take his vision. "In order to save our people from conquest and subjugation, Rome demanded the end of my father's reign. He was put to death, and his heirs, myself and my nephew, were taken away. I was brought here. They took Diethelm to Rome to serve the new emperor. So you see, I have no love for Rome. She has taken everything from me; my sister, my father, my home, my people…." Adalbern shook his head. "Enemies we might have been once. But we are not any longer." He turned to look at Mederei. She watched him with tears streaming down her cheeks. Reaching out, Adalbern gently wiped the tears away.

"Could you love me now?" he asked softly.

Mederei did not answer. She stared up at him with large, miserable eyes, searching his gaze. He felt her lean in and followed suit. Before their lips met, someone cleared their throat at the opening of the alcove. Mederei withdrew quickly, turning back around to face the alcove wall.

Irritated, Adalbern looked at the intruder with a scowl. Geraint the bard smiled at him briefly. "Beg pardon," he said. "But master Aetius is looking for you, Batavian."

"Why?" Adalbern demanded.

Geraint shrugged. "I did not ask."

Muttering darkly under his breath, Adalbern stood and dusted himself off. He glanced briefly at Mederei, but she had resumed her staring at the vine-covered wall. Still muttering, Adalbern made his way back to the party.

Geraint stepped aside to let the big man pass, smiling genially up at him. The smile vanished as soon as the German was out of earshot.

"What are you doing?" he hissed at Mederei.

"Nothing," Mederei answered blankly, distantly.

"Really? N—"

"It was nothing!" Mederei snapped. She whipped around to glare at him. Geraint could say nothing else, so he scoffed, turned on his heel, and stormed from the garden. Behind him, Mederei turned and buried her head in her hands.

"Oh! Bard!" Porcia said as she spied Geraint return to the hall to pick up his lyra once more. "Bard, have you seen Mederei?"

"The woman is in the gardens," Geraint answered, his performance mask on once more. "Observing the roses."

"Thank you," Porcia said, smiling up at him before vanishing from the room. Her father and soon-to-be husband were loudly chatting to one another and she had the chance to escape. Geraint watched her walk brusquely from the room. There was another thing he could use.

Porcia stopped once she was in the centre of the garden, looking about her in search of the British gladiator. She resumed her walk when her search revealed nothing. A small panic had settled in her stomach before she stumbled across Mederei, lying on her side in the alcove, trembling.

"Mederei," she breathed. She ran forward to kneel at Mederei's side. "Mederei! It's me. It's Porcia. Mederei?"

The woman remained unresponsive to Porcia's speech, so the girl reached out to touch Mederei's shoulder. Startled, Mederei twitched and turned. Porcia jumped backwards. She offered an apologetic smile.

"Forgive me," she whispered. "I didn't mean to startle you."

"Porcia," Mederei said. She sat up properly and smiled slightly. "I'm sorry. Are you all right?"

"I was to ask you the same," Porcia said. "You look unwell."

Mederei looked at the ground a moment before sighing. "I am tired, my wounds ache, and tonight I was forced to dine with those who would revel to see me dead."

"Not all of us," Porcia whispered, casting her eyes down to the grass. "It would have broken my heart."

"Oh, Porcia," Mederei hauled herself to her feet, feeling dizzy with fatigue. She walked over to the girl and wrapped her in a tight embrace. "I did not mean you. I'm sorry."

"No," Porcia said, shaking her head. Her voice sounded thick. "It is right that you hate us. What did I do to stop the slaughter? Nothing. I am a coward."

"What could you have done?" Mederei asked. "You are one amidst thousands. Even I could have done nothing."

"I was so afraid, Mederei," Porcia said, bursting into tears. "So afraid." She looked up at Mederei. "I admire you so much," she said. "I wish I had known you as a free woman, that we might have gone for long walks in the countryside together. I would call you sister, and…" Porcia could not finish her thought. Her attempt to control her tears ended in hiccoughing sobs. Mederei laughed softly and brushed the strands of Porcia's thick black curls from her face. "You can call me sister now, if it pleases you."

The sobs stopped and Porcia looked at her with large eyes. "May I? Do you mean it?"

Mederei nodded. "I mean it."

"I always wanted a sister," Porcia said. She smiled.

"You have one now. I don't know how long for, but…" Mederei shrugged. "For what time I have left, we will be sisters."

Porcia hugged Mederei close and the Briton marvelled at how petite the girl was. At her age, Mederei had been huskier by far.

"We will be sisters forever," Porcia said.

Mederei smiled. She envied Porcia's wide-eye naiveté. Her own had been stripped from her when she was ten. It was then she learnt how cruel the fates were. Porcia would learn too. Still, the girl was young. Let her have her dreams while she could. Mederei ran her fingers through Porcia's hair as they embraced.

It came suddenly, the spell that took Mederei's legs from her. Her head spun, feeling impossibly light. Then the world went dark, and she felt nothing at all.

Porcia struggled beneath Mederei's sudden dead weight. She lowered the woman as gently as she could onto the ground. "Mederei?" she whispered, tapping the Briton's face. "Mederei?" Then, "Mederei!"

Though she breathed, Mederei did not stir. Panic sat cold in Porcia's belly. She looked around her. There was no one in the garden. Indecision kept her only a brief moment before she took off running.

Adalbern had once again been shoved to the side line of the conversation. He stood apart from Aetius, holding an untouched cup of Roman wine, simultaneously observing the revelries and paying little attention to them.

"Adalbern," Porcia said as she breathlessly ran to him. "Help! Please!" She spoke quietly, but found it impossible to hide her distress. "It's Mederei. She's collapsed."

Adalbern did not bother to seek permission. In an instant, he set aside his wine and strode quickly from the room, Porcia trotting to keep pace behind him. They came to the alcove, where Mederei lay on the grass, her eyes closed and her face ashen.

"Fetch Vitus," Adalbern told Porcia. She nodded, and ran back to the party. Adalbern went to Mederei's side and checked her breathing. It was a little strained, but regular and even. He placed a palm on her forehead—a little too warm, but that was to be expected of a body in the middle of healing itself. He checked his bandages. They were all firmly in place.

"What's going on?" Vitus demanded as he arrived on the scene.

"I don't know," Adalbern replied. "Porcia?"

"She just collapsed," Porcia said, looking wan. "We were talking and then... she just... she dropped." The girl turned her large eyes to Adalbern. "Will she die?"

Adalbern sighed and sat back on his heels. "No," he said at length. "I don't believe so. In all likelihood, it's exhaustion. I have seen the wounded collapse on a march. Still, I would like to go back with her and ensure that there are no infections."

Vitus nodded. "I would appreciate that. You may use my wagon. I will obtain the necessary permissions with Aetius."

"I'm coming too," Porcia said.

"You shall have to ask your father, dear," Vitus said.

Porcia raised her brows, turned, and walked smartly back to the party. Vitus watched her a moment with a smile. He turned back to the healer. "Do you need help?"

"No," Adalbern replied. "I can carry her."

"Good. I'll have my servants bring the wagon around. I will accompany you, if only to ease Aetius's mind. Besides, my wife is bored and would infinitely prefer her bed."

Nodding, Adalbern lifted Mederei and stood. Avoiding the party, he walked to the entrance of Lilius's expansive house. Vitus went in search of Aetius.

"I was promised an audience with my champion this evening," Porcia said, sounding more authoritative than Vitus had ever thought possible for the meek girl. He joined the group of men, which included Lilius and Aetius, just as she spoke.

"My dear," Lilius began.

"It's all right, Lilius," Vitus said. "She can come if she wishes. I promise to keep an eye on her. Besides, she is hardly the kind for mischief."

"You Gauls are entirely too lax with your women," Lilius noted. Still there was no way for him to protest against the good-natured man before him.

"For which my wife is very grateful," Vitus said, motioning to his wife. She glided to his side. "Come, love," he said. "It is time we were home." He turned and, his arm around his wife's waist and hers around his, they walked away. Vitus paused a moment to look back at Porcia. "Coming, my dear?" he asked.

Porcia looked at her father and at her betrothed. Neither offered admonishment and so she scurried forward to join Vitus and his wife.

"Association with that Briton is turning your daughter wilful, Aetius," Lilius muttered to his companion. Aetius grunted.

"I'll take care of it," he said. He drained his wine and signalled to a servant to fetch him another.

Vitus watched Adalbern as the German sat in the wagon, still holding Mederei. The man's eyes were closed and he leant against the wall, his shoulders square. A small tick in his jaw indicated his anxiety. Porcia sat beside him, looking impossibly small next to his imposing mass. The young woman nibbled absently at her bottom lip as she gazed out of the window.

"This shall be a very dull audience," Vitus noted to Porcia. The girl turned to him with an uncomprehending frown.

"Your champion will not likely wake this evening."

Porcia smiled. "I think my father would prefer she not speak to me," she said.

Vitus rumbled a soft laugh. "You might be right about that, child."

"How do you do it?" Porcia asked. "How do you send people to die?"

Vitus remained silent a moment. "Most of the people who come to me are criminals; rapists, murderers, and the like. They cannot live in civilized society. I cannot feel remorse at the passing of evil people."

"And Mederei?"

Vitus sighed. "Not all gladiators die in the arena, or because of it. Some, a few, live on and retire wealthier than you could ever imagine. In fact, the lure of wealth and prestige is beginning to draw in competitors who have committed no crime."

"Only the desperate elect to die in the arena," Adalbern rumbled from his seat, his eyes still closed. "Their crime is poverty."

"That's not always true."

"And Mederei?" Porcia asked. "What was her crime?"

"She attacked her previous owner. Actually, all of them," Vitus said. "Or so I hear."

Adalbern scoffed, opening his eyes to look at Vitus. "Only in Rome would defence be considered offence," he said. "I have no doubt that her masters deserve death more than she does."

"You don't know it was defence," Vitus said.

Adalbern's soft brown eyes hardened. "You and I both know what Rome seeks from its slaves. You cannot tell me those men did not try to rape her."

Porcia gasped.

"Come now," Vitus said. "Such language in front of a good Roman girl."

Adalbern grunted. He returned to his repose, closing his eyes again. Vitus shook his head and turned his attention to the passing city as the horses plodded obediently forward through the quiet streets, his mind slipping into quietude. He had spent his life running the ludus and training the gladiators. Never once had he questioned his role. He had trained murderers to die. Many of them were given good deaths. How could he feel remorse for that? What guilt could there be found in his deeds? Yet now, confronted by a woman who loved her country more than herself, who had been thrown to him for fighting for ideals, for the dream of a Britain free from Roman occupation... Had not Gaul once dreamt the same dream? What life would Vitus have had if the great king Vercingetorix had defeated Caesar's siege? What laws would he now live under? Would they truly be better than Roman law?

So deep in thought was Vitus that he did not notice the wagon stop. Only when his wife touched his arm did Vitus rouse himself. He smiled at her and at Adalbern.

"You know where to go?"

"I do."

"Naturally, anything you need will be provided. I will see my wife to bed, then join you. I trust you can look after Porcia until I return?"

"I have no cause to distrust him," Porcia said, smiling. "Adalbern is a man of uncommon honour."

"I have heard that said of the Batavi."

Adalbern said nothing. He stood and stepped from the wagon. His ever-present guards stepped down from their positions clinging to the back of the wagon and moved to flank him. Adalbern muttered darkly, but otherwise ignored them. He waited for Porcia to disembark before striding off to the infirmary, Porcia and his guards in tow.

The servant Gaius awaited them in the infirmary, standing to attention when Adalbern walked in.

"Master healer," the boy said. "Do you require a bath for the Woman?"

"No, Gaius," Adalbern said softly. Vitus's serving staff was small, and he was well acquainted with them all by now. "But some freshly boiled water would be a good idea. Best to bring a bucket. I will be making more poultices."

"Of course. I shall bring the usual list of herbs."

"Thank you."

The boy bowed before scurrying off to attend to his tasks.

"They know you well here," Porcia observed.

Adalbern grunted. "As they should. I've been here so often, Vitus should just hire me permanently."

Porcia smiled. "That would give Father a stroke."

Adalbern smiled at her. "On the shelf there," he said as he laid Mederei down on a central table. "There are towels. Would you please bring me three small cloths and four large towels?"

"Of course."

Porcia moved to do as she was told. She looked back as she gathered the requested items. Adalbern's attention was only for Mederei. He moved slowly as he worked, oddly gentle for his appearance; a bear with its cub. Smiling to herself, Porcia returned to Adalbern and laid the towels on the next table over. She stood aside to observe.

Moving carefully, Adalbern checked Mederei over, seeking any obvious signs of new injury or infection. Finding none, he removed her dress at the shoulders.

"What are you doing?" Porcia asked.

"I'm certain it was exhaustion that brought Mederei to collapse," Adalbern replied. "But infection may have played a part. I must check all her wounds to ensure there is none. Come. I will show you."

Porcia moved closer as Adalbern peeled back one of the shoulder straps on Mederei's dress and began to unbandage the wound at her shoulder. Porcia gasped when the bandage came free to reveal a cut that had been stitched closed. Bits of grey-green poultice clung to the stitches and to the linen that had affixed it in place.

The serving boy returned with two buckets of boiling water. He placed them down and unstrung a large satchel from his side. He placed the satchel on the workbench that ran the length of the wall near the door.

"Thank you, Gaius," Adalbern murmured as the boy turned to leave. The boy smiled at Adalbern and said fondly, "You are welcome, Master Healer."

"Gaius's great-grandfather fought Rome," Adalbern said. "They were once powerful aristocrats of the Senoni. The war cost them a great deal, and the family was brought low and made servants to families Caesar had brought to his side. That boy might have been a prince."

Porcia remained silent. She had no words.

"They still have the heads," Adalbern said, smiling as he dipped a cloth in one of the buckets and began to carefully wash Mederei's wound.

"Pardon?"

"The Gauls used to take heads as trophies in battle. They preserved them in pine oil to be displayed to guests of high reputation. Gaius's family still has a few of those heads, stowed in a dug-out cave beneath their home."

"Rome outlawed the keeping of such trophies," Porcia said. She shuddered. "It is a barbaric practice."

"Is it more or less barbaric than watching warriors die for sport?"

Porcia looked down at the ground and Adalbern sighed.

"I'm sorry, Porcia," he said.

"No," Porcia whispered. "You are right. Rome's claims of civility are greatly exaggerated. We are but barbarians of a different kind."

Adalbern watched Porcia a moment. "Not all," he said, his voice returning to its normal, deep gentleness. Porcia lifted her head to meet his gaze. He offered her a small smile, which she returned.

"Here," Adalbern said, returning Porcia's attention to Mederei's wound. He brought one of the large candles that lit the room closer so that Porcia could see. "Redness is normal. The wound is fresh after all. Some puffiness is also to be expected. However, if the wound looks overly swollen or if it oozes cloudy liquid, it may mean an infection is setting in."

"What about clear liquid, like here?" Porcia pointed to the near end of the wound.

"If the humour is clear, then it means only that the body is healing. So, as you can see, this wound looks as good as we might hope, given the circumstances. The clear humour is a good sign. I might be able to remove the bandages altogether in a day or two for this one. But for now, I'm going to reapply the poultice and bandage it again."

"What poultice?"

"I'll show you."

They moved over to the work bench and Adalbern unpacked the satchel the serving boy left behind.

"On the third shelf down, you should find a mortar and pestle," Adalbern said. "Bring it, please."

Porcia did and Adalbern selected his ingredients. "Witch hazel," he said, picking up a piece of bark, "draws moisture out of the wound, helping prevent infection. Comfrey root keeps the inflammation down, making it more comfortable and less tender for the patient. And this is something I picked up while campaigning with our parent legion: calendula leaves. The flowers grow well in the southern reaches of Gaul, not so well in Batavia. We imported them dried at home, but the fresh leaves work best."

"What does it do?"

"It speeds healing," Adalbern replied. "The amounts of each ingredient in this poultice will vary according to what each wound requires most. Now, Mederei's shoulder wound is clean and doesn't appear to be affected by infection at all. So, we need only a little witch hazel." Adalbern took up a strange, bow-shaped blade and cut a relatively small piece of the bark. He chopped that piece thoroughly and tossed the tiny pieces into the mortar. "Mederei is asleep and does not have any social engagements after tonight, so we do not need much comfrey root either."

"Would you not want to keep the swelling down as much as possible?" Porcia asked.

Adalbern shrugged. "That depends on the physician. My sister believed the body did what it required in order to heal itself. She was loth to intervene unless absolutely necessary. Since she taught me most of what I know, and she was very successful as a healer, I follow that philosophy. We will, however, use a fair amount of calendula leaves. The faster her skin heals over the better it will be." Adalbern threw in the rest of the ingredients and picked up the mortar.

"May I?" Porcia asked, holding out her hands. Smiling, Adalbern held out the mortar and let her crush the ingredients.

"Because the calendula is fresh, you should not need to add much water. You're aiming for a paste that will spread well."

"So... like this?"

Adalbern checked. "No. See how it crumbles off the edge of the pestle? It should be almost like goo."

"Like tree sap?"

"Like tree sap. Yes."

"All right."

Porcia worked the pestle diligently in the mortar and Adalbern returned to Mederei, rewashing the wound in preparation for the new batch of poultice. Porcia watched him work in silence until she felt the poultice was ready.

"Like this?" she asked.

"Like that. Come, you put it on and I'll show you how to prepare a bandage."

Under Adalbern's careful instruction, Porcia examined and treated Mederei's wounds. Only two others had required stitches and were therefore the most at risk for infection. Not one was infected, however, Adalbern noted with satisfaction. When the last bandage was applied, Adalbern straightened. Only then did he notice Vitus standing in the doorway, watching them.

"How long have you been there?" Adalbern demanded, scowling.

Vitus put both hands up with his palms facing Adalbern. "Peace, Master Healer," he said. "Not over long. Long enough, however, to note your patient instructions." He turned to Porcia. "So, what do you think, my dear? Is Adalbern worthy of the praise my fighters give him?"

"A finer healer I have never seen," Porcia said with a smile.

"Aye, well," Adalbern said gruffly. "I had help."

Vitus rumbled a laugh. "And?" he asked Adalbern.

"There is no infection," Adalbern said. "It was exhaustion, I'm certain of it."

Grunting, Vitus stepped into the room. "So what now? Bedrest?"

"Ample bedrest, and good food. Plenty of it. Her body is under considerable strain at the moment. She will need to eat well."

"My fighters always eat well."

Adalbern shook his head. He turned back to Mederei, reattaching the shoulder clasps of her dress. "Speaking of bedrest," he said as he lifted the Briton from the table. "It's time we found her some."

Vitus nodded. "I will unlock her room."

Cradling Mederei in his arms, Adalbern followed Vitus out of the infirmary, Porcia half a step behind. They walked in silence. It lasted until Mederei lay in her bed, Adalbern adjusting her blankets around her. Porcia and Vitus watched from the entrance to the room.

"These quarters are far more comfortable than I imagined," Porcia murmured to Vitus.

"Mederei is the star of this school," Vitus answered. "She has an adoring crowd who send her many things. She has made me wealthy. And I treat my fighters well. They live a good life here."

"While it lasts," Porcia whispered.

Vitus nodded. "While it lasts."

"There is nothing else for me to do, Vitus," Adalbern said, moving around the bed to the door. "I can escort Porcia home now."

"I will have the wagon take you home." Vitus put up a hand when Adalbern started protesting. "I know your fondness for walking, even if it is just to irritate your guards. But my thoughts are for Porcia."

"I cannot argue with that," Adalbern said. "Thank you."

Vitus waved his hand vaguely. "Hardly. I'm sure I would have lost more fighters were it not for your aid. Come. The wagon awaits."

Adalbern spared one last glance back at Mederei before stepping from the room and permitting Vitus to lock the barred door. He said nothing as he followed Vitus to the front of the ludus where the wagon indeed waited. Vitus helped Porcia in before turning to Adalbern. "I will send payment to Aetius in the morning."

Adalbern shrugged.

"Out of curiosity, do you see any of the payments I make to Aetius for you?"

Adalbern scoffed. "None. But I am a hostage, and I must earn my keep."

Vitus shook his head. "I will have a word with him."

"Do not bother," Adalbern said. "I don't care either way. What am I to do with the money?"

"Whatever you wish, Adalbern. That is what money is for."

Adalbern smiled. "I am happy if Aetius takes the money. I am larger than your average Roman, and I eat more. It must be expensive to keep me."

Vitus laughed. "Indeed! Well, in that case, I shall send you a gift as well as payment. Aetius cannot complain then."

"Unnecessary, Vitus, but appreciated."

"Well, it is the least I can do. Have a safe ride home. No doubt I shall see you both again. Goodnight."

"Goodnight," Adalbern said, climbing into the wagon.

"Goodnight, Vitus," Porcia called from inside.

"Goodnight," Vitus answered. He watched the wagon pull away from the compound before making his way to bed.

Porcia watched Adalbern as the wagon jostled over the rutted roads. "You love her, don't you?" she asked.

Adalbern looked sharply at her.

"Don't lie, Adalbern. A woman knows these things."

Frowning, Adalbern said nothing. Unable to bear the knowing in Porcia's gaze, he dropped his eyes down, examining his hands.

"It's all right," Porcia said. "Your secret is safe with me." There was a brief silence before Porcia spoke again. "Have you told her?"

Adalbern glanced up at Porcia, then back at his hands. "Not in so many words," he said gruffly.

Porcia nodded. She reached out and took Adalbern's hands. "You know Ambrosius and I mean to escape with her," Porcia whispered. Adalbern nodded, taking Porcia's hands in his own.

"Will you not help us?"

Adalbern sighed. He let her hands go, leaning back against the wagon walls and staring up at the ceiling. "I can't," he answered.

"Not even for Mederei?"

"Rome has my nephew. I dare not."

Porcia let her gaze drop. She fiddled with the silver rings that adorned her thumb.

"I will tell no one. If you manage it, I will feign ignorance. But I cannot abandon my nephew to Rome. I cannot be a part of your schemes." Porcia looked up to see Adalbern's features twisted, a mask of torment. "What would they do to him if I am discovered?"

"To ask you to abandon your nephew was… I had forgotten. Please. I did not mean to cause you distress."

Adalbern knelt before Porcia and took her hands in his. "I hope you succeed," he said. "I hope that you, your brother, and Mederei find freedom in northern Britain. It will give my own captivity some pleasure to imagine her happy amongst her people again. So please, in whatever plots you make, be thorough. Get her home."

Porcia reached out and touched Adalbern's cheek. "But you will be parted," she said. "I have seen how you gaze at her."

"She escapes or she dies. Either way we will be parted. And she will be happy. To be free again, to be home, that is what Mederei wants. I could not claim to love her and be willing to deny those to her."

Porcia smiled. "Oh, you *do* love her!"

Adalbern rose, sliding back onto his seat. "With all that I have," he whispered. He closed his eyes.

Porcia said nothing, but she did not stop her observation of the hostage that she had come to regard as family. The corners of his mouth tugged down, exaggerated by the shadows, a picture of misery in the dim light. She resolved then and there, she would do all she could to free Adalbern also.

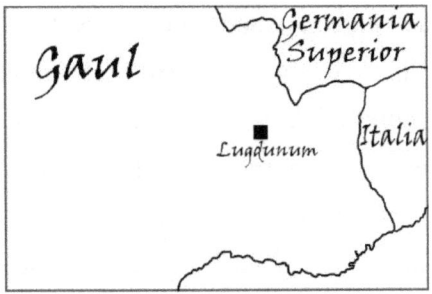

## 72 AD, WINTER, LUGDUNUM, PROVINCE OF GAUL

"Vitus," Lilius said, smiling broadly. "I have come upon the grandest idea for the games in the summer."

"Oh?" Vitus said, putting down his pork.

"Indeed, it has occurred to me that it has been ten years since Rome defeated the foul red witch from Britain. We must celebrate that achievement."

Geraint fumbled his strings, his heart violently fluttering against his chest. He recovered quickly, and only Ambrosius seemed to notice the musical error. Geraint ignored the Roman youth as he cocked his head to look thoughtfully at the bard.

Porcia's gaze was fixed on Adalbern, who had tensed. His food forgotten, Adalbern stared hard at the table, listening.

"Do you mean to have my Woman be the British war queen?"

"A fine thought, no?"

"May I remind you of the forty-two gladiators slain by six Britons due to her leadership?"

Lilius's smile slipped a little. He frowned. "That is true. A dangerous woman, that. Perhaps we should have a dramatist play the part of the shrieking harpy? Yes. Have a dramatist ride in on a chariot, and have him ride out again once his part is played."

Chatter stopped as Adalbern stood suddenly. Not looking at anyone at the table, he snatched up his cup of wine and stormed from the room.

"What ails him?" Lilius asked once Adalbern was out of sight.

"The Batavian healer does not think well of the games," Vitus answered with a shrug. "He thinks them a barbaric practice."

Lilius snorted. "Barbaric indeed!" he said. "A rich judgement from a northern savage."

Again, Vitus shrugged. "I have not met one healer who was not of the same opinion."

"They should not grumble about what keeps them employed."

"There are enough infections and ailments to keep healers busy. I dare say they would welcome the easing of the burden of caring for wounded gladiators as well. Besides which, the Woman and the healer are good friends."

"Does that not concern you?" Aetius demanded.

"Should it?" Vitus asked him. "It is Adalbern who has treated almost all of her wounds since she came to me. They are both strangers in a land not their own, here not of their choosing. It is only natural they would become friends."

"You do not think that they are... intimate?"

Vitus laughed. "And what if they were? What business is it of mine? Life is short and hard for a gladiator. As long as she does not fall pregnant, let them find what fun they can, I say."

"And if they plot against you?"

This time Vitus scoffed. "What would Adalbern do? Rome has his beloved nephew. Does he seem the kind to risk his blood in that fashion?"

"No," Aetius admitted.

"So, Vitus," Lilius interrupted. "What do you think about my proposition?"

"I think in order to do that kind of reenactment, we will require a larger arena."

"We can build a temporary one on the plains outside the city."

"I do not have enough fighters to build an army."

"We will buy more."

Vitus sighed. "It would probably please the Romans in the crowd," he admitted.

"Excellent! Leave the planning to me, Vitus. I will have these games mark the first day of my wedding celebration. It will be an affair talked of for years to come!"

Geraint listened with interest, though he kept his head down, watching his fingers move across the strings of his lyra, as if concentrating hard on his music. The conversation meandered away from talk of gladiatorial combat and Geraint focussed more fully on his tunes. He played for another hour before setting aside his instrument. Another musician would take his place for a while, and the dancers would come. Geraint estimated he had roughly two and a half hours to himself. He wandered the halls of Lilius's home.

He stopped at the entrance to the interior courtyard. There, Adalbern sat on a stone bench, his head in his hands. Even from here, Geraint could see that he trembled. He approached.

Adalbern lifted his head the moment he felt another presence in his space. He scowled up at the bard who had interrupted him.

"You appear distressed, Adalbern of Batavia."

Adalbern turned his head away and said nothing.

Sighing, the bard took the bench opposite the German hostage. For a time, he did not speak. He simply sat and observed Adalbern. "Is it the Woman?" he asked softly at last.

The shortest of glances and the barest of nods confirmed Geraint's guess.

"Lilius seems intent to see her dead," he managed to say.

"I imagine he fancies her a bad influence on his betrothed."

A small flash of a smile crossed Adalbern's face. "I imagine so," he replied. Thinking about Mederei brought fresh hurt and Adalbern struggled against it.

"I understand you have a nephew?" Geraint asked.

"Aye," Adalbern said. "He is all that survives my sister."

"Younger or older?"

"My sister? Older, by roughly eight minutes."

"A twin?" Geraint smiled. "Your poor mother."

This produced the desired effect. Adalbern laughed. He nodded. "You don't know the half of it."

"Mederei has a sister," Geraint said. "A girl three years her junior."

Adalbern's smile slipped.

"A beautiful girl, with hair the colour of flame, and eyes like a cloudy sky." Geraint observed Adalbern carefully as he spoke. "She's mad, though. Rome came to their home and razed it to the ground. She was seven years old when they rode through, out for British blood. She lost her mind that day. Were it not for Mederei... Well, I do not know what would have become of her."

"Did she tell you this?" Adalbern asked. Mederei often spoke of the beauty of her island, but had offered nothing about her family. Geraint shook his head.

"Her story is well known," he replied simply. "Do you love her, Adalbern?"

The question took the Batavian man by surprise. He blinked. His brows collapsed as he scowled at Geraint. "Why?" he demanded. "What's it to you?"

"Nothing," Geraint replied. He leant forward and said, "Everything."

"If you are looking to fight for her affections—"

That was too much for Geraint. He laughed, again taking Adalbern by surprise.

"No," Geraint explained. "No, no, no. Gods no!"

"Then where do your enquiries tend, Bard?"

Geraint grew serious. He leant in again. He sighed. "My name is Geraint."

"Yes, I know."

Holding up a hand to silence Adalbern, he continued, "Of the Caledonii."

Adalbern tensed.

"I was once the shield-bearer for the chieftain of the Caledonii, leader of the British resistance in the north. Mederei was taken by Rome in an ambush, and my lord, Rhys, sent me to fetch her back. I chased her here to Lugdunum and here I have stayed, trying to find a way to bring Mederei home, as I swore to my lord I would."

Swallowing, Adalbern leant back, staring at Geraint. "Is this some sort of trick?" he whispered. "Has Aetius put you up to this to test me?"

Geraint shook his head. "No. I tell you this in earnest. But no matter how I look at the problem, I cannot seem to find a way to take her safely away. Not without help. Adalbern…"

"Don't," Adalbern said. "Don't ask it of me. I cannot help you. I dare not."

"Why not?"

"Rome has my nephew!" Adalbern hissed. "Would you ask me to abandon him to punishment for my crimes? Because that is what Rome would do."

"If I can save your nephew," Geraint said, "would you?"

"Save him? He serves the emperor. How could you possibly free him?"

Geraint shrugged.

"And where would he go? He could not return to his people, he—"

"Britain," Geraint said. "He would go to Britain. The north of that country is still free."

Geraint's interruption silenced Adalbern. He saw in his mind's eye he and his nephew reunited in the highlands of Britain, free from Rome and Roman corruption. The boy stood on a craggy hill, overlooking the famously long lakes of that region. Beside him stood Mederei, her sorrow gone from her countenance, the weight of captivity lifted from her shoulders. The image was so visceral and so compelling it brought tears to Adalbern's eyes.

"How can you free him?" he whispered.

"I do not know yet," Geraint said.

Turning to his thoughts again, Adalbern struggled against the discomfort in his chest. Hope and despair battled for the greatest share of his heart, and their battle rattled through him. Again and again, his mind showed him images of the woman he loved, and the boy he loved, laughing, and free.

"Promise me," Adalbern said. "Swear to me you will do everything you can to free him."

"I swear I will give my life to the task. I would die rather than return to Britain without him."

"How do I know I can trust you?"

"Ask Mederei about me. She knows me well."

Adalbern nodded. He regarded Geraint carefully. He had never seen the man look so earnest. The Britons were much like the Gauls; a guileless people who were not particularly adept at telling lies. They wore their passions on their sleeves and, until Rome, had never thought anyone else would do differently. Increasingly cynical though they were becoming, most still had difficulty perfecting the act of lying. Adalbern could not detect any deceit on the bard's part.

His mind flew to his nephew, labouring for the emperor. The idea of the boy spending his whole life in servitude to the emperor of Rome was unthinkable; not now, not that there was some hope of rescue. What if this was Adalbern's only chance to free the boy? What if he turned this offer down and condemned his nephew forever? What would Diethelm desire?

Freedom.

The thought came through so strongly, Adalbern was not certain that it was his own. He looked at Geraint, who sat in silence, watching him. At length, he nodded. "I will help you," he said. "But so help me, if you prove in any way duplicitous, no amount of running shall save you from me."

Geraint smiled faintly. "I would not dream of it." He stood. "We will speak again. Thank you, Adalbern."

Adalbern nodded. He watched Geraint as the Briton walked back to the dining room and his lyra. The Batavian's face betrayed nothing, but in his chest, his heart sang with something he thought long ago forgotten.

Hope.

"What were you talking about?"

The unexpected sound of a man's voice in the short hall between the inner courtyard and the house made Geraint jump. He looked to see Aetius leaning against the wall, eyeing him suspiciously.

"Master Aetius!" Geraint said, grinning. "The shadows suit you well. I did not see you!"

Aetius did not return the smile. He watched Geraint, wearing his suspicion plainly. Judging from his speech and demeanour, Geraint guessed the man was drunk. Aetius raised his brows, expecting an answer.

"We were discussing the Woman, of course," Geraint said amicably. He had long ago learnt that the secret to lying successfully was to skirt the truth as much as possible. "He's grown quite fond of her, and finds the prospect of her gory death difficult to bear."

"Does he now?"

Geraint shrugged. "I do not know her half as well, and it hurt my heart to hear of Lilius's plans for her. I dare say many a man will feel the sting of her death. She is popular, particularly amongst the Celts of the region."

Aetius narrowed his eyes at Geraint, examining him critically. Geraint returned the man's suspicious regard with an open face and small smile; a simpleton's expression. The simple were very rarely liars. After a fruitless search, Aetius grunted. He turned and made his unsteady way back into the house and to the dining hall. Geraint gave himself a moment to collect his wits before following.

"Hello Woman," Vitus said, smiling sadly at the woman as she approached. "How are you?"

"My wounds ache," Mederei answered seriously. "But I am otherwise well." Her breath frosted in the chill air. Mederei, being of British blood, had little difficulty with the chill of the Gaulish winter. Unlike many of her peers, she still elected to walk outside during breaks in training. Gifts of thick furs had been plentiful and so she walked in relative comfort.

"Adalbern is here," Vitus said. "He wishes to examine your wounds. I have shown him into your chambers as he did not feel he required the use of the infirmary."

Nodding, Mederei turned to cast a longing glance over the frost-covered garden in which she so often took solace. "Winter is the most beautiful of seasons," she murmured.

"I find it abhorrent."

"How, when everything is so quiet and restful, clean with frost and snow? How, when there is the promise of new life in the bite of the air?"

"Fighting has made a romantic of you, Woman."

"Perhaps. It has, after all, impressed upon me the beauty of impermanence. I will die, sooner rather than later. This may be my last winter. How could I not love it?"

Vitus clamped his mouth shut to guard against the apology that desperately wanted to escape his lips. He had intended to tell her that the gladiators had all been rented out for a games not one was likely to survive, but found he could not. Not at present.

"Adalbern awaits."

Mederei nodded. She turned away from the gardens and walked reluctantly inside. Vitus watched her until she vanished inside the ludus. He sighed and rubbed his face. Being a master had never been difficult until Mederei came to his school.

Adalbern straightened as Mederei walked in. She slipped the furs she had around her body off and walked to the fire that blazed cheerily near the foot of her bed. The cold had turned her cheeks pink and the rest of her pale as snow. A lovelier face Adalbern had not ever seen. He took a moment to gaze at that face. Grand games were planned in the summer. He might never get a chance to see her alive again.

"I have come to tend to you," Adalbern said.

Mederei did not look at him. She nodded absently, still staring at the fire. "My mother once said you could divine the future from the dance of flames," she said absently as Adalbern approached. "But I have not her powers, it seems. All I see are flames eating wood."

"Perhaps there is something to be divined even in that," Adalbern murmured. He took her gently by the arm and sat her down on the end of her bed.

"And what would that be? Rome will consume all?"

"Or Rome will consume herself. Flames devour all, even to its own detriment. Perhaps these flames are telling you that one day, even Rome will fail."

A small smile touched Mederei's lips. She turned to look at Adalbern, her eyes far away. "Your optimism is astounding."

"It's all I have left." Adalbern stared into Mederei's eyes, trapped by them, for a long while. "Will you let me tend to you?" he whispered.

Wordlessly, Mederei nodded. She took her hair, grown long now, and pulled it aside. Adalbern slowly untied the dress at the shoulder and let it fall, revealing a sizeable bruise around a small cut. A training wound. He reached out and gently touched the bruise, inspecting the cut. Mederei drew a sharp breath and straightened.

"I'm sorry," Adalbern said.

"It is fine," Mederei answered. "In a strange way, I've come to enjoy the pain. It reminds me that, if nothing else, I am still alive."

"Take care to stay that way," Adalbern said. Mederei smiled, she closed her eyes as he turned and began drawing out phials of liquids and small jars of balms from his satchel. "This will sting."

Mederei twitched as Adalbern wiped her cut down with a tincture that smelled of roses and wood sap. It stung enough to bring sharp tears to Mederei's eyes. Long ago rid of any embarrassment at weeping openly in front of the Batavian healer, Mederei let them trickle down her still cold cheeks. The stinging faded as Adalbern applied one of his balms. Taking up another, he applied it to the bruise and began to gently massage it in, taking care to avoid the cut. Mederei winced as he worked.

"I'm sorry," Adalbern said, wincing himself every time Mederei twitched.

"It must be done," Mederei answered.

Adalbern worked slowly. He wanted to remain in Mederei's company for as long as possible. His gaze and hands strayed from the bruise, moving to her neck. She bowed her head slightly as he began to massage the muscles there.

"I have a question," Adalbern said, finally moving away from Mederei. He fetched a clean linen from his satchel, folded it twice and pressed it against Mederei's wound. He reached over and pulled out some bandages.

"Oh?"

"Do you know Geraint?"

"The bard? As well as one might, I suppose. He comes often for a visit and we talk over wine some."

Adalbern frowned. Was she telling the truth? Or was she trying to protect his identity by playing along with his charade.

"Is it a southern name, Geraint?"

There was a barely perceptible tensing of Mederei's shoulders before she answered, "It is a British name, and not an uncommon one at that."

Adalbern frowned slightly as he noticed the muscles at her shoulders bunch. She was hiding something.

"What other Geraints do you know?" he asked, hoping that his question was not so obtuse that she could not guess that he knew or, at least, had been told Geraint's true identity.

"One. He was the shield-bearer of my lord, Rhys. A good man, though we did not often agree." She turned to Adalbern, questions in her unguarded gaze. Adalbern smiled a little. Geraint had been telling the truth. He could be trusted.

"Why do you ask?"

Adalbern shrugged. "I was curious, is all. Geraint is not a popular name amongst the Gauls, with whom the southern Britons share a close kinship. I was wondering if, therefore, it was a more northerly name."

Mederei turned back around, remaining silent as Adalbern bandaged the linen to her shoulder. Her heart beat frantically. It was clear Adalbern knew who Geraint was. The question was now how did he come to learn this information, and who else knew?

"I will not betray you," Adalbern whispered in her ear, his fingers resting along her clavicle. "I could not. It would be to betray myself."

Mederei turned, twisting her entire body to face him. She remained silent, searching Adalbern's eyes for any hint of deceit. She could find none. Adalbern did not shy from her gaze. He returned it, not bothering now to mask his affections. He let his fingers run over her exposed skin to her throat. Her cool skin flushed with heat and her breathing deepened, growing faster. Her pulse ticked visibly beneath her pale skin.

"Mederei—" Adalbern began. His words were cut short when Mederei pressed her finger to his lips.

"Don't," she whispered. "No professing your love, Adalbern. I could not bear it."

The words cut. Nevertheless, Adalbern nodded. He let his hand drop and pulled away.

Mederei did not let him. She took him by his shoulders, turning him to face her again. Before Adalbern had time to begin a protest, her lips were on his and he understood. He could have Mederei if he pretended that love played no part.

Still, for his part, Adalbern made love that afternoon.

"How is it?" Vitus asked from the door to Mederei's cell. Adalbern straightened, packing away the last of his phials.

"Not as bad as you had described," he replied, forcing himself to appear calm and guileless. "It was mostly bruising."

"She's asleep?"

Adalbern nodded.

"It could not have been so minor if she sleeps now."

"Honestly, the treatment probably hurt more than the wound itself. Pain is exhausting." Yes. Pain. Adalbern shook his head. "And she had been training this morning. She likely needs the rest due to that alone."

Vitus nodded. He observed Adalbern a moment. There was no mistaking the Batavian's affections, from the frequent glances at the Woman to the tenderness in his voice when he spoke of her. The poor fool was madly in love. Vitus sighed and rubbed the side of his face.

"Listen," he said to Adalbern as the man walked past him out of the cell. "You and the Woman may do whatever you wish to in private, but let me caution you against losing your heart, Batavian. She is a gladiator, Adalbern. You will long outlive her."

Adalbern frowned down at Vitus. He looked back at Mederei's sleeping form.

"No, Vitus," he said quietly. "I will not."

Adalbern turned and walked away. He met with his guard at the entrance to the ludus and marched with them back to Aetius's house. Vitus watched the man go, sadness falling heavy on his chest. He was Gaulish, and had grown up with tales of warriors laid to waste from a broken heart; strong men who withered and died for want of an impossible love. Adalbern had admitted his own doom, and Vitus found his usual indifference to the fates of others lacking.

"I hope, for your sake," he whispered before closing the cell door, "That you do."

The games had been set. Mederei would not live past the close of summer.

Mederei lay on her side, pretending to sleep. She felt calmer now, as she had the first time she had lain with the Batavian healer. That was usual. What worried her, however, was how contented she felt, and how her heart ached when his warmth left her. She knew, though could not bring herself to admit, that laying with Adalbern was more than just the product of human need. It was her heart as much as her body that craved his touch.

*The Batavi are our enemies*, she thought, forcefully trying to remind her of their part in the subjugation of Britain and the destruction of the Magni Ceni. But Adalbern had addressed that already, and his story bounced around in her mind, mocking her attempts at remaining indifferent to him.

"He is not British," she whispered. The voices in her mind could not counter this, but they mocked her still, showing him standing on one of the craggy peaks of the north, the wind in his brown hair. His bearing was powerful and noble, the bearing of a free man in charge of his own destiny. It shocked her how much she wished this vision could be truth, that he could go to Britain and live free, no longer captive to a black-hearted empire.

"Magog," Mederei prayed. "Is this vision from you? Would you welcome a son of Batavia into your embrace? Help me, Magog, mother of my island. I am so confused."

But the mother of Prydein could not hear Mederei's tearful prayers, and she refused to stop the relentless march of the visions of the Batavian in Britain. His image danced through her mind, stern and proud and at home amongst the wilds of northern Britain, until her spinning mind could no longer compete with her exhaustion. No clearer on the path she was to take, Mederei fell to sleep and dreamt of home.

## 72 AD, SUMMER, LUGDUNUM, PROVINCE OF GAUL

Mederei stared at the new, temporary arena from her position amongst the ranks of the make-shift British army. She knew nothing of the upcoming fight save that she was expected to play the part of a British warrior; one amongst many. The arena was full, the audience screaming in their anticipation of the coming slaughter. Mederei detested them. She looked to the podium where sat Lilius, Aetius's family, Adalbern, Vitus and the visiting lanista from Rome. Mederei's eyes stopped on Porcia. She sat next to Lilius, with her father on her left. Tears streamed openly down the girl's face, her dark eyes fixed morbidly on the scene below.

Mederei tried to offer the girl a reassuring smile, but that only served to increase the sobbing.

The loud groan of the doors across the arena from where Vitus's gladiators stood announced the arrival of the opponents for these games. The crowd's pitch and fervour increased as infantry and cavalry dressed as Roman soldiers poured into the arena. The crowd was so loud Mederei could not hear the dramatists announce the rival army. One gladiator stood out. He rode on a strong Iberian horse, wearing the uniform of a Roman general and a helm that had a shining bronze mask attached—Creon, an Iberian fighter who had returned from retirement.

Before the flood of gladiators, two slaves pushed forward a large contraption made to look like a heap of stones. A thick plank of wood stood straight up from the contraption. Tied to the bit of wood was a young woman in rags, her thin, almost skeletal arms tied high above her head; a head which was covered by a large hessian sack.

The crowd quietened as Lilius stood. All the gladiators turned to face Lilius.

"Welcome," Lilius said, "to my summer games!"

The crowd roared.

"Today Romans fight Britons! As we know, the British consider their accursed island a goddess. They refer to it as 'She'. So, to honour our British gladiators, we have brought them their goddess. The winner of this fight gains not just their lives, but also Britain!"

Lilius gestured and one of the slaves that had pushed the contraption scrambled up the thing. He whipped the covering from the woman's head.

The air left Mederei's lungs in one sharp breath and the tumult of the arena ceased, falling now on deaf ears. Her knees gave way as her eyes fell upon the woman. It was not a woman, but a girl, with vacant grey eyes and hair that sparkled, even now, like fire in the morning sun. Despite the gaunt face, Mederei recognized her right away.

"Modron," she whispered as Gandwy caught her, preventing her collapse.

"No," Geraint whispered to himself when the bag was removed from the girl tied to the pole.

Adalbern turned to him with a frown. He did not need to ask Geraint any questions. The bard's ashen features and shocked expression told him all he needed to know. Hair the colour of flame. This was Mederei's sister.

Adalbern sought Mederei's form in the crowd of British gladiators standing in the arena. He found her, her eyes fixed on the girl tied to the pole, the devastation of her revelation twisting Mederei's features into a contortion of agony.

Adalbern's heart dropped into his stomach.

Lilius smiled. "Ah, but Rome has danced this dance before!" he said. "Let us now remember it!"

He sat down, smiling ear to ear.

The sound of a horn echoed around the arena and behind the cluster of British gladiators, the doors to the arena opened again. This time, a chariot entered, carrying a dramatist dressed in a woman's garments, wearing a long wig of unsightly horse hair dyed a foul orange colour.

It took Mederei some time to realize that something was happening. She tore her eyes away from her sister's slack-jawed face and scowled as they fell upon the chariot. Her blood turned to ice as the chariot turned and the dramatist addressed the Britons. His face had been made up with ludicrous face paint, and he spoke with a grating falsetto.

"My countrymen!" he said.

There was no mistaking who this man was supposed to be—a caricature of Boudicca, a mockery of Britain's most renowned queen designed to denigrate and demoralize. Mederei would have none of it. They would regret the mocking of her mother.

"No," she growled. Before Gandwy could react, she strode forward, forcing herself through the crowd towards the chariot.

"Mederei!" Gandwy hissed, trying to follow. He was not swift enough.

"Today we face the prodigious manhood… I mean might… of Rome," the dramatist shrieked. He had not noticed Mederei's approach, or perhaps thought her next action so unthinkable that it did not dawn on him to be concerned. He still performed his speech even as she climbed onto the chariot and threw the driver from the carriage.

"Today we—Hey!"

The crowd hushed as Mederei ripped off the man's wig. He stared at her in shocked disbelief, unable to react as she took a step back, raised her leg, and kicked him full in the chest. He tumbled backwards over the yoke of the chariot and hit the ground hard. Mederei took up the reins and whipped the horses back into action. The dramatist had no time to scream before the chariot ran him over, a wheel snapping his neck.

Her face set with terrible resolve, Mederei expertly drove the chariot around the group of Britons.

"My fellow countrymen," she barked, addressing the gladiators with such authority that every single warrior straightened. Mederei observed them with a stern gaze. "Rome believes itself master of our island. But they are small men. Cowardly men. Men afraid to face our warriors in honourable combat. They know they would lose! How could it be otherwise, when they cower before even our women like curs?

"Indeed, such small men are they that no amount of ravishing could so much as tickle a woman. Not like true British men! Behold, so small are they that they resort to the rape of children! They burn our homes and crops in an effort to subjugate the British spirit. But it will not be done! These unloved sons of rats will never have our sacred island, so long as one Briton lives to resist them. These soft southern bastards are too spineless for our land. They are paltry imitations of men!" Mederei turned the chariot, making such a tight turn the thing threatened to tip.

"Too long have our kin languished under the yoke of terrified tyrants! No longer! No more! Harken to me, warriors of Britain! Fight! If the lure of freedom is not strong enough, then let the heat of vengeance be! I am the mother of raped daughters! I am the queen of a devastated people! And I fight now to feed my island Roman blood!"

Mederei turned the chariot once more.

"Nothing is safe from Roman pride and arrogance. They will deface the sacred and seek to devour our island. Win the battle or perish; that is what I, a daughter of Britain, will do."

Once again, Mederei turned the chariot, this time whipping the horses to speed around the arena walls. She drew her sword and held it high.

"Prydein am byth!" she roared. "Prydein am byth!"

Gandwy stepped forward, his blood heated by her words, her manner so like her mother he was transported back to the fateful battle against the druid-killer. He drew his sword. "Prydein am byth!" he bellowed. He caught Mederei's eye as she galloped past him to the rear of the British gladiators. They nodded to one another, a silent understanding.

"Prydein am byth!" Mederei yelled again. This time, the Britons who had once cowered beneath the approaching foe stood tall, their shoulders square and their expressions proud. They drew their weapons. "Prydein am byth!" they roared in unison, their deep voices echoing through the arena as if the very sand answered their cries. Mederei turned her chariot to face the enemy squarely.

"For Boudicca!" she screamed. The horses bolted forward and the Britons broke into a run, parting to let Mederei through.

Gandwy ran to meet her and she extended her arm. He caught it and she pulled him into the chariot.

"Break the wall," Mederei said.

Gandwy grinned. Knowing her plan, he leapt from the chariot onto the axle and ran expertly up the yoke as if he had been born to chariot climbing. Mederei followed, running close behind. The pair leapt onto the horses; Gandwy on the right and Mederei on the left. They slashed through the straps holding the beasts to the yoke and turned their horses aside. Too late did the gladiators on the opposing side see the chariot speed unguided towards them. They broke rank.

Mederei's smile was vicious as she watched the carefully trained phalanx collapse moments before the chariot crashed into the opposing gladiators. Moments later, a wave of Britons did the same, their painted blue torsos a stark contrast against the red fabric and brown leather armour of the Romans.

"Pretty words," Vitus murmured as he watched. He glanced quickly at Adalbern, who sat still as stone, leaning forward and watching. The man looked like a fortress on the verge of crumbling.

Mederei ducked the javelin launched in her direction by the enormous man on the Iberian mount. She snarled and kicked her horse. Around her, the battle raged. All discipline in the ranks of the Roman army had vanished. Without their schemes, the odds of British victory were substantially higher. The Britons had two mounted warriors, trumping their one. Still, Creon was not cowed and he kicked his horse into action.

They met in the centre of the arena. The man swung a heavy sword at Mederei's throat. Mederei lay back as the blade whistled over her. She reached out an arm as she passed, not to try and stab her opponent, but to wrap around his torso. She twisted, leaping from her horse and flying over his, dragging him easily off his mount. They hit the ground hard. Fighting against lungs shocked by the impact, Mederei stood first, and drew her other blade.

"Want to play the part of the druid-killer?" she demanded of the man. "Then learn what our island and her queen would do to you!" She leapt forward, her blades flashing.

Her opponent was strong and fast. Mederei's only hope was to wear him down or cause him to err. Her two blades were like whips they moved so quickly. They trapped his blade against the sand. For it, Mederei earned a hard backhand across her face. It was forceful enough to stagger her and she shuffled back.

"Suetonius Paulinus defeated the screeching harpy," the man said from under his mask. "And she fled like a whipped bitch."

Mederei snarled. She attacked. "The coward never met her sword," Mederei growled at the gladiator as she pressed her two blades against his single blade. "You will meet mine!"

They separated and returned, separated again and circled. In simultaneous action, they engaged again.

"Correct me if I'm mistaken, Lilius," the lanista from Rome enquired of the governor. "But did not the Romans win that battle?"

Lilius stared down at the arena in disbelief. The Britons clearly had the upper hand, their fiery blood ignited by the impassioned cry of the Woman. His eyes fell upon her, her battle against her much larger opponent strangely even. This was not the plan. The Britons needed to be taught their lesson. He signalled to the two guards he positioned in the audience earlier with a quick wave. The soldiers nodded, threw aside their cloaks and hefted large javelins.

Movement in the stands caught Mederei's eye as she ducked the wide swing of her opponent. She danced beneath the man's arm and twirled away. Checking on the crowd, she saw two Roman guards heft thick javelins. Her heart skipped as she thought they might take aim for her. But their attentions were not on her. Mederei followed their lines and time slowed.

Her opponent rushed her. Mederei did not let him start his swing. She kicked him full in the chest and he flew backward, landing hard on his back. She turned and ran, lifting a round shield from the sand near its dead owner, a Briton who stared up at the Gaulish sky unseeing. She threw it.

Her timing was sublime. The first javelin, which would have struck her sister's skull, instead hit the spinning shield and fell quivering to the ground. The second javelin, however, found its mark. The thud and crack of the weapon piercing Modron through and striking the wood behind her could be heard over the din of combat.

"No," Mederei whispered. "No!" She ran forward, blind to all else in the arena. She did not hear the sudden silence fall over the audience as she scrambled up the false rocks. Unthinking, she struck the javelin with her sword, cutting the shaft neatly. Then she cut the bonds that held Modron's hands above her head. Modron slumped, Mederei catching her. Slowly, painfully, she slid her sister off the javelin. Her legs buckled and she fell to her knees, cradling her sister to her.

"Modron," Mederei whispered. She gently brushed some of Modron's fiery hair from her face and the girl's grey eyes fluttered open. Their usual distant haze faded as the girl looked up at the woman holding her. Seemingly unaware of the wound that gushed blood, Modron smiled. She lifted a delicate hand and touched Mederei's cheek gently.

"Found you," Modron murmured, talking through the blood welling in her throat.

Mederei smiled though tears streamed down her cheeks. She took her sister's hand and pressed it more firmly against her own face. "You did," she said.

The light in Modron's grey eyes faded, though they remained fixed on Mederei. The girl's hand went limp, held to Mederei's face only by Mederei.

Modron shivered, then was gone. Mederei felt the loss as if her own soul had been ripped from her chest.

Throwing her head back, Mederei screamed.

The scream stopped everything. All gladiators, no matter which side they represented, ceased their fighting and turned. Even the birds in the nearby glades silenced their singing. Gandwy had just defeated his enemy, taking his head when Mederei's scream reached his ears. The scene that met his searching gaze stole his breath.

Mederei knelt on the top of the Roman contraption, her sister's body held close. On the wooden pole was stuck a thick javelin, cut short and covered in blood. He guessed what had transpired immediately. His blood ran cold.

The silence did not last long. The gladiator chosen to play the part of the druid-killer saw his chance to win the upper hand and thus the battle at last. He lifted his sword and attacked the nearest man—Gandwy. Taken by surprise, Gandwy reeled back, narrowly missing a disembowelment. Taking their cue from Creon, the rest of the Roman gladiators renewed their fights.

Mederei dimly heard the sounds of fighting recommence behind her, but it felt distant and dull, as if heard from underwater. It did not matter. Nothing reached her. She held Modron to her breast, rocking the girl as if she merely slept. But Modron's grey eyes were open, staring up at Mederei, never to see again. "Forgive me," Mederei whispered. "Mother, forgive me. I have failed you. I have failed you both."

A cry cut short behind her roused Mederei and the slow fire of grief turned ire grew in her gut. She laid her sister's body down, closed her eyes, and arranged her body in the manner of the dead. She rose slowly. Looking out at nothing in particular, Mederei reached across and gripped the bloodied handle of the javelin stuck into the wooden post. She yanked, pulling the weapon free, and turned.

Gandwy could not recover his footing. He stumbled back under the brutal onslaught of the man dressed as the druid-killer, barely managing to avoid the blows. He did not notice the body that stopped his retreat. He toppled backwards, his arm flailing. It was the opening his opponent had been searching for. A swift flick and Gandwy's throat opened, spraying hot red blood over Creon's breastplate.

Creon smiled smugly as he watched the Briton collapse. The smile vanished as he spied Mederei flying through the air towards him. Creon had no time to react as Mederei flew, a javelin in one hand and a gladius in her other. She landed, plunging the spear into his chest and striking with both knees at the same time. He fell back, Mederei landing atop him. She rolled off. She did not release the javelin as she rolled. The combination of the strength of her fury and momentum picked Creon off the ground and threw him.

Creon landed hard on his back, the javelin still deep in his chest. He could not breathe, the world spun as he grappled with the pain. He blinked as he felt himself rise, lifted up by the neck of his breastplate.

"This is what awaits Rome, druid-killer," Mederei hissed. She swung her gladius and removed the man's head. She released his breastplate and let the body slump. Striding forward, she caught his rolling head, and turned to the podium. Though the occupants remained in their seats, she saw no one but Lilius, the man responsible for organizing these games. The man responsible for the murder of her sister.

Thought did not heft the head in her hands, nor did it launch it with all of Mederei's strength at the governor. It was all done automatically. No words accompanied the projectile, but the force of all of Mederei's grief, rage, and hate accompanied it. It never hit its intended target. The man ducked the head, and cowered as it bounced off his seat back with a sickening crunch. Only when the head stopped rolling did he uncurl. He rose slowly, rage turning his face purple.

"Guards!" he bellowed.

The doors to the arena opened and one full maniple of Roman soldiers marched into the arena. Lilius turned and stormed from the podium, descending the stairs with a speed that ought to have been impossible for his bulk.

The gladiators in the arena knew what the presence of the Roman soldiers meant. The battle was over. Seven of the remaining eight gladiators threw down their weapons. The eighth waited, her head bowed, her weapon still in her hand. She remained perfectly still, save for the twitch of her coiled muscles. Rage and madness emanated from her, an invisible field that not one Roman soldier dared cross. They surrounded her, but gave her a wide berth.

No one moved as they awaited the governor.

"No!" Porcia gasped when Lilius appeared, stomping from one of the entrances carrying a lash. Before anyone could stop her, Porcia rose and scurried after her betrothed.

"Porcia!" her mother and brother cried in unison.

"Damn it," Ambrosius hissed. He rose, closely followed by his mother and ran after the girl.

Aetius snapped a hand around Maxima's elbow. "Sit back down," he commanded. His wife would not obey. Not this time. She yanked her arm free and followed her son.

Adalbern stood, meeting Aetius gaze with an impassive expression, but his eyes promised bloody murder. Aetius uttered no command to the Batavian, watching him sourly as the broad-backed man followed his wife. He turned back to the arena to watch the events unfold.

Mederei felt, rather than saw, Lilius's arrival. She lifted her head to meet his gaze. The fire that blazed in her eyes gave the governor pause. He stopped mid-stride before drawing himself together and standing tall. He looked at the body of the young British woman atop the constructed set piece.

"Rome has killed Britain after all. Now, lay down your weapon, slave," he commanded.

Mederei did not answer. Her expression did not change. She simply stared at Lilius, hefting her gladius as if to test its weight. Lilius let the coils of his lash drop. His grip tightened on the braided leather handle.

"Your impertinence will be punished," he said. "But I will treat you more leniently if you drop your weapon."

A small smile spread slowly across Mederei's lips. It was a mirthless smile; a mad smile. Her fierce eyes flashed and she leapt forward.

"Guard!" Lilius shrieked, his voice breaking as if he were little more than a young boy first coming into manhood.

The soldiers reacted immediately. The insanity of Mederei's grief paid no heed to the fact that she was outnumbered one hundred and forty to one. Her target was Lilius, and she saw naught but him. She stepped forward, swaying on her feet; a mad gait to match her mad mind. Three steps more, and the soldiers swarmed over her and despite badly wounding four, she was captured and restrained, held fast by three soldiers, one grabbing her hair and yanking so that he might press a knife at her throat. A shadow fell over her and she moved her eyes to it. Lilius stood over her.

"Go on, my dear," he crooned, "struggle. Nothing would give me greater pleasure than to permit this soldier to open your throat."

Mederei only stared.

"No?" Lilius asked. He smiled and looked her over. "No matter. This sand will still taste your blood."

He reached out with one hand, sliding it up her front to the rough-cut collar. He grabbed a hold and tugged hard. It took three tries, but once the fabric ripped, it came away with little resistance.

"Turn her over," he commanded. Two more soldiers rushing in to help the three men grab Mederei and turn her around, exposing her back. One man held her at the end of each of her limbs and stretched her out like a starfish.

The whip cracked as it struck Mederei's naked flesh, sending a spray of blood across the forearms of the men holding onto her wrists. Mederei uttered no cry, giving no indication of her pain but the strong contraction of her muscles. Already weak from the various wounds acquired this fight, it took no more than three lashes before she stopped reacting altogether. Twice more the lash scoured her back with barely a twitch.

Lilius's expression was ecstatic as he flicked the lash back for another strike. He pulled, only to find the lash stuck. He turned.

Porcia stood, one foot pressing hard on the whip, keeping it from moving. Her stance and expression were defiant, her gaze holding his in an uncharacteristic display of strength.

"Enough!" Porcia said.

The shock of Porcia's insolence lasted only a brief second before anger replaced it. Lilius lashed out, striking Porcia hard across her cheek with the back of his free hand.

"Dare you speak to me like that," he spat as she tumbled to the ground. He took a step forward and stopped. Ambrosius and Maxima had arrived, running to Porcia's side and helping her up. The Batavian hostage also arrived, and he stepped menacingly between the governor and Porcia. He said nothing, but his brown eyes were now hard and cold, promising hellish retribution if Lilius moved one bit closer to the girl.

For a long moment, there was silence.

"That's enough now, Lilius," Vitus said as he walked past Porcia, Aetius at his side. "You've made your point."

Lilius looked at Aetius. "You need to teach your daughter some respect!" he spat.

"I will," Aetius said. "I apologize for this spectacle, Governor."

Snorting, Lilius looked from Aetius to Adalbern to Vitus. He snorted again, tossed his bloodied whip onto the sand and stalked out of the arena. "Clean up this mess and get the menagerie!" he snapped as he disappeared from the arena.

Adalbern watched him leave before turning back to collect Mederei. She was not where the guards had dropped her. Frowning, Adalbern followed the tracks in the sand to find Mederei crawling on her belly, struggling towards the structure upon which her sister lay. Her strength gave out before she reached the false rocks and she fell into the sand, one arm outstretched, striving even in her unconsciousness towards her sister.

It took a moment for Adalbern to move. He strode forward, the fierceness of his features replaced by sorrow, and removed his tunic. He wrapped it around Mederei's torso before lifting her. He turned and saw Gandwy's body lying not far away.

He looked up at one of the soldiers. "Give them a good burial," he murmured to the young man. "They fought bravely today."

Pale-faced, the soldier nodded. Adalbern nodded in return, turned and left the arena, Aetius's family in tow.

"Come on, Aetius," Vitus said. "There are exotic dancers from Africa to dance in the arena soon. Let's get some refreshment and retake our seats."

Aetius grunted, not trusting himself to speak in his current state. He permitted Vitus to lead him out of the arena as the soldiers began the arduous task of removing the day's corpses.

Only Romans watched the dancing. The Gauls of Lugdunum did not return to the arena for the afternoon entertainments. Instead, they stood vigil outside the ludus, waiting silently for news of the Woman.

Inside, Adalbern worked frantically, preparing his tools and poultices, balms and bandages. Outside the door of the infirmary, the gladiators not involved in the day's fight gathered in the training yard, sitting in groups but not speaking to one another. Gandwy's death had shocked many of them. He was close to retirement, and one of the better fighters. He had been with the ludus since Boudicca's defeat some ten years ago.

The gladiators watched as the servants entered, carrying large cauldrons of steaming hot water and exiting with cloths soaked in blood.

"Hush now," Maxima said, soothing her sobbing daughter. "It will be all right."

Porcia did not answer. She let her mother hold her close, while she held a sack of shaved ice against her bruised cheek. They sat on the bench at the far end of the infirmary, watching as the shirtless Batavian worked. Ambrosius sat with them, but apart, staring glumly down at the floor.

"He's going to make her marry him, you know," he said.

Porcia squeezed her eyes shut, shuddering at the thought. Maxima could say nothing. In all likelihood, her son was correct. Aetius was ambitious, and a familial connection to a governing official would aid his plans. The man cared more about his social standing than anything else.

The family fell into silence, save for Porcia's sobbing.

"The third pot, the brass one, is salt water," Gaius said, pointing.

Adalbern barely glanced up. "Thank you," he said.

"Here," the servant said. "I can thread that needle. Tend to Mederei."

The boy gently took the needle and thread from Adalbern's shaking hands.

"Thank you," Adalbern said again. He turned and took up a cloth, dropping it into the steaming salt water in the brass pot.

The boy nodded. "She was always kind to me," he said. "Some gladiators… some of them forget they are just slaves, slaves like me. They get cruel. Not Mederei, though. She always spared some kind words for me, and always in my mother tongue."

Adalbern smiled slightly as he began to wash the blood and grime from Mederei's back. "She prefers Gauls to Romans," he said.

Gaius laughed softly. "And Britons to Gauls." He pulled the thread through the eye of the needle, set it aside and picked up another. "How many do you need threaded?"

"All of them," Adalbern said.

The door creaked open and Adalbern glanced briefly to find Geraint standing at the entrance to the infirmary.

"I have come to lend my aid," Geraint said.

Adalbern nodded and Geraint stepped into the room, closing the door behind him.

"What do you need?"

"You could start mixing the poultices," Adalbern said. "The mortar and pestle is with the ingredients on the workbench."

Geraint nodded. He went immediately to the bench and, with Adalbern's guidance, mixed the first poultice.

"The girl," Adalbern asked, when Geraint delivered the first small pot of medicinal paste to the surgeon's table at which Adalbern worked. "The one Lilius had killed. That was her sister, wasn't it?"

"It was," Geraint croaked, his voice little more than a whisper.

Silence fell as Geraint moved back to the workbench to mix the next batch.

"You told me once her story was well known."

"Yes. The whole world must know it by now."

Adalbern nodded. He did not pause in his work, washing Mederei's back with the hot salty water and rinsing the cloth in the pot, turning the water in it bright red.

"Gaius," he called softly.

"Yes?"

"I need more salt water and a fresh cloth."

"Right away." The boy put down the needle and thread and took up the pot. He exited the room to tip the bloody water on the rose bushes that grew near the door before running with the empty pot to the kitchens where more water was heating in anticipation of Adalbern's needs.

The gladiators gathered there winced at the water, which was so red it ran opaque.

Inside, Adalbern took up the first threaded needle.

"She's not from the north, is she?" Adalbern asked as he began to stitch the first of the lash wounds.

"She is a woman of the north," Geraint snapped. He sighed and his voice softened. "But no, she was not born in the north."

Again, Adalbern nodded in answer to Geraint's admission and silence fell in the infirmary.

"Her mother," Adalbern said. "She led the British resistance against Rome ten years ago." It was not a question.

"Yes."

There was no pause in his work as Adalbern pulled Mederei's sundered flesh closed. "Boudicca's daughter," he whispered. He finished stitching the wound, washed his hands, and picked up another needle. "My father fought her," he said to Geraint. "The British queen."

Geraint grunted, not pausing. "That is the least surprising thing about you, Batavian," he said.

Adalbern's lips twisted slightly. "He had a different memory of that fight than Rome's."

This did capture Geraint's curiosity. He looked up briefly. "Oh?"

"My father recalled that woman being of fierce countenance, and beautiful beyond measure. 'Like a stormy sea,' he said, once. That fight was the beginning of the rift between the Batavian cohorts and our legion."

"How so?"

Adalbern shrugged. "A difference of philosophy. Father did not mind the battle itself, but what came after was inexcusable. There was no honour in Rome's actions."

"The druid-killer knew her daughters had escaped him," Geraint said. "He embarked on a campaign of slaughter in the hopes of ending her line forever. He should have come north. I'd have put my spear through his skull."

Adalbern grimaced and shook his head. "Boudicca's daughter," he whispered again.

Geraint looked at him.

Gaius returned with a fresh pot of steaming salt water and the conversation about Mederei's identity ceased. Adalbern finished washing Mederei's back with the saline solution in silence before Gaius brought the next of the threaded needles to him.

"Will she be all right?" he asked as Adalbern took the implements. "She will live, right?"

Adalbern did not spare a glance at the boy. "If she dies, it will not be her wounds that take her."

Gaius stared up at the tall German with wide, uncomprehending eyes.

"Heartbreak," Geraint said softly, "can take even the strongest warrior under. And Mederei has been through much of it." He shook his head. "With Lord Rhys dead, and now her sister taken from her, her reasons for living have been snatched away."

Geraint did not miss the twitch in Adalbern's hands at his words. Neither did Gaius. The boy placed a comforting hand briefly on Adalbern's forearm and tried to smile up at him. Adalbern nodded and returned to work.

"Porcia," he said softly. "Geraint needs help. Do you remember how I mixed the poultices last time?"

The young Roman girl lifted herself from her mother's embrace and stared a moment at Adalbern. She nodded and slid from the bench at the end of the room and walked slowly to the bench where sat the ingredients, and the mortar and pestle.

"Witch hazel to dry the wound," she murmured before setting aside her grief and focussing on the task.

"Good," Adalbern said. He stitched carefully, making sure that the split skin lined up well before pulling the thread taut.

"Do you think you can get her on her feet again?" Geraint said after a protracted silence.

"Again, it will not be her wounds that take her under."

"Lilius is leaving for business to Rome in three weeks. Aetius is going with him," Geraint said, dropping his voice so that only Adalbern could hear. "I told him I would likely see him there. I'm leaving for Rome in two days myself to try my luck finding work as a bard there. Perhaps for the emperor himself."

The meaning of the words was not lost on Adalbern, but whatever spark they lit in him, he did well not to show it.

"Is that so?" he asked, disinterestedly.

"Yes. I need Mederei on her feet before I leave."

Adalbern nodded. "I am doing what I can."

Another long silence followed, during which Adalbern finished the stitching and Porcia brought him the poultice she made. Adalbern checked it carefully before smiling at the girl.

"Well done," he said. "You might make a decent healer yet."

"Perhaps I might make my living doing this one day."

The silent implication hung in the air; *One day, when I escape this life.*

Adalbern smiled softly at her. The smile slipped as he turned back to Mederei, painting her back with a thick layer of the goopy medicine.

"Gaius, her clothes?"

"Already here," the boy answered, pointing to a neatly folded pile of clothing on the near end of the work table.

"How long?" Adalbern asked Geraint.

"Pardon?"

"How long do you think Lilius and Aetius are planning on being away?"

"They plan to spend only a fortnight in Rome," Geraint said. "Lilius wanted longer, but Aetius was concerned about being away for too long. He wanted to take his family with him."

Porcia started and looked up at Geraint, her eyes wide with terror.

"Lilius instead wanted to have the wedding a week before he left."

"No," Porcia whispered. She looked back at her brother, who approached. "I cannot marry him. I cannot." Fresh tears filled her eyes.

Ambrosius wrapped his arms around his younger sister's shoulders. "You won't," he whispered fiercely. "I swear it. You won't."

"We have no plan," Porcia said. She pulled away and turned to face her brother. "We have no plan to escape. You said we'd be away when father next goes on business! His next trip is after the wedding!" Panic took hold of the girl and her breathing quickened. "I can't marry him. I can't! It will kill me. Ambrosius... Ambrosius help me! I can't breathe!"

Ambrosius caught his sister as her knees gave way.

"I can't breathe."

"Porcia," he said. "Porcia, be calm!"

"Porcia!" Maxima ran to her daughter, taking her by the shoulders and shaking her. "Porcia! Pull yourself together!"

"Mother," Porcia whispered, before bursting into fresh tears.

Maxima pulled her daughter close.

"Please," Porcia begged through her tears. "Please, please, please, please..."

Movement diverted Geraint's eyes from the spectacle of Porcia's grief. He looked up to meet Ambrosius's eyes. There was something hard in the boy's gaze, some rock of determination that had suddenly aged him.

Adalbern paid no heed to anyone else in the room as he gently bandaged Mederei's wounds and slowly dressed her.

"I have to take her to her room. Gaius?"

"I'll fetch the key-bearer," the boy said, drawing his attention away from Porcia's hysteria.

"I'll come," Adalbern replied. "It will be faster."

The boy nodded and Adalbern lifted Mederei into his arms.

Not sparing a glance for anyone, he followed the boy from the infirmary. He blinked rapidly as he stepped out into the late afternoon sun. The air inside the infirmary had been so heavy with grief, Adalbern had forgotten that such a thing as the sun existed. A soft sound of shuffling feet alerted him to the presence of other people in the outdoor training area of the ludus; his eyes confirming it as they adjusted to the light.

The training area was full, those gladiators who had been spared this fight stood, each one facing the infirmary door. None smiled. Their eyes were fixed on Mederei's form, limp in Adalbern's arms.

Izem walked forward. "Will she live?" he asked softly.

"If heartbreak does not take her," Adalbern said. "It was her sister," he explained when Izem raised his brows.

"Her sister? The fire-haired girl?"

Adalbern said nothing. He moved forward, following Gaius, whose posture exuded impatience as he waited for the German healer. Izem stepped back, giving room for Adalbern to pass. The other gladiators did the same, stepping aside in silence. Their expressions were glum.

Ignoring them, Adalbern delivered Mederei to her cell, opened by the key-bearer, and laid her gently onto her bed. With Gaius's help, he covered her with a warm blanket.

"Is there really nothing left for her to live for?" the boy asked Adalbern, once the work was done. Adalbern turned and sought a chair, which he found at the beautifully crafted table in her cell; a gift from a Gaulish carpenter. He sat and rubbed his face with one hand before nodding.

"Yes," he said at last. "She once had the promise of freedom, but with both her lover and her sister dead, I don't know that will be enough now."

Gaius went to Mederei's side and gently moved her hair from her face. "I don't want her to die."

Adalbern scoffed. "Neither do I," he whispered quietly.

"Neither do I," Vitus said from the door. Adalbern jumped to his feet and Gaius gasped, spinning around.

"Did I startle you?" Vitus asked. His wife appeared from behind him.

"How is she?" she asked, pushing past her husband to glide into the room.

"Alive," Adalbern answered. "For now."

The woman went to Mederei's side and fixed the blankets around the Briton.

"You look exhausted, Adalbern," Vitus noted.

"I was working a long time."

"All afternoon, Izem tells me."

"Her wounds were deep."

Vitus nodded. "You will, of course, be compensated."

Adalbern shrugged, turning his attention back to the woman unconscious on the bed. Vitus sighed and entered the room. "Do all Germans wear their hearts so fully on their sleeves, Adalbern?"

Adalbern scowled at him.

"It is obvious to anyone with eyes that you are in love with this woman."

Grunting, Adalbern shrugged. "Why would one not dare show their affections? What possible benefit would it serve?"

"You do know that this was doomed from the start, don't you?"

A soft, sad smile touched Adalbern's lips. "The heart wants what it wants," he said softly. "Even if it's impossible."

"Disdain hurts less," Vitus noted.

"But the pretence of it does not. I would grieve all the same at her passing, whether I let myself show my love or not."

Vitus had no answer to this, and so turned his attention to his wife, who sat by Mederei's bed and watched her pale face. He went to his wife's side and placed a hand on her shoulder.

"She looks younger when she sleeps," the woman murmured.

"Come now," Vitus said softly. "It's almost time for dinner, and Lilius expects us."

"Lilius," his wife said, shaking her head.

"I know," Vitus murmured. "But he is governor."

"More's the pity."

"Enough now. Go dress."

Vitus's wife sighed and rose to her feet. She paused in front of Adalbern as she walked from the room. "Thank you, for taking such good care of her."

Adalbern offered a small smile. "Such that it is."

"It is more, I am sure, than anyone else has done since she was taken as a slave."

Not waiting for Adalbern's reply, she glided from the room to do as her husband bid. Vitus walked to Adalbern. "My wife's heart is almost as soft as yours."

Adalbern flashed a smile.

"Take care, Adalbern, that your soft heart does not lead you into foolishness."

There was no flicker in Adalbern's expression as he turned his gaze from Mederei to Vitus. "Rome has my nephew," he said. "Whatever foolishness my heart may desire is not greater than my love for him."

Vitus stared a long time at Adalbern, who boldly met his gaze. At length, as if satisfied, Vitus grunted and walked to the door.

"Maxima is ready to take her children home. They're in the courtyard with the carriage. I'll have them wait."

"I'd rather walk."

Shrugging, Vitus stepped through the door. He waited for Adalbern and Gaius. Casting one last look at Mederei unconscious on her bed, Adalbern left the room.

"Come, Gaius," Vitus called softly. He waited for the boy to exit Mederei's cell before closing the gate. His gaze flickered to Adalbern briefly.

"Your tunic is covered in blood," he noted.

Adalbern did not appear to hear him, his attention was back inside the cell. Vitus sighed and shook his head. "Goodnight, Adalbern."

This time Adalbern turned to Vitus. The slave master looked tired and unhappy. No doubt he had to do a lot of talking to calm Lilius's temper, perhaps saving Mederei's life.

"Goodnight, Roman," Adalbern replied, unable to keep the bitterness from his voice.

"I'm a Gaul," Vitus whispered as he watched the German walk wearily away.

Adalbern paused at the ludus gate. Gathered there in large numbers, the Gaulish citizens of Lugdunum stood in silent vigil. A soft murmur moved through the crowd when he appeared. Adalbern looked down at himself. He was indeed covered with blood.

Grimacing, he braced himself and stepped out into the crowd, his ever-present guards at his back.

"Does she live?" a sickly young woman clutching a child to her asked as Adalbern passed.

He turned to her, meeting her wide, hopeful eyes with a blank expression. He nodded. "Yes," he answered softly. "For now."

Another murmur made its way through the gathering. The woman reached out and grasped Adalbern's sleeve. Gripping it tight, she looked up at him and said, "Thank you. Bless you. Bless you."

Tired and unsure in his suddenly surreal surrounds, Adalbern nodded at her and continued forward. The crowd parted before him, each person murmuring a hushed "Bless you" as he passed. Some reached out to brush his forearms.

It was a long, strange walk lined with worried Gauls before Adalbern arrived back at Aetius's house. The house was silent and dark. Dead-eyed servants opened the door for Adalbern. One of the girls looked as if she had been crying.

"What's going on?" Adalbern murmured to her. The servant shrugged in return, but did not offer an explanation. Adalbern could guess. No doubt Aetius had a few words for his family. Sighing, he stepped into the house and made his slow way to his room. Unable to keep his eyes open, he slipped off his bloody tunic and fell face forward in the bed. He fell to sleep before his head hit the pillow.

## 72 AD, ONE WEEK LATER, LUGDUNUM, PROVINCE OF GAUL

"Adalbern!"

The German twitched, slowly opening his eyes as a cacophony of sound ripped into his sleep. Groaning, Adalbern lifted himself up to find Ambrosius holding a flickering candle at his bedside. Behind him, Porcia held onto her brother, looking terrified. Outside, the sounds of an angry crowd moved throughout the city.

"You sleep like the dead!" Ambrosius hissed.

"What is going on?" Adalbern demanded.

"The city's gone mad," Ambrosius said. "They're rioting in the streets, destroying everything. The city guard cannot maintain control."

Adalbern scowled and slipped from the bed. He grabbed a fresh tunic and pulled it on, tying it with a sturdy leather belt.

"We're leaving," Ambrosius said flatly. "You're coming."

"I can't!" Adalbern hissed, spinning to face the Roman youth in surprise. "My nephew!"

"There you are," Geraint said as he strode into the room. "Are you ready?"

"We're ready," Ambrosius replied in a harsh whisper. "Except the German."

"You must," Geraint said to Adalbern.

"My—"

"I will meet you in Britain with your nephew, I swear it," Geraint said. "Right now, I need you to keep your vow. With the city in uproar, this is Mederei's best chance at freedom. She is in no state to fight her way through this. She will need you to care for her until she can."

"But Rome—"

"This is the plan," Geraint said to Ambrosius, cutting through Adalbern's protests. "I'm headed to Lilius's house to help him protect it. Most of the city guard are there, leaving ample opportunity to flee the city." He turned to Adalbern. "My protection of Lilius's home will absolve me of any suspicion. I will offer to ride as fast as I can to Rome to appeal for aid on Lilius's behalf. That is how I will find your nephew. Vitus has taken the gladiators to aid the city guard. The ludus is mostly deserted. Now is the time to extract Mederei."

"How? It will be locked."

Geraint smiled. From his boot, he produced a key. "I am a bard, a shield-bearer, and a pick-pocket." He handed the key to Adalbern. "This will get you in, but I suggest you make it look like the gates were forced. That way they can blame it on the rioters."

"You've really thought of everything," Ambrosius said, shaking his head.

"I have had much time to ponder Mederei's rescue. Now, listen closely. The riot will not last long. Take weapons, you may need to defend yourself."

"Where is Aetius?" Adalbern demanded.

"Gone to Lilius's. He's instructed Maxima and his children to stay in the house and keep all the lights out."

"Where is Maxima?"

"Asleep."

Adalbern stared at Geraint.

"I may have offered her an old British medicine, to calm her nerves. She's in a safe room and very warm. She'll sleep only until morning."

"We have to go," Ambrosius said.

Geraint nodded. He led the way to the front door of Aetius's house. He peeked out. "The coast is clear," he said. Ambrosius nodded and, lifting a small pack from the shadows near the door, turned to offer his hand to his sister.

"This is it, Porcia," he said. "Our chance."

Her face twisted in a strange mix of terror and hope, Porcia took her brother's hand. They ducked out of the door.

"One last thing," Geraint said to Adalbern. "You must make your way to Helinio. You are looking for a Belgian fisherman. You will recognize him. He will likely as not be gambling on the docks. He will also be wearing a pendant with this symbol on it."

Geraint placed a painted pebble in Adalbern's hand. Adalbern looked at it, noting the scratched lines on the rock.

"He is my cousin, and hates Rome almost as much as I do. He will take you across the strait. I am trusting you with the most valuable thing Britain has ever had. Keep her safe, Adalbern. I promised my Lord I would see her home, and I meant it. If your care fails, you will not be spared my wrath."

"Me with your queen and you with my nephew," Adalbern said. "It seems we must rely on each other."

Geraint grunted. "Good luck, my German friend. We might not see the empire crumble, but here's to our own small victories."

Adalbern smiled slightly. "Good luck to you, too. Gods willing, we will see each other in Britain."

"Gods willing."

Adalbern slipped from the house and joined Ambrosius and Porcia. "Ready?" he asked them.

They nodded in unison.

"Good, stay close."

Keeping as much to the shadows as possible, Adalbern led the way through the rioting city to the ludus.

"Damn everything," Adalbern hissed. He pulled his head back around the corner and rested his back on the stone wall of the house he, Mederei, Ambrosius, and Porcia were hiding behind. The excursion to the ludus had been uneventful. Their return, however, was fraught with danger. They snuck through the streets like thieves, hoping the shadows and the riots would conceal their passing.

"They've guards on the gates."

"So what now?" Ambrosius demanded. "We fight our way through?"

"We might have to."

"German!" a voice hissed from the alley across the road. Adalbern looked across with a deep scowl. It vanished as he spied Gaius in the shadows. The young Gaul's face was smeared with soot, making the boy's white grin ghastly in the dim light. Gaius waved Adalbern over.

"You cannot be serious," Ambrosius whispered as Adalbern straightened. "He's from the ludus. He'll give us away!"

"No," Adalbern said. "Not Gaius. I know this boy. Come on."

"Are you sure?" Porcia asked.

Adalbern nodded. "I'm sure." He turned to Mederei, who rested against the wall, her eyes closed as if she was sleeping.

"Mederei," he said, touching her shoulder. Mederei's eyes flickered open.

"I'm here," she murmured. "I'm awake."

Adalbern nodded. "Follow me."

Mederei wearily pushed herself off the wall and turned. She took a step forward. Her legs gave way and she fell. Adalbern caught her before her knees hit the ground.

"Sorry," Mederei mumbled.

"It's all right," Adalbern replied. He pulled one of Mederei's arms around his neck, wrapped an arm around her waist and lifted her to her feet. "I have you," he said gently. "Come on."

With Adalbern's help, Mederei made it across the road into the alley, where Gaius patiently waited. Porcia and Ambrosius followed closely behind.

"Come," Gaius said to Adalbern. "I know a way out of the city."

"The gates are all shut," Ambrosius growled.

"Not gates," Gaius said. "Tunnels. Come!"

"Tunnels?" Porcia whispered her question to her brother. Puzzled, Ambrosius shook his head. With no other option open to them, they followed Gaius through the rioting streets of Lugdunum.

When they reached their destination, a small stone house with a thatched roof, Mederei was breathing heavily and entirely unable to stand.

"We need to rest," Porcia said, moving to Mederei's side and gently pulling the Briton's hair away from her face. "Mederei's in no state to keep running."

"In here," Gaius said. He opened the wooden door of the house and raced inside. Lifting Mederei in his arms, Adalbern followed, having to duck to avoid smacking his forehead against the lintel.

He paused once inside. Gaius was in the tight embrace of a broadly built Gaulish woman; his mother, presumably. The woman looked up, fixing Adalbern with hard grey eyes. They shifted to the woman in Adalbern's arms.

"This is her, then. The Briton?"

Adalbern nodded. "Please," he said. "We need to get out of the city. We need to get her home."

The woman nodded curtly. "So I hear." She released her son and crouched down to look the boy in the eye. "You are certain you want to do this? The repercussions should you be caught are dire."

Gaius nodded. "I know. But she needs our help, Mother. I could not call myself a Gaul if I did not do what I could to defeat Rome."

"Oh child, some monsters are too large to be slain."

"Then let me at least wound it."

The woman smiled and brushed the boy's blonde hair from his eyes. "My boy, you are so much like your father." Standing, the woman turned and pulled some blankets from a stand. She lay them across the small bench that regularly served as a bed.

"Put her here and rest your arms while I gather some supplies."

Adalbern immediately went to the bench and laid Mederei on it. He adjusted the blankets around her.

"We just need an escape," he said, turning back to the woman. "We need nothing else of yours."

The woman scoffed. "An escape we have. But you will not get far without help. Now sit a moment. It will be some time before the guards realize that any one of you is missing. I have some food to share. Sit. Eat."

"We don't—"

"Sit," the woman said again, her voice sharpening. "It is an affront to gods and men to refuse hospitality."

Properly chastised, Adalbern walked to the open hearth and sat on the packed earth there. Porcia and Ambrosius followed suit, huddled close together for security.

"Gaius," the woman said gently. "Fetch the ponies and bring them to the entrance. That girl is in no state to be walking to Britain."

Smiling, Gaius nodded at his mother and ran into a small, dark door on the side of the house.

"I am Genofefa," the woman said as she handed out dishes. "My ancestor fought with the great chief Vercingetorix against Rome. He lost his life at Alesia."

"I am sorry," Adalbern said. "I have heard of that battle. I am told the Gauls fought bravely."

"Indeed we did," Genofefa said, smiling sadly. "And it goes some way in explaining my willingness to help. Our family has a long-held vendetta against Rome."

"There are thousands of families with similar feelings, I understand," Adalbern said, smiling.

Genofefa scoffed. "I know your story, German," she said as she spooned steaming hot leek and mutton compote. "I know your auxiliary was Rome's favourite."

"We were," Adalbern replied. "Once."

Genofefa turned to serve Porcia and Ambrosius. "Your honesty is appreciated, Batavian."

"I have no need to lie. My sister was murdered by Rome, my father put to death for defending our people. My nephew is hostage to the emperor. Whatever favour once given my people, I have no love for Rome."

"No indeed."

"The horses are ready, mother," Gaius said quietly, panting the words as he tried to catch his breath. He had run fast and far.

"Good. Good lad. Now come and eat."

Gaius obediently sat at the hearth, joining Adalbern. He smiled up at the man before descending on his bowl of compote like a ravenous fox. All her guests now eating, Genofefa sat and served herself. The sounds of the riot echoed into the small home, growing or lowering in intensity as the angered mob moved through the city.

Gaius finished eating first. He disappeared again into the side room, returning moments later with a large knapsack bulging at the seams. "Ready," he announced to the room.

Mederei stirred and Adalbern abandoned his meal to go to her side.

"Where are we?" Mederei asked as Adalbern came into view.

"A friend's house. Come, sit up. I'll get you some food."

"It's all right," Mederei said, her eyes closing again.

"No," Adalbern said firmly. He wrapped his arm around Mederei and pulled her upright. "You need to eat. All this running around will increase the risk of infection, and you will need the strength to fight it. It will not do to lose you before we reach Britain."

Mederei opened her eyes again. "Why are you helping me?" she asked. "Why are you risking so much?"

"You know why," Adalbern whispered in return.

Mederei opened her mouth to reply and, finding her voice absent, shut it again.

"Eat," Adalbern said. He turned to fetch his unfinished meal, but was instead confronted with a full bowl of hot compote held by Genofefa.

"I think I understand you better now, Batavian," the Gaulish woman said as Adalbern accepted the bowl. "And now I believe you."

Adalbern had no response, so he turned to Mederei and placed the bowl in her hands. "Can you eat?" he asked. "Or shall I feed you?"

"I am not a child," Mederei replied. Though her hands trembled violently, Mederei took up the spoon and slowly ate her meal. Adalbern remained on the floor by her side until she finished. He took the bowl from her and set it aside.

"You must go now," Genofefa said. "The fighting has slowed. The city will be subdued come dawn. Gaius!"

The young Gaul stepped up. "Don't worry mother. I'll be back before the sun is up." He turned to Mederei. "Can you walk, my Lady?"

Mederei smiled at him. "Lady? Hardly. But yes, I can walk. The meal was most fortifying." She looked at Genofefa. "Thank you," she said. "I am glad to see that even under Rome's heavy thumb, Gaul has not forgotten herself."

"Gaul never will," Genofefa replied. She walked to Mederei. "For as long as there are Gauls living."

Mederei smiled and shakily rose to her feet. "This gladdens my heart."

Genofefa smiled back at the young woman and pulled her into a gentle embrace. "I know who you are," she whispered to Mederei. "And Britain needs you. Remember your Gaulish sisters when at last you are free from Rome. Remember us, and help us as I have helped you."

"You have my word," Mederei replied. "If Britain is free, we will lend our strength to Gaul."

"Thank you."

The women separated. Adalbern rose to his feet. "We need to move," he said gently.

"Follow me!" Gaius said. He disappeared once more into the side room. Adalbern lifted the bulging knapsack and hauled it onto his back. He turned and held his hand out to Mederei. Hesitating only briefly, Mederei took his hand and permitted him to aid her forward. Still silent and huddled together, Porcia and Ambrosius followed.

The side room proved to be little more than a large pantry, but one of the wooden shelves had been dragged across the floor, revealing an open trapdoor. Orange light from torches flickered, revealing the circular opening.

"Down here," Gaius said, disappearing into the hole.

Adalbern peered down. "That's a sizeable drop," he informed his companions. "I'll lower you all down. Come."

"Mederei first," Porcia said.

"Ambrosius first," Adalbern replied. "He has a weapon. Should there be guards in those tunnels, you'll need someone with a weapon in the lead."

"There are no guards down here," Gaius scoffed from below.

Grinning, Adalbern replied, "Nevertheless, Ambrosius first. Then you, Porcia. Then Mederei. I will follow."

Shrugging, Ambrosius stepped forward. He placed his hands on the ground and swung his feet in. "Need help?" Adalbern asked. Ambrosius grinned up at him before letting himself fall. Moments later, the sounds of thudding feet and a small grunt echoed out of the hole.

"Are you all right?" Porcia asked breathlessly.

"Fine," Ambrosius answered. "It's uh… it's a long way down."

"Down you go," Adalbern said to Porcia. He knelt by the hole. "Give me your hands. I'll lower you down. It'll shorten your fall."

Porcia did as she was bid, grasping Adalbern's strong forearms as tightly as she could. She squeaked as her feet left solid ground, and when they met it again.

"Now you, Mederei," Adalbern said.

There was no argument or complaint from the Briton as Adalbern held out his hands to her. She took them without hesitation, and entrusted her weight to their strength. She hit the ground lightly, nevertheless tipping to the side upon landing. She rested against the cool stone wall of the tunnel that yawned endlessly beyond the reach of the torchlight. Adalbern landed beside her. He blinked as he looked around at the tightly packed stone of the tunnel. A short way down, a small alcove in the wall revealed a wooden chest. Such alcoves appeared regularly in the stonework.

"What are those?" Adalbern asked as he stepped over to Mederei.

"Hmm?" Gaius asked, then, "Oh. The chests? Heads. Heirlooms of our families glorious past, before Rome and the death of honour."

"Heads?" Ambrosius said. "Actual heads? Of people?"

"Of course," Gaius said, frowning at the young Roman's horrified expression. "We keep them in pine oil. The man with the most heads was the mightiest warrior and given all the honours of his people. We were that family. Once."

Adalbern lifted Mederei into his arms. "We'll make better time," he murmured to her. Knowing it for truth, Mederei did not argue, even permitting herself to rest her head against Adalbern's clavicle.

"Let's move," Adalbern said to the group. His voice was sure and commanding, but his heart beat frantically against his chest. It was not the thought of encountering the Roman guard in these tunnels that sent his blood racing, but the silent sign of affection—real or imagined—in Mederei letting her head rest against him. He kept his screaming joy silent as the group moved swiftly through the dark.

"My ancestors built these tunnels in the time of Caesar," Gaius whispered as he walked, a torch in hand. Ambrosius held the other. "They suspected his offers of peace were little more than lip service designed to mask his ambitions."

"They weren't wrong," Adalbern noted.

"No," Gaius said, "they weren't. They used these tunnels to smuggle goods and people in and out of Roman controlled territory, but as more and more chieftains began to submit, the tunnels were forgotten. Only a few families use them now."

Adalbern grunted. He did not have the energy for words. Mederei's weight seemed to be growing, and his arms ached.

The quiet darkness of the tunnels swallowed all sense of time and direction. The group followed Gaius's torch as the boy navigated the various twists and turns.

"It's a damned warren in here," Ambrosius growled as Gaius turned down another corner. He noted the various branches of the tunnel, wondering if they should have actually turned left at the previous junction.

"That's the idea," Gaius said. "Only Gauls know the way through. Any Roman trying to find their way would wind up hopelessly lost."

"It's clever," Adalbern grunted.

"We're almost there."

True to Gaius's word, Adalbern thought he spied a wash of dark blue in the distance.

"Kill the flames," Gaius whispered. He dropped his torch into a small barrel of water hidden behind a depression in the rock wall. "I doubt the entrance is being watched, but just in case."

Ambrosius sighed, looking longingly at the comforting golden light of the torch before dropping the thing in the water. The group remained still a moment, giving themselves time to adjust to the dimness. The torches now extinguished, the end of the tunnel was easier to make out, the blue of the night sky contrasting against the black of the tunnel. A soft nicker from the small, cave-like opening put a smile of Gaius's face.

"Good news," he whispered. "The horses are still here. Come on."

The group crept forward, tense with the threat of discovery and capture. Not a Roman was in sight when they exited the tunnels, only three horses, one carrying large bags slung either side of its withers.

"This is where I must leave you. Mother will need help. The horses are not big, but they are strong, hardy, and willing. They will carry you far. Stay away from the roads. Travel at night. Light no fires."

Adalbern smiled at Gaius. "Such was my plan," he said.

"It was something my father once told my uncle," Gaius said. "He told me it was something his father told him. Now, I suppose, it is family wisdom we offer to all who pass our way. I don't even know if it's good advice. I've never been out of the city."

"It is very sound advice," Adalbern said. "Your grandfather was a very wise man."

Gaius smiled up at the big man. "I'm going to miss your visits to the ludus, Adalbern of Batavia. And you, Lady Mederei. You were always kind to me."

"Set me down please, Adalbern," Mederei said. Adalbern obliged. Mederei walked the few steps to stand before Gaius. She smiled softly at him. "And you to me, Maelyn," she said. "If ever the fight in Gaul wearies you, find me in Britain. You will have all the honours worthy of your high family."

"Maelyn," Gaius said, puffing out his chest. "Maelyn." He shook his head. "Safe home, Mederei, champion of Britain. May we meet again, free at last."

"Free at last," Mederei murmured. She bent over and kissed the crown of Gaius's golden head. "Goodbye, Gaius. Thank you for everything."

Gaius smiled at Mederei. He retreated a few steps as Adalbern approached. "There are only two horses for riding," the Batavian said to Mederei. "Will you ride with me?"

Mederei nodded and permitted Adalbern to guide her to a horse. With his aid, she mounted.

Ambrosius and his sister mounted the other horse. Lastly, having taken up the reins of the pack horse, Adalbern hauled himself up behind Mederei. He turned back, nodded his thanks to Gaius, and urged his horse forward at a swift walk. When next he looked back, Gaius had gone, and barely anything could be seen of the small opening into the Gaulish tunnels.

"Mederei," Adalbern asked after a while. "What does Maelyn mean?"

"Little prince," Mederei answered, a smile touching her voice.

"Ah," Adalbern said. "That would please him."

Mederei chuckled and the group fell silent. They walked their horses until the first blush of colour reached the horizon. Sheltered behind an ancient mound surrounded by equally ancient trees, the group rested until nightfall.

## 73 AD, AUTUMN, HELINIO, CANANEFATES TERRITORY GERMANIA MAGNA

Adalbern did not care to disguise himself as he walked the wharf at the port of Helinio. He was a German, in German territory. The chances of any of the Roman guard stationed there recognizing him were so slim as to be non-existent. Mederei walked at his side, her hair a strange orange colour. She had bleached it with lye and lime juice in an effort to disguise herself. It was effective. Any description of her that was circulating certainly would not describe a woman with sun-coloured hair.

Ambrosius and Porcia, notably Roman and unable to disguise the fact, remained behind, waiting in the home of the fisherwives; a collection of Belgic, Gaulish and German women who had lost their husbands at sea and now made a living fishing and repairing nets. They had been told of the arrival of Adalbern and Mederei beforehand in a message sent by Geraint. The crafty shield-bearer of the Caledonii had thought of everything.

It didn't matter that it took them over a year of running to reach the port town of Helinio, with illness, hunger, and desperate avoidance of Roman search parties necessarily slowing them down. When they arrived at Helinio, the fisherwives immediately took them in, though they had been waiting long.

Three men sitting at a barrel, throwing bones, caught Adalbern's eye; the one in the middle in particular. He looked surprisingly much like Geraint.

"May I join you?" Adalbern asked after the last lot of winnings were collected.

"For an aureus," the man in the middle said gruffly, not looking up as he gathered his marked bones.

"Will this do?" Adalbern asked. He tossed the small stone Geraint had given him onto the table. Fate smiled as the rock landed marked side up. The man stopped shuffling his bones around and looked up sharply.

"Caesar's hairy scrotum," he said.

Adalbern raised his brows. That cuss was new to him.

"That Caledonian bastard was telling the truth."

"He's your cousin, is he not?" Adalbern asked.

"Doesn't mean I trust the slimy cur," the man said. He stood. "I'm Senne of the Belgae."

"Adalbern of the Batavi."

Senne's eyes shifted to Mederei. "Lady of the Isle," he said. "It is indeed an honour."

Mederei met the man's searching gaze evenly. "Long without a woman?" she asked tartly as his eyes traced the lines of her body. "We passed several places where affections can be bought. Should I point them out to you?"

Senne's companions snickered and the man scowled at her. "Geraint didn't lie about you either," he said sourly. "Pretty face, tongue of acid."

Mederei shrugged. "Like all weapons, used only when deserved."

Senne grumbled and sat down. "Find a seat, Adalbern of the Batavi," he said. "You've bought your way in."

As the men gambled, Adalbern probed Senne a little. "Tell me, Senne, how is it that you came to this agreement with the Caledonian rogue?"

Scoffing, Senne replied, "Lost a bet. You?"

"Lost a war."

The snickers at the gambling table ceased. Senne looked at Adalbern, no trace of mirth—sarcastic or otherwise—cheapened his expression. "Yes," he said. "I heard about that. A damned shame. We were almost free."

"Almost."

They gambled more. More than half the day passed before Senne stood. "Bah!" he declared. "I've nothing left, you salty bastards!"

"Your fault," one of his companions replied. "You made some very poor choices."

"Bah!" Senne said again. "Come, German," he said to Adalbern. "Buy me a drink to ease my misery. I've got to be out first thing in the morning to catch my livelihood, and you've much to learn about fishing."

"Thank you for the game," Adalbern said to Senne's companions before rising to his feet. The men grunted their response, then promptly ignored Senne and Adalbern.

"I was told there would be four passengers," Senne said in halting Gaulish.

"There are. We've left two with the fisherwives."

Senne shuddered. "A saltier group of women I've never met."

Smiling, Adalbern declined to respond.

"You understand that I cannot take you all the way across the channel," Senne said.

"Geraint said you would," Mederei interjected.

"Like I said, a slimy cur. I can't. But, I can get you out far enough to board a small crossing vessel."

"I don't know how to sail," Mederei whispered to Adalbern.

"You need only one skilled sailor to pilot this boat," Senne said, looking at her.

"What kind of boat is it?" Adalbern asked.

Senne shrugged. "A boat. Belonged to a smuggler by the name of Helmutt."

"What happened to this Helmutt?"

"What else? Rome happened. Captured him last month as he was bringing weapons across to Britain. They had him drowned just off the wharf. Tied him to a box of rocks and sent him into the deep. He was my brother."

"I'm sorry," Adalbern said.

Again, Senne shrugged. "It is done. It also means that if I can get one over Rome, I will, but I will not risk my neck for it."

"That is fair."

"So, can you sail?"

"I can," Adalbern said. "The Batavi were born for the water. Swim or sail, we can do it all."

"I bet," Senne said. He pointed at one of the boats; a large, flat-bottomed fishing vessel with a serpent painted on the butt. "That there is mine. *Serpentina*, I've called her. No reason, I just liked the name. Be here at dawn tomorrow. I'll load you in and take you to Helmutt's boat, come back with barrels of fish, and these idiotic Romans will be none the wiser. Agreed?"

"Agreed."

"See you on the morrow, Batavian." Senne turned to Mederei. "My Lady," he said, before turning abruptly right and heading into the public house sitting on the wharf.

"I dislike him," Mederei said, pursing her lips. Adalbern laughed a soft laugh.

"Come on then," he said. "Let's find some food."

A loud, frantic banging on the door woke Adalbern moments before dawn. He slipped from under the blankets he shared with his three companions, grabbed his shirt from the hook on the wooden wall and walked to the door.

Mederei, Porcia, and Ambrosius all sat up.

"You have to move," Senne said, sliding into the room as soon as Adalbern opened the door. He paused and stared at Adalbern's half-naked form briefly, before turning to Mederei.

"Centurions," he told her. "They're looking for a German and a Briton travelling together, possibly in the company of two young Romans." He waved quickly at Porcia and Ambrosius. "Hello, two young Romans."

Mederei threw the blankets aside and rose from the thick straw that served as a mattress. "Then we must move."

"They will be inspecting the boats. You must find a way to get on the moment they're done inspecting mine. Now collect your effects. Get to the docks. There is no way for me to check to see you're aboard without appearing suspicious. I'll be sailing at dawn whether you're on or not."

Adalbern nodded.

"Good." Senne departed as abruptly as he arrived, vanishing into the night from the small shack near the home of the fisherwives. Adalbern turned to Mederei and shrugged. He pulled his tunic on. "Get your things," he said. "Let's go."

Senne had spoken true. The wharves were alive with activity as sailors and centurions mingled, the centurions barking orders, the sailors protesting in various states of drunkenness and or wakefulness.

Mederei and Adalbern, with Porcia and Ambrosius, hid behind crates in an alley beside a brothel near the wharf, close enough to the *Serpentina* to run to, if the centurions would only turn their backs.

"There are so many of them," Mederei whispered. "How are we to get past them all?"

Adalbern chanced a glance at the scene. It appeared hopeless. The centurions had split into groups, three details searching the ships, and at least five pairs watching the wharves and surrounding areas.

"We need a distraction," Adalbern murmured. He scowled as he turned over possible scenarios in his mind.

Ambrosius lifted his head and took in the scene. There was no way to the ship without being seen. The centurions needed to be drawn away from the *Serpentina* long enough to buy them all time to run across the wharf and onto the boat.

"There's a sewer," Mederei whispered, pointing to a round hole with a grate over it behind barrels near the mouth of the alley.

"That's a little close," Adalbern growled. "I don't like it."

"But it will undoubtedly lead to the ocean. We can get to the ships without having to cross the wharf. It's less risky than running for it."

"We'll still need a distraction to keep eyes off us while we board."

"Ambrosius, where are you going?" Porcia whispered harshly as her brother left her side.

"I have an idea," he whispered in return. "I'll be back soon."

"Ambrosius!" Porcia hissed, but he paid her no heed, disappearing into the night and around the back of the brothel.

Porcia turned to Mederei, eyes wide. Mederei shrugged at her and offered a sympathetic smile.

Ambrosius tapped lightly at the large window at the back of the brothel. Moments later, the shutters flew outwards. The young woman wore a deep scowl, which changed to an expression of surprise when she spied the young Roman looking sheepishly at her.

"Is the Madame in?" he asked in hushed tones.

"A strange time to be looking to buy," the woman responded, also hushed.

"I'm actually looking to help friends."

"What is it?" a gruff voice demanded. A tall, slender woman with long blonde hair marched into view. Her eyes locked with Ambrosius's and she raised an eyebrow at him.

"Forgive the disruption," Ambrosius said. "But I need help."

"Oh?"

"Please, let me in to explain."

Intrigued, the blonde woman nodded to her younger counterpart, who stood back from the window. Ambrosius gratefully hauled himself into the brothel.

Seeing his chance, Adalbern ran across to the sewer grate. A centurion stopped at the mouth of the alley and peered down just as Adalbern reached his new hiding spot. The German tensed behind the crates near the sewer grate, every muscle aching for release, his mind screaming with the terror of getting caught. Moving slowly, he reached for the sword at his side. Apparently satisfied that there was no one there after all, the centurion grunted and moved on. Adalbern relaxed briefly. He quickly checked the wharves for any prying eyes before wrapping his hands around the bars in the grate. Bracing himself, he hauled the grate up.

Years of exposure to salt and sun rusted the grate and ate at the cement holding it in place. It lifted easily. Adalbern paused as the grate came up, tensing as the noise stopped his heart. It was not heard over the din on the wharf, however, and after a tense moment, Adalbern relaxed again. He raised his eyes to meet Mederei's. He started to beckon her over, but the appearance of a young woman from behind the brothel stopped him.

Seeing his gaze shift, Mederei turned. A young woman crept rapidly to her side.

"You are Mederei?" the woman asked.

Mederei nodded silently.

"Ambrosius said that he has a distraction for you. He says you should get to the ship. He will wait until it has been investigated before creating his diversion so you can board. He said you would recognize it when it happens."

"Board?" Porcia asked. "Without him?"

The woman turned to her and offered a sad smile. "Porcia, I assume. He told me to tell you that he loves you very much, and that he can live happily knowing you're free from the clutches of your betrothed, but he cannot go with you this time."

"No!" Porcia breathed, tears striking her eyes, blurring her vision. "I cannot go without him! We were supposed to escape together!"

"Here," the girl said. She removed a small necklace from her neck. "He gave me this to give to you. He said it was a promise. He'll find you in Britain, but you must get there first. He would die, he said, to see you married to the man... Lilius? Is that the right name?"

Porcia nodded, barely containing her sobs. She took the necklace.

"It really is the only way, Porcia," Mederei said. "We will be caught otherwise. Adalbern and I will be put to death, and you will never be free. You must leave without him."

"But we were supposed to escape together," Porcia said, tears at last escaping the prison of lashes. She looked up at Mederei. "He's always been there for me. I don't know that I can be without him."

"He is here for you now," Mederei said, gently wiping a tear from Porcia's cheek. "He is giving you the best gift he knows; freedom."

Porcia nodded. She swallowed back her tears and turned to the young woman. "Please tell my brother I will wait for him. Tell him he must hurry to Britain."

The woman smiled and nodded. She glanced at Mederei before turning and scurrying back to the rear of the brothel.

Mederei placed a comforting hand on Porcia's cheek. "You are lucky to have a brother who loves you so," she said. Porcia nodded, but did not look comforted.

"Now, come," Mederei said. "We must get to the boat."

Mederei turned and checked around the crates to ensure that the alley was not being watched.

"The coast is clear. Quickly!"

Porcia hesitated only briefly before running across to Adalbern, keeping low to avoid being seen. With Adalbern's help, Porcia lowered herself down into the hole and vanished from sight. After a quick check again, Mederei ran to Adalbern.

"Where is Ambrosius?" Adalbern asked. Mederei grimaced and shook her head. Adalbern understood immediately and his brows rose in surprise. He looked down at the dark alley and a soft smile touched his lips.

"Aetius wanted his boy to be a man. And now he is. I doubt Aetius understood what he wished for."

Mederei smiled, but said nothing. She lowered herself down into the hole, landing on the carved stone ground and very nearly slipping on the slime that had grown there.

"Careful," she whispered up to Adalbern. "It's slippery here."

"It stinks," Porcia added.

Adalbern landed shortly thereafter, dragging the grate back over the hole. He winced as the noise echoed in the sewer, hoping it was not heard by unfriendly ears. He turned, slipping. Mederei's quick strength saved him from a fall.

"Thank you," he murmured.

Mederei nodded.

"Let's go."

Porcia glanced up at the grate, hoping to spy her brother one last time before turning and following Adalbern. She smiled in the darkness when she felt Mederei take her hand. She squeezed it in thanks.

They did not walk far before Adalbern stepped knee-deep in salt water. He paused, Mederei crashing into him.

"Sorry," they mumbled in unison.

"We're at the ocean," Adalbern said. "It must be high tide. The exit is likely underwater."

"I can't swim," Porcia whispered, her pitch rising in panic.

"It's all right," Adalbern said, reaching out to her. "I can, and the end of the sewer cannot be far. If you can hold your breath, I can take you out."

"How?"

"Hold tight onto my back."

Porcia stared at the dark figure that was Adalbern. "You're mad!" she hissed. "We'll drown."

"We won't," Adalbern said softly. "Swimming with weight is something all Batavi know how to do. I can swim in armour. I can swim with you on my back."

Porcia shook her head.

"You must trust me, Porcia."

"I trust him," Mederei said. "If nothing else, trust that. Trust that I would not leave my sister in the hands of a fool."

Porcia looked at Mederei, whose hand she still held. She felt Mederei squeeze it and she squeezed it in return.

"All right," she said.

"Good. Now take a hold of my shoulders," Adalbern commanded.

Porcia did as she was told.

Adalbern walked forward, one hand above his head to gauge the height of the ceiling. He walked three steps.

"All right," he whispered to Porcia. "This is where we go under. Mederei?"

"I'm right behind you. I can make it out."

"Ready, Porcia?" he asked the trembling girl.

"No," Porcia squeaked.

"Deep breath. Hold on tight. We'll be out before you know it."

Porcia nodded, took a loud breath in, and squeezed her eyes shut. She forced her panic down as she submerged, praying to all the gods she knew, and a few she didn't, all the same.

Her lungs burned by the time they broke the surface. She tried to cough, but Adalbern covered her mouth, and she swallowed back the coughing, wincing in pain. She turned to Adalbern who pointed up. They had come up just beneath the wharf where the gangplank to board the *Serpentina* rested. Directly above, five centurions shuffled as they marched up the creaking plank.

Mederei breached the surface shortly after and received Adalbern's hand over her mouth as well. She looked up, nodded at Adalbern, and he slowly removed his hand. She drew in a quiet breath, ignoring her lungs' painful cry for more air. The three of them hovered under the dock, clutching at the barnacle-encrusted wood to save their limbs.

"I'm cold," Porcia whispered through chattering teeth.

"I know," Adalbern replied. "Me too. Hold on tight. We'll swim to the far side of the boat the moment—" Adalbern did not get the chance to finish the thought. A ruckus on the wharf drew his attention.

"Help!" Ambrosius' voice sounded from the door of the brothel. "They're in here! They have my sister! Centurions! Help!"

Mederei smiled, her aching lungs preventing her from laughing. "Clever boy," she whispered.

Adalbern nodded. Porcia stared at the underside of the dock in the direction of her brother's voice, tears streaming down her cheeks. The sound of armoured boots pounding down the gangplank above him turned Adalbern's eyes upwards. The detail of centurions was disembarking, drawn to the brothel before which Ambrosius stood, screaming in a pretence of panic.

"I see an anchor cable," he whispered to Mederei. "Off the starboard bow. If we swim under the boat we won't be seen."

"Hurry," Mederei answered. "My limbs are going numb."

Adalbern nodded. "Hold on tight, Porcia. We're going under again."

Too cold to form a vocal response, Porcia nodded.

"On the count of three. One, two..." Adalbern took a deep breath and submerged. Mederei followed.

The cold of the Atlantic waters drove the strength from her limbs, burning her lungs and scrambling her mind. Mederei fought through the pain and kept Adalbern's feet firmly in her sights. She followed him up, struggling over to catch the thick rope that ran from the ship to the anchor. Her limbs near useless, she followed the rope to the surface.

"Gods," she whispered, trying to control her spasming lungs in an effort to remain quiet.

"Climb," Adalbern said. "Quickly. They'll soon find we're not in the brothel."

The commotion on the wharf seemed to have died down somewhat, though Adalbern could hear the startled cries of the prostitutes as the centurions made a thorough search of their house. A high pitch scream cut through the night, then a bright, earnest female voice shrieked, "That way! I saw them! They went out the window!"

Grinning, Adalbern helped Porcia up the rope, with Mederei following. "Be quick," he said.

He watched them climb before hauling himself out of the water.

Keeping on their bellies, Mederei and Porcia dragged themselves on the deck, grasping the bitt to which the rope was attached. Mederei lay flat and scanned the deck as Porcia panted and trembled beside her. Adalbern pulled himself up beside Mederei, also keeping his belly on the deck.

"There," Mederei whispered to him, pointing one cold-blue finger to a small hatch. Nodding, Adalbern began to slowly crawl across to it.

"Come on, little sister," Mederei whispered to Porcia. She started Porcia on her way by dragging her. Together, they crawled to the hatch. Not hesitating, they crawled inside, headfirst. Propped open by a long wooden stick, the hatch provided just enough room for Adalbern to squeeze through, though the effort scraped his skin. He winced as the cold air and salt water seeped into the cuts, but uttered no sound, even as he fell onto the hard floor.

Mederei helped him to his feet before turning to Porcia. The young woman's lips were blue, and she trembled violently, her teeth chattering.

"Clothes off," Adalbern whispered. "We have to take these off and huddle together."

Porcia stared at him, her eyes expressing disbelief though her face was frozen in a neutral expression.

"What?" Mederei hissed.

"The water will make you cold and you'll freeze to death. We need to conserve our heat. Clothes off. Now." Not waiting to see if his companions complied, Adalbern began to disrobe, hauling the wet, cold clothes off his body as quickly as possible.

Mederei watched a moment before turning back to Porcia. She nodded at the girl. "He's probably right," she said quietly.

"I can't!" Porcia hissed through lips that could not move.

"Then you will freeze," Adalbern said. Mederei and Porcia looked at him. Naked and bathed in the moonlight, Adalbern waited expectantly.

"Turn around," Mederei told him.

"This isn't the time for modesty," he replied.

Mederei gaze turned to a hard glare. Sighing, Adalbern turned around. "Hurry up," he mumbled. "You aren't the only ones to feel the cold."

Mederei turned back to Porcia. "Come on," she said. "I'll lie between us if it will make you feel better."

Porcia nodded. With Mederei's help, she disrobed, her borrowed fisherwives's dress made impossibly heavy with water. She curled up as it fell to the ground with a wet smack. Mederei followed suit.

"Can I turn around?" Adalbern asked.

"Not yet," Mederei answered. She gathered up the dresses, squeezed as much water out as possible and hung them against the ropes and baskets located in a corner of the relatively small storage space. She returned to her place in front of Porcia, in order to shield her from Adalbern's gaze.

"Now you can," she said.

Porcia need not have feared Adalbern's eyes. They were only for Mederei. He paused, absorbing her form, her nakedness a distraction from the danger they were all still in. Her brows arched in response to his searching gaze, but the small smile that tugged at the corners of her lips belied some slight pleasure at his open admiration of her.

Swallowing back his desires for now, he gathered some coiled ropes and barrels and arranged a small cubby for them to hide in; a means of concealing themselves from prying eyes and containing as much body heat as possible.

"In you go," Mederei whispered to Porcia. Moving quickly, Porcia crawled into the space and curled up on her side. Mederei followed, Adalbern close behind. Settling in, Mederei wrapped one arm around Porcia and pulled her close.

"It will be all right, little sister," she whispered to the girl. "We're safe for now. Sleep. I'll be here when you wake."

Too exhausted to argue, Porcia closed her eyes, letting Mederei's words, and the heat of the Briton's body, lull her to sleep. She was drifting away even as Adalbern settled in beside Mederei.

"Almost home," he whispered in Mederei's ear as his arm snaked across her waist. Mederei shifted slightly as Adalbern pressed his body against hers.

"Almost," Mederei whispered back.

In the darkness of the hold, Adalbern smiled. He pressed his lips against Mederei's shoulder, then let his head rest beside hers. Comforted by her presence, Adalbern fell asleep.

## 73 AD, AUTUMN, CITY OF ROME, ROME.

Geraint squinted as Emperor Vespasian's carriage rolled by, followed by an enormous entourage. The boy Diethelm was easy to pick out. He was an exact copy of his uncle, though blond and still caught in the delicate hands of youth. The boy walked with a straight back and a grim face, looking incredibly German despite his Roman garb and haircut. Of the young men the emperor had taken under his wing, Diethelm was the broadest.

Keeping his eyes on the boy, Geraint made his way through the bustling crowds of Rome. Seeing his chance, he pretended to stumble, crashing into a farmhand dragging a cart. He spun wildly out onto the road as the cart upturned, disturbing the emperor's train of retainers, before falling face first onto the paving.

"Forgive me!" he said as he felt several pairs of hands lift him up. He looked up, searching for Diethelm's face amongst the crowd of boys who had come to his aid. He found it and smiled. The smile was rewarded with a frown.

"I'm so sorry," he said. "I was distracted. I should have paid more attention to my footing. Goodness, but I am unused to such crowds."

"It's all right," one of the boys said, his accent exotic. "It happens more often than you would think."

"There are too many people in Rome," Diethelm added. He bent down to pick up the objects Geraint had dropped as he fell.

"Here," the boy said. He straightened as he looked down at the objects he retrieved. A small whittling stick covered in cut marks, a worn-out coin purse, and a large silver ring. Diethelm paused. He recognized that ring.

"Oh!" Geraint said. "My things! Thank you, boy."

Reluctantly, Diethelm handed over the objects. He looked up into the Briton's eyes and found them twinkling.

"That is a beautiful ring," Diethelm ventured.

"Isn't it? It was given to me by a German friend." Geraint watched Diethelm closely, pleased to see a small start. Good. He understood. "I was supposed to give it to his nephew, but goodness knows where that boy is." Geraint's lips split into a lazy grin. "I'm to take the boy home, you see."

"Oh," Diethelm answered softly.

"Get out!" A praetorian guard ordered, grabbing Geraint by the shoulders and shoving him off the road.

"Pardon me!" Geraint exclaimed. "I am sorry! So sorry!" He continued to mumble meaningless apologies and platitudes as the shorter Roman guardsman attempted to loom over him, scowling. Satisfied that the interloper had proved himself meek, the guard turned and marched back to his post. The procession of the emperor resumed. Geraint watched them go, before turning and helping the poor farmhand with his upturned cart.

## 73 AD, AUTUMN, HELINIO, GERMANIA MAGNA

A loud protestation woke Adalbern and Mederei. They turned to look up at the hatch and tensed. The shadow of a centurion lay across the barred opening in the dull dawn light.

"You've already searched the damned boat!" Senne bellowed. "And you move so damned slow that if I let you on again I'll miss the bloody tide! Now I have to sail. I have to catch my fish, or there'll be nothing to pay Rome's ridiculous taxes and you'll get no salary!"

"Was this boat searched?" a voice asked.

"Yes sir," another answered. "Last night."

A pregnant pause followed before the first unfamiliar voice said, "Fine. Go catch your fish, you drunkard. May the sea take you."

"Aye," Senne answered. "If only to free me from your imperial meddling. Now, get off my boat, or would you like to join my crew and help me fish?"

"Watch your mouth, fisherman, or you'll join your brother." The speaker nevertheless disembarked, his heavy boots shaking the plank as he did. Several more sets of footsteps followed.

"Aye." Senne's muttering echoed into the hold. "After I slit your throat."

Below, Adalbern forcibly relaxed his muscles. He sighed in relief and glanced over at Mederei. She smiled at him before closing her eyes. A few moments of Senne shouting orders and the scurrying of feet on deck and soon the boat began its gentle rocking as it headed out to sea.

"Are the clothes dry?" Mederei whispered. Adalbern sighed. He did not want to move. Mederei's body was warm and agreeable against his. She smelled pleasantly of ocean brine and, oddly enough, flowers.

"Wake Porcia," Adalbern said. "I'll check."

"Thank you."

Grunting a response, Adalbern slid out from the cubby of barrels and ropes he had made to check on their clothing.

"No," he whispered. "They're still damp."

"Damn it," Mederei's muffled response came from the cubby. It was closely followed by a groan from Porcia.

"It'll have to do. We'll be boarding the new ship soon, I imagine. Here," Adalbern said, tossing the clothes to the cubby entrance. "Get dressed."

A hand shot out of the cubby and dragged the clothes in. Adalbern smiled as he pulled on his trousers and laced them shut. He straightened as Mederei crawled out of the cubby, still naked.

Unabashed by her nakedness, Mederei straightened and stretched. She noted Adalbern gaze and did well to conceal a smile at the pleasure of his appreciation. Her mind turned to Rhys and the feeling of pleasure immediately vanished, replaced by guilt. She turned away and dressed, wincing at the cold cloth against her skin.

Adalbern felt her change in mood, and he turned away, walking to the hatch and staring up.

"We're ready," Mederei said softly from behind him. Adalbern looked briefly at her to confirm before turning back to the hatch.

"Senne?" he asked. He waited. "Senne? Senne!"

"What?" the Belgian snapped.

"Is it safe to come out?"

"Yes, yes."

Adalbern grunted. He reached up and pushed the hatch open, hauling himself up easily. He turned and helped Porcia and Mederei.

Mederei murmured her thanks before walking to the stern of the boat. The coast of Germania Inferior had all but faded from sight. She turned to the bow and saw nothing but ocean. Her heart thrilled all the same. Home. It was so close.

"Senne tells me it's three days sailing to landfall in the north," Adalbern said, coming to stand beside her. "Probably more, since our boat is small and not likely to pick up much speed in these waters."

"Four days," Mederei murmured, her eyes never leaving the horizon.

"We're coming on the boat," Senne said loudly, breaking the spell of hope. Mederei turned back to him as he pushed on the rudder, his two shipmates working silently to bring the fishing boat alongside the small smuggler. The Belgian fisherman nodded towards the starboard side, where sat a very small boat.

"Glad it's still here," Senne said, grinning. He shrugged when Adalbern raised his eyebrows at him and said, "The anchor wasn't quite long enough to catch the floor. I was hoping it hit the rocks there."

"All right," Adalbern said. He turned to look at the boat bobbing in the choppy waters. "It's not much," he noted.

"Smaller boats are hard to spot," Senne said. "Perfect for smuggling."

"Smaller boats are easier for the sea to swallow," Adalbern countered.

"It's that or you swim. Take your pick."

Adalbern sighed and shook his head. "There is no choice, is there?" he muttered.

"Can you sail her?" Mederei asked. Her voice trembled, tightened by the uncertainty of the powerful hope that welled in her throat.

Adalbern nodded. "Yes. Yes, I can sail her."

A small smile flashed across Mederei's face and was gone. Adalbern reached out and covered one of her hands with one of his. "We will get you home," he assured her.

"You'll want to head northwest," Senne said approaching the pair with a large net in his hands. "When you spy the coast, turn north and follow it until you see no signs of life. But be careful, I smell a storm coming."

"The day is clear," Mederei noted.

"It is now. But weather on the sea can turn on a spindle. And I smell a storm."

"Let's hope you're wrong," Adalbern said.

"We're in place," one of Senne's crewmen said, sounding bored.

"Well slide the plank over, then," Senne growled at him. He turned back to Adalbern and Mederei. "This is where we part ways. Good luck German, and to you, Lady of the Isle. I shan't miss that sharp tongue of yours, but your face was pleasant enough."

Mederei rolled her eyes and walked to the gangplank. She stopped and indicated to Porcia, who stood forlornly by the mast of the fishing vessel, looking back at the barely visible coastline of Germania Inferior. It took the young Roman a moment to realize that Mederei was trying to get her attention. She walked over.

"He's all right," Mederei murmured to the girl. "He's clever enough to avoid trouble."

Porcia smiled sadly at her. "Still," she said, "I miss him."

"You will see each other again. For now, let's get you as far from your betrothed as possible."

The sad smile Porcia wore immediately brightened. "Yes," she said. "Let's."

Taking her hand, Mederei turned and led Porcia carefully over the gangplank. Years of running the length of chariot draught-poles put Mederei in good stead, but Porcia had not had a British childhood, and struggled to keep her footing. She squealed and screamed as the rocking boats shifted the gangplank to and fro. Mederei's assurances did nothing to stop her heart from pounding wildly or the screams that leapt from her throat independent from her will.

It did not take long to cross, though to Porcia it felt an age. Adalbern followed easily, jumping onto the deck of the smuggling vessel and quickly taking stock of the layout of the vessel. It was familiar; a Cananefates river boat.

"This was not made for the ocean," Adalbern growled to himself.

The sounds of the gangplank dragging across the wood of the deck turned Adalbern's head.

"I honestly wish you luck," Senne called. "And when you return to Britain, you tell my bastard cousin I did exactly what he asked."

"Not exactly," Mederei murmured to herself. She raised her voice to call back, "Thank you, Senne. I will bless your memory the day my feet touch British soil." Quietening again, she said, "And the gods help you if I drown."

"Plan on a haunting?" Adalbern asked her, waving as the *Serpentina* began to move away from their boat.

"Never doubt the shade of a vengeful woman," Mederei answered, smiling.

Adalbern scoffed a laugh and said, "I'm going to get us going."

"There's food down here," Porcia said, standing at a small hole, holding the hatch open. "It's mostly bread and cheese, but I see olive jars."

"I'm less inclined to haunt," Mederei noted.

Adalbern laughed. "All right, let's go."

Under Adalbern's stern but patient command, they caught the wind and began to sail towards the coast of Britain.

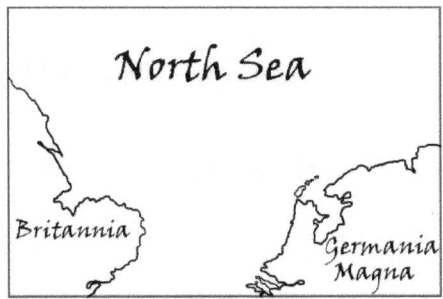

## 73 AD, THREE DAYS LATER, NORTH SEA, NEAR THE COAST OF BRITAIN

Adalbern scowled as he looked north. "I do not like the look of those skies," he growled.

"I do not like the look of that ship," Mederei answered, standing on the prow, staring at the southern horizon.

"What?" Adalbern demanded, turning around. A string of curses followed. "Roman," he spat.

Mederei grimaced. "I thought it might be. Do they so frequently patrol the strait?"

"With any number of peoples trying to escape Roman oppression, I imagine so."

"They're gaining."

Adalbern swallowed. He watched the vessel approach.

"What do we do?" Mederei asked, her voice soft. When Adalbern did not answer, she turned to him.

His brown eyes remained fixed on the Roman ship, hard as flint. Behind the eyes, Mederei could see his mind working. After a long moment of silence, he turned his gaze north. "Do you trust me, Lady of the Isle?" he asked Mederei, turning to her.

Mederei met his gaze evenly. "Why?" she demanded, suspicion making her words hard.

Adalbern turned north again. "Do you trust me?" he asked again after a long pause.

Catching on immediately, Mederei paled. "You mean to lose them in the storm."

"Yes."

Mederei observed Adalbern as he gazed intently at the approaching dark grey wall. "Yes," she whispered. "I trust you."

Turning to Mederei, Adalbern smiled, the corners of his eyes crinkling. "Good," he said. "Bring Porcia up. I'm going to need help."

Mederei nodded. Before she moved past Adalbern, she reached out and touched his forearm. Adalbern's skin tingled beneath the soft stroke of her fingertips. He stared down at his arm, mind suddenly blank.

"All right, then," Mederei said as she helped Porcia out of the hatch. "Tell us what to do."

"You're responsible for the mast," Adalbern replied, rousing himself. "You'll need to work together. Keep the sail as steady as possible, but if that mast breaks, you let go of the ropes, do you understand?"

Mederei and Porcia exchanged a glance. They nodded at Adalbern.

"Good." He took a hold of the rudder. Glancing behind him at the Roman vessel, he pulled on the steering oar, turning the nose of the boat north. A cold wind from the approaching storm buffeted his skin. "Gods keep us," he whispered as the first of the heavy raindrops struck the boat.

The mast broke a mere three hours into the storm. The groan of the thick wood as it splintered and toppled could not be heard over the violence of the water as it surged in great waves that continually threatened to tip the little river vessel. Mederei clung to the balustrade as her feet once again left the deck. Porcia screamed, the sound drowned as the boat crested the swell, inviting a flood of saltwater to crash over it.

At the steering board, Adalbern clambered around, using whatever he could to keep his balance, to keep the boat afloat and headed in more or less the right direction.

"There!" Mederei screamed as the boat righted again. Through the haze of rain, she could see the rocky shore of Britain. "There!"

Adalbern could not hear her cries. That he looked up was nothing more than coincidence. He cursed violently, pulling hard at the oar to take the boat to sea again. The storm had pushed them farther and faster than Adalbern had anticipated. They were too close to the shore. In this weather, the rocks there would surely spell death.

The fight with the steering oar lasted not five minutes. Unable to bear the strain, the wood snapped, sending Adalbern face first onto the deck.

The boat spun out of control.

Running to Mederei, Adalbern bellowed, "Hold on! We've lost our steering. We're going to run upon the rocks."

"What?" Mederei yelled back, not hearing. Adalbern grabbed her hands as they gripped the rails.

"Hold... On..."

Understanding, Mederei nodded. Her eyes followed him as he stumbled to Porcia to relay the message. The girl shook her head vigorously, her face ashen and eyes wide despite the rain. Adalbern began his explanation again. Before he could finish, the boat tipped, slammed against a rock by the angry sea. In the blink of an eye, Adalbern vanished, thrown from the boat by the impact.

"No!" Mederei barked. She released her hold on the rails and let the shuddering of the boat throw her to Porcia. Slamming into the balustrade on the port side, Mederei searched desperately for Adalbern in the frothing water.

A loud crack alerted her to the imminent destruction of the boat. The bow was wedged hard on a rock, the stern twisting madly in the water.

"Jump," Mederei said to Porcia.

"What?" the terrified girl demanded.

"Jump! Clear the wreck!"

"I can't swim!"

"There's no choice!" Grabbing Porcia's hand, Mederei leapt from the deck, dragging the Roman girl with her.

Panic drove Porcia to cling to Mederei, climbing the Briton as if that might gain her some respite from the sea. All it served to do was push Mederei under. Porcia's climbing stopped suddenly, and Mederei forced herself to the surface.

Opening her eyes, she saw Adalbern, Porcia clinging to him now.

"Swim!" Adalbern commanded. "Aim for that rock." He pointed to a northern outcropping of stone at the far end of the small bay. He did not wait to get confirmation. Porcia's panic was dragging him under, and he needed to get to shore as quickly as he could. He started swimming, Porcia worming around, trying to find the most secure purchase on his soaked body. Swallowing water, Mederei followed, her eyes firmly on that northern outcropping, the place where ocean met home.

The swim to shore was the hardest of Adalbern's life. Porcia did not weigh much more than the armour he was accustomed to swimming in, but armour did not move quite so much. Pauldrons and vambraces did not wrap themselves around his throat, cutting off his air supply. And he had never before swum in a storm, pushed and pulled by waves more vicious than he thought imaginable. He quickly learnt to let the waves push him to shore, giving him moments of rest.

Still, his arms ached and his lungs burned. He swallowed more seawater than he thought he could take. He had never panicked in the water before, but the thought of drowning very nearly overwhelmed him. Though it hurt, he thrilled when the waves threw him into shallow water, scraping his knees and shoulder. He could touch the sea floor with his feet and forced himself to stand. Fighting the rain, and with Porcia clinging like a limpet, Adalbern struggled to shore, his heart leaping as he felt the water levels drop. Though he fell often, hope kept Adalbern moving forward.

Halfway up the shore, just clear of the highest of crashing waves, Adalbern fell onto his hands and knees. Coughing up water, Porcia finally released her grip on him and slid to the ground.

Sitting up, Adalbern looked around. He tensed. Mederei was nowhere in sight.

"Mederei?" he called.

Caught by his cry, Porcia sat up. She looked around frantically as she scrambled to her feet, Adalbern immediately after.

"Mederei!" Adalbern bellowed, his eyes scanning the crashing waves for any sign of her. "Mederei!"

"There!" Porcia screamed, pointing.

Adalbern's stomach twisted as he saw Mederei; a pale, limp form flung by a wave. Without thinking, he bolted forward, running back into the stormy water in an effort to retrieve Mederei.

He did not have to swim very far in order to reach her. The storm had thrown her slack body towards the shore. He reached out to grab Mederei, only to have a wave draw her under. Not waiting, Adalbern dived. He grabbed Mederei by the shoulder of her dress and dragged her back to the surface. Wrapping one arm around her chest, he swam back to shore, the strain of his efforts contorting his face.

Porcia was at the waterline to help drag Mederei onto higher ground the minute she saw Adalbern begin his swim back. Fuelled by fear, Porcia managed to drag the heavier woman to the grass that grew over the far dunes.

"She's not breathing!" Porcia screamed through the rain. "Adalbern! She's not breathing!"

"Out of my way," Adalbern snapped, pushing Porcia away so that he could tend to Mederei. He slapped her face in an effort to bring life back into her again.

"No!" he said. "You are not going to die here. You are not! Wake up!" He slammed a fist hard onto her chest. "Wake up!" He pounded her chest again. "Don't you dare. We did not weather all of this just for you to die. Now, wake up!"

Mederei's lifeless form did not move, save for the full body jolt every time Adalbern struck her chest with his fist.

"Wake up!" the force was gone from Adalbern's voice. He stared down at Mederei, a terrible numbness creeping through him. "Please," he whispered. He lifted Mederei and held her close. "Please wake up. Please."

As if hearing his pleas, Mederei convulsed, spitting water out of her lungs. She coughed and drew a deep, painful breath. Adalbern pulled away, holding Mederei up to him as he looked at her face. Her eyes fluttered open briefly and the smallest of smiles touched her lips before Mederei fell limp again. She was unconscious, but she was breathing.

Relief more powerful than any storm surged through Adalbern. He pulled Mederei to him once more and wept. He did not notice Porcia wrap her arms around him and Mederei both.

They stayed there, Adalbern holding Mederei, Porcia holding them both until the storm began to subside. The violent lashing of rain slowed and lightened to a heavy drizzle, and while the ocean was still in turmoil, the skies had ceased their angry howls. The cold, sharp end of a spear at Adalbern's throat lifted his head. He followed the length of the spear to meet the steel grey eyes of an angry Briton, her face tattooed blue.

"Help," he whispered in Gaulish before he fainted.

# 73 AD, WINTER, SOMEWHERE IN TAEXALI TERRITORY, FREE BRITAIN

It hurt to breathe. That was the first thing Adalbern noticed as his mind crawled towards the small light of life. It hurt to breathe, and someone was singing to him. Then he felt the cold cloth on his forehead. The light in his mind's eye grew suddenly and he blinked.

"Mederei," he croaked as he gazed up at the woman tending him. She looked down and smiled.

"I'm here," she said, her voice calm and soothing. "Welcome back. You have slept long."

Adalbern let his eyes close again, savouring the feeling of Mederei's fingers caressing his cheek.

"He'll recover, then?" Calgacus asked from the door, startling Mederei. She immediately withdrew her hand from the German's face.

Nodding, she answered as nonchalantly as she could. "Yes. He'll recover. Thank the gods. The Batavi are famously tough bastards."

Calgacus smiled. He took the time to observe Mederei. She wore the same face as the girl who was stolen away by Rome, but so much about her had changed. The hard lines that a lifetime of hate and grief had etched into her features had softened somewhat. The grief was still there, deeper than before. But the hate had vanished, replaced by something less volatile. Resolve, or something close to it.

"It's all right," Calgacus said at length. "That you love him," he explained when Mederei frowned at him. He nodded his head at the man on the bed. "You've been through much with him."

"I don't—"

"Mederei," Calgacus said softly. "It's all right. Rhys would have wanted you to be happy, not to spend your life in miserable isolation."

Standing abruptly, Mederei put aside the cold water and cloth. "I have to go," she said. Calgacus did not argue with her, standing aside as she brushed past him in a rush to escape their conversation. He watched her leave the round hut given over to the Batavian's care. When she left his sight, he sighed and shook his head, taking up Mederei's duties in caring for the unconscious German.

"You poor bastard," Calgacus said to Adalbern. "You're going to have a hell of a time with that one." He picked up the wet cloth and pressed it to Adalbern's feverish skin.

The small cairn that marked the beginning of the Taexali burial grounds had long ago grown wild, though it was now hidden by the layer of snow that sat atop it. Mederei stood at its end, staring down at the raised earthen mound, tears streaming down her face. She had not had time to mourn Rhys properly, and even still, it was not grief at his passing that prompted her tears, but guilt.

She had lain in his bed, accepted his love, and even promised herself to him in marriage, but she had not loved him. She knew this now.

Calgacus had guessed correctly. Mederei loved Adalbern. The strength of her feelings towards him surprised her. Now that she knew love, she knew that she did not love Rhys. She had admired him. She had loved the idea of him, and the opportunity for a free Britain he represented. But of the man, she had not loved him, not in the way he loved her, at least.

"Oh Rhys," she whispered. "I'm sorry. I'm so sorry." Falling to her knees, Mederei let the storm of emotions inside her come flooding out. The dam had burst, and she no longer had the strength to keep back the tide. Her body shook as she keened by the grave, belonging to a man no one remembered any more.

Adalbern awoke the following morning, starving. It was not Mederei by his bed, but a dark-haired man with a young, if careworn, face and bright eyes.

"Mutton," the man said, lifting a bowl in his lap. "Its delicious scent will wake even the heaviest sleeper. Good morning, Adalbern, son of Civillis, who was king of the Batavi."

Adalbern stared mutely at the man, whose cares vanished in a bright, boyish grin. "Mederei and Porcia have been very free with information. I am Calgacus, chieftain of the Caledonian Federation, and the leader of the British resistance against Rome."

Adalbern struggled into a sitting position. He accepted the proffered bowl of lamb in broth. "Thank you," he said, his Gaulish hesitant.

"Mederei also told me you speak Gaulish well enough to understand the language of this isle."

Adalbern nodded. He spooned a small chunk of mutton into his mouth. No sooner had the tender meat touched his tongue than his stomach growled, loudly demanding as much food as possible as quickly as possible.

"Eat slowly," Calgacus advised, "despite the advice of your stomach. If you eat too quickly, you will regret it. You have been under for a long while. Awake enough to eat, though I wouldn't really call that awake, on occasion. Your stomach has known only broth."

"And Mederei?"

"Three days, though she was not allowed out of bed until a few days ago. She was never grumpier than the months she was relegated to bedrest."

Adalbern grunted and shovelled more food into his mouth.

"It was quite the risk, sailing to the heart of the storm."

Adalbern stopped eating long enough to answer, "It was that or be caught by Rome. We struggled so long to escape. I could not let her fall back to them. I could not."

A soft smile touched Calgacus's lips and he nodded, as if confirming something to himself. A sparkle of mischief danced in his brown eyes. It was obvious enough that Adalbern forgot his meal a moment.

"What?" he demanded.

"You love her," Calgacus said. It was not a question.

The statement robbed Adalbern of his appetite. He turned his eyes away from Calgacus's face and stared down at the contents of the bowl in his lap.

"You have your work cut out for you," Calgacus said.

Adalbern looked up again, scowling in confusion.

"Mederei is wracked by guilt," Calgacus said. "For my brother," he said with a shrug when Adalbern's confused frown only deepened. "To whom she was betrothed," Calgacus prompted.

The confusion vanished immediately. "Oh."

"She is as stubborn as they come, Batavian," Calgacus said.

"Yes," Adalbern agreed, a rueful smile pulling at the corners of his lips.

"She also loves you."

This caught Adalbern by surprise. He blinked stupidly and frowned. "No," he said quietly. "No, she does not."

"Yes," Calgacus said. "Yes, she does. But she fears dishonouring the memory of my brother. She fears love, too, I think, or the risk of losing it. She's lost too much already."

Adalbern nodded. "We all have," he whispered.

"Yes," Calgacus answered. "I like you, Batavian," he said suddenly. "You have an honest way about you, and I appreciate that. So, I'm going to help you."

"Help me?"

"Make Mederei your wife."

Adalbern stared incredulously at Calgacus.

"You do want to marry her, don't you?"

"Yes." The response was rushed and breathy, as if escaping before the man speaking it could gather control of himself.

"Good. Then you must follow my instructions to the letter. Understood?"

Adalbern nodded.

"Excellent. You can start by finishing your breakfast."

## 74 AD, Spring, Caledonia, Free Britain

Frustration followed Adalbern like a cloud of marsh flies since the journey to Caledonia. He could find no time to speak with Mederei alone. Whenever the opportunity arose and he approached her, she would excuse herself to attend to some chore or other.

The German, unused to such staunch resistance, became less and less subtle in his approach. Whenever he and Mederei were in the same space, people would excuse themselves, smiling or giggling, in a grand conspiracy to marry Mederei to their new German inhabitant.

It amused Calgacus no end, but even he called an end to the games when he noticed how hard Adalbern took each failure. He sat with Mederei one night at dinner, waiting patiently until she had finished instructing Porcia on the hairstyle of choice for that evening. Porcia had decided that she admired the style Mederei wore; one favoured by high born Gauls, and Mederei's mother.

"There," Mederei said. She turned Porcia around so that she could inspect the Roman girl's handiwork. "Well, you could use some practice, but it looks very well this evening."

Porcia smiled. "Thank you," she said sweetly.

"You're welcome. I imagine many a young man will be begging your hand for marriage by the end of the night."

The smile on Porcia's face fell.

"You need not accept such proposals, little sister," Mederei said softly.

Porcia looked up. "No?"

"No. Not every woman is suited to marriage. You can choose to remain unattached forever should it please you."

"You say that, but—"

"Porcia," Mederei said firmly. "No one has claim over you but you. This is not Rome. Here in Britain, women are masters of their own fate."

Her smile returning, Porcia threw her arms around Mederei. "Thank you," she said.

Mederei nodded. "Now your friends are waiting. Go on."

Taking her shell comb from Mederei, Porcia scurried to the end of the table, where a small gaggle of similarly-aged girls awaited their newest friend.

"She's settling in to British life well," Calgacus noted casually. "Still a little timid, though."

"The Roman in her is hard to wash away," Mederei answered. "But it is not all bad. Clearly, not all Romans are evil."

Calgacus smiled. "Not words I'd ever expect you to say," he said. Mederei scoffed.

"And what of Germans. Are they evil?"

Scowling, Mederei turned to Calgacus.

"I've been watching you two," Calgacus said, tilting his head towards Adalbern, who was sitting with a group of seasoned Caledonian warriors, and not a few women interested in taking what Mederei so stubbornly refused. "Mederei, he loves you."

Mederei turned away.

"You are my sister," Calgacus said. "And it breaks my heart to see you languish in this self-imposed prison you have concocted. I know you love him. I don't understand why you continually deny him, deny yourself."

"Calgacus, I cannot—"

"Yes," Calgacus said, cutting across her excuse in a firm tone. "You can. More to the point, you must. He is the hereditary chieftain of the Batavi. Have you any idea what an alliance with those warriors could mean in our fight for Britain?"

Mederei's gaze shifted to Adalbern, who showed absolutely no awareness of the very interested women around him. He kept his conversation primarily with the Caledonian warriors.

"Think about it," Calgacus asked.

Mederei did not answer. Her eyes were on Adalbern. Smiling to himself, Calgacus kissed her gently on her temple before returning to his position by the aged druid who had served his family so well.

"Playing match-maker, Calgacus?" the druid asked mildly.

Calgacus grinned. "In the game of love, my friend, I am king. Watch. There will be a wedding before the summer is out."

Though blind, the druid turned to Mederei, who was still gazing at Adalbern. Calgacus's eyes were on the German. He watched as Adalbern noticed Mederei's attention, doing a double take when he realized she was watching him. He offered her a smile, small and unsure.

Her returning smile was also small, but sad.

A young woman keen on the German playfully shoved his shoulder, breaking the small magic that was the eye contact between two people who desperately loved one another.

Calgacus grinned wildly behind his cup.

"I told you," the chieftain said. "A wedding by the end of summer."

The dinner had been loud, as it always was with the Caledonii. Life was short and hard. Good food and good company were cherished dearly. Now, however, with a good number of diners asleep on the tables, the chairs, and the floors of the hall, silence reigned. Mederei had retreated from the noise somewhat, eschewing conversation after she had her fill of food. She sat instead by a window, gazing up at the moon. It was full and round and had touches of peach in its light—the lover's moon.

Though she tried hard to recall Rhys, every thought of him was disrupted by memories of Adalbern. For such a large man, he was always gentle. His touch had never been hard or greedy, even when falling to his desires. His eyes, hard when angered, were always soft and sad when they fell upon Mederei. She wondered how a man could be both a bear and a doe. Yet Adalbern was. And, she loved him for it. Sighing, Mederei rose to her feet and made her way quietly from the hall.

Adalbern's eyes snapped open the moment he felt the air shift. Someone had moved, and it changed the entire mood of the place. He watched, his face shadowed by a great post, as Mederei made her slow way from the hall.

He rose, then paused. She would surely turn away from him again, would she not? But she had smiled at him this evening. Surely that meant something? Indecision froze him in place until, deciding that he may never have an opportunity like this again, Adalbern went after her.

Calgacus grinned to himself from his position on the bench where he pretended to sleep. "I win," he whispered, before shifting position and closing his eyes. He was snoring in minutes.

Mederei paused, hearing the crunch of stones behind her. She was being followed. A soft smile lit her face as her heart leapt. It was Adalbern. She knew it. Changing directions, Mederei headed not to her own bed, but out of the village, and down a barely visible track towards her favourite childhood haunt.

She paused every so often, hoping for the tell-tale sign of her German shadow. When she heard it, she continued on. Upon cresting a small hill, Mederei stopped walking. Standing in the moonlight, she looked down into the small valley where grew a sacred grove. She closed her eyes when she felt the heat from Adalbern's body at her back.

"This was my favourite place as a child," she said quietly. Not waiting for Adalbern's response she walked down to the grove. She paused and looked back to see Adalbern still standing at the crest of the hill. She smiled and entered the grove.

A small spring trickled with a merry sound from a crack in a large moss-covered stone. The water carved a miniature creek into the ground and disappeared underground again. The crunch of rock and leaf told Mederei that Adalbern had arrived.

"I would come here whenever I got angry. So, a great deal." Mederei turned and smiled at Adalbern, who could muster no response but to stare at her.

"When I was troubled, I would imagine that the spirits in the fallen leaves would help. I would speak my troubles to one of them, and put the leaf on the water and watch it take my troubles away."

"What would you tell them tonight?" Adalbern asked, his deep voice so soft it was almost a whisper.

"That I am afraid," Mederei answered. "That if I let myself love again, Rome will come and take it all away." Her voice trembled when next she spoke. "And that would break me."

Mederei did not turn to Adalbern when she felt his hands slide across her waist. She instead closed her eyes, letting tears fall, and leant back so that she rested her back against Adalbern's torso.

"Rome may come," Adalbern murmured. "And they may take everything that you have. But they are not here yet. There are still nights free from Rome, where joy and love can bloom. If Rome does come, if I am slain and you are not, you will still have had those nights, that joy, this love."

Quiet sobs escaped Mederei, and Adalbern gently turned her to face him.

"Mederei, I love you. I loved you the moment I laid eyes on you, standing like a queen before her court on an auction block. I will love you whether Rome comes or no. Rome has already taken so much. They will not deny me my love. I will not let them. They will not have that victory."

"Adalbern," Mederei whispered. She had not the words to speak her mind, so instead she stretched up and took his lips with hers. They kissed long by the babbling spring.

"Mederei," Adalbern said when the kiss ended. "I know I am not a Briton. I know I am an exile with nothing to offer. But I have love. And I will honour and cherish you for whatever days I have left. Please." He sank to his knees. "Would you honour me, and consent to be my wife."

Smiling through her tears, Mederei stroked Adalbern's face. "Yes," she whispered. "Yes, I will be your wife, and gladly."

This time, it was Adalbern's turn to weep. The tears struck his eyes without warning, but he cared not. Rising to his feet, he pulled Mederei in a close embrace. They stayed that way, savouring each other's warmth, until their tears calmed.

"Come," Adalbern said, taking Mederei's face in his hands. "You have filled this spring with grief in years before. Let's now show it joy." He kissed Mederei—a kiss that filled her with sudden fire.

Beneath the glow of the pale lover's moon, Mederei and Adalbern made good on their pledges to one another.

# 74 AD, Summer, Caledonia, Free Britain

Calgacus stood on the hill watching Porcia, Mederei, and Adalbern as they walked through the herd of horses, trying to find a suitable mount for the Roman girl. Beside the Caledonian chieftain stood Drustan, a Brigantian who defected when Venutius failed to rid the tribe of Roman interference, and one of the best fighters in the Caledonian ranks.

"She was never this affectionate with Rhys," the man noted, his arms folded across his chest as he watched the three walk through the horses.

Smiling, Calgacus noted how Mederei and Adalbern walked together, hands clasped as if it was their last walk.

"She has the most beguiling laugh," he told his surly companion. "It's bright and contagious. Do you know, I do not recall ever hearing it before? Look at them. They are well-matched, are they not?"

"He is not even British," Drustan answered.

"After a lifetime of grief and misery, my sister is finally happy, Drustan." Calgacus turned to the warrior.

"And what of Rhys?"

"My brother loved Mederei with all his heart. He lived for her rare smiles. If you think he would begrudge them now simply because they are not for him, when he is dead and cannot indulge them, then you do not know my brother half as well as you think."

Drustan grunted. "We'll be overrun with Germans."

"Good. That will double our fighting force."

"We are fighting for Britain."

"Yes, we are. And when Rome is gone, we will rule by British law, German and Caledonian alike. Do not fear the Germans, Drustan. The Batavi have Gaulish heritage, after all, and they hate Rome as much as we do. They are not our enemy."

Again, Drustan grunted. He turned away from his chieftain when Mederei's laugh echoed up to his position. A small smile tugged at his lips.

"You are right," he said. "She has a pretty laugh."

Mederei and Adalbern were wed the following week. Calgacus, long expecting the nuptials, had already made most of the arrangements. All that truly remained was the hunt for the wedding feast, and the weaving of Mederei's dress.

The festivities were loud and filled with bright light. The aged druid, though he grew increasingly frail, presided over the ceremony with Porcia at his side. The Roman girl had abandoned her gods and sought to learn from the druid. She proved to be an apt pupil, taking up the healing arts as if she had been at them her entire life. Her chosen path also put an end to the numerous marriage proposals that had plagued her since the day she arrived in the Caledonian village. Her heart, mind, body, and soul now all belonged to the secrets, and no man could come between her and the spirit world.

A month following the wedding, Adalbern and Mederei returned from one of their long morning walks to find a large contingent of Germans awaiting them in the village centre.

"What is all this?" Adalbern demanded of Calgacus, who stood at the head of the group wearing a bright grin.

"My Lord Adalbern," an enormous, grey-haired German said, walking forward. Adalbern recognized him; Chlodulf. Adalbern's jaw fell open slightly. "We have come by order of your mother, who had demanded that her son and his new wife be granted their wedding gifts as is our tradition." Chlodulf looked around Adalbern and smiled at Mederei. "My Lady," he greeted.

He turned his attention back to Adalbern, who remained in shocked stillness. Unable to contain himself, Adalbern wrapped the man in a tight embrace. "It is good to see you again," he said in German.

"And you, lad," Chlodulf replied, clapping Adalbern on the back. "Let me look at you." Pulling away, the man placed a burly hand on Adalbern's shoulder and looked him over. "Your father's son, and there's no doubt. Congratulations, my Lord. Your wife is very beautiful."

"Yes," Adalbern murmured. "And more besides."

"Come then! We have gifts for the bride and groom!" Motioning with one hand, Chlodulf turned. The first man walked forward, bearing an over-sized shield, gilded with swirling designs, and painted with enamel. Adalbern recognized it immediately.

"For the bride," Chlodulf said.

Mederei stepped forward cautiously and accepted the gift.

"The shield of the Batavi, made for Waldeburg and carried down her line. Wife of our chieftain, this shield is a symbol of your position amongst the Batavi."

"Thank you," Mederei murmured.

"Brygda wished she could present it herself, as is tradition. However, she feels she had a better purpose helping Batavian warriors escape Rome and come to Britain to fight for her son. She hopes she will be forgiven."

Mederei nodded. "How could it be otherwise? Surely her son has acquired his courage from her."

"There can be no doubt. She is a formidable woman. Now, for the groom," Chlodulf continued. He beckoned again, and another man walked forward, this time carrying an axe. Adalbern recognized this as well. Axe and shield had hung in his father's hall, above his seat. The sight of the ornate weapon brought tears to his eyes.

"His father's axe, made by Cerdic the Carver for Eberhard, the first of his line, symbol of the kings of the Batavi."

Adalbern took the axe carefully from the bearer. He stared down at it, silent in remembrance of his beloved father and his beloved home.

"Your father would be proud of you," Chlodulf said gently. "And find you more than worthy of this axe."

"I miss him," Adalbern whispered back, offering the older man a sad smile. He felt Mederei's gentle touch on his arm and turned to her. He took her hand and pulled her close.

"These gifts are grand indeed," he said, turning to Chlodulf.

"We're not finished, yet!" the man replied. He beckoned again. "Gifts now from the chieftains of the Chatti Federation!"

A soft nicker pulled Calgacus's attention away from the informal ceremony happening in the village centre. He spied a horse with two people on its back, a young lad, caught between child and man, and an older man with a very familiar face indeed. Calgacus grinned widely and quietly excused himself. None noticed. He slipped away to greet the riders.

"And at last," Chlodulf said. "From the king of the Frisians, who is grateful to the son of the liar who saved his life." He beckoned again.

Two warriors strode forward, each holding the leads of proud black horses, their manes long and thick. One had a white blaze on her black head, the other had nothing disrupting his gleaming coal coat.

"A mare and stallion, for the bride and groom."

"This is generous beyond imagining!" Mederei gasped.

"Aye, well, the old goat is very grateful," Chlodulf said. "And perhaps a little indulgent."

Adalbern laughed, still holding his father's axe. "My friend, how am I to keep all of this?" he indicated the pile of jewels, weapons and other gifts bestowed upon him and his new wife.

Chlodulf shrugged. "Not my problem," he said. "But an empty belly and want of mead is. Let's drink!"

"Wait!" Calgacus said, pushing through the crowd. "I have one last gift." He grinned at Adalbern. "Adalbern, husband of my sister, let it be known that when a Briton makes an oath, he keeps it."

Adalbern scowled in confusion at Calgacus.

Grinning wider, Calgacus stepped to the side. Adalbern looked behind him at a sea of Germanic warriors, until they too, turned around and slowly parted. Shock knocked the air from Adalbern's lungs when the parting crowd revealed a familiar bard, who stood behind a lanky youth.

"Diethelm," Adalbern whispered. He absently handed his axe over to Mederei and walked forward. "Diethelm," he said again, joy swelling his heart so that he feared it may burst. The boy took a few cautious steps forward, before breaking into a run. Adalbern matched him, and the pair crashed into one another, each weeping uncontrollably.

"My boy!" Adalbern said. "My brave boy! You're here! You're here!"

Diethelm could not respond, so savage were his sobs. Adalbern pulled him yet closer. "My nephew! My boy!" he whispered over and over again.

When their tears subsided, they pulled apart.

"Sorry for weeping," Diethelm said quietly with a rueful smile. He wiped the tears away from his cheeks. "I did not think I would see you again."

"I had hoped," Adalbern said. He did not bother to clear away his tears. Feeling Mederei at his back he moved so that he could introduce her. "Mederei, this is my nephew. Diethelm," he said, "this is Mederei. She is my wife."

Diethelm looked at Adalbern in surprise. He smiled. "I am honoured," he said.

Mederei stepped forward and pulled Diethelm into a tight embrace. "Thank the gods you are all right," she said. "Your uncle would not speak it, but your fate has been weighing heavily upon him. Welcome to Britain, Diethelm. Welcome home."

"Home," Diethelm whispered. He began to weep again and Adalbern wrapped one arm around his wife, and one around his nephew and pulled them both close. There they stood for a time.

"Bah!" Chlodulf said, wiping something from his eyes. "*Now* can we drink?"

# 83 AD, MONS GRAUPIUS, CALEDONIA, FREE BRITAIN

They stood upon the hill, watching as the Roman army drew close. Venutius, though unable to aid in this battle, or even hinder the approaching army for fear of Roman retribution, had at least sent warning to his old allies that Rome was marching to do battle with them. News of the attack had not been unexpected. It had been many years since Rome had come north.

Mederei was surprised it took them this long. It had been almost ten years since Rome last made a serious attempt at conquering northern Britain. She glanced across at her husband, who sat on his mount before the Batavian cavalry. Time had turned the hair at his temples grey and deepened the lines around his eyes. It did nothing to mar his stern, handsome features, or dull her love for him.

Germans from all over Germania Inferior, and no small contingent from Germania Superior, had fled to Britain in the hopes of living free from Roman oppression. They now formed a large part of the fighters for the Caledonian Federation; an invaluable part of the British resistance. As their chieftain, Adalbern elected to lead them in battle, as his father had done.

Riding in the ranks was Diethelm, old enough now to do battle, and still angry enough to want it. The lanky youth had broadened into a strong man, threatening to overtake his uncle in height. He had settled well into British life, being familiar with his Gaulish heritage, which was similar enough. He was even wooing a British girl. Several of them, in fact. Few could resist the stern lines of his handsome face, so like his uncle's.

Adalbern turned to meet his wife's gaze. He offered her a tight smile before he turned back to the approaching Romans. The plan had been his. The Caledonii and their allies had no hope of winning against Rome in open combat. If it was truly a free Britain they craved, they would have to fight differently, in a way Rome had no experience with. They would have to wage combat by night, in the shadows, by the cover of trees. His idea, to draw the Romans over the hill into the forest behind, had first been met with resistance. It was Calgacus who saw the wisdom in it.

"We are fighting to win the war, not the battle," he had said.

So the war council conceded the point. If things went poorly, Rome would have the day. But they would not win the night. They would be chased, harassed, starved and startled until, tired of the tricks of the north, they fled. It could take months, Adalbern warned; years perhaps. But Rome would not be able to resist the wraiths the Britons would make of themselves.

Mederei's heart pounded, matching rhythm with the armoured boots of the Roman army. It did not stop pounding when that army halted, their number stretching far back across the plain. A man approached; no doubt the governor of the Roman province of Britannia, Gnaeus Julius Agricola.

Calgacus followed suit, Adalbern close behind. Mederei left her position at the head of the women she led; women she had trained herself for almost ten years. They had lost much in the violence of Rome's occupation of their island—husbands, children, land, dignity. Young and old, broad or slender, these women stood against their oppressors with a fierceness few other warriors could match. Their anger undulated around them, a shield of battered British pride.

Agricola lifted his face a little, so that he might look down upon the warriors who approached. It was quite a feat, as not one of the warriors stood shorter than he.

"We have come," he said in a strangely nasal voice, "to make you civilized. Submit now, and we shall be lenient. A tithe, and men for our armies, nothing more."

"You have come," Calgacus answered with an easy smile, "to test your mettle against the last of the free British and to steal our tin. Do not pretend civility has anything to do with it. Turn around, Roman, and we shall spare you much humiliation."

Mederei smiled, watching the governor try and rein in his temper. "You will rue your arrogance, Briton," he said. "Very well, since you refuse to listen to reason, begin your prayers to whatever gods still listen now that your druids are gone."

Mederei twitched. The scourging of the Isle of Môna had helped draw warriors to her mother's side more than twenty years ago. It was a cruel blow to the British heart.

"Our druids shall outlive you, Roman," Calgacus said. "And history will remember it." With nothing more to say, Calgacus turned his horse, and with his entourage, returned to the ranks.

Mederei dismounted her old black mare and permitted it to be led away. She looked at the women under her command. There was nothing she could say that could allay their fears, or heal their hurts. Rome had taken so much from them, and yet they stood now, bent, wounded, but unbroken.

Mederei found she had nothing to offer her courageous amazons.

Instead of rousing words and grand speeches, Mederei simply smiled at her warriors, a smile that promised mischief and blood to those who were yet to discover their secret—the secret that was a British woman's strength.

Backs straightened, eyes hardened, and one by one, these brave women warriors smiled back. They knew a woman's strength. Soon Rome would as well.

Mederei turned to face the forthcoming battle, preparing for the signal to attack.

"Prydein am byth!" Calgacus roared as he raised one hand.

"Daughters of Britain," she called. She looked back at her troops briefly.

"Remember yourselves."

# EPILOGUE

Tacitus writes of the terrible loss of British life and the grand Roman victory won by his uncle at the Battle of Mons Graupius. In the wake of that fight, he writes, the rest of free Britain was subdued and Rome had, at long last, conquered the whole of the island.

Shortly after the Battle of Mons Graupius, Emperor Domitian recalled Gnaeus Julius Agricola to Rome, where he received great honours, leaving Saulltius Lucullus in his place as governor of the troublesome province of Britannia.

Rome advanced, reaching as far north as Cawdor. Their stay was exceedingly brief. The following year, driven by constant raids and missing supplies, Rome was forced south again, to the fortress at Pinnata Castra.

Agricola, it is noted, had a falling out with Domitian, who felt betrayed by the former governor of the Province of Britannia. It is claimed that the emperor discovered Agricola's assertions at having subdued the Britons false, for the northern tribes never submitted to Roman rule.

Two years after the Battle of Mons Graupius, Rome withdrew from the north entirely, dismantling Pinnata Castra before the fortress was even complete. All Roman occupants withdrew to a frontier they considered defensible. Hadrian's Wall was later built on that line.

Constant raids from the free people of the north proved too costly to Rome, and for all of Agricola's claims of a monumental victory, his successors proved unwilling to strike further north than Hadrian's Wall until the construction of the Antonine Wall in 142 AD. Two decades later, Rome once again abandoned the north and retreated to Hadrian's Wall.

In 209 AD, Septimius Severus attacked the far north in a disastrous attempt to win the island. He was forced to retreat once again to Hadrian's Wall. Septimius died before he could try for the north once again, and his plans to attack were abandoned by his son, Caracalla.

No other attempts were made.

Rome never conquered the north.

# TEIR GÖRUOR6YN YNYS PRYDEIN.

vn onadunt ewei uerch seitwed

a rore verch usber

a mederei badellua6r.

- Trioedd Ynys Prydei, Llyfr Coch Hergest, c. 1382 AD.

## Three Amazons of the Island of Britain:

The first of them, Llewei daughter of Seitwed;

and Rorei daughter of Usber;

and Mederei Badellfawr.

- The Welsh Triads, Red Book of Hergest, c. 1382 AD.

# ACKNOWLEDGEMENTS

This book would not have been written were it not for the love and encouragement of friends and family who believed in me. Your constant support and encouragement helped me struggle through the long days when I felt like giving up.

Thank you to my parents, who have supported this insane dream of mine since I first decided to make writing my career. I cannot imagine having made it without you there.

Thank you to my three beta readers, Mum, Dad, and my good friend Éric, who helped make this manuscript readable and made me believe it possible that I would see this novel in print.

To Caroline Fréchette and the remarkable team of editors at Renaissance Press, you are wizards. Thank you so much for believing in this story enough to take it on, and for putting in the work to make it sing.

I also owe a great deal to my good friend Professor Paul Birt, who, in his time at the Ottawa Celtic Chair, exposed me to the wondrous world of Celtic Studies. I am now a lifelong student, infatuated by these ancient peoples and their remarkable cultures, and I do not regret it.

Lastly, to my readers, old and new, who have stood by me and supported me, encouraged me and helped me to believe that I was, in fact, a writer: you are the reason I continue to write. Thank you so, so much for all you've done for me. I hope this book is worthy of you.

All my love,

Sonia

# about the author

Born in 1983 and raised in various countries around the globe, S.M. Carrière has always felt drawn to epic tales of heroes and villains. An avid reader herself and despite always writing, she did not think of becoming an author until her final year of university, when she found herself compelled to the craft (when she ought to have been studying). She self-published her first title, The Dying God and Other Stories, in 2011 at the urging of a friend, and has not stopped since, publishing one book each consecutive year.

Falling in love with speculative fiction was easy for S.M. Carrière, and she has since become very involved in the speculative fiction community in her current city of residence. Ottawa. She founded Silver Stag Entertainment to share her love of genre books and films and can be frequently seen on that youtube.com channel discussing them.

Not content with merely writing, and 'youtubing,' S.M. Carrière has also indulged her love of fine art, picking a paint brush up for the first time in many years in 2014. Her portfolio of drawings and paintings grows steadily.

S.M. Carrière is also an avid martial artist, studying Northern Mantis Kung Fu and Chinese Kickboxing with Wutan Canada, and taking up western equestrian martial arts when she has the time.

And, after all of that, if she has a moment or two, she can be found curled up with a hot cup of tea, a meaty red wine or a smooth whiskey and enjoying a good book… or playing the Xbox.

# If you liked this, check out these other Renaissance titles!

## The King in Darkness by Evan May *Supernatural Suspense*

Adam Godwinson, former priest, isn't sure what he believes in anymore. These days he deals in used books at a small store in Ottawa. But an old text, written in an unfamiliar language, is about to change that forever. Adam now finds himself the target of a powerful conspiracy. These shadowy figures, wielding abilities he can't understand, want to cleanse society of its sins – even if that means destroying it. Adam will have to figure out what he believes in to have a chance to save himself and the rest of the world.

## The Admirer by Aurelia Osborne *Historical Mystery*

Rose Fraser has been given the opportunity of a lifetime: the chance to go to London as a debutante for the London season. She is nervous yet excited at the idea. However, her excitement soon fades away when she starts receiving threats in the form of intricately folded, anonymous notes. Feeling trapped, unable to go to the police, she turns to the only person she thinks can help her: her most serious suitor, private investigator James Grey. But will he uncover the truth before things take a turn for the worse?

**The Family by Choice series** by Caroline Fréchette

*An action-packed, fast-paced series about*
*superpowers, crime, survival, and responsibility.*

Alex Winters is a young man involved in organized crime who also
has the ability to manipulate fire. Through various confrontations
which put him and his loved ones in danger, he learns that there is
more to life than just survival.

**Here's what people are saying about it:**
"I loved this. If you like dark fiction, supernatural, and a good dose of
action, then try out this series. You will not be disappointed."
*I Heart Reading book reviews*

"Caroline Fréchette is one of my favourite fantasy writers in the
National Capital Region. (...) The story has a great pace and the strong
writing makes them an easy read."
*Apartment 613*

"While I find this series to be a quick read, it is also an incredibly good
read."
*Geeky Godmother reviews*

Renaissance Press was founded in May 2013 by a group of friends who wanted to publish and market with a new business model.

As authors ourselves, we wanted a company that treats its authors like family, and for the authors to be involved in every step of the process. Their input is highly valued, and they get final say on how their book looks and feels.

At Renaissance, we value community and diversity. We are committed to working with local authors, events and companies to knit the literary community closer together. It is also very important for us to prioritize underrepresented voices.

Above all, we are passionate about books, and we care as much about our authors enjoying the publishing process as we do about our readers enjoying a great, professional quality and affordable product on the platform they prefer.

Our catalogue is eclectic because we love different things, and we only publish the books we fall in love with.

renaissancebookpress.com
info@renaissancebookpress.com

# Did you enjoy this book?

Independent authors and publishers rely mostly on word of mouth publicity.

Please consider helping others discover this title by posting a review of it online, on Amazon, Goodreads, a blog or social media.

www.ingramcontent.com/pod-product-compliance
Lightning Source LLC
Chambersburg PA
CBHW072020020726
47501CB00006B/1889